"COME HAVE A SEAT, STEPHEN," RUDY SAID. "BE MY GUEST."

Rudy spread his hands to indicate free seats on either side of him. A chill ran through Stephen, paralyzingly cold, and it said *nobody wants to get too close to him. Everybody else is afraid of him too.*

There was something strangely compelling about Rudy's eyes: a fire not previously there, a force behind them that seemed to draw Stephen forward despite himself.

Slowly, he obeyed.

"It's good to see you," Rudy said, grinning. "How've ya been?"

Stephen shrugged. It was as if somebody had him hooked to invisible strings; had it been left to him, he wouldn't have been able to move at all.

"I suppose that you've been wondering where I've been." Rudy laughed out loud. "I've been traveling. A trip and a half." He wrung his bone-white hands. "A great and mysterious journey.

"I've gone all the way in." Rudy's voice was hypnotizing, like the hiss of a cobra over cold slit eyes. "I've gone all the way into the darkness. And do you know what I found there?

"*The other side.*" Rudy's face, as he said it, was a terrible thing to behold. "The proverbial light at the end of the tunnel, my friend: a place beyond your wildest dreams.

"I think I'd like to take you there . . ."

THE
LIGHT
AT
THE
END

John Skipp/Craig Spector

BANTAM BOOKS
TORONTO • NEW YORK • LONDON • SYDNEY • AUCKLAND

THE LIGHT AT THE END
A BANTAM BOOK 0 552 17269 7

PRINTING HISTORY
Bantam edition published 1986

Copyright © 1986 by John Skipp and Craig Spector
Caricature of Craig Spector and John Skipp by Leslie Sternbergh

Bantam Books are published by Transworld Publishers Ltd.,
61-63 Uxbridge Road, Ealing, London W5 5SA,
in Australia by Transworld Publishers (Aust.) Pty. Ltd.,
15-23 Helles Avenue, Moorebank, NSW 2170, and in New
Zealand by Transworld Publishers (N.Z.) Ltd., Cnr. Moselle
and Waipareira Avenues, Henderson, Auckland.

Made and printed in Great Britain by
Hunt Barnard Printing Ltd., Aylesbury, Bucks.

To Marianne and Lori, with whom we are in love,

and

To the Creator, who gives us the Light
By which we more clearly see the Darkness.

Acknowledgments

The authors would like to thank the following for loving, supporting, and/or putting up with us during the writing of this novel:

Lou Aronica, our editor, who tampers with nothing and makes only the best suggestions; Adele Leone and Richard Monaco, our agents, who push for us like crazy; T.E.D. Klein, late of *Twilight Zone*, who gave us our break and encourages us still; Educated and Dedicated messenger service, who provided the background for this novel and got us through the lean years; our parents, who kept the faith; Dennis Etchison, Harlan Ellison, Stephen King, Gardner Dozois, and Karl Edward Wagner, who took a little time out for kind words and advice; and the city of New York, where anything can happen and probably will, for showing us the bottom line.

We'd also like, with a minimum of redundance, to give special thanks to Shirley, Charley, Gram, Dave, Tappan, Beth, Joel, Bob, Richard, Amy and Alan, Leslie and Adam, Matt, Krafty Polekat, Kim, Pete, Gail, Rick, Mindy, Shelley, Allison, Roy and Lauren, Mark, the rock mafia, Cubby, Glen, Tony, Max, Curtis, Cuz, Tommy and Cathy, Steve, Steve, Steve, Steve, and the city of York, Pa.

There are roughly fifteen billion other wonderful people we'd like to thank, but we only get one page. You know who you are. Thank you.

Prologue
On the Dark Train, Passing Through

When all the lights went out, Peggy Lewin was alone in the third car. She had been trying to immerse herself in *Love's Deadly Stranger*, trying to drive away thoughts of that bastard Luis and their miserable "night on the town," vainly fighting back tears. Now the paperback sat limp and forgotten in her hand, and all she could think about was how frightened she had suddenly become.

"Oh, Christ," she moaned softly into the darkness. Slowly, she set down the book and reached into her purse, groping for a moment. Her fingers closed around the Mace and remained there while her eyes cast blindly from corner to corner and a voice in her head whined *it's too late to be taking the subway alone, that cheap bastard, wouldn't even pay for a cab, goddamn it!*

Peggy squeezed the Mace for reassurance, tried to control herself. Light from the tunnel strobed in through the windows, playing across billboards for El Pico coffee and Preparation H. A nervous giggle escaped her. It was buried under the roar of the train.

Should I get up? she wondered. *Find some people, some light?* She stood, shaky, in the center of the aisle, and looked in either direction. Darkness. A sigh escaped her, and she moved to the security of the metal holding post on her right: a pretty girl, slightly overweight and modestly trendy, willing slave of Manhattan's you-gotta-look-good prerogative, wishing suddenly that she'd played down her curves. Who knew what kinds of creeps rode at this time of night?

The dark train pushed forward, racing toward the southern tip of Manhattan Island. It struck her that they

1

would be rolling into 42nd Street any minute now, and that even though Times Square wasn't the greatest place in the world at 3:30 in the morning, it had to be better than this. There'd be a cop or something, anyway. There'd be light.

There'd be hope.

"Hurry up," she almost prayed. "Oh, hurry up and let me out of here."

As if in answer, light flooded the car from either side. Gratefully, she moved toward the center doors, watching the pillars whip past, the regular hodgepodge of derelicts assembled, the long TIMES SQUARE 42 ST. sign, more pillars, an officer, more pillars, more pillars, more . . .

. . . and she realized that the train wasn't going to stop, and she pounded against the glass with her fists, a mute sob welling in her throat as the station whizzed by . . .

. . . and in the last moment of concentrated light, before darkness engulfed her once again and completely, she saw the man standing in the space between cars, staring in through the door.

Staring in at her.

And she saw the door slowly open.

"It ain't stoppin', Jerry! Check it out!"

"Yeah, I see it, man," he answered, but Jerry wasn't watching that at all. His eyes were on the big black cop, smiling coldly, while his mind worked. "Yeah, officer. Why doncha go find out what's wrong with ol' Pinhead, the conductor? Lights go out, train don't stop . . . looks like a job for the *police*, ya know it?"

The cop frowned, nervous and torn. On the one hand, something was definitely wrong. On the other hand, skinheaded punks like these guys formed their own category of bad news. Sure, one of 'em couldn't even sit up right now, might start pukin' any minute; and the one with his nose against the glass looked too stupid to worry about.

But he'll be right there if this Jerry creep starts anything, he noted, unconsciously fondling the butt of his gun. *And Jerry-creep probably will.*

There were two other people in the car: two little middle-class hippie throwbacks, probably never been so glad to see a cop in their lives. They were huddled together in the corner by the door, eyes full of mute appeal. Jerry had been giving 'em grief before the lights went out; their up-raised voices had drawn Officer Vance in from the last car, where he'd wearily been trying to rouse a crashed-out derelict.

If I leave now, Vance knew for a fact, *these boys are dead meat. Not that it makes that much difference to me. But, dammit, then I will have to book Jerry and his bozo friends, chase 'em halfway to Hell and back on this friggin' blacked-out train. Oh, Jesus.* Thoughts of switchblades in the darkness made him very, very nervous.

He had pretty well decided to stay when Peggy Lewin's scream ripped into their ears from five cars ahead. The two hippies jumped a foot a piece and came down hugging each other like pansies in a high wind. Something in Vance's chest tightened up and froze; that was not a natural scream. He quickly glanced at Jerry's face and saw that the fucker was smiling.

"Sic 'em, baby!" Jerry yelled. "Woof woof woof! It's Police Dog!" His dimwit buddyboy guffawed, steaming up the window. Vance felt like knocking their heads together.

Then Peggy Lewin screamed again. This time it was worse. Much worse. It wailed out and out, as though her soul had been soaked in gasoline and lit, sent howling out of her mouth to shrivel and die in midair. Even Jerry shut up for a second.

Even Jerry had never heard such terror.

"Damn," Vance hissed. He had no choice. Peggy Lewin had made up his mind for him. Choking down fear, he drew his revolver and started running toward the front of the train. When Jerry refused to get out of the way, Vance knocked him on his ass and kept going, just as the tunnel swallowed them again.

"I HOPE IT GETS YOU, TOO, YOU BLACK BAS-TARD!" Jerry bellowed in the fresh darkness. Vance bit back a response, by now scared half out of his mind. The screaming had stopped, but somehow that was not reassuring.

I hope it gets you, too. The voice rang in his ears. Like the scream. Like the roar of the train. *You black bastard!* It hurt to be hated so automatically, so completely, on the basis of so very little: uniforms, pigments in skin. The fact that he did the exact same thing did nothing to dampen his rage.

I'd love to blow you away, white boy, Vance thought bitterly as he came to the door. *Blow you right the hell off this world.* But the girl, if that was what it was, might still be alive. He was compelled to check it out.

The door slid open, and he stepped into the space between cars. The wind blasted into him, and the metal platform pitched and buckled beneath his feet. Carefully, he reached over and opened the door to the next car, moved from blackness to blackness to blackness, pausing nervously on the other side.

The car was empty. Silent, but for the ever-present thunder. No, *more* than silent and empty. *Dead.* Suddenly, Vance was overwhelmed by the feeling that he was riding in a dead thing, already beginning to rot, kept in motion by a power not its own.

Vance knocked on the conductor's door. No answer. He rattled the lock. "*Sid?*" he called. "*You in there?*" No answer. Something damp and chilling uncoiled in his gut.

What the hell is wrong with this train? he wondered, and then forced himself to keep moving.

A man named Donald Baldwin was slumped in the driver's seat, one hand dutifully on the throttle, staring straight ahead. The lights from his instruments were the only working lights on the train; they cast bright reds and yellows on all the shiny spots and streaks in his clothing.

The door to the engineer's booth was locked from the inside. Any driver with half a brain kept it locked on night runs, because you were a sitting duck in there, and only lunatics rode at night anyway. If you were crazy enough to be there in the first place, you could at least minimize your risks.

Tonight, Don Baldwin had been grateful for his half a brain. Right after leaving 51st Street, something started to rattle at the door. Not just the train shaking around; something was trying to get in. Don didn't know why he thought some*thing* instead of some*one*, but he did, and it scared the bejesus out of him.

He had tried to raise Sid, his conductor, who sat in a similar cab toward the middle of the train. No answer. He couldn't even be sure if the intercom was working. *Goddamn train is falling apart*, he silently groused. *Whole goddamn transit system*. He got a sudden vivid flash of Sid and Vance, just hanging out, the exact kind of lazy-ass spear-chucking bastards that were dragging the subways to ruin. *And me with a nutcase at the door*, he moaned. *God damn it*.

Don lit a cigarette, his twenty-third of the night. He always smoked a lot on night runs; it killed time, and what else could you do? Even with his side window open, it filled up with smoke pretty fast in there.

He never saw the mist drift in, under the door.

He never even knew what hit him.

By the time Officer Vance reached the car where Peggy Lewin lived and died, the back of the train was already filling up with rats. They were gray, squat, bloated little bastards with red, gleaming eyes, and they came up through the floor like maggots out of pork. As though they'd been there the whole time. Just waiting.

The derelict that Vance failed to rouse was still sleeping, decked out on the cool curved plastic of the seats, thick in his own smells. The rats had found him.

Just as Vance had been found by the dark shape in the doorway. The shape that motioned toward the dead thing at its feet, and impaled him with its luminous eyes.

"Cigarette?" Jerry was kneeling in front of the two wimps, grinning unpleasantly. They shook their heads, blubbering. He smacked the taller one across the face, eliciting a yelp. "I didn't ask if you *wanted* one! I ast if you *got* one!"

The taller wimp, William Deere by name, shook his head more emphatically and whimpered a little. First time he'd ever wished for cigarettes, too. Big night for firsts. Fortunately, his friend Robert had one; the little longhair pulled a Tareyton out with shaky fingers and handed it to Jerry.

"What the hell is this?" Jerry took it, inspected it in the light from the tunnel. "Tareyton. These any good?"

"I like 'em," Robert said, risking a chummy grin. His NO NUKES T-shirt was plastered to his back and armpits. He was remembering a movie he saw on TV once, with Tony Musante and Martin Sheen playing badass teen psychos who terrorized sixteen people on a subway car. It was called *The Incident*, and it had made him swear that *he'd* never be intimidated like that. *He'd* never simper and squirm and let some tough guy take him apart piece by piece.

He had fooled himself about that for a long time. No more. If Jerry wanted to take Robert apart, Jerry could go right ahead. Robert wasn't going to do shit. Robert was going to risk a chummy grin.

"Great," Jerry said, grinning back. "You got anything else I might like, baby boy?" Robert's smile dried up, and he reached into his pockets.

"You, too, doll," said Jerry's stupid friend, coming over to join in the fun. William Deere nodded now, exercising his neck far more than his spine. He echoed his friend's gesture, coming up with eighty dollars in crisp twenties.

"Hot damn! Moses, you done good by us." Jerry punched William in the shoulder affectionately. "Yer buddy didn't do so hot, though. Wassa mattah, little Jesus? Nobody givin' at church?" He grabbed Robert by the collar and started to hoist him out of his seat.

Then the door at the front of the car slammed open, and Vance reappeared, still holding the gun. There was something stiff about his movement as he came toward them. And his eyes gleamed red, like a rat's.

They hit 34th Street just as the first shot went off, striking Jerry's asshole friend in the forehead and spinning him backward. Light flooded the train, illuminating the brains and blood that spattered the back wall. Jerry jumped back, freaking. William and Robert squealed like pigs.

Jerry's remaining friend, the drunk and sickly one, looked up in time to see a nightmare appear in the door behind Vance. He groaned, assumed he was delirious, and lost it all over the floor. Vance pumped two bullets into him, rolling him off into his own vomit, face first and forever still.

"Jesus!" Jerry screamed. He pulled a very nasty blade from his back pocket and flicked it open, brought it to rest against William Deere's throat. The gangly hippie came up with ease, back pressed against Jerry's pounding chest. "One more step, man, this boy gets his throat sl . . ."

Vance's next shot smashed William Deere's nose on its way out the other side. The body jerked once and then sagged in Jerry's arms. He pushed it away with a tiny animal sound and ran screaming toward the cop.

To his credit, Jerry was every bit as tough as he liked to act. He took one in the belly and one in the right lung, crawled ten feet on his knees and buried the blade in Vance's thigh before drowning in his own blood. Vance watched, blank-faced, not even seeming to feel the pain.

"Take it out, please," said a voice from behind Vance. A voice of unspeakable calm and remorselessness. A chill, serpentine hiss. A whisper of graveyard breeze.

Vance dropped the gun, gripped the handle of Jerry's switch with both hands, and pulled it wetly out of his leg. He straightened. The knife hung poised in front of his stomach.

"Now in," said the voice, and Vance plunged the point into his navel.

"Now out." The blade slid away with a puckering sound.

"Now in."

Officer Vance was slopping viscera all over his boots by

the time Robert finally lost his mind. The young man bolted from his seat and attacked the end door, pissed himself and didn't even know it. The door slid open almost by itself, and he staggered out into the space between, wind and thunder pounding at him as he screamed, "HELP ME! HELP ME! OMIGOD, YOU GOTTA . . ."

Then the last of the empty 34th Street platform disappeared, and he was screaming at a wall in total darkness. His hands gripped the metal chain guardrail and clung to it with everything he had.

Robert dimly heard the door slide shut, and leaned against it with a sigh of relief. The sound of Vance mechanically disemboweling himself could no longer be heard, and that was good, because if Robert had had to listen for one more second, he would have jumped.

Jumped . . .

Robert looked down. Even in the dark, even half-insane, he could tell that the ground was moving by very quickly. The part of his mind that still worked weighed his chances of survival. Not too good. He began to cry.

Oh, Jesus Christ, they're dead, they're all dead, I'm gonna die! His thoughts tumbled all over each other like the bodies behind the door. The floor, split down the middle, wanted to rip his legs off and eat him alive; but he was losing his grip on the chain and the world. His strength was slipping away; he was sagging, sagging . . .

The door rattled in front of him. Not *the* door, behind which the cop was still carving himself like a Christmas turkey and the walls were wearing William's face. Not that one.

The other one.

The one that led to another car.

The one that led to escape.

Robert half fell across the platform, grabbing hold of the door latch and pulling. A crack appeared. He gibbered and extended its dimensions, struggling to his feet . . .

. . . just as the dark train entered the 28th Street station, flooding him once more with light . . .

. . . just as a rat the size of his foot squeezed through

the crack, chittering in its own obscene tongue. Robert shrieked and booted it right into a pillar, slamming the door shut abruptly. He imagined that he could hear a thousand furry, filthy little bodies slamming against the other side, trying to reach him.

Then, beyond imagining, he felt the red eyes boring into the back of his head. The window went cold, and he recoiled from it. The door slid open without resistance. And a hand . . . ancient, horrible . . . reached out for him.

Without hesitation, he jumped.

Robert experienced a moment of remarkable freedom, of triumph. Then he hit the first pillar and his neck snapped, mercifully, like a twig. He was dead before most of the damage was sustained.

It was the best he could have hoped for. Under the circumstances.

It was taking a joyride on the dark train tonight, cold steel slicing through the underbelly of Manhattan. Just as it had twenty years before, and twenty years before that, when the whole system of subterranean labyrinths was fresh and marvelous, before the taking-for-granted and the turning-to-shit. *The more things change, the more they stay the same*, it thought, savoring the brute constancy of humans and their achievements, no matter how far through the ages they slithered.

It was over 800 years old, and didn't look a day over seventy-five.

Someone was giggling and whining in the conductor's booth: crawling with spiders that nobody else could see. The ancient creature was amused, as usual. Boundlessly, terribly amused.

The dark train barreled down corridors of endless night, heading toward 23rd Street and beyond. In the engineer's booth, Donald Baldwin stared vacantly out at the tunnel, fingers locked on the throttle, cigarette butts stuck to the spilled Pepsi and blood at his feet. In the light from the tunnel walls, the meaty expanse of his throat twinkled and gleamed. And the controls cast bright reds and yellows on the shiny wet spots and streaks in his clothing.

As they approached 23rd Street, Don Baldwin's dead fingers pulled back on the throttle, and the dark train began to slow down.

Way at the front of the downtown platform, Rudy Pasko was defacing subway posters. *Evita*'s eyes became two blackened pits.. Blood rolled from the corners of her mouth in bold streaks of Magic Marker. The microphone stands had been turned into an enormous penis. And in large jagged letters, on either side, Rudy wrote:

SHE EATS THE POOR
AND MAKES SHELLS OUT OF HER LOVERS

There was no joy in it. Rudy scowled at his handiwork for a moment, then moved down to see what he could do with Perdue's Prime Parts. A cigarette dangled from the arrogant slash of his mouth. His eyes were dark, set back with mascara in the pale, bony face. There was an unpleasant tic around the right socket: too much speed, too much pent-up rage and despair. His hair was a bleached blond rockabilly pompadour. He was dressed entirely in black: tight jeans, artfully ripped sweatshirt, spiked wristbands, leather boots.

Like Peggy Lewin, Rudy's latest romance had come to a less-than-spectacular conclusion. Unlike Peggy Lewin, Rudy had not been drained of all blood and flung from a speeding subway. Also unlike Peggy Lewin, Rudy harbored no sugary illusions of love. Only nasty ones.

Which was why he had the terrible fight with Josalyn. Which was why she threw him out of her apartment. Which was why he woke up his so-called best friend Stephen in the middle of the night, threatening suicide or murder or worse. Which was why he waited, alone, for the RR train to come, while Steve the Sap was no doubt putting some coffee on the burner.

Curiously, now that he *was* alone, Rudy's mind was almost completely silent. He stared at the twins in the poster, Smilin' Frank Perdue and this enormous fucking sheep, and cracked up. The fight was forgotten. He thought only of those two ridiculous mammals, and how to enhance their appearance.

Rudy was applying a business suit to the sheep's likeness when the dark train rumbled into 23rd Street with a ratlike squealing of brakes. He shrugged, beyond caring, and quickly added a pinstriped tie. "A masterpiece," he proudly proclaimed.

The dark train ground to a halt and glared at him with its two blank eyes. Rudy took a last drag of his cigarette and chucked it onto the tracks. He leered at the man in the driver's seat, slipped him the finger.

Donald Baldwin leered horribly back.

The doors opened, and Rudy noticed that there were no lights on the train. Then a very bad rush hit him with alarming force, and he staggered back a bit, puzzled.

It's nothing, he told himself. *It's nothing. Let's go.*

He moved toward the open door, and the hair started to prickle on his arms. Rudy felt himself tightening up involuntarily, but he didn't know why. His steps grew suddenly timorous, uncertain, and then the second rush hit him like a fist to the belly.

"Jesus!" He doubled up slightly and stopped, just staring at the blackness inside the car. *What's happening?* his mind wanted to know. He hung there, frozen.

The doors started to close.

Purely by reflex, Rudy jumped forward and grabbed for the opening. The doors flew open at his touch, and he hustled inside.

The doors closed.

Rudy watched them, panting. He pressed his face to the glass, took a last look at the Perdue twins. Suddenly, they weren't very funny anymore.

Something moved behind him, and he turned.

The dark shape stood in the middle of the aisle, winking at him with luminous eyes. "*How do you do,*" it whispered, and light sparkled on the long sharp teeth.

As the dark train resumed its terrible, downward roll.

The Writing on the Wall

BOOK I.

The Writing on the Wall

CHAPTER 1

Light struggled gamely against the storefront window with the words MOMENTS, FROZEN embossed on its filthy surface. If Danny'd ever scrubbed the sucker, the light just might have prevailed. But New York City grit is feisty, pernicious, and only a few diffused beams clawed their way into the shop.

Inside, Danny Young was thumbing through old movie posters, as usual. There was a little dust on Marilyn Monroe's showgirl thigh; he brushed it lovingly away. Her angelfood face was so luscious, so tragic, that he found himself lost there for a moment, his four eyes gazing into her own.

He pushed his wire-rimmed spectacles up on his nose, ran a hand through his quietly receding hair. He was a tall, gangly man who seemed flash-frozen in 1968: flannel shirt, Grateful Dead T-shirt beneath it, jeans that were a threadbare excuse for a thousand-odd colorful patches. His love of the fantastic, of make-believe, was stamped all over his long, clownish features. He couldn't tell you what he had for breakfast yesterday, but he could tell you every bit player's name in the original *Thief of Baghdad*: a movie made before he was born.

"Oh, Marilyn," he moaned, bending close to her, romantic. "I would have respected your intelligence! I would have given you serious, challenging roles! I would have done *anything* . . ."

She smiled tenderly, understanding.

". . . to have you smile at me that way in real life!" He peeked around the room, a bit guiltily, though no one

15

else was there, then he pulled the poster toward him and gave Marilyn a large wet smack on the lips.

And, of course, someone walked through the door.

"Oops!" Danny cried, dropping her like a hot potato. He flipped quickly ahead to a shot of King Kong and looked up, embarrassed, at his customer.

Only it wasn't a customer. At least, the odds were against it. It was Stephen Parrish; and while Stephen was a regular to the shop, he rarely if ever bought anything. He mainly just liked to hang out and talk, obsessively, about the strange concerns of young media freaks: movies, music, comics, books, and video.

Danny liked Stephen, even though the kid didn't know when to stop sometimes, and his dress was a weird blend of punk and preppie that came off looking silly as a six-legged beagle. True, he'd stopped combining LaCoste shirts with spiked wristbands; but he still seemed perpetually out of place, as if he were followed through life by the caption, *What's Wrong With This Picture?*

It was sad, but Danny could forgive him. Some good ideas always got batted around, and Stephen definitely knew his trivia. Every once in a while, Danny even saw some dollars out of the bargain.

But this morning, Stephen looked pale and haggard, not well at all, from Danny's perspective. *It's been that way ever since he started hanging out with that graffiti asshole, the pseudo-poet with the black eye-liner . . . what's his name?*

"Have you seen Rudy?" Stephen asked suddenly, as if in answer.

"Nope," Danny replied. "But have you seen this?"

He reached into the next rack of posters and pulled out a beautiful coup: Dwight Frye as Renfield in the original *Dracula*, climbing up from the ship's hold with crazed eyes and a lunatic's laughter.

Ordinarily, this would have made Stephen's eyes pop open. But Stephen just muttered, "This doesn't make sense," and went right back out the door.

"Nice seein' ya!" Danny called after him, then

shrugged and scratched his balding head. "Wo
up his ass," he mused. *Probably Rudy, three times*
came unbidden from out of the blue. It made him la
but it wasn't really very funny.

It was depressing, in fact.

"Oh, well," Danny sighed, turning his attention back
to Renfield. "I suppose we'll just have to ask The Master,
won't we, if we want to know why Stephen is hunting a rat."

Renfield's eyes, twinkling with secret knowledge,
reflected on the thick glass of Danny's spectacles. And
faintly, in the back of the shopkeeper's mind, played that
mad and discomfiting laughter. . . .

Stephen Parrish moved briskly down MacDougal
Street, eyes scanning the sweltering crowd. Ninety-five
degrees out and stickier than a bitch in heat, but the
sidewalks were still crawling with life. Tourists, students,
frustrated artists and burnouts: all parading through the
Village like there was nothing better to do, sweating their
silly asses off.

*We've probably got everybody in the western world
here today*, Stephen thought, *except Rudy.*

So where the hell is he?

There were several conflicting tides rolling through
Stephen right then. The one that had stayed up all night for
nothing was tired and pissed. The one that worried
throughout was worrying still. The forever-voice of Reason
was recycling old, lame explanations. And other voices,
which made *no* sense, demanded to be heard nonetheless.

Rolling in separate directions like that, his thoughts
were taking him nowhere. He crossed Bleecker Street with
the traffic, saw nothing useful, and decided to just sit in the
park for a while. *Maybe I'll run into him there*, he thought.
Or somebody who's seen him.

But I doubt it.

Sweat gathered in the short dark hair around his
temples, ran in rivulets down his back and sides. He kept
close to the wall, in a thin band of shadow. It helped, but
not much.

THE LIGHT AT THE END

There was a pizzeria on the corner. An extra large bottle of Coke, with ice cubes all over it, danced in the back of his mind. Stephen moved toward that cold vision, smiling a little. For a moment, thought gave way to more basic biology.

Then he passed the newsstand, and the *Daily News* headline screamed out for his attention. He stopped dead, staring. The Coke was forgotten. And something far colder flooded him with a terrible, dawning realization.

It was raining Frisbees in Washington Square Park, but Stephen didn't notice. Even when one zipped by an inch from his ear, he remained oblivious.

Same went for the kids who were illegally whooping it up in the fountain; the cops who had to chase them out, even though they were roasting themselves; the jazz trio in one corner, the guitarist whacking off his Les Paul in another; the stand-up comedian surrounded by his howling, hysterical audience; the loose joint salesmen, rip-off artists, roller-skating homosexuals in tights, and would-be intellectuals of every shape and description. Not even the promise of a thousand ripe halter tops, dancing in the sun, could pull Stephen away from the nightmare.

He took another absent swig of his beer and read the article again.

8 DIE ON TERROR TRAIN

Subway Ride Through Hell
Leaves No Motives, No Clues

"Police today are at a loss to explain the deaths of 8 people found slaughtered on a downtown RR train this morning. Nor can they explain why the victims—five youths, a transit patrolman, the motorman, and one unidentified man who appears to have been eaten by rats—all died in such horribly different ways.

"And the lone survivor—the conductor of the

train, whom TA spokesman Bernard Shanks de-
clined to identify—has been hospitalized for 'complete psychological collapse.' The man, who was
taken from the scene of horror at 5:17 this morning, is not currently regarded as a suspect.

"A police spokesman stated that 'we are still
looking for a motive in what is certainly the most
bizarre, horrible tragedy in recent memory. . . .'"

There was more, but Stephen had already gone over it
ten times in the last twenty minutes. All to no avail. No
matter how hard he tried, he couldn't find the black hole
that appeared to have swallowed his friend.

And yet he knew that it was there.

"Dammit, Rudy," he moaned, low in his throat.
"Where are you? What happened?" He felt dizzy and weak,
and he wanted to cry; but the tears, like the answer, refused
to come. He was no closer to the answer than he'd been at
5:00 this morning, when the coffee was just beginning to
grow cold.

CHAPTER 2

Joseph Hunter was hunched up behind the wheel of
his delivery van, his muscular frame fighting for air space in
the cramped cab, just waiting for the light to change.
Midtown traffic being what it was, he'd been stuck on the
same block of 38th Street for the last ten minutes. *Fucking
gridlock*, he thought to himself. *If I don't get out of here
soon, I'm gonna drive right over somebody's car.*

There were a lot of cars blasting by on Fifth Avenue.
Joseph watched them wearily, trying to guess which one

would be blocking the intersection when the light changed. "Who will die?" he asked them, indifferent. A black Volvo's brakes squealed with terror.

His beeper went off.

"Oh, God *damn*!" he growled, reaching down quickly to silence it. He hated the thing, its insipid *meep meep meep*ing sound. Like the alarm clock, the telephone, the school bells of his youth: it was the shrill, insistently whining voice of civilization itself. He hated the way that it dug into his side, clinging to his belt like a blood-bloated parasite, nagging like the world's tiniest Jewish mother.

Most of all, he hated the fact that his livelihood depended on it.

Joseph shut the beeper up with a slap of his hand, unclipped it from his belt, tossed it contemptuously onto the dashboard. He was just reaching for his Winstons when he heard the scream.

He glanced immediately at the rearview mirror. When she screamed again . . . it was a woman . . . he pinpointed her: pretty, fashionable, middle-aged, waving her arms and running up the sidewalk toward him. She screamed again.

Joseph whirled around, trying to figure out what was going on. Then he saw the skinny black dude flying through the crowd, clutching something that might have been a football to his chest. Except it wasn't.

It was the woman's purse. And she'd never be able to catch him, no matter how loud she screamed.

"Son of a bitch," Joseph mumbled under his breath. He threw the van in park and jumped out, the door slamming shut behind him.

All the way to the curb, he couldn't stop thinking about his poor crippled mother and the punks that messed her up. He couldn't stop thinking about how much he hated New York, the human garbage that infested its streets. His mind was moving rapidly . . . much more rapidly than his feet. He pushed himself to go faster.

Out in front of the neighborhood deli that bore his name, an old man named Myron was busily sweeping the

walk. He refused to look up at the source of the screams.
He kept his eyes on the pavement, the end of his broom,
and the never-ending filth and debris at his feet, cursing
quietly in Yiddish. He was, like most people, afraid.

That was why he didn't see the enormous form of
Joseph Hunter barreling out of the street. He didn't see the
wild-haired giant bearing down on him like a nightmare
Paul Bunyan, eyes flaming, beard bristling. Not until the
broom was snatched from his hand did he look up; and then
there was nothing to do but watch.

"Excuse me," Joseph said. The wormy little purse
snatcher was almost upon him. He reared back with the
broom, settled into a Reggie Jackson stance, and waited
three seconds.

"Now," he whispered; and when the guy was even with
him, Joseph broke the broom handle squarely across his
forehead.

Everything went flying at once. The purse did a triple
somersault and landed flat on its side with a mute *wump*. Its
snatcher went over backwards, feet whipping out from
under him, a little louder but no less dead to the world
when he hit. The severed end of the broom spun crazily
over the backed-up traffic and *ping*ed off the roof of a
parked car on the other side of the street.

Myron's arms were beginning to flail when the woman
rushed past him. He stepped back to avoid a collision, and
the next moment found him holding what was left of his
broom.

"Thanks," Joseph muttered, and turned away.

The woman had retrieved her pocketbook. It was
clutched to her bosom like a baby as she pushed past the
little storekeeper again and started kicking her would-be
assailant. *"Take that, you lousy prick!"* she shrieked, nailing
him low in the belly with the point of one expensive Italian
high-heeled boot.

"Jeezis, lady!" yelled some guy from the crowd,
grabbing her from behind and holding her back with some
difficulty. "He's already unconscious, fercrissake! You wanna
kill him or something?"

"*You're goddamn right I do!*" she bellowed, and a small crowd began to applaud. The woman flailed out with her right foot, but the guy had dragged her out of range. "*Let me go!*" she screamed, and caught him in the shin with her heel. He yipped like a puppy with a stepped-on tail and obliged her. The crowd went nuts.

Myron was speechless. The dead broom was still clutched in his hand. He let it drop and peered, birdlike, into the sea of faces. Looking for the mountain man.

But Joseph was already climbing back into his van. The light had just turned green, but nobody else had tuned into that yet. He slammed the door shut behind him, slammed into gear, and slammed his foot down on the accelerator.

Luckily, no one was in his way.

"Lucky for you," he growled at no one in particular. A pedestrian thought about crossing in front of him, thought better of it, and jumped back quickly. Joseph ignored the outstretched finger and rumbled past.

It wasn't until he'd cleared the intersection and gone halfway to Madison Avenue that Joseph Hunter allowed himself the slightest trace of a cunning grin. It disappeared as quickly as it came.

"So you flattened him out, huh?" There were a few drops of ale on Ian Macklay's blond mustache. He brushed them away with long, delicate fingers and grinned ferociously at his friend.

"Uh-huh." Joseph shrugged, as if it were nothing, but the tiny smile on his face betrayed him.

"Well, good!" Ian brushed the long blond hair back from his thin, intense features. He drained his mug, pounded it against the table for emphasis, and cleared his mustache again, blue eyes twinkling mischievously. "*All* the little predators should be so lucky! WHAP!" He pantomimed a mighty swing. "Sons of bitches might think *again* before . . ." He paused a moment, puzzlement in his eyes. "On the other hand, he might never think again at all. Joe, you didn't kill him, did you? Knock his brain out of its socket, or anything?"

"If he had a brain," Joseph said, "I might've."

"Well, fuck him, then. Bash his head in!" Ian laughed and reached for the pitcher, emptied it into their mugs, and raised his for a toast. "To streets that are free of monsters and maggots!" he cried. They drank to it.

But when the empty vessels came down, their eyes were sober and serious. For a moment, the sounds of the bar took over. They listened like men in a dream.

There was an argument brewing at the barstools by the door. Some guy with a buzz cut and leather biker jacket had just spilled his Budweiser all over some other guy's pants, and now everyone else was starting to take up sides. Joseph and Ian watched the bartender reach for something under the counter, and Ian said, "It's time to go."

"Where?"

"Under the table."

"Bullshit. I'm still thirsty."

"If it gets too hairy in here, you're gonna hafta tuck me under your arm and run."

"Bullshit. If it gets too hairy to drink in here, you and I will just have to kill 'em all. Order up another pitcher, all right?"

"Right." Ian rolled his eyes and laughed, a little desperately. He was not a very large man—a full foot shorter than Joseph's 6'3" stature—but what he lacked in size, he made up for with audacity. "HEY, WAITRESS!" he shouted at the top of his lungs. "WE NEED ANOTHER PITCHER OF BASS ALE HERE!"

All eyes turned to the little guy with the big mouth and his even bigger buddy. The argument stopped dead for a second, distracted. Their waitress, a tall, vampish girl with long black hair, nodded quickly and hurried out of the firing line.

When the stares had lasted just a little too long, Ian smiled and waved impishly. People went back to their own business; New Yorkers are notoriously good at that. Ian didn't fail to point that out with amusement.

"Yeah," Joseph grumbled. "Like today. If I hadn't stopped that guy, everybody woulda just let him go.

Nobody wants to put their ass on the line for anything, you know? That's why this is such a sick city."

"That's why they had you shipped in here at an early age. They knew you'd grow up to be Batman." Ian winked and leered. Joseph groaned and muttered some expletives. The waitress came back with a full pitcher.

"This one's on me," Ian informed them, digging into his pocket and whipping out a ten-spot. Joseph started to protest. Ian pshawed him. "I don't want to alarm you," he added to the waitress, "but this man is secretly The Defender: an amazing new superhero."

Joseph buried his face in his folded arms. The waitress pretended to be amused, gave Ian his change, and headed for a nice safe corner. Ian socked his friend lightly in the shoulder and said, "Drink up, champ. There's crime to fight."

"Aw, cut me a break. . . ."

"No, seriously! I'll be your teenage sidekick, Butch Sampson. We'll strike terror into the hearts of . . ."

"*Can* it, Ian! You're makin' me feel like an idiot. Cut it out."

Ian shut up, and silence reigned. After a moment, he gingerly refilled their mugs. Joseph stared at the table, stony-faced. Ian sighed deeply, lit a cigarette, and said, "I'm sorry. It's not funny. I know."

And it wasn't, because Joseph was retreating back into his mind now, and it was not a happy place. Ian could only watch his main man slip away, guess at the scenarios playing out behind those eyes. His mother's vicious beating? His own helplessness, when he found out? The helplessness of living, trapped, with her twisted and broken remains? Or was he back in his van, reliving the frustration, flooded by the knowledge that he and he alone would act?

Suddenly, Joseph looked up. His eyes were red-rimmed and weary as they focused on Ian's. "I just want out," he said, and the pain in his voice was contagious. "I just want out of this cesspool. Back to the hills or something. I dunno. Just . . .

"Anywhere a man can *breathe*, damn it! *Clean* air!"

Without even thinking about it, he lit a cigarette. Ian was politely silent. "Where you aren't stepping in someone's piss every time you turn around! Where people don't eat each other for lunch and then go back to the office, you know?"

"Yeah, man. I know." To the best of Ian's knowledge, that was the longest speech Joseph ever made. He was not about to break the flow.

"I just gotta get out. I can't take it any more." He took a long cold swig of his ale, wiped his mustache. "And I can't be knockin' people over the head all the time, either. I don't wanna be anybody's goddamn superhero. I just . . ."

"Want out."

Joseph nodded, eyes averted. Ian wasn't about to ask *well, why don't you just go?* He knew the answer to that one, alrightee.

And it went, very nicely, without saying.

On the subway home . . .

Joseph Hunter, alone in a hot, grimy car with twenty other people who were also alone. No major problems: no threats, no delays, no multiple slayings. Just too much time to think, as they rolled over the bridge into Brooklyn.

On the street . . .

Joseph Hunter, scowling against the ruin. Teenagers, hawking bad drugs and blow jobs, dotting the sidewalk like garbage bags in groups of three to five. Grandmothers, huddled behind shuttered windows. The twinkle of cabs and taverns. The occasional glint of steel.

Joseph Hunter. Leviathan strides against the wasteland. Angry. Alone. Pausing in a battered, poorly lit doorway. Withdrawing his key. Engaging the lock.

In the stairwell . . .

Alone. Mounting the stairs, dragging his weight through the blue light of fading fluorescent bulbs. Hand sliding on the rail. Eyes smoldering. Joseph Hunter, coming to a stop in front of his apartment. And waiting.

At the door . . .

Thinking. Too much. Saying *I don't want to go in*

there. Knowing *I have nowhere else to go.* Hanging in the space between shadow and darkness. Thinking, but knowing. Reaching slowly, once again, for his keys.

Inside . . .

Darkness, almost total. A thin wedge of light, on the wall in the hallway. Across from the bedroom. Its door, open a crack.

She's asleep, he thought. He hoped. Moving quietly inward. Sidestepping the coffee table. Closing in on the television set. Flipping it on, with no volume.

Floorboards creaking, as he moved toward the refrigerator. Shushing himself with a whisper. Opening the door. Brightly lit, for a moment. Withdrawing a can of Bud and popping it open.

From the bedroom, a moan.

Damn. Eyes clenched. Refrigerator door, swinging shut. Back to darkness.

Another moan. Louder.

A semi-articulated sound. Movement: a shifting on sheets, the old bed groaning.

A semi-articulated sound.

"Joey?" Her voice, as he'd heard it all his life. Until the beating. *"Joey?"* Her voice, ringing in his ears.

A semi-articulated sound. Her voice, the voice of memory, receding. Receding, as the sound in the room took over. A sound that few would recognize, saying something that only he could understand.

Calling his name.

"Joey?" A semi-articulated sound.

Then she began to cry.

Damn. Moving quietly toward the coffee table. Taking a long pull before setting the beer down. Moving toward the light.

The darkness, vibrating, as he moved. *Too much beer.* Thinking to himself, as he moved.

Crying, ahead. *Not enough,* he thought. Longing for the beer on the table behind him. As he moved.

In the doorway . . .

Joseph Hunter. In the thin beam of light. Hesitating,

once again. Listening. Fighting the impulse to run, to leave her, to find some kind of freedom from the burden and the pain of it. Shuddering. And stepping forward.

Into the room.

In the bed . . .

She lay. Shivering, under her pile of blankets. Scrawny, pale, prominently veined and horrible: a shadow of herself, stark as a solitary detail in the light from the bedroom lamp. Fear in the eyes: modulating, as recognition struck, into a kind of relief.

Not an enemy, he could almost hear her think as she closed her eyes. *My son,* as she rolled over, sighing as a full human might. *Not one of them.* Then still. Very still.

In the doorway . . .

Joseph Hunter. Not moving. Barely breathing. Knowing what he knew, full well. And unable to touch her. Unable to comfort her. Unable to find it in him.

Standing. Watching. Waiting.

Until she was asleep. Lingering, even then, until he was sure that she would stay that way.

Wishing she would stay that way forever.

And then moving back into the darkness.

Alone.

CHAPTER 3

Upstairs, a phone was ringing. Josalyn Horne paused in the front doorway and winced; there was no doubt in her mind that it was hers. There was also little doubt as to who it was. "Oh, no," she muttered, slamming the door and starting to run up the stairs.

An automatic response. Less than ten steps of the way up, she stopped, catching her reflection in the stairwell window: an attractive young woman, with fashionably short dark hair and finely chiseled features, looking more distraught than she liked to or deserved.

Josalyn smiled ruefully, her eyes flicking upward toward the sound. "Drop dead," she said, taking a moment to readjust the weight of her backpack. Then she started back up again, taking her good old time about it.

The phone continued to ring. She tried to ignore it. She tried to think about the desk she'd be sitting in front of for the next five hours or so. She tried to concentrate . . . absurdly, as she'd be the first to admit . . . on how tired her legs were as they hauled her up the stairs at a deliberate snail's pace.

The phone continued to ring. She gritted her teeth against the sound. It rang again. She got to the second floor landing and stopped, leaning against the rail and wiping moisture from her forehead. *I'm not going to hurry*, she told herself sternly. *I'm not going to . . .*

The phone rang again. She let out a little scream and rushed to the second flight of stairs, rounding the corner and climbing again. The phone continued to ring, louder and louder as she got closer and closer to the apartment door, fumbling with her keys and cursing under her breath.

Josalyn tripped on the last step and almost fell flat on her face. Her keys dropped to the floor. She picked them up angrily and hastened to the door, unlocking it in one swift motion and throwing it open.

The phone rang again, unquestionably hers now. She threw on the lights and made for the kitchen. Her white cat, Nigel, gave her one wide-eyed glance from his place in the middle of the floor and skedaddled. She nearly tripped over him, yelled, "Oh, Nigel!" and reached for the receiver . . .

Just as it cut, in mid-ring, to silence.

"Sonofabitch!" she hollered, lifting the receiver and putting it to her ear. A dial tone. She slammed the receiver back down and leaned against the refrigerator, fighting back tears.

Nigel watched her for a moment in silence, then made

his way cautiously over to her feet. He rubbed himself against one nylon-stockinged ankle, a calculated gesture of friendliness. She didn't nudge him away. He took this as a good sign, repeated the performance; then, glancing quickly up her skirt, he turned for another pass and quietly mewled.

"Oh, Nigel," she cooed, gently dropping to her knees beside him. He purred, a sound like a tiny fur-covered outboard motor. She scooped him up and held him to her breasts, softly squeezing. "I'm sorry I yelled at you. I'm just not in a very good mood."

Nigel struggled a little, looked her in the eyes, and mewled again. She understood. "Hypocrite," she said, setting him down and then standing with a tired, motherly grin. "You just want something to eat, don'cha?" He meowed, loudly this time, and circled her feet as she moved to the cupboard.

Josalyn withdrew a can of 9 Lives Western Menu from the shelf, set it down on the counter, and started rooting in a drawer for the can opener. "This is going to be tremendously exciting," she informed him. He meowed in agreement. She laughed, feeling better already. "John Wayne used to eat this stuff by the case."

Nigel reacted indifferently to this piece of information. It occurred to her that he didn't know John Wayne from a hole in the wall, and that, in essence, she was just talking to herself. She shrugged, equally indifferent, and continued to dig until she found the opener, while Nigel meowed ever more loudly and began to pace at her feet.

"You're all alike, you know it? Men are all alike. I don't care what species they are." Nigel, unfazed, continued to whine. "See? It's just 'gimme gimme gimme.' You don't care about my needs. You don't care about my problems. All you want to do is sleep with me and eat my food."

The can came open. Josalyn wrinkled her nose, but Nigel seemed to find it quite stimulating. "Mmmmmm, boy," she said, trying to conceal her distaste. He started to go wild on the floor; this time she *did* knock him aside with one foot. "Hold your horses, asshole. Don't get so uppity. When was the last time you made *me* dinner?"

She smiled, slightly; it faded. This whole happy encounter had been, she knew, just a diversion. In the end, it had brought her right back to where she started: with the phone, and the man on the other end.

No, scratch that, she amended. *Make that the* child *on the other end.* She smiled again, ruefully. Just then, Nigel reasserted himself at her feet. "Oh, yeah," she mumbled, absently picking up the cat bowl from the floor, filling it up with Western Menu, and putting it back down again. The cat let out one last meow of anticipation and set upon the food in earnest.

Josalyn watched him chow down, his back to her, as if to say *you're dismissed.* It reminded her of the look on Rudy's face after one of his selfish sexual performances. After a half-hearted premature ejaculation (his standard offering), he would slide out from between her legs and roll away from her; in that moment, she would catch a glimpse of his eyes . . . just a flash, before he pulled away.

Only on their last occasion in bed had she figured out what his eyes were saying.

They were saying *I got mine, bitch. Get out of my face.*

It made her furious, just thinking about it. Furious with Rudy, but that was the least of it. Mostly, she was furious with herself for ever having let that soft-headed, brainless prick through the door in the first place.

She turned to stare at the phone, practically daring it to ring. It hung there: silent, white, innocent as a baby's first tooth. She shook her head, tried to clear it. When that didn't work, she moved to the living room and stood foggily in front of the stereo.

Dan Fogelberg was gathering dust on the turntable. She'd put him on last night, after the big to-do with Rudy. It harkened back to happier days . . . less complicated ones, anyway . . . and helped her to get the tears out of her system.

She slapped him on again, cueing the needle by hand. She was not very good at it . . . it always made her nervous . . . and the involuntary shaking of her hands didn't help.

When the phone rang, she almost ripped the tone arm from its socket.

"DAMN IT!" she screamed. The needle dropped to the middle of the first song. She went to fix it, trembled in a mad sort of paralysis, and then just let it go. The phone rang again. A cacophony of voices howled through her brain like a tornado, and she wrestled with them. The phone rang again. And again. And again.

Finally, when she could stand it no longer, she moved back to the kitchen and brought the receiver to her ear.

"Hello?" she said, painfully aware of the weakness in her voice. It misrepresented her position. It didn't belong. It made her angrier still.

"Josalyn?" She jumped at the sound; it was not the voice she expected to hear. "I don't believe it! Do you know that I've been calling all day?"

"Uh . . ." she droned, mentally off-balance. "Who is this?"

"It's Stephen!"

"Oh." Her thoughts snapped back into place with a nearly audible click. "Hi," she said, thinking *so this is how you try to get back into Josalyn's good graces. So we're still in kindergarten, after all. You bastard*.

"Hi," Stephen said. "Uh . . . listen. Is Rudy there?"

What? she thought. It took her a second to answer. "No," she said finally, "he isn't, and . . ."

"Well, have you seen him? Talked to him? Anything?" There was something desperate in his voice. Josalyn wondered briefly what Rudy had told him, what kind of story he got, and the anger flared up like a Roman candle inside her.

"Listen," she said. "Rudy is a very bad subject for me right now. I don't want to talk about him. I don't want to think about him. If I never see or hear him again, I'll still have seen and heard too much. Now, if you don't mind . . ."

"But you don't understand!" Stephen cried, his voice

stripped of veneer. "Rudy has disappeared! I can't find him anywhere!" And then, seeming to realize that he'd begun to sound melodramatic, "I think that . . . something might have happened to him."

"Stephen, *you* don't understand." Her voice was cold; she felt it was a definite improvement. "I don't *care* what happens to Rudy. Rudy can jump off the nearest bridge, as far as I'm concerned. He's a pig, and I hate him, and that's all there is to it. If you want to find him so badly, you can call almost any other number in New York and have a better chance of it. Because he's not going to be here. Never again. Do you understand me now?"

"Josalyn . . ."

"What?" He seemed to be on the brink of tears. She tried not to let it bother her.

"Josalyn . . . did you hear about the murders last night?"

"*What* murders?"

"On the subway. On the downtown RR train, to be specific: about 3:30 or 4:00 in the morning. Eight people were killed. Horribly. Are you interested now?"

"Not really," she said, but a little something in her voice betrayed her.

"It's the train he would have taken. I know it is. He was on his way to my apartment. He called me from the station. . . ."

"What did he tell you?"

"Well . . ." Stephen hesitated for a moment. "Just that there was a big fight, and that . . ."

"That I was a cunt, right?" Josalyn could no longer contain her fury. "*Surely* he couldn't have left out the undeniable fact that I'm a cheap, stupid, naive little farm-girl cunt who thinks that her shit smells like roses! *His words*, Stephen! Do you see why I don't want to talk about it?"

"But . . ."

"If Rudy was on a train where eight people were killed, then I'm sorry, but I think he's probably the one who did it. Why don't you just call the police?"

"*What?*"

"He's the only person I know who's nasty and vicious enough to do anything like that. What were they: Grandmothers? Babies? That sounds just about his style."

"Josalyn!" Stephen sounded furious now, as well. *That makes two of us*, Josalyn thought with a grim kind of satisfaction. "Do you know anything about this story?"

"No, and I . . ."

"*One of the people was eaten alive by rats!*" Stephen yelled, and it came through the receiver with such force that Josalyn shuddered despite herself. "*Do you think that Rudy could possibly have done that?*"

"It wouldn't surprise me," she said, trying to sound cooler than she felt. "To be perfectly honest with you . . . and no offense, Stephen . . . they're the only kinds of friends he deserves."

"I don't believe this!" Stephen was screaming. "Rudy could be dead, and you don't even care!"

"That's right. I don't." Come to think of it, she actually felt as cold as she sounded. She felt nothing at all.

"You're every bit as big a bitch as Rudy said you were!"

"If you're stupid enough to believe that, Stephen, you're stupid enough to believe anything. How about this one? Rudy is Jesus. Rudy walks on water. Rudy . . ."

"I don't believe this!" Stephen yelled for the last time. There was a loud click, followed by silence. Blessed silence. Josalyn felt like spitting on the receiver, decided it was pointless, and hung up with a hand that shuddered in deliberate spite of herself.

"Jesus Christ," she thought out loud. It was so absurd: even if it were true, the timing was unbelievably, riotously funny.

It's like Glen, she thought suddenly. The thought sobered her, and her mind drifted back to her tenth grade year. She had been going with this guy named Glen Burne . . . another self-styled poet, of course . . . and finally just decided that she didn't want to see him any more. He was a nice enough guy; it wasn't a matter of

bastardliness, like Rudy; there weren't any fights, any bitter
points of contention, or anything of the sort.

But he burned like Rudy. The memory made her
shiver, as though she were standing over Glen's open grave
again, a chill wind blowing in her face. *He was so sad, so
strange, so obsessed with darkness. He took the whole
weight of the world on his shoulders and let it crush him
into the ground, a little deeper with every step.*

She hadn't been able to take the constant depression.
That's what it had come down to, finally. She'd had a lot of
optimism in those days, a lot of faith, and she didn't like the
way he walked all over it without even trying. He was the
kind of guy who couldn't pass a flower in the field without
dragging out the tortured metaphors: it would remind him
of innocence lost, martyrs on crosses, butchered babies
stacked through the war-torn ages. He would say it all
offhandedly, as if those were the things you were *supposed*
to be thinking every time you saw a fucking flower in a field.

It had finally become too much for Josalyn, and she
had resolved to break off with Glen . . . gently, of course
. . . on the very next day.

That was on April 26th, 1978. She remembered the
night distinctly. That was the night that, at roughly the
same time she arrived at her decision, Glen Burne quietly
went up to his room and hung himself from the rafters, a
seventeen-page suicide poem set neatly on his desk,
immaculately printed on his mother's flowered statio-
nery. . . .

Josalyn pulled herself out of her thoughts forcefully,
returning to her kitchen in the present. Suddenly, the room
seemed too stark, too white, as though she were having an
acid flashback on the set of a Stanley Kubrick film. She
leaned against the counter dizzily, and a low, husky moan
escaped her.

It's been so long, she flashed. *So long since I've thought
about him.* His face lingered on the big screen behind her
eyes, larger than life and stronger than the grave. It smiled
at her, full of woe, and turned to stare off into space. She

shook her head to clear it, and Glen's face disappeared . . .

. . . and suddenly it was Rudy's face that she saw, his typical arrogant sneer plastered across it like the pancake makeup he used to make himself more ghastly white than even God, or whatever, had intended him to be. Rudy, with his cold eyes as black as the tips of his Magic Markers, mocking the world with every glance.

And in that moment, she knew that Stephen was right.

"Oh, *shit!*" she whined, slamming her fists down on the counter. "*Why,* God? Why does this always have to happen to *me?*" Once again, the anger overwhelmed the sorrow. "It's not *fair!*" she yelled, not thinking about her two dead poets, though their faces ran together in her mind to form one perfect, grinning skull.

She was thinking about what a phenomenal guilt tripper God is, pointing his fat little finger, bringing sweat to palms that in no way deserved it, laying on trauma like the world's biggest Jewish mother. Was it her fault that Glen was too weak and self-absorbed to survive? Was it her fault that Rudy was too much of a bastard to put up with for one minute more? Was it her fault that they'd gone and purchased such nasty fates for themselves?

NO, God damn it! NO! her thoughts screamed, almost audibly. Her eyes snapped shut, squeezing out hot tears that she was barely aware of, she was so royally pissed.

Without thinking, she reached a trembling hand into the refrigerator and pulled out a bottle of Vola Bola Cella. She'd been saving it for a special occasion, and by God, this had to be it. After all, it wasn't every day that your lousy ex-lover got eaten alive by rats, or whatever the hell happened to him. She let the door slide shut behind her absently, not even bothering with a glass, just popping the sucker open and taking a long, cold pull off of it.

The wine was sweet, strong. It went straight to her head like a helium balloon. She teetered slightly on her feet, steadied herself with effort, took another hefty swig, and waited for the second rush to tear through her system.

When it subsided, she felt much better. The shaking

had quieted: the voices and pictures had backed off; the kitchen looked normal again. She smiled wanly at nothing in particular and moved back to the living room, where ol' Dan Fogelberg might as well have been back in his record jacket, for all she'd heard of him.

"Oh, damn," she said, shrugging. She took another hit of Vola Bola, set the bottle down, and cued up the album again. This time, with a couple of belts in her, it was no problem. She giggled a little, mostly at how high she had suddenly become, and sauntered casually over to her desk.

Before her, the various facets of her project were arrayed in consummate order. To the left of the typewriter, the first nine pages of her thesis were facedown and neatly stacked; half of page ten was jutting out of the typewriter, awaiting completion; to the right sat an index-card file with more than a hundred entries, all clearly and sequentially catalogued. Next to that was the filing cabinet that held the lamp, the ashtray, the box of heavy white bond paper, and a host of reference books (philosophical tracts, *Webster's New Universal Dictionary*, the current *Writer's Market*, etc.). And on the bulletin board above the desk, an outline of the thesis and the book that should result from it . . . plus a check list of the myriad essays and articles that she planned to spin off from there, slanted toward everything from *New Age* magazine to *Psychology Today*.

Josalyn Horne was nothing if not methodical in her work; and though she was possessed suddenly with the devilish urge to just tear it all up and scatter it around the room like confetti, she knew that the next five hours would find her poring over it, refining it, and whipping it into shape, as methodical and orderly as ever.

"If I'm not too ripped," she qualified aloud, then laughed and amended it: "I damn well better not be." Still, she moved to retrieve the bottle from its place beside the stereo before sitting down at the desk, taking just a sip this time, and turning to the opening page of her manuscript.

NIHILISM, PUNK, AND THE DEATH OF THE FUTURE read the bold print at the center of the page. *Catchy title*, she kidded herself, and then lapsed into absolute seriousness. She stared at the title for almost a minute before taking another long pull from the bottle and lighting her first cigarette of the session.

This is the payoff, she told herself silently. *My meal ticket. My baby. My rite of passage.*

If I pull it off, I won't have to worry about needing a good man . . . assuming, of course, that there is such a thing . . . to take care of me. Because I'll be taking care of myself.

And if I ever actually do find a good man, she added, *I'll be able to do it on my own terms. Or at least be able to negotiate the terms. And, God, what a precious, rare commodity that is.*

She raised the bottle in a one-way toast, glass clinking against thin Manhattan air, and took another short swig. Then she set it down, resolutely this time, and tried to focus on the words poised awkwardly in mid-sentence, halfway down the length of page ten.

After a while, she began to write. And kept it up, doggedly, for the specified five hours, before shutting off the old Smith-Corona and cashing in her chips for the night.

That night, she did not dream.

CHAPTER 4

In the tunnels . . .

The old Number 6 train rumbled away from the light of Union Square Station, dragging itself painfully into the darkness uptown. The usual number of passengers were on board, doing their midnight ride; atrocity tends to attract as many people as it scares away. Much to the disappointment of morbid thrill-seekers, nothing spectacular was going to happen to them. They would get where they were going, and that would be that.

A few of the more astute commuters would notice the abandoned station, smothered in darkness, that hung to either side of them as they rolled down the tracks between. If they were quick, or particularly observant, they'd notice the signs on the walls: EIGHTEENTH STREET, bold-lettered in white against the long black rectangles. They'd notice the debris on the platforms, the general state of disrepair, the fact that nobody's made a habit of getting on or off there for a long, long time.

They wouldn't notice the figure that lay sprawled in the corner of the uptown platform, surrounded by rusting trash receptacles. They wouldn't see it writhing in the grip of a nightmare, twitching like a man on a gas chamber floor. They wouldn't see the rats that were gathered around it, caught between hunger and an almost religious awe.

They wouldn't know that it dreamed.

Meanwhile, halfway across the Atlantic, something awakened in the cargo hold of a freighter bound for Europe. It smiled like an old man who'd just proved once again that his bowels still worked. It stretched. It sighed.

It climbed out of its coffin.

To its ears, the sound of the ocean was a beautiful thing. Such power. Such mystery. Such agelessness. It felt a kinship with those pounding waves; its life, too, was moved by the moon into patterns of endless recurrence.

The thing in the cargo hold scanned its surroundings with grinning, luminous red eyes. It estimated that there might be 80 to 120 people on board. They should last the voyage.

Although it expected to be very hungry tonight. Traveling did wear on one so.

And after all, it thought, *anyone who's lived 800 years is entitled to a little excess.*

CHAPTER 5

"**Y**our Kind Of Messengers, Inc. Can I help you?" The phones were ringing off the hook, and the sweetness in Allan Vasey's voice was almost purely a matter of routine. Had to be nice to the customers, man. At all costs. You had to keep them happy. In fact, just this morning, he'd pinned a bogus memo up over the dispatch desk: it said BE POLITE, OR WE'LL KILL YOU. Signed, *The Management*. At least two of the people who came into the office weren't sure that it was a joke.

"Jesus Christ, I never seen such a rush!" Tony yelled from the chief dispatcher's seat. He seemed upset; but Allan knew that Tony wouldn't have been happier if you laid two lines of coke out for him and gave him a fifty-dollar raise. It had been a miserable slow summer for the business, and any action was good action when you'd been staring at a dead switchboard for nearly a month.

Your Kind Of Messengers, Inc., occupied a renovated storefront on Spring Street, in SoHo. Despite its bare-bones economy, it was a fairly cheery place: large bay windows for the sun to shine through, plants on the ledge, good people working both the phones and the streets. The dispatch phones sat in a line on the western wall, directly opposite the messenger check-out counter, with the customer-line desk between.

Chester and Jerome were bogged down with calls from clients: law firms, p.r. firms, publishers, fashion designers, art galleries, advertising agencies. It seemed like every client on the books had been waiting all summer for this morning; the sudden volume was staggering. Allan had no choice but to assist them, leaving poor old Tony to dispatch it all.

The only messenger in the office was a new guy. He stood at about 5'9" in his roller skates, wore a light tan jumpsuit that contrasted sharply with his black messenger bag. He eagerly watched the runs pouring in, waited for his share of the pie. Your Kind Of Messengers worked on a commission basis: the more you worked, the more you made. He was ready for some money.

Allan hung up the phone and absently massaged his brow. A headache was coming; he could feel it building up behind his deep-set brown eyes. He let his hand slide down his face, tug briefly at his neatly trimmed and mahogany beard. He glanced at the economy-sized bottle of Tylenol next to the phone, decided against it for the moment, then snatched up a pair of tickets from the desk and handed them to the roller-skating messenger.

"Here's two for you, Doug," he said. The messenger smiled appreciatively. "Not too bad for your second day, huh?"

"It's great," Doug replied, taking the runs and copying the information onto the sheet of paper in his battered clipboard's grip. "Love it."

Allan turned back to his phone. The customer lines had mercifully stopped ringing, for the time being; only the messenger lines were lit, seven flashing buttons on hold. Seven guys, calling in from all over the city, waiting for something to do.

He picked up the receiver and punched in the first button. "Your Kind. Who?" he said.

"This is Vince," answered the little voice over the phone. "Listen . . ."

"Where are you, Vince?"

"Uh . . . Grand Central." Vince sounded impatient. "Listen, don't you guys have any work? I mean, I'm gettin' tired of being told to . . ."

"Hold on, Vince," Allan said, pushing the hold button. If there was one thing he didn't need, it was idiots like that to contend with. Vince's light blinked cheerily, like a Christmas tree bulb. Allan punched in the next line.

"Your Kind. Who?"

"Hunter, up at Columbus Circle."

"Hey, boss! How ya doin'?"

"Alright." Even on the phone, Joseph Hunter was a man of few words . . . most of them surly. "Let me talk to Chester."

"You got it, champ." Allan put him on hold, called across the room. "Hey, Chester! Hunter on seven-oh!"

"Wait 'til I finish with this jerk," Chester called back, holding the phone away from his mouth. Then he turned back around and said, "Vince, you always got an excuse for everything. You know that? Always got a fuckin' excuse."

Allan couldn't hear the response, but he knew that Vince must be laying it on heavy. Chester's broad shoulders were slumped in resignation, his head shaking back and forth slowly, eyes rolling in the dark face. He flashed a pained glance at Allan. Allan nodded and mouthed the words *I know, man*. Chester straightened in his chair and cleared his throat.

"Hey, man. I don't wanna *hear* that!" Chester cried, exasperated. "I wanna know why it took you two hours to get from Manhattan Harbor to 57th Street, you know? I mean, did you get out of the van and just push it up the street yourself?"

You could hear Vince from across the room.

"That's bullshit, bro'," Chester intoned. "That's bull . . . no, man, I *don't* have anything on my desk . . . I . . . listen, pad'nuh. If I *did* have anything, I wouldn't give it to you. You are the slowest motherfucker I ever seen!" Jerome got off the phone, looked at Chester, looked at Allan, and started to laugh. "Now . . . hey. *No*, man! Now you just drop by the office with your manifest. I wanna make sure that people been *signin'* for this shit, you ain't just been dumpin' it in the river or somethin'."

"Hunter on seven-oh," Allan reminded him gently. Chester nodded and squared his shoulders.

"Come into the office, Vince . . . no. Come. In. To.

The. Office. Vince. That's all . . . no . . . goodbye, Vince . . . *goodbye*, Vince!" He slammed down the phone and turned wearily to his compatriots.

"Man, if there's one thing I don't need," he moaned, "it's Vince."

"Vince is the worst," Tony contributed, turning from the phone for a moment. "A real scumbag."

"You know what he said?" Chester exclaimed, throwing his hands up in the air. "He said they had him carrying coffins! I mean, what the hell does that have to do with anything? Why did it take you two hours to get halfway across town? Two hours! Can you believe that?"

"Hunter on seven-oh," Allan said for the last time.

"Soon as I get another driver, Vince is *gone*," Chester concluded, insistent. "That boy is O-U-T." Then he picked up the phone again and punched Joseph's button. "Hunter?" he said. "Hey, babe. You don't know how good it is to talk to somebody sane. . . ."

"That's what *you* think," said a voice from the doorway. Allan turned and saw Ian walking into the dispatch room. Ten o'clock in the morning, and Ian was already dripping with sweat, pasting the long hair to his head and staining the blue work shirt in innumerable places. His messenger bag dangled at his side from the shoulder strap; his clipboard was already in hand. "Hey, who's the spaceman?" he jibed, glancing at Doug.

"Hey, Ian! How's it goin', boss?" Allan called, flashing a toothy grin. Then he addressed the question. "That's Doug Hasken, ace skating messenger."

"Pleased ta meetcha," Ian said, grinning. "Are you for real?"

"You bet," said Doug.

"What happened to your clipboard? Looks like it got fired out of a cannon."

"I use it to direct traffic," Doug quipped, emphasizing this with a swinging motion. "Cabs, especially."

"Him, I like," Ian said, turning to Allan. He flashed a wildass grin and continued. "Hey, I just thought I'd drop by, since I was in the neighborhood and my beeper went off."

"You ready to do some work, buddy?" Tony asked, holding up a handful of tickets. Ian's eyes widened, and he nodded in mute astonishment. "One, two, three, four, five, six, *seven* runs for you, buddy. I'll tell ya, we're goin' off the wall in here."

"Seriously," Allan said, massaging his forehead again, "this is the busiest we've been all summer. If it would just keep it up . . ."

"I could get that condo in Florida," Ian cut in, "instead of sucking gravel for lunch every day."

"It's just the economy," Allan went on. "If you want to know how the country's doing, just check out how many runs are going out. We're one of the best economic indicators there is."

"Who is?" Jerome wanted to know. "You and me?" He was a handsome, fair-skinned black man with a decidedly effeminate air about him. For Jerome, every week was Gay Pride Week, and he didn't care who knew it.

"Nobody's talking to you, Mary," Tony informed him gruffly.

"I told you not to call me Mary. My name is Jerome."

"Anything you say, Queen Mary."

"If nobody's making any money," Allan resumed, unflustered, "*we're* not gonna make any money, 'cause they're not gonna be sending anything anywhere."

"Well, somebody's doin' *something*," Ian asserted, busily copying the runs onto his manifest, "because I am definitely making some money today."

"Enough for a couple of six-packs on Friday night?" Allan sidled up to the counter conspiratorially. "Maybe go back down in the dungeon again?"

"You know," Ian said thoughtfully, "Poot the Barbarian hasn't hacked up anybody in . . ."

"Three weeks," Allan completed the sentence for him. "And I've added a couple of new rooms, a few more magic items. . . ."

"Ah! Renovating, eh?"

"You won't even recognize the place."

"What on earth are you talking about?" Jerome was feigning petulance. "You have a dungeon in your basement, or something?"

"Yeah," said Ian. "It's green, and slimy, and . . ."

"Do you tie people up there?" Jerome asked, eyes brightening. "Do you hold them in chains?"

"You'd like that, wouldn't you, Mary?" Tony commented over his shoulder.

"I'd like to wrap *you* up in chains," Jerome countered, "and flog you silly."

"I bet you would, bitch. I bet you would. . . . Hey, Ian! You gonna sit on those runs all day, buddy? Let's go!"

"Right!" Ian started writing hurriedly again. "So it's Dungeons and Dragons on Friday night. My place again?"

"It already looks like a battlefield, so I don't see why not." Allan winked, and they shared a grin. "Think we can get Mr. Hunter to play?"

"Is he still on the line?" They turned simultaneously to look, but Chester had just hung up the phone.

"Now, that guy is *good*," Chester proclaimed. "I don't hafta worry about Hunter. He's okay. He does his work. But fuckin' *Vince* . . ."

Everybody started rolling their eyes. Chester was going to be on a Vince-trip all day, and it was only ten after ten.

"All he kept sayin' was '*Coffins*, man! *Coffins!*' I mean, who cares about coffins?"

Allan and Ian looked at each other, two minds that liked to play with the fantastic. Two sets of eyebrows raised at the same time. A matched set of evil, obsequious leers.

"Our master," said Allan, rubbing his hands together in toadyish abandon.

"Count Vampiro," said Ian, with fawning adoration in his voice.

"What a lovely bunch of coconuts we've got to work with around here," Tony griped, lighting up a cigarette. "I kid you not, buddy."

"Don't these guys ever do any work?" Doug asked Tony. Tony shrugged.

"No," said Jerome with perfect diction. "They're too busy serving Count Vampiro."

"Nobody's talking to you, Mary. . . . Ian! Get outta here, buddy! Doug, you too!"

"I'm going!" Ian grabbed his clipboard, stuffed it into his bag, and ran for the door, Doug skating up in hot pursuit. Allan watched them, and a weird flash of trepidation struck . . . a shapeless fear, with no identifiable cause, that suddenly loomed up inside him like a monster from his imaginary dungeon.

A sense of impending doom.

He started to say something, but the door slammed shut behind them. Allan stood there, frozen, the bad rush just sitting in his chest like a rotting thing. *Was it for me, or was it for them?* he wondered, staring at the closed door. *Or was it just random paranoia?*

He was dimly aware of Chester's voice, going on and on behind him.

Saying, *"Coffins,* man! Can you believe that?"

As a chill moved up his spine like a snake.

CHAPTER 6

At about 3:30 in the afternoon, Stephen Parrish resolved to call Josalyn again. He'd been all over the Village until almost four in the morning, checking every possible hangout, and come up with nothing. He'd finally dragged himself home and collapsed in defeat, slept through the rest of the morning, and awakened at a quarter to two: bleary-eyed, cranky, and not at all rested.

He'd gotten dressed, made a cup of instant coffee, and gone down to the corner for the *Post* and the *Daily News.* The subway murders were relegated to small boxes in the lower left-hand corner of the front page: POLICE SUS-PECT DEMON CULT IN SUBWAY SLAYINGS for the first, SUBWAY PSYCHO'S CALL . . . "THE DEVIL MADE US DO IT!" for the other. They did not make him happy. He bought them and took them home.

He read them. They were nonsense, pure and simple. Stephen was amazed that the ruse had made it past the copy editor's desk. Obviously, some fruitcake had called in, dubbing himself High Priest of the Luciferian Order, and claimed to have orchestrated a blood sacrifice to the Dark Prince Himself. The police were checking on it, on the off chance that there might be something to it; but Stephen's opinion was that "Lord Blood" (as this loony-tune referred to himself) was a sicko publicity-seeker, cluttering the trail with bad jokes and schizophrenia.

But . . . how could he know for sure?

For all he knew, Lord Blood was not only as weird as he seemed, but even *weirder*. For all he knew, the guy might be a cover for a real group of Satanists, or mobsters, or terrorists, or whatever. For all he knew, it could have been the C.I.A.

The big question in his mind was beginning to be *what difference does it make? If someone got Rudy, it doesn't really matter who it was. Does it?*

In truth, he didn't really have any evidence that Rudy was on the train at all, just a gut feeling that got harder and harder to hang on to as time dragged by. By 2:45, Stephen was more than half convinced that he'd been making a complete arse out of himself . . . that Rudy was out somewhere, sleeping it off, and just not bothering to call.

Which led to the next question: *why, exactly, should I care? Why should I break my neck looking for someone who wakes me up in the middle of the night, says he'll be right over, and then doesn't so much as call for two days?*

By 3:15, Stephen had decided that Josalyn was right, and he was wrong: Rudy was a pig. He had no respect for anybody else. He was completely selfish, completely wrapped up in his own cynical world. He treated other people . . . other *artists*, even . . . like trash, and he had a ridiculously inflated sense of his own importance. An ego as big as a Buick. And he wasn't all that great, really, when you came right down to it.

Stephen felt extremely guilty, then. He felt like an idiot for letting Rudy jerk him around like that, and he felt even worse about jumping all over Josalyn. She was a nice enough girl, and she certainly wasn't stupid: she'd seen through Rudy before he had.

And so it was that, at roughly 3:30, Stephen decided to call her up and apologize. *It won't be pleasant,* he told himself, *but I really have to do it. It's the least I can do, considering how I've behaved.*

He started pacing around the apartment, trying to figure out how to approach it. Should he just say *I'm sorry* and forget about it? Should he try to joke around with her, stay within her good graces if it wasn't already too late? And what if she wasn't willing to talk with him? Could he blame her? Not really.

By 3:40, he'd given up on the idea. It would probably just blow over, and the situation was already awkward. Why make it worse? He spent another ten minutes, just trying to assure himself that he'd made the right decision.

Then he tried to think of something to do.

He went downstairs and checked the mailbox. His weekly check from Mom and Dad was there. As an unemployed art school student (who needed lots of time to pursue his main interest, which was writing), it seemed only right that they should cover his rent, tuition, and all other expenses. *This will come in handy,* he thought. *I'm down to thirty bucks.* Then he went back upstairs.

Half an hour later, after another cup of instant, he decided that writing might help him work off some of his nervous energy. The only problem was, he didn't know what to write about. There were a couple of stories kicking around in his head, but he didn't quite know where to start with any of them.

He tried to come up with something new, but it went nowhere. He threw out the sheet and put in a new one. He stared at it for a long long time.

When 5:00 rolled around, Stephen put on his jacket and headed for the store. He decided that a nice long walk might do him some good, help him clear his mind for this story he was trying to write, help him to relax. He wanted desperately to be a writer . . . a *great* writer . . . but he just couldn't seem to concentrate. Too many distractions. He made a private vow to let nothing disturb him until the story was complete.

By 5:15, he was calling Rudy's house from a Bleecker Street pay phone. Nobody answered. He decided to get a Coke or something and try again later. Just knowing that Rudy was alright would certainly ease his mind.

By 9:30, Stephen had decided that Rudy probably wouldn't be out on the street tonight. He headed home to do some serious writing: a great new idea came to him at McSorley's, swigging ale . . . actually, just some insights into collegiate behavior. Their sexual problems. How hard it all was. That kind of thing. It wasn't a story, but it could be turned into a *great* one, if only he could think of some way to tie all the pieces together.

By 10:30, Stephen Parrish was fast asleep in his bed. He decided that the story could wait until tomorrow. He was really, really tired.

It had been a long, hard day.

CHAPTER 7

By 10:30, Danny Young was munching popcorn in the front row of the St. Marks Cinema and waiting for Werner Herzog's *Nosferatu* to start. It was only the tenth time he'd seen it, and he couldn't wait. "Ah, this is gonna be great," he said to no one in particular, and kicked his scrawny legs like a little kid on a swing.

The black couple on his right, busily rolling up joints for the performance, took one look at him and busted up laughing. He smiled back, ebullient, and did a series of elaborate dance steps from his seat.

"Wha'choo *on*, bro'?" the guy wanted to know, brandishing a fat joint of what looked to be high-grade Hawaiian. "It's got to be better than *this*, thass all I got to say."

"Oh, I don't know," Danny answered. In truth, all he had was some mediocre Colombian. *But, hey, why spoil the illusion?* he thought. *That's what going to the movies is all about!*

He didn't notice the girl coming up on his left until she was almost next to him. He turned, going on the chronic movie-goer's sixth sense; but when he saw her, something else went off in his mind.

I've seen her before, he thought. *In my shop, maybe. Or maybe it was the last time I saw* Nosferatu, *with Jay and Brenda. I'm not sure. But I know that I've seen her before.*

He certainly couldn't forget that face: the large, dark eyes, surrounded by broad patches of black makeup in the shape of bat's wings; the broad features, made almost gaunt by highlights and a thin layer of whiteface; the thick black hair, streaked with blue, styled like Magenta's in *The Rocky Horror Picture Show*; the gaudy purple of her full, arrogantly set lips. He certainly couldn't forget this girl, perennially dressed in red and black flowing garments that only partially obscured her extravagant curves.

No, there's no doubt about it, he mused, watching her approach. *She's the one.* It suddenly occurred to him that there was only one empty seat in the front row, that it was currently occupied by his pack and denim jacket, and that she was going to ask if anyone was sitting there. He cleared his throat in advance and waited for her to reach him.

"Anyone sitting there?" she asked, pointing at his belongings.

"Not at all," he said, piling his things quickly onto his lap. "Sit thee down." Without a proper explanation, his heart was beginning to pound.

"Thanks," she said, complying. While there wasn't any

gushing of eternal gratitude, he figured that she probably
wasn't pissed off at him, either. *Maybe she'll share a doobie
with me, once the show gets going,* he thought, checking in
his pockets for the joints he knew were there with suddenly
clammy hands. Quite involuntarily, the movie screen in his
head started showing clips from a new art-porno film in
which he and she were the stars. He closed his eyes and
tried to stop the projector, but some pretty hard-core
scenes played out before he achieved any measure of
success.

Danny chanced a quick look over at her. She sat, eyes
trained on the blank screen, expressionless. He assumed
that she hadn't read his mind and relaxed a little, but the
sight of her hit him with a burst of renewed imagery.

You don't get laid enough, he reminded himself
sternly. *That's not good. Nonetheless, it is the way it is.* He
helplessly allowed one more seamy shot to flash before the
shout went up from behind him and the lights began to
fade. . . .

"Alright!" he cried, as darkness enveloped the theatre.
And the horror began.

When the uptown RR pulled out of the 8th Street
station, there were only two people left on the platform:
Louie, who was passed out some twenty yards from the
southern mouth of the tunnel, and Fred, who was staggering around in a considerable stupor, looking for money that
people might have dropped. Neither Louie nor Fred had
held any gainful employment for the last eight years or so.
Both of them smelled like ripe sewage on a hot plate. The
uptown passengers on the RR were extremely glad that
Louie and Fred had decided not to join them.

Louie snored while Fred dragged his gaze along the
concrete floor. It didn't look promising for the great white
hunter: if he found more than fifteen cents, he would have
to consider himself lucky. Maybe . . . he wasn't quite
sure . . . that'd give him enough for another bottle of
muscatel, if he got Louie to chip in. . . .

There was a sound from the mouth of the tunnel. At
first, Fred thought that it was just his buddy, shuffling

around or something. But when he heard it again, he was looking directly at Louie, and Louie didn't seem to be moving at all.

"Whuzzizit?" he mumbled, wiping his eyes with a grimy paw. He staggered a little further down Louie's way, and that was when he saw it.

Sitting at the very edge of the platform, right next to the far wall, was a wallet. Even from that distance, with his vision swimming like an Olympic gold medalist, Fred had no doubts as to what it was. It looked pretty fat, too, and Fred couldn't figure out for the life of him why he hadn't noticed it before.

"Oboy," he said, making a jagged beeline toward the black leather goody. He briefly considered waking up Louie, but decided against it. *Piss on 'im,* he thought. *Gonna drink the whole bottle myself.*

He was almost up to the edge of the platform when the first wave of irrational fear hit him. He shrugged it off, having learned long before to ignore anything that didn't get him drunk. There was a gold buckle on the wallet; it twinkled in the overhead light like the wink of a harlot.

He was seduced. The wallet was so close now that he could almost smell the leather. He stumbled up to the yellow safety line, dropped to his knees, and reached out slowly with one trembling hand.

"Oboy," he said.

And then the hand whipped up from below: so cold, so fast, that Fred barely had time to gasp before it took him by the wrist and yanked him, head-first, toward the rails. . . .

Two joints and more than half a film later, a strange thought came together in the back of Danny's mind. Though it had nothing to do with what was on the screen at the moment, he found himself remembering the scene where Nosferatu's ship docked . . .

. . . his ship full of rats . . .

. . . and he thought about the subway murders from a couple of days ago: the ones that made all the papers. He seemed to remember something about rats in that story, too: somebody eaten alive, speculation that a large number of rats were brought on board by Satanist crazies, or something. . . .

What if. . . . he thought, and then stopped himself. It was too crazy to even consider, beyond a shadow of a doubt. And yet.

And yet.

Sitting in this theatre, surrounded by crazy people, with Klaus Kinski's two monstrous fangs staring him in the face, it suddenly didn't seem any stranger than the fact that James Watt was once Secretary of the Interior. Suddenly, with a rush that bordered on cold certainty, it seemed ridiculously clear that vampires were riding the subways and feeding on hapless commuters.

Danny giggled nervously. He looked at Nosferatu's face and cracked up completely. People on either side of him turned to see what could possibly be so funny; he waved them off with helpless little sweeps of his arms. *Oh, it's so obvious, it's almost obscene!* he thought, and then broke out into fresh, hysterical gales of laughter.

The girl on his left, with the bat-wing makeup, grabbed him by the arm and started to shake him. "*What's going on?*" she hissed, eyes red and glassy from Danny's two joints and God-knew-what-else she might have done before the show. On her face was a mixture of annoyance and amusement; she wanted to know why he was laughing just as badly as she wanted him to shut up.

"I'm sorry," he whispered back. "I'll be quiet." And started giggling again.

"No, wait a minute." The smile had taken over her face. "I want to know what's so funny."

"Uh . . ." The words froze on the way up his throat. *She'll think I'm a fruitcake,* his rational mind informed him. *She'll say* uh-huh, right, *and move to the back of the theatre.* But then he looked at her again . . . not just her physical appearance, but the way she was leaning toward him now, her eyes almost flaming in their twin pools of dark design . . . and he reconsidered.

Fuggit. One fruitcake to another. He shrugged his shoulders, not giggling now, and leaned toward her with one hand cupped between his mouth and her ear.

"You might think this is silly," he whispered, "but I'm beginning to suspect that there's a vampire running around in the subways."

She didn't move. Danny, too, was fixed in position, with his face half-buried in her hair; and because he couldn't see her awed, almost beatific expression, he had no idea as to how she was reacting. For a long moment, he sat in tense, motionless apprehension, wishing that he knew what went on in her mind.

And it was funny, because when she turned to him with lowered eyelids and a crafty smile on her purple lips, the first thing she said was, "You know, I was just thinking exactly the same thing."

For another long moment, their eyes were locked.

An understanding passed between them.

"Later," she whispered finally, bringing one finger to her lips. They turned, secretly smiling, and went back to the movie.

On the screen, an actor was pretending to drain blood from an actress who was pretending to die; but for the first time in Danny Young's life, he saw it as though it were actually happening. As though it were *possible*.

And for the first time in ten viewings of *Nosferatu*, he was genuinely scared to the bone.

Louie wasn't sure, at first, what woke him from the sleep of the mortally wasted. It happened suddenly; no dreamlike segue between his own little world and the big one outside his head, no break at all between total unconsciousness and as much attention as he could muster. Suddenly he was awake, staring bleary-eyed at the empty platform.

Alone.

"Wuh," he mumbled, wiping something wet from his mouth. Liquor and drool. It left a thin, glossy smear across his dirty hand. He wiped it on the hair that spilled down into his eyes, and looked around the platform again.

Dimly, in the back of his mind, it occurred to him that something was missing. He didn't know what it was, but it was there; or, rather, it was *not*. Louie grimaced, perplexed, and scratched absently at his itching scalp. His brain, pickled by the years, refused to cooperate.

And then he heard the sound that awakened him. Echoing crazily from the depths of the tunnel. Cutting off sharply, as if by a switch. And erupting again.

A scream.

Louie dragged himself forward for about a yard before he could get to his feet. It came again . . . horrible, tortured, pleading . . . and stopped abruptly. He craned his neck, stumbled, and fell on his face. For a second, he forgot where he was, then remembered; his ears pricked up like a dog's, and his bowels threatened to let go in terror.

But the screaming had stopped.

"Fred?" he whispered.

Then, from somewhere deep in the forever darkness, a low rumbling: faint at first, but slowly gathering force as it drew closer and closer to where he lay, trembling, on the cold concrete. The rumble became a roar, like thunder. For the second time today, Louie pissed himself; but this time he was awake, and whimpering, as two bright circles of brilliance glared out of the tunnel like a pair of hellish eyes.

And as the express train hurtled through the 8th Street station, Louie was not at all sure whether the puny screams that he heard were a last dying echo from the shadows beyond, or whether they were his own.

"The thing I don't understand," she said, "is why it's just starting now. Why now?"

"Why not?" he answered, glib. "Good a time as any."

"No. I mean, did he just move to New York two days ago, or has he been hiding out for a while?"

"I don't know. A lot of people move here every day." He paused to scratch his chin, a gesture of deepest concentration. "Maybe it's just a tourist."

"A tourist?" She laughed, beaming, and brushed a dark lock of hair from her eyes.

"Yeah. He pops into town, takes a room under the wine cellar at the Plaza Hotel, sleeps all day, and paints the town red at night."

"Oh, Jesus." She shook her head and gave him a look that said *I don't believe I'm walking with this guy*, then laughed again. "Paints the town red. Jesus. You're insane, did you know that?"

Her name was Claire De Loon; or at least that was what she'd have had him believe. She said that she lived on MacDougal Street, just south of Houston, which was good news for Danny: it put her within four or five blocks of his shop.

Another happy development for Danny, were it to be true, was that Claire seemed to like him. It was evidenced by her laughter, the sparkle in her eyes, by the fact that she'd told him so much about herself . . . even if some of the details, like the name, were bogus—if nothing else, then by the fact that they were going to Cafe Reggio for cappuccino together.

It was good news for Danny because he had definitely taken a liking to Claire De Loon, or whatever her name was. *She's a real character*, he thought fondly as he watched her walk beside him. The jiggle of her breasts was an awesome thing to behold. She moved with unmistakable New York bravura: a swagger just this side of haughtiness.

But the clincher, without a doubt, was their little psychic link. There must have been half a million girls in the city who could make him do a double-take; very few of them, however, would be apt to get the same flash at the same time, and fewer still would be willing . . . no, make that *eager* . . . to talk about it. Especially when it was as weird a flash as this.

"Well, then," Claire continued, "he might be gone by now. Nobody else has been killed, have they?"

"Not that I know of . . . but it's an awfully big city."

"I know." She looked wistful. "I hope he isn't."

"Isn't what?"

"Gone," she said. "I hope he didn't pick up and leave."

"*Why?*" He gaped at her with honest incredulity.

"I've always wanted to meet a vampire," she answered, matter-of-factly. Then, with a cryptic little half-smile, "I think they're sexy."

"And you think *I'm* crazy!" He smacked the flat of his right hand against his receding hairline. She put on a mock-pouting expression. "This is not a *nice* vampire, Claire. It feeds people to its pets."

"Well, you know how monsters are." Grinning.

"Yeah, but . . ." he started, and then grinned back. It was too ludicrous a situation to get all worked up about. Danny threw up his hands, conceding, and then thought of an even more ludicrous twist to throw in.

"How do we know," he asked, "that it's even a *he*?" She looked up, startled. He smiled triumphantly and continued. "How do we know that it's not some withered, two-thousand-year-old bag with warts all over her?"

"No, no, no," she insisted, repressing a giggle. "Vampires are eternally young and eternally beautiful."

"Oh, yeah? What about Nosferatu? He wasn't so cute."

"That was only a movie."

"Oh. Right."

By now, they were almost across Astor Place, the small plaza that splits Park Avenue South into Fourth Avenue and Lafayette Street, and 8th Street into St. Mark's Place. In the center of the plaza, an enormous cube was balanced on one of its corners. A bunch of enterprising young punks were spinning it around and around: in a sense, that was what it was there for. Participation Art.

On one side of the cube, the word IMAGINE was rendered in large, spray-painted letters. It happened shortly after John Lennon's senseless, pathetic murder. Nobody had seen fit to paint over it.

New York City loves its graffiti artists.

They crossed in silence, watching out for the cars that blasted by with little or no regard for pedestrian safety. There was one singularly deranged taxi driver who must have been doing 60 mph; he seemed to be deliberately bearing down on them. Danny took Claire's hand and took off running. She followed, not resisting. The cab missed them by less than two feet.

"CRAZY BASTARD!" Claire yelled from the safety of the curb. The cabbie shouted something back, swallowed

by the sound of his own squealing tires. She flipped him the
bird as he raced into the night, then laughed and turned to
face her companion.

Danny let go of her hand, feeling suddenly awkward . . . presumptuous, even. It took a second before
he realized that she hadn't minded; by then, it was too late
to just grab it back again. *You putz*, he informed himself
silently, and hoped for a lot of traffic when they hit
Broadway.

They resumed their pace, heading down 8th Street
toward Greenwich Village. For the moment, they remained silent, immersed in their own internal dialogues.
Neither was sure as to what the other one was thinking. If
they'd known, they would have been amazed by how strong
their psychic link actually was.

Because they were both thinking about the same two
things: the vampire in the tunnels, and what it would be
like to sleep together. For Danny, the priorities were
reversed, but that hardly mattered.

But since neither of them knew for sure, neither one
dared or cared to say anything. Then, because he sensed
that the silence had become overlong, Danny cut off his
train of thought and cleared his throat loudly.

But before he could think of something ridiculous to
say, they heard the voice shouting from down the block,
near the subway entrances. The words were drunken,
slurred, more than slightly hysterical. As they drew nearer,
they listened carefully to what the voice was trying to say.

". . . DOWN THERE! IZ'WUZ DOWN THERE,
AN' IT GOT FRED! OMMA . . . OMMAGOD, IT WAS
. . . HE WAS SCREAMIN', AN' I . . . OH, LORDY,
SUMPIN'S *DOWN THERE!*"

They stopped dead, turned to stare at each other
apprehensively. Claire asked him quietly if he heard that.
He nodded, mute.

And though it was a warm night, they shivered, as
though a cold hand had reached up from Hell to take the
two of them in its grip.

CHAPTER 8

In her dream, she was standing over Glen's open grave again. A thin wet mist descended from the sunless heavens of a chill gray autumn sky. Josalyn was smoking a cigarette, cupping it in her hand protectively as she stared down at the coffin in its hole of mud and formless shadow, watching the scattered clods of dirt on the fiberglass lid lose form themselves as the rain slowly, painfully, broke them down.

Inside, she felt cold: cold as the rain, as the sky, as the grave. No tears. No sorrow. Nothing but a sense of flat, stupid finality: life as a series of elaborate, meaningless figures on a mathematician's blackboard, rendered in chalk and wiped away by a clumsy block of wood and felt and padding.

It's so stupid, she thought, staring down at the muddy pools on the coffin's lid. So stupid, and pointless, and cruel. She'd have liked to know what she'd done to deserve this, what crime so heinous that it demanded this smack in the face, this deliberate blow of her belief that life was good and sensible and fair.

But she knew the answer, no sooner than the question was posed. Nothing. She'd done nothing, short of being born in a world that had long before lost its bearings and gone cartwheeling off toward madness and oblivion— perhaps at the time of the Apple, perhaps even earlier than that.

She mused, sight unfocusing, turning inward. She was only dimly aware, in the back of her mind, of something stirring in the hole at her feet. It didn't fully register until,

58

with a loud snap of splintering wood, something burst through the lid of the coffin.

Josalyn stared down at the grave in horror, frozen. *The cigarette slipped from between her fingers and tumbled downward, a slow-motion spinning that seemed to go on forever.*

From the grave, a rotting skeletal arm projected upward, clawing at the air as if to rip bleeding holes in the sky. A tiny cry escaped her throat, and the mouldering hand froze, clenched like the talon of a great winged bird. Then slowly, slowly, it twisted itself around so that the back of the hand was facing her. The index finger, its broken end dangling from a few strands of greenish flesh, straightened and then curled back toward the palm. Repeated the gesture. Repeated it again.

It beckoned to her.

NO! *she cried silently, no wind in her lungs.* NO! She spun, eyes snapping shut reflexively, and something was there: something warm and comforting, wrapping itself around her and holding her tightly. She shivered, blind and terrified; she whimpered, deep in her throat; she nestled against the figure that held her and understood, though foggily, that it was a man. A good man. She let herself go, and huge gut-wrenching sobs escaped from her mouth, smothered in the warmth of her protector.

It's alright, *a kind, soft voice assured her.* It can't touch you now. It can't hurt you. *And though she could still feel that skeletal arm, trying by its sheer presence to claw through the back of her skull and take her, consume her, she also knew that the dead thing was losing its power. That the voice wasn't lying. That she was, in fact, safe.*

Oh, thank you, *she whispered, pulling her face away from the man's chest and opening her eyes to see him . . .*

. . . and suddenly she was alone, in her apartment, with the typewriter quietly humming on the desk before her as she jotted down something in her notebook with a finely sharpened No. 2 pencil. Life is good, *she rendered in tight, elegant longhand.* Life is sensible. Life is fair. . . .

The phone rang. She jumped, and the pencil went

flying out of her hand. She watched it spin through the air like her cigarette on its way to the grave, with the same slack-jawed expression of horror on her face.

She watched the pencil imbed itself point-first in the hard wooden floor, sticking straight up like the needle of a compass pointing north. Trembling for a moment. And then standing completely still . . .

. . . as a dark pool of blood began to spread across the floor, slowly at first, then more and more quickly . . .

. . . as a mocking, sneering, inhuman voice from somewhere in the room breathed the words you were expecting company? *into her ear and began, horribly, to laugh and laugh and . . .*

Josalyn awakened, screaming, into the otherwise silent darkness of her bedroom, alone.

It was the first, and the mildest, of the dreams.

CHAPTER 9

At 11:08 the following morning, by the company time clock, Allan took the call from Rosa, the woman who lived downstairs from Joseph and watched his mother during the day. Rosa's English was poor, and the fact that she was crying and lapsing sporadically into Spanish didn't help, but Allan got the message loud and clear.

He hung up the phone, feeling like he'd aged a hundred years in the last three minutes. His breakfast started to churn sickly in his stomach; sweat covered his forehead like a thin sheet of ice; he reached for his pouch of Captain Black tobacco with a trembling hand, tamped it into his pipe, and just stared at it for a long unhappy moment.

Jerome was the first to notice that something was

wrong. He'd just been clowning with Allan a few moments before, and everything'd been hunky-dory. He could only think of one thing that could bring a dispatcher down that fast.

"Did somebody get hit?" he asked, remembering the squealing taxi brakes that had brought his own career as Ace Bike Messenger to an inglorious end.

Allan turned quickly, disorientation stamped on his features. "What?" he said, and then the statement registered. He grinned vaguely and shook his head. "No, no. It was . . . well, nobody got hit, exactly, but . . . uh, beep Hunter for me, will you?"

"Joseph?" Jerome didn't get it "What . . ."

"Beep him." Allan lit the pipe and made every attempt to steady his voice. "His mother just died. I've got to tell him."

Joseph Hunter was standing in a phone booth on the corner of 8th Avenue and 42nd Street, the dead receiver still clutched in his hand. He stared out through the glass, seeing nothing. His mind was elsewhere.

When his beeper had gone off, he'd been cruising up 8th with a vanload of prints for some European film festival. His mind had been riveted on his environment at that point; like most cities, New York demands that you drive like a ruthless maniac with metal teeth and eyes on all four sides of your head. Joseph was accommodating: cutting people off, swerving madly from lane to lane in an effort to pass everybody on the road, shouting at people when they didn't get out of his way. Death had been the farthest thing from his mind.

When his beeper had gone off, he'd suspected that the guys in dispatch had something else for him to pick up. He'd had no idea that it would be this heavy.

She's dead, said a voice in his head that sounded like it must be somebody else's. He felt detached from the thought, from the very idea of it. *She's dead*. It had to be somebody else's life that he'd just been listening in on.

Automatically, his free hand dug into the pocket of his

jean jacket for a cigarette; he spent about thirty seconds trying to light the filter before he realized what he was doing.

"AARRGH!" he bellowed, tossing the useless smoke to the floor. He looked at the receiver as if it were a pigeon turd that had landed on his sleeve, slammed it down onto the hook, and stormed out of the booth.

Back on the sidewalk, surrounded by the gaudy sleaze of West 42nd Street . . . peep shows on top of live sex acts on top of $1.99 porno triple bills, all flashing their multi-colored marquees to sucker in the scum of the earth . . . Joseph was overwhelmed by the urge to just reach out and smash something. It didn't much matter what: a wider selection of eminently smashable things could not have been assembled for love nor money. All he had to do was wait for a little provocation.

Normally, he wouldn't have had long to wait. There was something daunting, however, about a gigantic bearded young man who looked like he was about to explode. The danger light went on. Con men who would ordinarily try to sell him bad drugs, pictures of naked harlots, the naked harlots themselves, and other hot items gave him a wide berth, some actually stepping off the curb and into the street to get around him.

"Yeah, that's right," he said, too quietly for anyone to hear. "Back off." But as he spoke, the tears began to well up in his eyes. The shuddering seemed to start in his chest and radiate outward, like shock waves from a depth charge that somebody just set off in his heart. Before he fully realized it, he was practically doubled over by the force of his own massive sobbing.

And the same voice in his head came back, speaking like a stranger with a clearer view of the situation than anyone involved. *She's dead*, it repeated. *But that's what you wanted, isn't it? You wanted to be free of her. To live your own life. To get the hell out of this grimy insane asylum.*

Isn't that what you wanted? the voice insisted, point-blank, and suddenly it sounded like some cheap prick D.A.

that the State had sent in to break him down. It was the voice of his conscience being a cruel bitch, trying to make him squirm over crimes never even committed.

Isn't that what you wanted? the voice repeated, jabbing his chest with a long, bony finger. By then, he'd had just about enough.

"No," he growled through gritted teeth. He wiped the tears from his eyes with a painfully clenched fist and repeated the word. "No." It played over and over in his head, as though he'd spoken into an echo machine and then kept slowly turning up the speed and intensity so that it gradually rose in pitch, faster and faster, the word blurring into itself, a maddening cacophony that pounded against the insides of his skull . . .

Until something inside of him snapped.

Joseph Hunter turned then, shutting his mind off with an audible click. He began to move east on 42nd, toward his parked and waiting van, with a chill and deliberate gait. Once again, the crowd parted before him with extreme caution in their sidelong glances.

About thirty yards ahead, an argument was brewing on the sidewalk in front of an adult novelty store. Out of the hundred-odd conversations going on within earshot, this one singled itself out for Joseph's attention. He moved closer.

"I WANT MY MONEY!" A white guy. Young. Very hip-looking, like he just got off the plane from California. Except that he was sweating, and his face was red.

"Hey, blood . . . you wanna try an' double it, doncha?" A black dude. Young. Very cool. In shades, so you couldn't see his eyes as he reached down to scoop up three cards.

Between them was an improvised Three Card Monty table: an open cardboard box on a trash can. Around them was the usual crowd of suckers and rubbernecks out on a lunch break, taking turns gawking and losing more of their paychecks than they could reasonably afford. There was easily three hundred dollars riding on this game, most of it California's.

"NO, MAN! I WON!" California was howling, pointing at the cards. Evidently, he'd picked the right one anyway.

"Yo, man. Chill out. Don't . . . ?" Monty began. He was starting to get nervous now. He took a short step backward: the cards in one hand, the money in the other.

"GIMME MY MONEY!" California yelled, making a grab for it. Two large black dudes started to converge on them from the gathering crowd.

"Cops," Monty said, kicking over the trash can and turning quickly away. The money was halfway to his pocket: his face was still half-turned, looking over his shoulder. He took one step, his head swinging back around, and walked face-first into something large and solid.

He looked up.

"How much money did you steal today, cocksucker?" Joseph inquired. A pair of tiny Joseph Hunters stared back at him, reflected in the mirrored shades. Monty smiled, innocent as dumplings, and started to back away. Joseph smiled and punched him in the head.

Large white teeth and dark sunglasses went flying through the air. The stack of twenties blossomed and dispersed like a bright green fireworks display, dancing in the breeze. California rushed forward. Monty dropped at his feet.

Joseph whipped around quickly. The dealer's two buddies were stunned, for the moment; *they* were the ones who were supposed to appear from out of nowhere when trouble arose. By the time one of them got it together to go for his knife, a large fist was already on the way.

The knife never left its sheath. Its owner's nose broke with a resounding crack, twin crimson geysers streaming from the wide, flaring nostrils. The man wasn't out, but he was hurtin' for certain; he dropped to his knees, clutched his face, and moaned into his blood-spattered hands.

The sporting thing to do would have been to leave him there for a moment, then come back to disarm him. Joseph kicked him in the stomach first, then turned to deal with the other one. It took just a second too long.

He didn't see the excited crowd, fanning out in a wide

semi-circle. He didn't see California drop to his knees, scooping up the fallen dollars. He didn't see the fourth dude that was coming up behind him, or the two cops that were running to the scene.

What he saw was a shiny, black, metallic blur, racing toward the side of his head. He brought one arm up reflexively to block it, and searing pain shot through his forearm. Before he could cry out, the pipe completed its swing, striking him just above the temple. His vision started to gray out, like a bad picture on an old black-and-white TV.

Then something hit him hard between the shoulder blades from behind, and he went over. He heard the shouting and commotion above him as if from a great distance: then it faded out altogether.

"He's just lashing out." Ian sighed wearily. "It's so obvious."

"I know," Alan agreed. "But what are we going to do?"

Ian shrugged, eyes downcast, and took a listless drag off his cigarette. They were sitting around the coffee table at Ian's one-room studio apartment. It was 1:30 in the morning, and Joseph Hunter had finally passed out on the couch, having drunk himself into his second oblivion of the day.

Allan set down his tobacco pipe and reached across the table for his brass dope-smoking bowl. "There's still a little bit in here," he said. "You want some?" Ian looked at it for a moment, then nodded and smiled wanly. "It's the most constructive thing I can think of to do at the moment," Allan concluded, passing the pipe.

Ian brought the stem to his lips and wrapped them silently around it. Allan was there with the lighter, flicking it on, and for a few seconds their faces were all highlights and shadow, like two characters making a deal by candlelight in an old *Prince Valiant* comic strip: Ian, with his wild blond hair and heavy mustache, struck an almost barbaric figure; Allan, with his dark hair cut evenly at the shoulders, his thin mustache and goatee, could have been a moneyed merchant of old, striking up an offer that no red-blooded mercenary could refuse.

Then Ian had the pipe lit, and Allan withdrew the lighter. The illusion ended: they were two young men in the twentieth century, half-stoned out of their minds, agonizing over somebody else's problems.

Ian took a hit and passed the pipe back to Allan. He sucked in sharply, holding back the cough that threatened to wrack him, and somberly shook his head.

"What?" Allan asked, taking his toke. The other paused for a moment, blew out a great cloud of smoke, and then leaned forward.

"Five hundred dollars," he said finally. "That's what."

Allan rolled his eyes and nodded solemn agreement. It had taken $500 to get Joseph out of jail this afternoon on charges of assault and battery. Because California had vanished after Joseph helped him out, there were virtually no witnesses who weren't either friends of, or afraid of, Three Card Monty and his boys. The cops had no choice but to book him, though they informed him confidentially that the charges would be dropped. It still cost him five big ones to get out.

"Thank God he had it," Ian continued. "I couldn't have helped him."

"Me either. . . . He makes more in a week than both of us put together!" They laughed, a welcome development. "Last week, I think he took home about eight hundred."

"Christ." That figure looked like the Holy Grail from where Ian was sitting.

"Yeah. But he has all kinds of expenses that we don't; gas, tires, repairs on his van, insurance. . . ."

"And funerals," Ian added. "Don't forget that."

"No. Christ." Allan looked over at Joseph's limp form, sprawled out on the couch. "I don't think I could forget that. I was the one who had to tell him."

"I bet that was fun."

"A joy unbounded."

"I'll bet."

"A regular barrel of monkeys."

"Oh, God." They laughed again, the way one laughs at dead baby jokes: nervously, guiltily, and helplessly. "Jesus Christ, I can't stand it," Ian concluded, when he regained his voice, then staggered over to the fridge for two more 16-ounce Buds.

"Thanks," Allan said, receiving his. They spritzed the cans open simultaneously, took identically long swigs off of them, then turned to stare at each other with grim smiles.

For almost a minute, there was no sound but the faint rumble of Joseph's drunken snoring. Ian took another swig off his beer and spoke.

"You know what I think?"

"What?"

"I think he should pack up his gear and get the hell out of New York, as soon as he can. I'd hate like crazy to see him go, but I think he'd be a lot happier almost anywhere else."

"Yeah." Short pause. "I think you're right. There's nothing, short of our smiling faces, to really keep him here, is there?"

"Nope." Another short pause. "Not that I can think of."

Another pause, longer.

"Do you think he will?"

"God, I hope so." Ian snubbed his butt out in the ashtray. "Before something else happens."

"What do you mean?" Allan's dark eyes were hidden in shadow, but Ian felt the bright glint of them just the same.

"I don't know," Ian answered. He was staring at the ashes, as if for a clue. Then, turning to meet Allan's shrouded gaze, "I really don't know."

CHAPTER 10

It watched her from the darkness of the tunnel.

She was a fat, ugly, middle-aged woman with a large, hairy wart displayed prominently on her left cheek. Her dress was preposterous: a shapeless mass of fabric that had once been brightly colored, but which had faded and worn away through the years into a dull, dingy opacity. Her hair hung lifelessly down either side of her face, the color of a healthy dog's stools.

Nobody was near her. A few others were gathered around the middle of the platform, near the safety of the turnstiles; they were not paying any attention to her. She had chosen to wander down to the end, with her grocery bags full of bric-a-brac in a clumsy pile at her feet.

She picked her nose with a flabby finger, indifferent to the reaction it might provoke. She flicked a dry, pale strip of mucus onto the tracks with a graceless minimum of effort.

It was sickened, watching her. It leaned against the cold wall of the tunnel, pressing its cheek against the moist stone, and contemptuous nausea bubbled up in its empty stomach. If the disgust could compete with the hunger, it would turn away now and leave this woman to some other ghastly fate.

But it was hungry. Oh, yes. Unbelievably, ravenously hungry. And this woman, unpleasant as she appeared, seemed to have an awful lot to offer in the way of food.

It considered snatching her from the platform, then decided against the idea. There were others . . . too many others . . . and it did not want to be seen. Not now.

Not yet.

It waited, watching. Two more people made their way

down onto the platform. They remained near the entrance, as well. It appreciated their good sense, in light of all the nasty horrible things that had gone down in the subway of late. It chuckled, more than a little mad.

And it waited.

Presently, a deep rumbling from the darkness behind it announced the imminent arrival of the uptown local. It ducked deeper into the shadows, waiting for the train to pass, and tried to figure out how to time its next move.

Within a minute, light began to creep along the rails, heralding the final approach. It hunkered back even further, into a niche; and as the train whipped by, the thing in the tunnels was quite certain that its presence had not been given away.

It waited for the train to screech to a halt before moving; even then, it moved as silently as possible. When it heard the doors slide open, it slipped quickly up to the back of the train, then sidled along the far side until it came to the space between the last two cars. It jumped up onto the metal platform. Crouched down, unseen. And waited for the train to start rolling again.

The waiting lasted only a moment.

Then, as the train disappeared back into the darkness, it rose to its feet. Slowly, very slowly, it opened the door to the rear car. Stepped inside. Closed the door.

And, barely realizing that it had done so, ripped the handle off in its hand.

Armond Hacdorian was a quiet, dignified, peaceful old gentleman of Rumanian descent. With his neatly tailored suit and carved walking stick, he bore more than a passing resemblance to Sir Laurence Olivier in *The Boys From Brazil:* the same fragile good looks, not so much withered as weathered and beaten by time.

He had suffered more horrors than most people would encounter if they lived to be two hundred. Armond was only seventy-five, however; and he expected to spend the next twenty years, at least, in an atmosphere of some decency and sanity. That would be sufficient, he felt. That would balance the scales.

If there was one more horror that Armond Hacdorian was *not* willing to suffer, it was the horror of being seated next to a young Neanderthal with a radio twice the size of his head. Not only did it offend his sensibilities; not only did it hurt his ears; not only did it seek to intimidate every other single person on the train; *more* than all of that, it threatened to make him angry.

And anger was something that he wanted no part of. Anger was something that he hoped to have outgrown, like the impulse toward cruelty, or his swaddling clothes. He had seen the wages of anger and its dark brethren. He had been through the wars, and the camps, and the purges. He had lost friends and family to Fate's brutal, arbitrary blade. And if he never witnessed another act of violence . . . even of the tiniest sort . . . then he still would have seen too much.

Rather than dicker with the boy, and endure anything from gross epithets to actual physical assault, he decided to move to the next car down. The boy could then listen to his rhythmic noise until every tooth in his mouth was shaken loose by it, for all it would concern Armond; though the Good Lord knew that Armond wished nothing but the best for the poor, misguided youth.

He got to his feet gingerly . . . it was difficult for an old man to keep his footing on a moving train, no matter what kind of shape he was in . . . and turned toward the rear of the train. One step at a time, holding always on to the handgrips that dangled from overhead, he moved slowly toward the door. Once, he glanced back at the boy and his radio. He met a cold, uncomprehending set of eyes, and kept moving.

The train was moving with merciful smoothness; Armond crossed over to the door without incident. *Now will come the tricky part,* he told himself. *Crossing to the next car while the train is in motion. I must be a stupid old man, to try such a dangerous thing.*

Still, the train was riding smoothly; and though the

split platform between was somewhat treacherous, shifting and bouncing as it did, Armond felt that he should have no problem with the help of the guardrails.

He stuck one foot out onto the platform and stood there, poised like a surfer. It seemed alright. He held on to the door frame and brought his other foot around. When both feet were on the platform, he reached over to the guardrail with his left hand, steadied himself, and pulled himself over to the door of the rear car.

There was nothing to it. Chuckling slightly, he reached over to open the door, pleasantly aware of his heart's quick pounding in his temples.

The door wouldn't open.

What? he thought, as the handle clicked futilely; and for the first time since he made up his mind to move, he was afraid. He twisted on the handle again, vainly, and grappled for a moment with panic.

It's alright, he thought. *I can always go back.* It seemed to help pacify the little voices that were gibbering in the back of his head, like the voices of people in cattle cars being led to the ovens. It seemed to calm them down.

He paused for a moment in the doorway, catching his breath and resting. When the rate of his heartbeat returned to normal, he took just a quick peek in through the window before turning to go back. . . .

The lights went out.

From somewhere in the darkness ahead, a fleeting movement.

What? he thought again. With his failing eyesight, he could only dimly perceive the shape on the right-hand side of the train. It seemed to be thrashing, making some sort of rapid movement, although Armond couldn't really tell if he was imagining it or not. He stared concertedly, trying to make sense of the shadow-play before him . . .

. . . *and then the lights flashed on again, and he saw the dark, slim figure standing over the enormous pale one, with its fat limbs kicking and flailing while the dark one leaned over and . . .*

The lights went out again.

"My God," Armond whispered. The shapes blended back into one again; he could no longer distinguish between them. He saw the one dark shape rise from the seats, hang there for a moment, and then fly to one side . . .

. . . as the sound of shattering glass drifted quietly to his ears like a distant, delicate music box . . .

. . . *as the lights came back on, and he saw the dark shape dragging the other one's throat across the windowsill, while hot blood gushed over the wall and the seats and into the tunnel beyond* . . .

. . . *as a scream strangled in Armond Hacdorian's throat, and* . . .

The light went off again.

And stayed that way.

There, in the dark space between cars, Armond Hacdorian stood with his face pressed against the window of the broken door. There, immersed in the wind and the roar of the train, he watched the monster feed. Unnoticed, he watched. Until it was done.

It was not easy for an old man to maintain consciousness under such circumstances, no matter what kind of shape he was in; but Armond managed to pull himself back into the car that he came from, find a seat, and ease himself into it before he blacked out.

Perhaps it was because he'd seen more horror than most people would if they lived to be two hundred; and, whether he liked it or not, he could handle it.

When it had finished with the headless, stinking thing beside it, the thing from the tunnels paused for a moment in bloated, almost drunken elation. Then, remembering its situation, it rose to its feet and looked out through the door to the next car.

Nothing. It appeared that no one had seen it. And that was very, very good.

It returned its attention to the terrible dead thing on the seat. There was blood everywhere. The rich, ripe smell burned in its nostrils, reawakening the hunger. But it had had its fill.

A strange idea came to it, then: something so marvelously, thoroughly twisted that it was amazed with itself for not having thought of it sooner. With a tittering, high-pitched giggle, it leaned over the corpse and dipped a finger into the jagged, dripping stump of the neck.

Withdrew the glistening tip.

Smiled.

And began to draw.

CHAPTER 11

On the newsstands the following morning, both the *Post* and the *Daily News* had a common message for their common readership, as expressed in almost identical headlines which could be boiled down to this: SUBWAY PSYCHO'S MESSAGE IN BLOOD . . . "I'M BACK!" Both were accompanied by a grainy black-and-white photographs of a figure under a sheet, being carried off a train by MTA workers with decidedly queasy expressions.

For the ghoulish delight of the millions who purchased these papers, there was another photograph to grace the story on page 3, just above the shot of the long-legged actress who proclaimed in bold type, "Playing WINGO Turns Me On!!!"

This was the shot of the writing on the wall: of large, ornate letters, gracefully rendered above a bloodstain roughly the size of an upright piano. A smiley face, also in blood, dotted the exclamation point at the end of the killer's pronouncement.

Easily half of the 600-plus commuters on the 14th Street subway platforms were taking in all the gory details while they waited for their trains. They were reading about the horrified group of teenagers who discovered the body, tearfully swearing to God that "we didn't do it"; they were reading about the sole witness, an old man who subsequently fainted and proved unable to give any description of the killer; they were reading about redoubled police patrols on the trains, a massive manhunt for "The Subway Psycho," and an appeal from the police and the MTA to avoid the trains at off-peak hours until "this nightmare is ended."

Because they were so busily engaged, very few of them noticed the figure staggering out of the tunnel.

Peggy Lewin: a pretty girl, slightly overweight and modestly trendy. Formerly a receptionist with a major New York graphics firm. Last seen over three days ago by an ex-boyfriend whom she referred to as "that bastard Luis."

Peggy Lewin, no longer pretty, staggered up the thin stairs that lead to the uptown platform. Half of her head had been staved in from the impact of being thrown from a moving train. Her neck was bent backwards and to the left at an impossible angle. Her right arm was crushed and dangling; her right leg, blackened and stiff. Her dress had been shredded in innumerable, revealing places, but it showed nothing that anyone would want to see.

Peggy Lewin, over three days dead, dragged herself up the last remaining steps and onto the platform, still shrouded in darkness. She fell back against the wall for a moment, panting, then pushed forward into the light.

The first scream rang out. Followed by another. Followed by twelve more, as startled eyes turned away from their papers and focused on the thing that shambled toward them, moaning piteously, coated with dirt and mottled gore.

Fifty people retreated, shrieking, on the already-crowded platform. From behind them, shouts of anger and excitement, as the throngs were pressed dangerously close to the edge. People coming down the stairways paused, gaping; a few of them ran back up the way they came.

The thing that had been Peggy Lewin continued to advance, waving its good arm as it reeled forward, dragging the bad leg behind it, hissing now through broken teeth. It advanced steadily, forcing back the crowd even further, until the front ranks broke and ran for the stairs as well.

Panic erupted. The screaming spread to the platform across the tracks, where commuters were swarming down to the end for a glimpse of whatever the hell was happening. On Peggy Lewin's side, people knocked each other over and trampled each other in the grip of mindless mass terror. The platform began to clear.

Something in Peggy Lewin's mashed, malfunctioning brain told her to escape. It didn't think to go back the way it came. It was incapable of that kind of thought. It saw, with its one still-functioning eye, that people were pouring up the stairs. Just as mindlessly, it decided to follow.

She pulled herself up the stairs, laboriously breathing, her ruined arm flapping at her side. Above her, she could dimly hear the screams, the sound of retreating footsteps. Her one eye rolled; her broken throat emitted a howl. However obliquely, the monster inside of her sensed that it had the people right where it wanted them. A vague feeling of victory flowed through her, mingling with the unbelievable pain of her broken body and what it had become.

Peggy Lewin reached the top of the stairs, struggled to pull herself upright, and headed for the turnstiles and the streets beyond.

"Jesus Christ," Ian droned, his voice barely more than a whisper. "What the hell is going *on* down there?"

He and Joseph had just crossed 14th Street to Union Square Park. They were roughly fifteen yards from the subway entrance when the first wave of howling humanity came surging up the stairs at a breakneck pace. Now they stopped, Ian grabbing his friend's arm involuntarily, as the hysterical stream continued to gush forth from below.

"This is *insane*," Ian continued, slapping his free hand to his forehead in disbelief.

"Let's go check it out," Joseph said. Ian looked up at him, stunned, and saw the cold set of Hunter's features. He smacked himself across the face again.

"What are you *talkin'* about . . . ?"

"I want to see what's going on."

"But . . ."

"I thought you said your name was Butch Sampson," Joseph said, and the delivery was so straight that Ian had to laugh. "Now are you gonna help me fight crime, or what?"

"What?" Ian said, but the point was moot. Joseph started to drag him toward the stairway. He shrugged helplessly and then cooperated, standing just behind Joseph as they hit the last of the fleeing crowd.

"DON'T GO DOWN THERE!" someone screamed as they muscled past.

"Bullshit," Joseph mumbled, and then they were at the mouth of the stairs.

Staring downward.

Halfway up, the dull semi-darkness of the underground gave way to sunlit radiance. Slightly below that halfway point, a dark shape made its way laboriously toward them. Joseph took two steps downward and squinted, but still couldn't really see what was coming. He called to Ian. Ian reluctantly came to his side.

"What *is* it?" Ian's whisper was nervous, sharp.

"I don't know," Joseph whispered back, "but I . . . *wait a second.*"

At the foot of the stairs, an amorphous black mass surged into view. A crowd, from the looks of it. It filled the passageway and then froze. A ripple of motion ran through it, and Ian noticed the glint of light off of eyeglasses, metal clasps, and something else. *A gun?* he thought, and then the sight no longer interested him.

Because the thing on the stairs let out a low, yowling cry; and with a massive effort, it dragged itself into the sunlight.

It screamed, then. It screamed the way Peggy Lewin screamed the first time she died: a high-pitched wail of agony that wound out and out, echoing madly, as though it had traveled all the way up from Hell to split the morning air. It screamed, and it whirled, and it dropped to its knees, weakly clutching the railing. Then it pulled its terrible face around to gaze, one last time, in the direction of Ian and Joseph and the sky.

And before their horrified eyes, Peggy Lewin's flesh began to pucker and sputter and turn a grayish green: the color of meat left to rot in the sun. Tiny patches of furry turquoise mold formed in the open wounds. She fell sideways, her head striking the stone step with a wet thud. She kicked once, twice. A last dying rattle poured out of her throat like sand. Then she was still. Forever still.

Peggy Lewin had escaped, after all.

CHAPTER 12

The story, in a highly abbreviated form, made it to the evening papers. Mention was made of a young woman who was found dead at the Union Square station, suffering from massive head injuries and numerous broken bones.

No mention was made of the fact that she wandered out of the tunnels, or that she was in such a state of decay that she had to be scraped from the steps.

"Are you sure about this?" Allan asked over the phone, a match's flame dancing nervously at his fingertips. He cradled the receiver against his shoulder and brought the briar pipe to his lips. Lord knew that he needed *something* to relax.

"I stood there and *watched* it!" Ian's voice was profoundly agitated, still wavering at the borderline of hysteria. "Hunter and I both! We watched this poor woman crawl up the stairs, hit the sunlight, and . . . poof! Just go down in a cloud of green gas!"

"You . . ." Allan began, but Ian would not be interrupted.

"When the smell hit, I wanted to run up the stairs and find a quick bush to puke in, that's how bad it was."

"Whoa . . ."

"And they're covering it *up*, goddamit! I don't know *why*, but they're covering it up, Allan! I mean, who are they trying to protect? Something like this happens, the people ought to know about it! You know what I . . . ?"

"Yeah, boss. I know. It's just that . . ."

"You don't believe me, right?"

"Well . . ." *How do I put this?* "If I were hearing it from anyone else, I'd be having an even harder time than I'm having now. That's all."

Ian seemed to consider this. At any rate, he paused for a moment; and when his voice came back over the line, it was a good bit calmer.

"Honest to God, Allan. It's true. You wouldn't have believed it if you saw it with your own eyes. . . . I'm having an awfully hard time believing it, myself . . . but it actually happened. There were cops there, just standing there with their jaws flapping. They didn't know what to do, either. It was . . ." His voice cracked, and Allan suspected that he'd started to cry. ". . . it was just so unreal. It was the worst thing I've ever seen. Worse than *Day of the Dead*."

"Jesus." From Ian, that was bad; he must have seen that film a hundred times.

"It was worse, because it was *real*. It was . . . well, you *know* what it was, don't you?"

Allan sat and thought for a moment, filling the room with clouds of aromatic smoke. He knew the answer that Ian was suggesting . . . *what looks dead, walks around, and decomposes when exposed to sunlight?* . . . and he wasn't lying when he said he'd have a harder time believing it from anyone else. But, dammit, how *could* he believe something like that? How could even a dungeon master, with one foot firmly planted in the shadowland of fantasy, suddenly rip down the veil and say that, yes, monsters *are* real? How could he say that?

"A . . . a vampire?" he said.

"You can bet your ass on it," Ian declared, "and come home with two." They laughed nervously. "Yes, sir. You can walk through the door with a full set of cheeks on either side if you push the buzzer that says VAMPIRE. Because that's exactly what it was, my man. No two ways about it."

"And Joseph agrees with your prognosis?"

"Oh, yeah. That's all we talked about all day. That's why we didn't show up for work; we just sat in a bar and drank 'til it came out our ears. Then . . . I guess it was about eight o'clock . . . he just got up and split."

"Did he say where he was going?"

"No." Pause. "Well, he said that he was going home, but I didn't believe him. And when I called out there, nobody answered the phone."

"That's probably the last place in the world he wants to be right now."

"Yeah." Alan heard Ian lighting something; he waited. "You know where I think he went?" Ian resumed.

"Where?"

"Well, I think we're gonna have to start calling him Joseph 'The Vampire' Hunter."

"*Whoa,* boss. Wait a minute. What do you mean?"

"I think he went to look for the thing that killed that woman." Once again, Allan got a cold rush up his spine. "I think he plans to track it down and destroy it."

CHAPTER 13

Stephen fidgeted nervously in his seat on the downtown side of the 42nd Street station, 6th Avenue line. There were a lot of unsavory characters out tonight, filling him with a low-level, numbing sort of dread. He didn't want to be the next victim of the Subway Psycho, or anybody else.

In the seat next to him, a black man in a nicely tailored suit was reading the *Post*. Stephen determinedly repressed the urge to peek over the man's shoulder. He had always hated those seamy scandal-rags; and he had, in his opinion, wasted enough time and money on them in the past week to last him the rest of his life.

Especially since they reminded him of Rudy, this week's Number One time-waster. Every time he thought about Rudy, anger smoldered inside of him like a hot coal. When he thought about all the *work* he could have done, if he hadn't been running around and worrying himself half to death! It was just infuriating, that was all. It was just intolerably, unforgivably infuriating.

That was why he'd spent the afternoon at the New York Public Library, ostensibly doing research for a new science fiction story. That was why he'd decided to treat himself to a nice dinner at Beefsteak Charlie's and the 7:15 showing of *The Dark Crystal:* an evening calculated to relax and reward him for all his fruitless effort.

It didn't work. He'd accomplished zilch at the library, of course; dinner at Beefsteak's wasn't nearly as much fun when you were alone; and *Dark Crystal* had left him with some extremely disturbing imagery. The essence-sucking scenes, in particular, were fraught with a horror that he'd in no way expected. They nagged at him now, though he didn't know why.

I wish the train would hurry up and get here, he thought, staring down at the tracks. Nothing had run their length in the last fifteen minutes. Slowly, the platform was beginning to fill with people, all of them strangers. *I wish I weren't alone*, he posed as a corollary to his first wish.

A noisy group of Latinos came down the stairs, laughing and gesticulating like crazy while one of them shouted out some story in Spanish. Stephen turned to look, and that was when he saw the woolly mountain of anger on his left.

That the man was blitzed, he had no doubt. That the man was fully capable of murder was equally clear. As Stephen stared, the man turned suddenly; and Stephen found himself looking into the coldest set of eyes he'd ever seen. The man turned away then, looking at something or someone down the platform, and Stephen shuddered with relief.

Thank God, he thought. *That man was terrifying.*

Then, barely discernible at first over the boisterous Latinos but quickly overcoming their chatter, came the sound of the train. It took a moment to figure out which way it was coming from. Stephen found himself looking both ways, as if his eyes could pinpoint the source of the rumbling; then, with a slow grin of dawning realization, he became certain that it was heading his way.

"Terrific," he said, pulling himself to his feet. He took a few steps in the direction of the tracks, glanced around at the others who were beginning to move forward, and . . . .

. . . roughly halfway down the platform, his pale features contrasting sharply with his customary black attire, was Rudy.

"Omigod!" he gasped, barely believing his eyes. "RUDY!" Rudy looked vaguely around, as though Stephen's shout had been an echo heard in a dream. "RUDY!" he repeated; and then the train plowed into the station, drowning out all other sound.

"Shit!" he yelled, audible only to himself. Hastily, he began to muscle his way down the platform. Some people didn't take kindly to it; he muttered a series of apologies that went unheard by all, save one.

The train screeched to a halt. Stephen realized that he wasn't going to get all the way down there in time. The doors slammed open; he moved quickly to the nearest one, then waited in extreme impatience for the five or six people in front of it to drag their asses on board.

He had completely forgotten the large, angry man who had frightened him mere moments before.

He didn't know that the man had begun to follow him.

Stephen boarded the train and proceeded toward the front. It was fairly clear sailing inside . . . most everybody was taking advantage of the available seats, leaving the aisles open . . . and he had made two cars' worth of progress by the time the doors shut and they began to roll.

He came to a door. He opened it. He stepped into the

space between cars and hesitated for a moment, unsure of his footing. It occurred to him that he had never trekked through a moving train before . . . had always considered it a reckless, foolish thing to do . . . and the realization unsettled him further still.

As a kid, Stephen Parrish had always been regarded as a wimp. In his pre-teen years, he sat home and read comic books while the other kids whupped the tar out of each other in contact sports and other forms of casual violence, or flung themselves bodily through the air via rope swings and high diving boards. When high school rolled around, the stakes of playing rough got increasingly higher; Stephen advanced tangentially into the worlds of science fiction and fantasy.

Now, as Joe College, Stephen had graduated to the realms of highbrow philosophy, New Wave culture, and moderate drug use. His earlier fascinations still remained . . . had expanded, in fact; and so with his fear of bodily harm, his recalcitrance in matters of even slight potential danger. New York City, in particular, had heightened his urge to seek escape from mortal terrors by the use of his intellect.

And here I am, he thought, still poised on the bucking, yawning sheets of metal where the cars joined together. It reminded him of standing on a two-by-four slung across a flowing stream . . . another activity which, as a child, he had always wanted nothing to do with. It had always scared the bejesus out of him.

Just as standing here was scaring him now.

So why am I doing it? he asked himself. *Why am I doing something so contrary to my own nature? Why is Rudy worth taking that kind of chance?*

Standing there, in the space between, Stephen found himself examining the nature of his strange friendship with the notorious Rudy Pasko. His mind ran over some of the more typical scenes that they'd been known to act out: Rudy, going off on a spiel that was half lecture, half mad raving, while Stephen passively absorbed it all; Stephen, admiring Rudy's latest piece of graphic poetry, be it on tenement wall or subway poster; Stephen, lending Rudy money that his parents sent, knowing full well that Rudy would never pay him back; Stephen, blushing in embarrassment, while Rudy introduced him to total strangers with caustic wit and derision; Stephen, envying Rudy's indomitable self-confidence, easy success with women, and relative success in the field, while Stephen himself eked out an existence as a lonely literary dilettante who barely even started his work, much less finished it; Rudy, strikingly handsome in the dim light of some Bleecker Street cafe, while Stephen wrestled with the impulse to reach over, to touch . . .

"Oh, *God!*" Stephen whined, suddenly hating himself more than he ever had before in his young, self-pitying life. He saw it all very clearly, all of a sudden. He saw himself in the subservient, stereotypically feminine role: wanting to be dominated by a stronger will, sucking up the humiliation like some fawning, insecure little chippie would suck up her macho boyfriend's semen on demand. Not request: *demand.*

He realized that what he'd wanted all along was Rudy himself, and that he had been willing to believe all the nasty lies that Rudy told about Josalyn because, in the final analysis, he was jealous of her.

It made him want to cry.

Suddenly, the platform between cars was monstrously stifling: a cage balanced precariously on the edge of a cliff, with the wind howling through it like all the demons of Hell joined together in song. He tried to hold back the tiny scream that trembled in his throat. He failed. And with a sudden, desperate effort, he yanked open the door ahead of him.

And stepped inside.

Of the thirty or forty people in the car, only a dozen or so turned to look as the door slammed shut behind him. None of them were wearing Rudy's face; the confrontation had not been forced. Stephen received this with mixed disappointment and relief.

The train rumbled into the light of the 34th Street station, dramatically slowing down. He staggered as the engineer jerkily plied the brakes, grasping for the nearest handgrip. Several people got up from their seats to stand in front of the doors, and Stephen briefly considered the idea of joining them, of getting off the train and letting Rudy roll right out of his life forever.

But something inside of him, one of his mind's wiser voices, told him to stay. *Go find him*, it said. *Calmly ask him what happened, where he's been. If he hands you some kind of arrogant attitude, turn around and leave. If he apologizes, or has some kind of legitimate excuse, forgive him.*

But whatever you do, keep your head on straight. Don't let him manipulate you.

Be strong. For once.

The train ground to a halt; the doors flew open. Stephen waited once again for the doorway to clear, then peeked out onto the platform to see if Rudy had disembarked. As far as he could tell, no. He decided to take advantage of the fact that the train wasn't moving, started walking once again toward the front.

Behind him, at the rear of the car, someone waited for Stephen to reach the next car before opening the door and slowly, cautiously, following after.

Stephen stepped into the next car just as the doors closed on 34th Street. His own door slammed shut behind him. Once again, numerous sets of eyes looked up to check him out; but this time, he saw only one of them.

One set of eyes, so red as to appear infected, staring up at him: hazily at first, then clearing into the sharp glint of recognition.

"Ah," said the owner, a thin smile cutting jaggedly across his thin, bone-white features. "Stephen."

"Rudy," Stephen said. It was barely more than a whisper. His heart seemed to have climbed into his throat and strangled the sound.

The train began to move. Stephen stumbled forward, nearly tripping over a businessman's briefcase. Rudy was watching him, head cocked to one side and grinning coldly, like a pet boa constrictor who's just been thrown a live mouse. Predatory. Reptilian. Amused. And totally in control.

"Come have a seat, Stephen," Rudy said. "Be my guest." Rudy spread his hands to indicate free seats on either side of him. A chill ran through Stephen, paralyzingly cold, and it said *nobody wants to get too close to him. Everybody else is afraid of him, too.*

"Have a seat," Rudy reiterated, patting the space to his immediate left. This time, however, though the smile was still there, it was not a request. There was something strangely compelling about the eyes: a fire not previously there, a force behind them that seemed to draw Stephen forward despite himself.

Slowly, Stephen obeyed.

Rudy watched. He nodded. His smile broadened, as though some wonderful thought had just occurred to him for the first time. Stephen saw him mouth something, but was unable to read it.

Stephen's hackles rose. He could feel the short hairs at the nape of his neck stiffen as the chill continued to flow through him. He saw now that Rudy was not only pale, but sunken to a deathlike pallor; and the darkness around those horrible eyes was not his customary makeup, but an actual discoloration of the skin. The sight was almost enough to make Stephen stop.

But not quite.

Stephen sat down beside Rudy, and at once the smell hit him: the smell of dampness and mold, the slightest trace of sewage wafting up and through it as though Rudy had been dipped in a septic tank. Stephen wrinkled his nose, but he didn't move away; to his horror, he discovered that he couldn't.

"It's good to see you, Stephen," Rudy said, grinning. "How've ya been?"

Stephen shrugged. It was as if somebody had him hooked to invisible strings; had it been left to him, he wouldn't have been able to move at all.

"Good." Rudy drew out the word, as if he were

savoring a fine wine. "I suppose that you've been wondering where I've been."

Stephen nodded, this time voluntarily; but the movement was sluggish, weak. Rudy grinned, watching him, then laughed out loud.

"I've been traveling, Stephen. A trip and a half." He tittered and wrung his bone-white hands. "A great and mysterious journey," he said.

His features grew wicked and patronizing. His eyes burned holes in Stephen's last vestige of self-control. He smiled.

"I used to fancy myself quite the connoisseur of darkness. I really thought I'd seen it all." An almost humbled expression flickered across his face and was gone. "The full depth and breadth of human depravity. The monster behind the civilized veneer! The skull behind the mask! I thought I knew all about it. I *thought* I knew. . . ." Rudy's eyes glittered darkly, madly, his voice a husky whisper. "But now I *know*.

"I . . . I've *changed*, Stephen." He laughed again, a piercing lunatic trill. "I've seen things in the last few days that you wouldn't believe . . . you would not *believe* it, Stephen . . . unless I showed you."

Stephen shuddered, eyes locked on Rudy's. It was like staring into a roaring furnace. There was something happening inside of them that inspired the same kind of awe and terror: a dance of destructive power so intense that its majesty outweighed the pain of bearing witness to it. Stephen's eyes burned, but he was powerless to look away.

Behind him, at the rear of the car, somebody stepped through the sliding door and stood there, watching. Stephen could not have been less aware of the fact.

"I've gone all the way in, Stephen." Rudy's voice was hypnotizing, like the hiss of a cobra over cold, slit eyes. "I've gone all the way into the darkness, Stephen. And do you know what I found there?

"*The other side.*" Rudy's face, as he said it, was a terrible thing to behold. "The proverbial light at the end of the tunnel, my friend: a place beyond your wildest dreams.

"I think I'd like to take you there."

Rudy reached over to take Stephen's arm. His hand was extremely cold.

Suddenly, the train began to slow down drastically. Without realizing it, they had gone all the way down to West 4th Street. Rudy looked up, startled, and his hold on Stephen was broken.

Stephen snapped back into ordinary awareness. All at once, the sweat welled up from his pores and soaked him in tingling dampness. A sharp breath escaped him, and he cringed from Rudy like a beaten puppy, eyes wide and full of terror.

"Omigod," he croaked. "Omigod, Rudy, I . . ."

Rudy whirled back around, lips curled in annoyance. He started to say something.

And then things started happening very quickly.

The train stopped. The doors opened. Next to the doors, directly across from Rudy and Stephen, a young couple was seated in nervous silence, watching the whole thing. The girl had an ornate, woven gold chain around her neck.

A large, muscular youth stepped up to the doorway. He took one look at the girl's necklace and, without hesitation, reached down and tore it from around her neck. She screamed.

"Hey!" her boyfriend yelled, half-rising out of his seat. Again without hesitation, the chain-snatcher smoothly drove one fist into the boyfriend's nose. There was a loud snapping sound, and the kid went flying back into his seat, blood flowing from his nostrils. The thief ran quickly out the door.

"Oh, holy Christ!" the boyfriend hollered, leaning forward into his cupped handful of blood. With his free hand, he reached into his back pocket and pulled out a handkerchief, which he promptly applied to his nose. By now, everybody in the car was watching the action.

But Rudy was leaning forward, red eyes wide and glazing over. His mouth opened a crack, and his tongue flicked out across the trembling lips. The air around him crackled like a static charge. His whole body shuddered, and he let out an unearthly moan.

Then, without warning, he surged out of his seat and grabbed the boyfriend's bloody hands. There was a brief, insane struggle. The girl screamed again. And again. And again.

"RUDY!" Stephen shrieked, his hands pulling down at the sides of his face, mouth and eyes locked in a rictus of stunned horror.

Rudy spun around, yanking free of the boyfriend. He had the bloody handkerchief in his hands. As if to stifle a scream of his own, he touched it to his lips and started backing toward the door, his expression twisted into something beyond rage, beyond madness, beyond any conceivable human emotion.

He was directly in the center of the doorway when the doors slammed shut, pinning him from either side. He screamed like an animal and struggled against them. They recoiled for a second, as if in pain, then closed on him again. Rudy writhed and flailed and twisted until he finally broke free.

The doors slid shut.

And Rudy disappeared into the West 4th Street station, leaving a carload of people behind him in stunned, astonished silence.

"Oh, shit," moaned the boyfriend, as he and his girlfriend collapsed into each other's arms and began to cry.

Stephen just stared at them. He stared at the blood on the floor. The train lurched into motion, and he stared at the pillars as they drifted slowly by like clouds on a windy day. He stared at his hands, shaking uncontrollably and knotting together like two awkwardly mating spiders.

Faintly, as if from a distance, the tiny voice of reason informed him that he was losing his mind.

Then a hand reached down to touch him on the shoulder. He looked up blearily into the face of the enormous shaggy man who had frightened him way back at 42nd Street, when fear had a different, lesser meaning. The man said something. Stephen had no idea what it was.

The man shook him then, and Stephen's mind began to clear. He heard the words, "I said, did you know that guy?" And, like a movement made in a dream, he felt himself nodding *yes*.

"At the next stop," the man said, and this time Stephen heard him clearly, "we're gonna get off and go for a little drink. And you're going to tell me everything you know about him. Okay?"

"Okay," Stephen said, as the tears started to trickle down the sides of his face.

Joseph Hunter nodded, squeezed Stephen's shoulder in a gesture of almost fatherly reassurance, and then turned to stare out the window into the tunnels of forever night.

BOOK 2

Sweet Teeth

CHAPTER 14

The West 4th Street station is a sprawling, multi-leveled subterranean structure of reinforced concrete and steel. At its deepest point, a good 60 feet below street level, run the trains of the 6th Avenue line: the D, the B, the F, and the JFK Express. On the top level, perhaps only twenty feet from the outside world, the 8th Avenue line veers over to the west, consisting of the A, AA, CC, and E trains. Both of these platforms are brightly lit, as are most subway stations; both are reasonably well-populated at all hours of the day and night.

Sandwiched between them is yet a third level, continuously rumbling from the tracks above and below it but bearing no rails of its own. It is neither well-lit nor populous; rather, it has the appearance of an empty warehouse, lined symmetrically with massive steel girders and periodic staircases on either side which, when standing at any point near the center, give it the appearance of infinite length, the far ends disappearing into darkness.

It is an ominous place, reeking of mildew and at least a decade's worth of wino piss. It is not the kind of place where anyone would care to linger, unless they were a bum seeking shelter from the elements, or a mugger waiting to drag some innocent into those boundless crosshatchings of shadow. Most people . . . most sane people . . . pass through this level with wrinkled noses, a sort of nightmare apprehension, and as much speed as they can muster.

It would not be a good place to die.

Deep in the shadows, next to a pile of human feces rendered odorless by time, Rudy Pasko leaned against a moist, grimy wall and played nervously with his hair, twirling and twisting it around one pale, bony finger. The bloody handkerchief sat like a lump at his feet, caked with dirt and saliva, discarded like an empty granola bar wrapper.

It was a snack, that's all: a little something to tide him over. He had snatched at it impulsively, like a kid passing by a candy store. He had fought over it like a dog vying for a bone, a pigeon desperately grappling for an old crust of bread.

And that was all it was, actually: a scrap tossed by Fate to make him crazy for a moment and further whet his appetite. It bothered him now that he'd gone for it so automatically, so instinctively . . . that the sight and smell of so little blood could make him lose control.

More than that, however, he was worried about Stephen. He could have kicked himself for talking so much, flexing his new muscles like that. It would have been just as easy to lure him somewhere, out of the simplest of pretexts . . . *let's go have a drink, Stephen, you wouldn't believe what kind of week it's been* . . . and laid it all on him after the fact.

How much does he know? Rudy asked himself, still twiddling absently with his hair. *How much did I tell him?* It angered him that his concentration was so scattered. Even now, less than ten minutes later, he could barely remember what he'd said.

The last several days had been, for Rudy, like an endless and incredibly potent acid trip. The same kind of insane sensory clarity. The same surreal disorientation. The same flood of images so powerful that they took on the aspect of Visions From God. And though he found the idea of God and the Devil laughable, he couldn't deny that the visions seemed to be coming from somewhere higher, or lower, than himself.

Rudy pulled away from the wall and stood in the middle of the vast second landing. To his sight, the shadows seemed to be crawling with a power and a life of their own, like blind protozoa slithering across the face of all earthly creation, invisible to the ordinary naked eye.

Maybe it is *alive*, he thought, chuckling quietly to himself. *Maybe the darkness* does *have a life of its own*. It made sense, suddenly. It made complete and utter sense. It moved from the realm of ideas to the domain of absolute certainty: another vision.

It served to explain his own strange new existence.

Rudy giggled aloud. It echoed off the naked walls, ghostlike as it bounced back into his ears. He grinned, entertained. It was all he could do to keep from howling like a wolf, filling the air with riotous sound. But that would bring the transit cops running, and force an unnecessary encounter that could blow his cover to smithereens.

"No," he whispered to himself, no longer giggling. "There'll be plenty of time for that later." Smiling faintly, wickedly. "All the time in the world."

Rudy Pasko listened to the thunder of a train overhead. He looked up, drawn by the power of it. Slowly, the sound of his footsteps drowned by the echoing roar from above, he moved toward the nearest flight of stairs. Slowly, he ascended them.

It would have been fun to ride the trains again tonight; the subways had always fascinated him, though never so much as in the last several days. But the newspapers he'd found abandoned in the stations, and his own recent encounter with Stephen and the bloody nosed boy, led him to believe that the streets would be far safer. The night was young, and the Village would be teeming with life at this hour.

Hot-blooded life.

Just waiting for his kiss.

Besides, he thought, *there's still the matter of Stephen. I'll have to get to him soon, before he puts two and two together. Not that that'll happen any time soon. Stephen's such a schmuck. He's probably shaking in his shoes right now, taking a couple Darvons from his asshole psychiatrist and sitting at his stupid typewriter.*

Rudy laughed, thinking about Stephen. What a wimp. What a spineless little jellyfish: afraid of life, afraid of death, afraid of sex, afraid of his own goddamn shadow. Rudy knew that Stephen wanted to get it on with him; he'd been playing with that for a long time, teasing Stephen subliminally with it, though the idea of actually bedding down with Stephen didn't interest him at all. It would be too easy, like seducing a twelve-year-old girl. It would be boring. No challenge. No risk.

But he has uses, Rudy added, reaching the top of the stairs and moving toward the ramp that led to West 4th Street and the great outdoors. *I like his parents' money. And who knows? He might make an excellent slave.*

The AA train rumbled away from the platform, covering the sound of his private laughter as he proceeded, shrugging his way past small clusters of people who completely failed to interest him. He looked up for a moment, and noticed a transit cop who was eyeing him strangely.

Fuck you, prick, Rudy thought, averting his gaze and continuing on his way. He felt the same kind of insolent paranoia that he used to feel while dealing drugs: an irrational, overwhelming distrust of anyone who looked at him askance, coupled with the desire to lash out and smash those prying eyes back into their sockets.

Rudy continued to walk, containing his fear and anger. He felt the cop's eyes burning into him from behind. He kept walking. Not until he reached the ramp and began to climb it did he turn around to look; when he saw that the cop was still staring, but had not budged an inch, Rudy laughed and nodded as if to say *yeah, clown, you just stare all you want*.

Then he turned, his white lips pulled taut in an unpleasant, vindictive smirk. Ahead of him lay the turnstiles, the token booth, and the stairways leading up into the night.

"I'm coming, Stephen," he said, in a sing-song. "I'm coming for you now.

"But first, I'll grab a little something to eat. Just a bite," he added, chuckling and running his tongue along the sharp incisors that were growing out quite nicely. "Because, *God*, am I hungry!"

And with that, he proceeded again toward the stairs and the first moon that he'd seen since the night that he died.

"In here," Joseph said, a bit impatiently. "Let's go."

He was practically dragging Stephen along behind him. As the shock began to wear off, and the original fear loomed up again, Stephen had become more and more reluctant to talk. Joseph had tried to be understanding for a while, as calmly pursuasive as he had ever been in his life, but this was the end of the line.

"No, I don't think . . ." Stephen droned, his eyes wide and timorous, pulling slightly against Joseph's grip on his wrist.

"*Now,*" Joseph said, yanking him forward with one hand, pushing open the door of the Blarney Stone pub with the other.

As the door slammed open, a number of old men looked up from their mugs and shots, eyes full of drunken disinterest. Two young couples in a booth near the back laughed boisterously, unaware of anything in the spinning universe but themselves. The bartender, a great burly Irishman with twinkling green eyes and massive sideburns, nodded and grinned at Joseph and Stephen, while cars collided noisily and exploded on the TV above his head.

Joseph nodded back, not smiling. "Two pitchers of Bud," he shouted over the noise from the tube, the laughing hyenas in the rear booth. The bartender made the A-OK sign with the fingers of his left hand and pulled two pitchers off the shelf with his right. Joseph turned back to Stephen, pointed at a table near the door, and said, "Let's sit here."

"Wuh . . . we don't really need two pitchers," Stephen said, allowing himself to be led to the table.

"Don't worry about it. I'll probably drink most of it myself. You just have what you want." Joseph pulled out a chair for Stephen, then crossed to the other side of the table and seated himself with a small grunt of weariness. "Sit down," he said.

Stephen sat. They looked at each other for a moment, then away; their minds were racing. The silence went on for nearly two minutes. Then a waitress emerged from the ladies' room, saw the bartender point at the two pitchers and the new arrivals, nodded tersely, and went to bring them their drinks.

"How ya doin', Joe?" she asked, setting down the beer and empty mugs. He shrugged, digging in his pocket for a ten spot. "Who's your friend?" she inquired further, looking from Stephen to Joseph and back again.

"Uh . . . Stephen," said the smaller man, trying hard to smile warmly. "Stephen Parrish. How do you do?"

"Alright," she answered, flashing a glance at Joseph that said *what's with the gimp?* He laughed and handed her the money.

"Keep the change, Rita," he said quietly. "Thanks."

Rita smiled, tucked the money coyly into her blouse, and sashayed back over to the bar. Stephen watched her move, more than casually drawn by the swivel of her hips. Joseph disinterestedly filled his mug.

"Are you a regular here?" Stephen asked.

"I'm a regular almost everywhere," Joseph answered, taking a long swig. He all but drained the mug, filled it up again, and set the pitcher down in front of Stephen. "Here. Have some."

Stephen nodded, saying, "Thanks," so quietly that even *he* couldn't hear it, and poured himself a mugful. He took a tiny sip, smacked his lips, and then took something close to a healthy swig. "Ah, that's good," he said, setting down the mug and looking at Joseph.

Joseph stared back coldly.

There was a long, uncomfortable silence.

"Okay, man," Joseph said finally. "Stephen, right?" Stephen nodded numbly. "Okay, Stephen. I want you to tell me about that guy you ran into on the train. Like, for starters, what's his name?"

Stephen hesitated. A mad thought flickered through the back of his mind. Then he cleared his throat and said, as calmly as he could, "Uh . . . Bruce."

"Bullshit."

"No, seriously! His name is Bruce. . . ."

"Then why'd you call him Rudy?"

"His name is *Bruce Rudy!*" Stephen yelled, aware of how absurd it sounded, how obvious a fabrication it was. And in the back of his mind, he was wondering *why am I saying this?* But he didn't have an answer.

"BULLSHIT!" Joseph shouted back, slamming his mug on the table for emphasis. In the space of a second, his right hand shot across the table to grab Stephen by the lapel and yank him forward.

"Now you listen to me," Joseph hissed, his face very close to Stephen's. "If you talk to me straight, you can go home to Mommy in less than an hour if you want to, or you can sit here and drink all night for free. But if you feed me this kind of crap, I'm going to snap your scrawny little neck in two. You got me? I'm going to twist your miserable head off if you don't tell me what I need to know. Alright?"

Stephen nodded rapidly, eyes bulging, unable to speak. Joseph held him there a moment longer than he needed to, getting a sort of cruel enjoyment out of it: and it occurred to him that he didn't much like this Stephen kid, the way he whimpered and stuttered and talked out his ass. He was kind of pathetic.

But he's the only lead I have, Joseph mused, letting go of the kid's collar.

Joseph thought back to the subway platform, to the oddly gripping sensation he felt when he first picked Rudy out of the crowd; there was something profoundly *wrong* with the spiky-headed little bastard, something that transcended fashion, or politics, or personality. It rolled off him in waves. Even blitzed, even from a distance, he'd felt it. And this sniveling collegiate twerp was his bestest friend. Stephen would tell him what he needed to know—or else.

Stephen slumped back in his chair, shaking and shivering. He reached for his beer and took a sloppy swig of it, getting his face wet. Tears gathered in the corners of his eyes. He brought a hand up nervously to wipe it all away, then snuffled and stared at the table.

"Let's try it again," Joseph said, no emotion in his voice. "What's his name?"

"Rudy." Stephen's voice was wobbly, weak. "Rudy Pasko. He's an artist."

"He's an artist," Joseph repeated, musing. "I bet he's just the greatest. Where does he live?"

"I . . . I don't know. . . ."

"Now, *listen* . . ."

"I DON'T KNOW!" Stephen screamed, collapsing face-first onto the table and sobbing hysterically. Joseph turned and looked at the other people in the bar. They were all staring now. *I'll let it go for now*, he decided, even though he knew that Stephen was lying.

"Okay, okay," he said. "So you don't know where he lives." Stephen's hysteria seemed to abate slightly, though he remained facedown. Joseph paused to light a cigarette, clear his mind, think of a more productive approach. The beer was catching up with him again, and he wanted to make the most of this situation before he passed out.

"Stephen, look," he said, reverting to his more compassionate voice. "I'm sorry. But I've got a bad feeling about this Rudy guy . . . the way he acted on the subway was *not normal*, you know? And . . ."

Stephen mumbled something into his hands.

"What?" Joseph asked, leaning forward.

It took a moment for Stephen to pull his face up from the table. His eyes were red and puffy; a nearly transparent pool of mucus had slid from his nostrils to the ridge of his upper lip; strands of shimmering saliva were draped between the teeth of his upper and lower jaws as he opened his mouth to speak, making his thin face look like something out of a Bernie Wrightson illustration. The face itself was flushed and stained with tears. Joseph couldn't help but feel the faint stirring of pity in his heart, looking at this guy.

"Yuh . . . you think th-that Rudy had . . . s-something to do with the m-m-*murders*, don't you?" It was almost an accusation. "You think he m-might have k-k-killed all those people!"

Joseph took a drag off his cigarette, saying nothing.

"Well, you're wr-*wrong!*" Stephen straightened, gathering the presence of mind to wipe the snot from his nose, and made every attempt to steady his speech. "Rudy's a little crazy, but he's not *that* crazy. He wouldn't do anything like that. He . . . he wouldn't. . . ."

"How well do you know him?"

Again, Joseph could see the internal struggle on Stephen's face, could see fact locking horns with convenient fiction. *Nobody wants to put their ass on the line for anything* was the thought that came instantly to mind, remembering his rap with Ian on the day that he flattened the purse-snatcher. Then he pulled back to the present and waited for whatever answer the kid decided to present.

But Stephen had opted not to answer at all. "You'd have to understand Rudy," he said. "Rudy's a philosopher. He really thinks about the things going on in the world today. He's got a certain way of looking at things. . . ."

"Yeah?" Joseph, trying hard not to show his dark amusement, refilled his mug.

"If you understood what Rudy's really like, you wouldn't think . . . what you're thinking." The sentence ended in an oddly clipped manner, as though Stephen had intended to say something else entirely, then thought better of it.

"Well," Joseph said, putting one elbow on the table and resting his chin on the fist at its end, "why don't you just explain him to me, then?"

Stephen looked away for a moment. When his gaze returned to Joseph's, there was something slightly different about it . . . a decisiveness, a willingness to talk . . . that hadn't been there before: as though he wanted to convince not only Joseph, but himself as well, that what he was saying was true.

"Can I have some more beer?" he asked. Joseph nodded, a slight grin on his face. Stephen lifted the pitcher, emptied it into his mug, drained the mug in one long shot, then refilled it from the second pitcher. Joseph was tempted to applaud; instead, he sat back in his chair, crossed his massive arms, and waited for the story to begin.

* * *

　　Nihilism is the branch of philosophy that negates the existence of absolute truth, or any knowledge thereof; it denies the existence of any order or meaning in the universe; it mocks any religious, moral, or social system that would seek to impose such order or meaning, on the grounds that such an imposition is purely arbitrary, a mental construct designed by the people in power to hold the rest of humanity in thrall. Therefore, a nihilist believes in none of the things that lend a sense of order or meaning to the bulk of humanity: hope, charity, courage, faith, love, harmony, cooperation, caring.

　　Josalyn paused at this point in her manuscript, pulling her fingers away from the typewriter keys to wrest a Salem Light 100 from its pack and bring it to her lips with trembling fingers. The machine hummed quietly in front of her, patiently waiting for her to decide on the wording of the next paragraph.

　　She lit the match, brought the dancing flame to the tip of her cigarette, and inhaled. The flame went out in a burst of cool, mentholated smoke. She watched the cloud disperse into nothingness, as Rudy and his philosophical pals would have the entire universe do, and grinned fiercely at the thought. *What assholes*, she thought; but, of course, she couldn't write that into her thesis.

　　Yes, she continued, imagining the words in neat double-spaced type on her college professor's desk. *Nihilists are angry, self-deluding assholes who would sooner deny all meaning than take responsibility for the condition of their world. If life is meaningless, they're off the hook; they can do any goddamn thing they like and not be taken to task for it, because nothing means anything anyway, and what difference does it make in the gaping black pit of infinity? Just sit back, pick your scabs, and pass the buck.*

　　She laughed aloud at the image. Maybe Dr. Mayhew would give her good grades for her courage and audacity, but she doubted it; the language was more extreme than she planned to use in any of her writings on the topic. Instead, she'd couch her observations in the same tidy, polite rhetoric that she'd used throughout her college career.

It was funny to think about how much she owed to Rudy, in regard to the paper. When she'd first started doing her research, she was dangerously close to defending nihilism as the proper response. Something inside of her . . . the bloodied baby Josalyn who refused to die, she supposed . . . still resisted the idea; but life at home and life in the newspapers had all but persuaded her to murder the child and abandon all hope.

Then she had met Rudy, and there was something so damned attractive about the way he packaged his anger that she forgot entirely about the paper for a while and just threw herself into *him*. Or he into her. Whatever.

That had lasted for about two months. By the end of that time, he had begun to get on her nerves. Such bottomless hatred she had never imagined, much less seen, in a human being. If she had wanted a living embodiment of the philosophy that intrigued her, then . . . God help her . . . she seemed to have found him.

Also by the end of that time, she had begun to write again. It pissed Rudy off. "What are you doing, fucking me or putting me under a microscope?" he'd shouted once, storming into her living room after finding several of his observations picked apart in her notebook.

She'd been speechless at that point. She hadn't been thinking about it that way at all; he'd just happened to bring up some points that she thought were worth mentioning, if only for their immense questionability.

Thinking about it now, however, she realized that Rudy had been right. She *had* been studying him. And as it turned out, that was good: it was the *only* good thing she'd gotten out of their miserable two months together.

I wonder if he's dead, she thought, snubbing out the cigarette in a pile of its own ashes. *And if he is, I wonder where he went*.

Soon . . . all too soon . . . she would know the answer.

Dorian gets all the gorgeous guys, Claire complained to herself silently. *All she has to do is toss that peroxide mop of hers around, leave her blouse half-undone, and come on like Debbie Harry in heat. It's all over.*

She was standing alone near the jukebox at the St. Marks Bar & Grill . . . or as nearly alone as one can be in a room that has exceeded its 250-person capacity by at least thirty people. They were pressing against her from every side, a sea of faces that extended all the way to the front door; but not a single one within reach was nearly as cute as the one that her roommate had managed to wedge herself against.

That bitch. Some people have all the luck, she continued, sullenly sucking on her Heineken with her eyes pointed in the direction of her shoes. Of course, she couldn't actually see them; that would be asking a bit much, wouldn't it? To be able to see all the way down to her feet? *Christ, I might as well be hanging out on the subway at rush hour, for all the fun I'm having.*

The gorgeous guy that Dorian was wedged up against had the kind of dissipated, lean, vampish look that really turned Claire on. Pale-skinned, dark-eyed, redolent with a sense of mystery and danger that expressed itself in his cocky stance, the cryptic nastiness in the way his mouth curled upward as he smiled. She'd only gotten a brief glimpse of him, on her way back from the bar, but that was enough; she wished Dorian would keel over dead, so that *she* could get a shot at him.

But no. Dorian would take him home, that little slut, and hump his brains out. Claire could see it now. She'd wind up sleeping with the headphones on again, trying to screen out the wild moans and whimpers from the next room. It was enough to make her take up prostitution: at least Dorian wouldn't be the *only* one shaking pictures off the wall 'til 6:00 in the morning.

Oh, well, she thought, draining the Heineken and

turning her gaze toward the cracked plaster on the ceiling. *There's always Danny. I could snag him in a second. Probably get a few free posters in the bargain.* It was a cruel thought, she admitted . . . she *liked* Danny . . . but there was no comparison. Paranormal connection or not, the guy still left a thing or two to be desired in the looks department; she'd take a stupid, meaningless night of continual banging with a guy as cute as Dorian's latest in a second, given half a chance.

I mean, she reasoned, *you only live once, right?*
Right.

Claire decided to go for one more beer, one more peek at Romeo, before checking out some other scene. It wasn't easy. She had to plow her way through half a dozen skinheads, twice as many trendies, and a gaggle of miscellaneous riffraff before she could even reach the point where she'd last spotted Dorian and the handsome hunk.

They were no longer there.

Figures, she silently bitched. She cast her gaze around for as far as it could go, but there was no sign of them. Knowing Dorian, they were probably halfway into the sack already. "Goddam," she mumbled, barely loud enough to be heard.

"Pardon?" said a voice from behind her. She turned to stare into the eyes of a pizza-faced preppie with moldy-looking teeth.

"Oh, fuck off," she suggested to him, elbowing past on her way to the bar and another sorrow-drowning bottle.

Or maybe a dozen.

At the Blarney Stone, an hour had passed since Stephen and Joseph first sat down. A lot had gone down in that time, the least of which was another pitcher of beer. Now they sat, staring dully at each other like a pair of frogs in formaldehyde, wondering how to wrap things up.

Stephen's discourse on the Gospel According To Rudy didn't carry much weight in the final analysis; not nearly as much as Joseph's description of the rotting woman on the Union Square steps. Every time Joseph closed his eyes, he saw her: the light green vapor that rose from her body as she lay, kicking and sagging into herself like a gouged inner tube, her flesh glossing over with mold and a thin layer of slime. While Ian had turned away, swallowing bile, Joseph had remained. He hung around while the crowd crept slowly up the stairs, gagging and fainting and shrieking anew at the sight and smell of her. He watched the police push the bystanders back. He watched them scrape her up.

The officer in charge, a young guy named Benzoni who was looking a little bit green around the gills himself, made Joseph agree that he wouldn't say a word to the press. "No problem," Joseph had said, and it wasn't.

He wanted the thing that had killed that poor girl. He wanted that thing for himself.

Which was why, after darkness fell, he decided to stake out the subways. Which was why, when he saw Stephen calling that Rudy cat on the platform, he decided to follow behind. Which was why, after that bit with the handkerchief, he no longer had any doubts as to who or what he was after.

"I'm sorry, pal," he said finally, pointing a drunken finger at Stephen. "But after what you saw, and after what I told you *I* saw, there shouldn't be any question. Rudy's the one."

"No." Stephen shook his head, eyes half-closed, expression blank. "No," he repeated, banging his mug on the table. "I can't accept it."

"It's true."

"I don't *care*. . . . I mean, I don't *know*!" His head was spinning, the world was spinning. He let go of the mug and gripped the edge of the table with both hands, as if that could make it stop. Too much beer, too much weird information.

Stephen had done his best to withhold as much information as possible. He had managed, for example, to leave out the fact that Rudy disappeared on the night of the multiple murders. It would only strengthen Joseph's case: a case already so strong that it would have been undeniable if it weren't so utterly preposterous.

In fact, he had found himself continually whitewashing everything that he'd said, and he wasn't sure exactly why. There was no question that Rudy was acting peculiar as hell; there was no question that he had scared the piss out of Stephen, although the details had receded into a fear-and-alcohol-induced fog, at least for the time being. *And that thing with the bloody handkerchief . . . Christ!* he thought, playing it back in slow motion on the Betamax of his mind, while the room lurched suddenly, sickly, to the left and proceeded to turn and turn and . . .

"No," he gasped again, knuckles turning white from the sheer effort of hanging on. He could feel his dinner come alive again in his stomach, trying to force its way back to the shrimp 'n' salad bar at Beefsteak Charlie's. The thought of throwing up made him instantly sicker. He wobbled in his seat, cheeks bulging, and groaned.

Joseph didn't see him. Joseph was busily writing something on a napkin, bent over the table. "I'll tell you what," he said, pausing to finish the line, still looking down. "If anything weird happens to convince you that I might be right, give me a call. Here's my number . . . whoa." He looked up to see Stephen, pale and sweaty, with one trembling hand over his mouth. "Hey, man. Are you alright?"

"No . . ." Stephen moaned through his fingers. He tried to get up and fell backwards into his chair, almost keeling over entirely.

"Oh, Jesus Christ." Joseph got out of his seat quickly and moved to the other side of the table. He grabbed Stephen by the armpits and hoisted him up. The chair fell over with a crash. Everyone in the bar turned to see Joseph dragging Stephen to the bathroom as fast as he could.

"He pukes on the floor, you're cleaning it up!" Rita yelled from somewhere behind them. Joseph responded by slamming open the door marked MEN with his shoulder, dropping Stephen to his knees in front of the toilet, and flicking on the light.

Immediately, the air filled with the sound of violent retching, the moist plunk of vomit against water echoing up from the toilet bowl. Joseph wavered in the doorway, staring stupidly for a moment, before leaving the room and closing the door behind him.

A brief flurry of one-man applause erupted from the booth in the back. Joseph turned a baleful eye toward the comedian, who stopped in mid-clap and turned quickly away. The only sound in the bar then poured faintly from the TV set: a Budweiser commercial, no less.

"This Bud's for you," sang the twangy C & W voice from the speaker as Joseph stomped back to his table, shaking his head at the absurdity. Rita came up behind him, also shaking her head, a repressed grin on her face.

"Where'd you find that guy?" she asked. "The Salvation Army?"

Joseph laughed sourly. "Oh, he's a real champ, alright. Lied his ass off to me all night, and then . . ." He stopped himself. *I can't tell her this.* "He's just a jerk."

"Tell me about it. Hey, you're not gonna leave him here, are you?"

"Call him a cab or something. He's got money. I paid for all the beer."

Rita nodded, keeping her amusement to herself. "You're done then," she said finally.

"Yeah," he answered. Then he remembered the napkin, still sitting on the table where he'd dropped it in his haste. "Almost," he added, picking it up and turning back toward the bathroom.

"What, are we out of toilet paper?" she called after him. He ignored her, striding up to the door. Opening it. And looking inside.

Stephen appeared to be just about done. His body no longer shuddered or heaved. His arms were crossed over the toilet seat, his head resting upon them. He could have been asleep.

"You alright now?" Joseph asked.

"Yeah." The voice was weak and breathy as it rang up from the toilet bowl. "I guess so."

"Well, here," Joseph said, sticking the napkin into

Stephen's back pocket. "My phone number. Give me a call when you wise up."

Then he stepped out and closed the door behind him again, leaving Stephen to think about it. He wasn't really angry . . . not nearly as angry as he *could* have been, considering the amount of garbage he'd had to listen to just to get one useful piece of information.

But he got it, and that was what counted. He got what he was looking for.

A name.

Rudy Pasko. The words felt nasty on his tongue as he mouthed them. *Rudy Pasko*. He could almost taste the dust.

"You're a real prince, you know it?" Rita yelled as he passed her on his way out the door. She pointed to the men's room with mock indignation. "A real friend of the animals!"

"Thanks, Rita," he called back, waving. "I'll see ya later."

"What, I'm supposed to be thrilled?" she countered. Then she smiled, making ready to wave in return.

But Joseph Hunter was already gone.

Okay, Mr. Rudy fucking Pasko, he thought, stepping out of the Blarney Stone and into the night. *I'm gonna find you. I'm gonna track you down and nail you to the floor, before you do it to anyone else. . . .*

The door opened.

". . . and that's when I knew that those people didn't know *anything* about fashion!" Dorian exclaimed, absently twisting the key until it yanked loose from the door. "I mean, they were *totally* ignorant!" She laughed wickedly, dropped the keys into her pocketbook, and stepped into the apartment.

Rudy followed her, nodding and smiling silently. He was barely hearing her words: absorbed by the motion of her infinitely layered hair, the sound of her blouse sliding against the naked shoulders beneath, the aura of vitality that surrounded her. It was amazing. It was enthralling. It was . . .

"Hey. Shut the door, alright?" She turned now, her eyes locked on Rudy's. He didn't notice her slight irritation, engrossed in the tiny lines that streaked the warm blue of her irises, emanating from the pupils like spokes on wheels. He got lost in their depth for a moment; her words didn't register at all.

"Are you deaf?" she said, and he snapped back into . . . what? Character? Circumstance? At any rate, he heard her; he understood what she'd been saying; he reached behind him to give the door a push, let it swing shut on its hinges with a screech that grated along his spine like a piece of steel wool. A grimace flickered across his face, then vanished as the lock clicked audibly shut.

Dorian was looking at him strangely. "I haven't had enough to drink tonight," he offered by way of apology, and grinned. She wavered for a moment, uncertain, then grinned back. *So he's a little weird*, she mused. *I can handle it*.

Dorian was not oblivious to the sense of danger around him. It was part of the allure. So many men were *merely* cute, *merely* interesting, *merely* endowed with money or drugs or a striking image. But Rudy was different; she could tell that from the moment she spotted him. The difference radiated from inside of him, a perverse magnetism that simultaneously attracted and repelled.

It intrigued her. It sent little rushes of excitement through her body that tingled in all the right places. She turned fully toward him and smiled now, her irritation of a moment ago forgotten. "Let me show you around," she said, extending her hand and winking seductively.

Rudy's mouth dropped open slightly. His heart was pounding in his chest, in his ears. There was a rasping, grating quality about it, like an engine that's low on oil. He couldn't believe that she couldn't hear it as she moved forward to take his hand, trembling with awesome exhilaration.

"God!" she cried out at his touch. "Your hands are *cold*,

lover! We're gonna have to do something to warm them up." Rudy nodded, eyes half-closed and dreamy, as she brought her other hand up to massage the white flesh, the long fingers, with a sensual circular motion.

They were both breathing heavily now, as though the contact had caused some unseen floodgates of passion to cave in, unleashing the tidal waves. Dorian looked up into his dark eyes and saw a swimming, infinite blackness; Rudy looked down into hers and saw shimmering oceans, vast and blue and pulsating with *life*, with *life*, with . . .

Her soft lips parted, as if for speech, but no words would come. She made a little clicking noise with her tongue, and the corners of her mouth lifted upwards hungrily. Her hands let go of Rudy's and moved to the sides of his face, cupping it gently, as she moved forward to press herself against him. Then, very slowly, she slid her tongue along his Adam's apple and up to the cleft of his chin, tarrying for a moment before taking his chin in her mouth and giving it a light, playful nibble.

Rudy groaned, low in his throat. His hands closed around her back, feeling the lithe muscles tremble at his touch through the sheerness of her blouse. She pushed forward with her pelvis insistently. His eyes snapped shut. He saw red, glorious red.

He would not be able to control himself much longer.

Josalyn was asleep, her consciousness trembling at the border between darkness and dreams. She shifted beneath the sheets, rolling over onto her back, legs opening slightly. Her soft lips parted.

She made a little clicking noise with her tongue.

At the foot of the bed, Nigel also stirred, awakened from a dream of his own. The soft white fur of his back stiffened slightly; the back arched. His claws came out, imbedding themselves in the blankets and hooking there like long, thin teeth.

Nigel pulled himself to a standing position. Something was happening in his little cat-mind that was utterly beyond

him. He moved with it, like a dancer responding to some
primitive beat. Very softly, he began to purr.

Then he moved . . . slowly, gently . . . through
the space opened up between Josalyn's legs. He stood,
looking over her with eyes that gleamed in the darkness.

Gleaming red.

Then he nestled down over her groin, curling up in the
way that cats do, his eyes never leaving her face.

The sound of his purring filled the room.

They were in bed now, Rudy lying prone on his back
while Dorian crouched over him. She had unbuttoned his
shirt to the waist and was running her tongue down the
length of his abdomen, lingering at the nipples to bite and
suck and tease. He writhed beneath her, running his fingers
through her hair and moaning with insane pleasure.

Her mouth moved down to the side of his belly now,
finding the line that arced inward to his crotch. She traced
it to the waistband of his pants, flicked her tongue beneath
the fabric; then, shuddering with hunger, she brought her
hands up to unzip him.

Rudy lifted his hips. Her hands came around under his
ass and quickly dragged the pants down to his knees. She
pulled away for a moment, bringing one hand up to brush
away the hair that had fallen over her face, and Rudy
settled back onto the bed.

"My God," she said, staring at the white, semi-erect
penis. It didn't look real. She had never *seen* anyone so
incredibly pale: the color of the walls, the sheets. It
astounded her.

Dorian took his penis into her hands. It throbbed
slightly; and she noted with pleasure that it was the
warmest part of his anatomy. Rudy moaned loudly as she
ran one sharpened fingernail along the aperture at its tip.
She smiled, and then took him into her mouth.

"Ohhhh," Rudy gasped as she began to work him. His
eyes were dry and luminous, red. His fingers dug into the
mattress, hanging on. His body shook uncontrollably. His
mouth opened wide, sharp teeth glistening in the dim light;

when he closed his mouth, the teeth tore into his lower lip, drawing no blood.

It was as though all the blood in his body, what little there was, had rushed down into his cock. He felt lightheaded, dizzy, on the verge of unconsciousness. Dorian held him upright at the base while her lips slid rapidly up and down the shaft, a tight and expert orifice. Rudy felt the thunder building up in his balls, more intense than any ten orgasms he'd ever dreamed of.

And at the same time, he felt the hunger washing over him, smashing against the whole of his body in an overwhelming blood-red tide. It sent a surge of renewed power into him, a lust more commanding than the sexual drive, merging with it into something beyond.

He reached forward to unbutton her blouse from behind. She shifted slightly, still sucking on him, to facilitate the operation. He took her then by the breasts and pulled her gently but firmly backwards. Her lips smacked as she disengaged, and then she was on her back beside him.

"Now," he said throatily, unbuckling her pants. Her hips uplifted, grinding at thin air. The garment came off in one smooth motion. He threw it on the floor and turned to her.

Her eyes were clouded over, pale blue and glistening. There was a warm, beautiful flush in her face, her neck, her breasts. Rudy could see the blood surging toward the surface, making her hot to the touch as she moaned for him, thrust herself toward his crotch, took hold of his prick with one hand and began to pump it.

Rudy's senses were swimming. He couldn't hold back another moment. With a tiny cry, he pulled her hand away and rolled on top of her, hearing her cry out something that he couldn't understand. Violently, he plunged into her. They gasped in unison, her body tightening around him, and launched into a mad, staccato rhythm.

It built. It built. She shifted herself so that her legs were sticking straight up, brought him in as deeply as he could possibly go. He collapsed against her chest, nearly swooning, as she humped at him with deliberate animal abandon.

And in the moment before he felt himself blacking out, he brought one shuddering hand up to jerk her head sideways, holding the face away by her beautiful hair, and buried his teeth in her neck.

In her dream, Josalyn was making love to somebody. His face was veiled by clouds, but his body was upon her, huge within her, as she ground and pumped against him. Something wild had come alive inside her, sending the blood racing through her veins, hammering in mad syncopation with the pounding at her loins. She gritted her teeth and whined desperately through them.

Her hands were clutching his back. She slid them up to his shoulders, his neck, the back of his head. She tried to pull him closer, to see him, to kiss . . .

. . . and the clouds parted, and she saw that it wasn't a man at all, and she suddenly began to scream . . .

. . . as the animal face descended upon her, blood and drool rolling from the contorted lips, the glistening fangs, the bone-white jaws that parted in lust and hunger . . .

. . . and she screamed, and she screamed, and . . .

Dorian's eyes were almost closed now. She was dimly aware of her body: the vigorous coitus in which it was still engaged, the sharp prickling at her jugular vein. She could hear the sucking and slurping in her ear, but it seemed to be coming from far away. And the warmth of Rudy's body was rapidly increasing; but she, herself, was going cold.

Her sharp fingernails were buried in Rudy's back. Thin trails of blood trickled from the broken flesh. She was only faintly aware that it was her blood, running from his wounds, and onto the sheets.

She moaned, almost silently. There was very little wind left in her. Her body had ceased to move of its own accord, bouncing against the mattress because *he* was humping her now, *he* was slamming in and out of her with frightening power, with the energy he had drained from her throat in hot glistening gouts of crimson that she could see from the corner of her eye.

The room was bright, too bright. Her head ached dully, a cold steel band of pressure, relentlessly tightening. She felt the teeth slice down her throat, opening a gash three inches long. It made a sound like tearing curtains, like a veil rent asunder to let the darkness stream in on leathery wings, a muted and pervasive beating that pulsed in her temples as she felt herself slipping away. . . .

Then Rudy's hand, still gripping her head by that beautiful, blood-matted hair, jerked violently to the side. And the neck snapped. And she gave herself over to the darkness completely.

"NO!" Josalyn screamed, jolting suddenly into total, terrible wakefulness. She sat bolt upright, wide eyes streaming as they stared into the darkness of the room, aware of a rumbling in her ears and a sharp pain in her groin.

. It took her a moment to realize what it was.

Nigel was still curled up in the space between her legs, his chin resting on her mons, the paws to either side. Because the room was too dark, she couldn't see the blood; but she felt his claws, having torn through the sheets, sunken deep into her soft underbelly.

While his eyes, red and luminous, stared into her own. And he purred.

"NIGEL!" she cried, reaching toward him quickly. He hissed, back arching, claws sinking deeper. She squealed with pain and swatted him across the face. He yowled, claws wrenching free with a wet shredding sound. Josalyn screamed, thrown forward by reflex, and grabbed him by the throat. Before he could respond, she hurled him across the room and into the wall.

"Oh, God, Nigel! Oh, God! Oh, God!" She collapsed forward, curling like a fetus, and cried violently into her hands. "Oh, God, I don't *believe* this!" she whined, and then words were no longer within her power.

Nigel hunkered down in the corner of the room. His muscles were tensed. His breath was shuddering, mad, incensed. He growled, low in his throat: a terrible sound. And he watched her, poised, as though he were waiting for a command.

"N-N-Nigel?" she whimpered, looking up through her fog of tears. Nigel growled again, baring his teeth. "Nigel, you . . . you're not *yourself*!"

He spat at her, hunkering lower.

"You're not *yourself*, Nigel!" she screamed, pulling herself to a half-seated position. "You're not . . . you're not . . ." She reached the point of hysteria, smashed through it like a train. "MY GOD, NIGEL, *WHAT'S HAPPENING TO YOU?*"

Nigel screamed, then: the sound of babies, tortured babies, with cigar butts being ground out in their eyes. It was the most unearthly, horrible sound that she had ever heard. It coiled out and out of him, forcing his head back like a coyote's, climbing higher and higher in range until it threatened to burst her eardrums, send blood surging between the fingers that she clamped now to the sides of her head, trying to shut out the killing noise, trying to ward off the madness that she was a membrane's thickness from being engulfed by.

"STOP IT!" she screamed. "STOP IT! STOP IT! STOP . . ."

Rudy awakened, suddenly, from the trance. For a moment, he didn't remember where he was. Then he looked down at the dead, bloody shape beneath him, and it all came back.

Dorian's neck had been twisted around so that her face was pressed down in her pillow, though the body was still on its back beneath him. Her throat was a raw meat canyon, open to the point where the broken bone protruded like a drainage pipe, emptying its waste into the river of blood that had finally ceased to flow.

Her skin was completely white . . . as white as his had been. He noted with surprise that his color had deepened, become more the color of flesh. He also realized, with a strange blend of horror and amusement, that he was still grinding on her automatically; and that he was still erect.

How long? he found himself wondering. *How long was I out? How long have I been . . . humping her like this?* He stopped himself, an act of will, because his body had locked itself into a rhythm that it could probably have maintained forever. He slid out of her immediately, crawling backwards off the foot of the bed and away from the corpse.

Naked but for the pants around his ankles, Rudy stumbled to the middle of the room: his penis caked with the dried lubricants of passion, pointing like a divining rod at his grisly handiwork. Every pore in his body seemed to open wide, screaming with life. He rubbed himself all over to ease the tingling.

Of all the killings that he'd done, this was clearly the most horrible. And yet . . . and yet . . .

"I feel great." He said it so quietly that it was barely audible over the roaring in his temples, the hot pulsation of blood in his veins. "I feel great," he repeated, as if to convince himself that it was true.

But he didn't need to. There was no doubt. He felt absolutely invigorated, absolutely without remorse. He felt, to his way of thinking, the way he should have felt *every* time he slipped it to some dumb cunt: the way he should have felt with Josalyn, and every other . . .

Josalyn. His thoughts backtracked, riveted on the word with unnatural intensity. *Josalyn.* It rang in his head like a sweet, clear bell. He remembered the night that she tossed him out, swearing at him, trying to make him crawl with the ferocity of her words. He remembered the way that she tried to make him feel small and shitty, less than a man: more like a mongrel, a lap dog, some tiny-brained bundle of Willingness To Serve, yapping and wagging its idiot tail every time she craved affection or understanding or . . .

Less than a man. The phrase rankled his ass, filled him with a hatred profound as the heavens. *Less than a man? I'm MORE than a man now! MORE than any pathetic, sniveling little human being!*

I'm MORE than that!

And God be damned if I don't prove it to you, bitch.

All the while that he was dressing, his mind was focused on Josalyn. That tart. That slut. That lousy collegiate whore. As he pulled up his pants and zipped them, he was seeing her: on her knees before him, the two puckered wounds in her neck standing out in sharp relief as she blew him with the abandon of the damned. As he put on his shirt, he was seeing her: her sallow flesh setting off the red luminescence of her undead eyes as she draped a royal robe around him, forever his servant, his jiz bag, his slave. And as he slipped on his boots, he was seeing her: the boot pressed into her face as she groveled in the dirt, begging forgiveness, pleading for the opportunity to go with him, to feed. . . .

Ah, yes, he thought, chuckling to himself. *The right to feed. A new issue for Gloria Steinem to champion, once she and the rest of those bimbos are mine*. He laughed aloud, an evil rippling against the silence. He laughed, and he laughed, and he laughed.

When he had laughed the image out of his system, he took one last glance at the thing on the bed before turning to leave the room. It was tempting to write, once more . . . to poke around in the wound until enough juice came out to compose with . . . but he dismissed the thought. *I don't want them to make the connection*, he thought. *I want them to believe that their "Subway Psycho" only kills in the subways*.

He was about to leave when yet another thought struck him: *what if she gets back up again? It happened to me; it could happen to her*. It was a disconcerting thought. On the one hand, she was beautiful, and great in bed: she'd make a welcome addition to any man's court. On the other hand, her neck was broken: he didn't know if he wanted to see anyone, beautiful or not, walking around like that.

Rudy walked slowly over to her. He took her head in his hands, tried to twist it back around. When her glazed, dead eyes met his, he jerked involuntarily.

And her head came away in his hands.

"Wah!" he yelled, dropping it like a hot potato. It bounced on the bed, hit the floor with a thud. Rudy backed away, disgusted, and hurried out of the room.

On his way to the front door, he noticed another open doorway in the apartment. A quick glance inside revealed a pale, familiar nightmare countenance that made him giggle when he saw it. He stopped in the doorway—the giggling giving way to howling now—and stepped inside.

The room was plastered with vampire posters. The first one, Bela Lugosi, leered at him in black and white with his ridiculous, limp-wristed predatory stance. Surrounding Bela were shots of Frank Langella, Christopher Lee, Klaus Kinski, Max Shreck, and Lon Chaney. In addition, there were half a dozen David Bowie shots, all of which clearly showed why he'd been chosen to play John Blaylock in *The Hunger*.

One more picture hung on the wall, a photograph in an expensive frame. The light glared across the glass. He moved closer, in order to see.

He smiled.

If only she knew, he mused, looking at the pictures of an attractive girl, dressed entirely in black and red, with the bat wings painted across her features. He had never seen Claire before, but he knew all too well what she was trying to be.

In fact, the entire room was a sort of shrine to vampirism, strewn with regalia from the popular mythology. Her bookshelves were cluttered with vampire titles: *I Am Legend, Interview With The Vampire, Salem's Lot, Dracula,* the whole Fred Saberhagen series. There was a candle in the shape of a human skull. There was a large mirror with a black tapestry slung over it, a bureau covered with conventional and theatrical makeup.

There was an inverted cross hanging over the bed; but

instead of Jesus Christ, Bozo the Clown was nailed to it, his red hair jutting out in either direction.

This is tremendous, Rudy marveled, clapping his hands with childlike glee. *This is really incredible. I'd like to meet this chick, whoever she is. I might even let her reign at my side.*

The thought inspired him. Up to now, he'd been thinking exclusively in terms of slaves. This vampire lover, however, set up another line of reasoning entirely. He played it over and over in his mind, excited by the prospect.

Why not? he thought. *Why not a queen? There are eight million people in New York City . . . more than enough for me. And with so many servants, I couldn't possibly keep track of them all.*

He moved to the bookshelf, perusing the contents. *Interview With The Vampire* stuck out in particular; there was something gratifying about the title, a touch of glamour to what he already knew was a superior status. "Why, yes, Johnny, I've killed over ten thousand people," he said out loud, imagining himself on the *Tonight Show*, Ed McMahon's mangled body at his feet. "And you're next."

He picked up the book, began to flip absently through it. His eyes stopped on page 83, riveted to a particular passage near the bottom of the page. He read:

> "Vampires are killers," he said now. "Predators. Whose all-seeing eyes were meant to give them detachment. The ability to see a human life in its entirety, not with any mawkish sorrow but with a thrilling satisfaction in being the end of that life, in having a hand in the divine plan."

That's nice, Rudy observed. *I don't know about this "divine plan" crap, but that's very, very nice. I like that.* He began to flip ahead, see what other gems of sterling wisdom the author had provided for him. . . .

. . . when there was a sound at the front door. *What?* he thought, his heart suddenly pounding.

And in that moment, quite contrary to his own desires . . .

He underwent a transformation.

Claire hesitated for a moment at the door, listening. She wouldn't have been surprised to hear them going at it from the stairwell. At the very least, she expected some kind of loud music, some laughter, some of Dorian's characteristic drunken shouting.

But she heard nothing. Absolutely nothing. And the absence of sound confused her.

Maybe they went to his apartment, she thought, but that didn't sound like Dorian. Dorian always had to flaunt her new boyfriends, invite Claire in for a naked peek before telling her to get out and change the record or something. *No, she would have definitely brought him here,* she confirmed with a nod. *So where are they?*

Claire fit her key into the lock, struggled for a moment to make it turn, and then pushed open the door. . . .

With a screech, something small and squat and dark rushed past her feet. Claire let out a screech of her own and stepped back, terrified, staring after it.

It was the largest rat she'd ever seen.

"Oh, my God," she breathed, bringing one hand up to her breasts involuntarily. She watched as the rat disappeared into the darkness of the stairwell, and fell back against the door frame.

"Dorian!" she called, backing nervously into the apartment. "Dorian, did you see that . . . ?"

Then she turned.

The words froze in her throat.

The door slid shut behind her, forgotten.

And she collapsed to the ground, unconscious, while Dorian's head stared across the floorboards at her with eyes of bright, forever-unseeing blue.

CHAPTER 15

It was now 2:35 in the morning.

Ian sat at the bar of the Shamrock Pub, alone. To either side of him, empty barstools jutted from the floor like black, bloated mushrooms on fat chrome stems. In his left hand was a cigarette with an inch-long ash. In his right was a red Flair pen.

Spread out before him were a series of notes and diagrams, drunkenly scrawled on the backs of several blank messenger manifests. He stared at them, red Flair poised, while his mind grappled with the details of the plan.

One of the pages was labeled TOOLS. On it, he had all the traditional implements of vampire-hunting: wooden stakes, mallets, crucifixes, silver bullets, garlic, holy water. To this, he had added an innovation or two: compact mirrors, to spot the monster by his absence of reflection; and, most important, a pair or more of data pagers, a dozen street guides, and the number of every subway pay phone in lower Manhattan.

As for the plan itself . . . well, it was an iffy proposition at best. It *could* work, if all went properly. Ian didn't doubt that. But it had some major holes in it, any one of them big enough for a full-grown vampire to slip through.

Twelve guys, say, Ian thought, musing over the notes on the page marked THE PLAN. *Split up into groups of three. A data pager in each group. We leave Joseph and two other guys in the van; the other three groups hit strategic subway stations around the city. When somebody spots the vampire, they beep everybody else. The number of the pay phone shows up on the data pagers; they look on their*

*charts for the location of the phone, then surround the area
within a three-stop radius in either direction. . . .*

Damn! Ian stomped on the barstool footrest in frustration, knocking the long cigarette ash onto his lap. *Goddamn it, this is never gonna work,* he added miserably, and
turned to the page marked PROBLEMS.

There were already more problems than anything else,
he noted; and he'd just come up with another. Running
down the list, they read:

1) Data pagers cost $150 apiece.
2) What if the phone's busy, doesn't work, doesn't
   have push buttons?
3) How does everybody get to the right station
   fast enough?
4) *What* twelve guys?
5) We don't even know what the vampire looks
   like.
6) Do we kill him right there on the platform, or
   what?
7) Who's gonna get the number of every goddam
   pay phone in lower Manhattan?
8) Where do you get silver bullets: a sporting
   goods store? Weapons cost money!

To all this, he now had to add:

9) Twelve people aren't enough to surround *anything* in groups of three!

"Well, that just about does it," he complained to
himself. "No way in Hell." Then, silently, *if twelve people
aren't enough to do it, then how is Joseph supposed to do it
all by himself?*

And how am I supposed to explain that to him?

The door behind him opened. He turned automatically, with a start; even after a dozen beers or more, his nerves
were still horribly on edge. Like Joseph, he couldn't close
his eyes without seeing Peggy Lewin's spontaneous decay.

Ian turned toward the door and watched as two large men stepped into the pub, wearing the orange Day-Glo vests, rubber boots, and grimy work clothes of the MTA. Their eyes shone white in their dirty faces, darting this way and that with an expression that took only a second to read.

Those guys are terrified. Ian stared at them for a moment, his jaw hanging slack. He felt like laughing, like curling up in a ball. He watched as the second man closed the door with a bang that made the first man jump. Ian jumped, too, then giggled involuntarily. His flesh was crawling.

He could feel their fear from halfway across the room.

He turned away abruptly, staring straight ahead. In the mirror behind the bar, his reflection stared back at him: a pale, ghastly mockery. He tried to grin reassuringly, the traditional hambone response to discomfort; but the face that grinned back at him was so drained . . . so *dead* . . . that his eyes snapped shut in revulsion. . . .

. . . *and Peggy Lewin was screaming, one eye rolled back into darkness, the other gone entirely, as the flesh surrounding her tensed jaws began to split and reveal the straining muscles beneath* . . .

"No," he whispered through clenched teeth, eyes snapping open again to rivet on his hands, clenched into fists on the bar before him. Behind, he could hear the two men, their steps slow and halting, as they made their way toward the bar. *I'm not going to look at them,* he told himself. *I don't want to see any more.*

But he found himself listening as they seated themselves about four stools down to his right, ordered double shots of Johnnie Walker Red with a pitcher of beer for a chaser, and . . . softly, tentatively . . . began to talk.

"Yo . . . T.C.?" This from the white guy, the first one in the door. He sounded, predictably, like Sylvester Stallone.

"Go ahead," his black companion muttered without much enthusiasm.

"It's . . . I . . . I don't know if I want to go back

down there again." The black dude let out a derisive snort. "No, really, I . . ."

"You had to go right up to that thing, didn't you? Shine your goddamn flashlight right in its face." He snorted again, furious. "You're one bad-ass dude, Tommy. You know it. You as bad as they come. . . ."

"Hey! You ran, *too*, buddy! Don't give me that crap!"

"I didn't even want to check it out, blood! *You* were the one who had to be so in-quisitive! *You* were the one . . ."

"Hey, just lay off me, would'ja?" The white dude, Tommy, stared sullenly down at his knees, grimacing. T.C. glared at him, then chugged heavily on his beer and ruminated. Finally, he spoke.

"I'm goin' back down," he said. "I can't be quittin' no job just because of this. I got alimony to pay. I got child support. I got bills crawlin' up my butt like you wouldn't believe. . . ."

"Yeah, yeah, but . . ."

"But *nothin'*, you stupid Pollack sonofabitch! Now, if Weizak wants to make some kinda big deal outta this, he can just deal with that thing himself! I just needed a drink to mellow myself out. Thass all."

"That fuckin' *thing*!" Ian glanced over and saw that they had both paused to drain their double shots in unison. Then Tommy slammed his empty glass down and said, "I don't even wanna *think* about it!" Ian looked quickly away.

What did they see? The question tugged at the base of Ian's brain like a spoiled brat at the hemline of his mother's skirt. He found himself grinning wildly, grinning at his knotted hands, while his mind repeated the question: *what did they see? What did they see down there?*

As the net closed inexorably around him.

One minute, he thought, *you're allowed the illusion that things are pretty much the way they've always been and always will be. Next time you turn around, some pinhead rips the world out from under you, and the weirdness starts pouring in from every directon. . . .*

Like these guys. If they didn't see the vampire down there, I'll eat my hat. I'll buy a hat and eat it.

* * *

In the tunnels . . .

T.C. Williams and Tommy Wizotski, cleaning up after a water main break on the Broadway line between 8th and Prince. Not thinking about the murders, the rumors of things even worse than death; not thinking about the bodies that sporadically turned up in one section of tunnel or another, even in the most ordinary of circumstances. . . . MTA workers stumbling into third rails, junkies and winos crawling down there to die. . . .

Not thinking about any of that.

T.C. and Tommy, drenched with sweat and filthy water, nodding at each other like conspirators do. T.C. and Tommy, leaving the mess behind them as they moved to a niche in the wall on the uptown side. Withdrew a joint of exotic pot, valued at $120 an ounce, from a grease-stained pocket. And proceeded to fire it up.

A train, rumbling toward them. Pausing to blow blue smoke defiantly against the approaching lights, laughing in the grip of a steadily mounting high, before pressing back into the niche and safety.

Glimpsing, in the moment before caution forced them to retreat, something small and pale that lay by the side of the shuddering rails . . .

. . . and then moving back, watching the faces in the brightly lit windows flash by, too quickly to be distinguished, as the train thundered past. Communicating with a glance, because words could not possibly cut through, while the joint passed back and forth in the constricted space of the niche. The first glimmers of fear, constricting that space even further . . .

. . . as the train continued to stretch out before them, a solid wall of power and motion . . .

. . . and then was gone, the last car whipping past them and off into the distance, leaving them bathed in dope smoke, darkness, and reverberating sound . . .

. . . that dissipated, gradually, into silence.

Moving, then, away from the wall. Stepping carefully

over the deadly third rail and into the center of the still-thrumming tracks.

Moving toward the thing. . . .

Ian had made up his mind.

They had been talking together for the last fifteen minutes. Little by little, the story was coming together, as the steady flow of alcohol began to loosen them up. But they were still beating around the bush, and Ian couldn't stand it much longer.

He closed his eyes. The darkness was softly spinning, but at least Peggy Lewin wasn't in it. *I'm going to regret this in the morning,* he informed himself, grinning lopsidedly. Then he opened his eyes, waited for the room to steady itself out, and motioned for the bartender.

"What are those guys drinking?" Ian asked, leaning forward and cupping his hand to his mouth. The bartender squinted at him darkly, suspiciously. Ian was confused for a second; then he rubbed his eyebrows and leveled a cold gaze at the man.

"Look. Just set 'em up with shots of whatever they're drinking," he said, "and bring me another pitcher, okay?" The bartender nodded, slowly, and turned away.

What does he think I'm gonna do? Get two big transit workers drunk, lead 'em out back in the alley, and mug 'em? Didn't seem too likely; they were both about six feet tall. *Probably thinks I want them to take me home,* Ian continued, laughing at the thought. *Christ. In a sane environment, that wouldn't even come into the picture.*

But this isn't a sane environment. The thought clung for a moment. *This is a place where bodies come climbing out of subway tunnels. This is a place where, if you have three guys sitting at your bar, chances are all three of them saw a monster today.*

Which reminded him. The bartender was setting up the shots now; the two guys were staring over with blank surprise. Ian motioned for them to wait a minute, then gathered up his belongings and rose from the stool.

God, this is going to be weird, he thought, and then he was moving toward them.

It was the head. Tommy had suspected it from the first glance. As they got closer, it became more and more evident that this was no handbag, no crumpled-up newspaper, no discarded underwear: none of the options that T.C. had stubbornly posed.

It was the head, all right. The one from the murder of a day before. Upside-down and at an angle, forehead half-buried in a pool of water, stringy hair dangling downwards. A dirt-caked expanse of blackness at the base of the neck, bone poking out and toward them like an accusing finger.

A large, hairy wart displayed prominently on the left cheek of its fat, lifeless face.

"Aw, come on, Tommy," T.C. had almost whined. "Leave it alone, now. I'm serious."

"Wait a minute. Just wait a minute."

"You don't wanna see that . . ."

And they had come closer, to within five feet of it. They had come closer, almost on tiptoe, as though they were afraid of awakening it.

Then Tommy had knelt down in front of it; and, pausing to make absolutely sure that T.C. was watching, he unhooked the flashlight from his belt. Flipped it on.

And shone its light into the dead thing's face . . .

. . . and the eyes shot open, twin crimson reflectors that stared blindly back at them, while the jaws widened into a silent, screaming rictus of horror. . . .

Tommy and T.C. had screamed then, too: sonic accompaniment to the soundless howl of the thing at their feet. The flashlight had slipped from Tommy's fingers and rolled, its beam trailing off into darkness and distance. Then they turned and ran, crazily: away from the nightmare, away from the tunnels, out into the street and the dull, comforting light of the nearest bar.

And into the tightening net.

* * *

Breaking into the conversation wasn't easy. T.C. and Tommy weren't inclined to talk. It took forty-five minutes, two more rounds of shots, and the story of Peggy Lewin to get anything out of them.

But by 4:00, when the Shamrock closed its doors for the night, they had discovered that there was, indeed, a lot to talk about.

CHAPTER 16

Night gave way slowly to dawn, the gradual blossoming of daylight into a heavily overcast sky. The city was sleeping, insofar as it ever does; and in the tunnels, even the dead were at rest.

In a small apartment on MacDougal Street, police were just wrapping up their interrogation of a terrified young woman named Claire Cunningham. The body . . . both parts of it . . . had recently been taken away.

Detective Brenner of Homicide was less than thrilled with the morning's events. The girl was in shock. She couldn't tell him anything. She said that she wasn't there, and he believed her; she said that she had no idea who Dorian Marlowe was with, and he wasn't so sure. *But what can I do?* he asked himself rhetorically. *I can't say a thing without her bursting into tears.*

Brenner left his name and number on the kitchen table, next to the phone. He told her to call him when she'd rested; he wanted to talk with her again. She barely seemed to have heard him. Her eyes were staring off into some dark space beyond. He shrugged, exchanged helpless glances with the remaining patrolmen, and ushered them toward the door.

There were several things about this case that bothered Brenner a lot: the fact that there were no signs of struggle; the staggering brutality of the murder itself; the conspicuous shortage of blood both in and around Dorian Marlowe's corpse. The fact that she'd been beautiful set off a little private pang, as well; but he'd seen more than his fair share of great-looking stiffs in his seventeen years on the force.

Worst of all was the similarity between Ms. Marlowe's death and the bag lady's from the day before . . . which led him, inescapably, to that whole bit with the "Terror Train." He knew that he wasn't the only one who would make that connection, and it worried him. The police commissioner was breathing down his neck, the mayor and the city council were about to shit Tiffany cuff links, the media were blowing it up into mythical proportions . . . and all Brenner was left with was a growing pile of still-warm corpses, an enormous deadweight that had been laid upon his shoulders.

He paused in the hallway, thumbing through a battered leather notebook. The "Terror Train" conductor was still in Bellevue, still a basket case: constantly slapping at himself while he whimpered and drooled. It was like somebody had taken his brain out, popped it in the microwave for three minutes, and then put it back in, completely cooked. They would never get a word from him, ever again.

Then there was the old man, Hacdorian. He was unhelpful to the point of evasiveness, but Brenner couldn't really blame him: old people were traditional targets for the vengefully, murderously insane. And checking on his records, it was clear that the poor bastard had already been through enough misery to last him for another two thousand years.

Which left him with Claire Cunningham: a nut case if ever there was one. Her bedroom belonged in next month's issue of *Better Homes and Coffins*. She was too shook up to talk right now, and he could understand it; but he wondered if she had anything up there to begin with. Bats in the belfry, maybe. Toys in the attic.

Vampires, he thought, snapping the notebook shut.

Vampires. Sure. Then he lit a cigarette and stepped out into the street.

The ambulance was just pulling away, replete with Dorian Marlowe's neatly bundled remains. Brenner scanned the crowd of rubber-necking well-wishers, pushing up against the blue police department barricades. A *News 4* van had arrived on the scene and was wrapping their broadcast. He was glad that he'd told his boys to keep their mouths shut.

"Vampires," he mused, poking his cigarette at the sweaty hordes. "*Here's* your goddamn vampires."

Claire sat alone on the living room couch. It took her a minute to realize that she *was* alone, and the cops were gone. The knowledge didn't affect her much, one way or the other. She was lost in the dull haze of her thoughts.

Four images in particular were haunting her. Dorian's head, of course, was first: she would be seeing that picture until the day she died. Second on the list was that guy at St. Marks Bar & Grill: the details were unclear, but the overall impression lingered on.

Third was the sight that greeted her when she stumbled into her bedroom, dragging herself off the floor and frantically calling the police. The disorientation ha[d] been overwhelming even then, but her eyes had not fai[led] to notice the item that lay sprawled on the floor beside [the] bed.

Interview With The Vampire by Anne Rice.

Claire had picked up the book and stared at [it for an] unknowable length of time. She had tried to read [the page] that the book was open to, but the words all ra[n together] before her eyes. It didn't matter.

After a while, she had closed it and [laid it] carefully on her bookcase. Then she had gone [to the] living room and waited for the police to [come].

It was something that she didn't me[ntion when they] questioned her. Like the guy at the bar[, she knew] exactly why.

Last, but not least, was the rat.

Fuzzy as it was, her mind had arranged these images into a neat cosmology: one that related back to the other night, and Danny. The vampire was here, in her home. She knew it.

And she knew that it was aware of her now. It had been in her room. It had left her a clue.

And, for some reason, chosen to spare her.

She was starting to nod out now, real sleep placing its demands on her stunned, scattered mind. Her eyes closed, and the world pressed its soft, insistent weight upon her like a mountain of cotton and chloroform.

Once, before she blacked out completely, she got a strong flash of something standing in the room with her. Some presence, powerful and unseen, just waiting for its moment to approach her. She struggled to open her eyes, but she couldn't. And then, in an instant, it was gone.

I've got to see Danny, she thought in the last second before darkness overcame her. *Maybe he'll know what to do.*

And then she was unconscious. At the table. In her apartment.

Alone.

CHAPTER 17

f a dream, in that
er worlds have
pull you. Inside
, at the top of the
the sound of voices.
e.
was getting closer.

Joey . . .

Joseph moved slowly down the staircase, squinting into the darkness at the bottom. Something was moving there: a lone figure, bent and shambling, that wavered painfully at the sunlight's edge. He took another step forward, crouched down, and peered closely, intently. . . .

That was when he recognized her.

No! he tried to shout, but no sound would come. He shuddered for a moment, paralyzed, and then started to move forward. But he was too slow, and it was too late . . .

. . . and his mother came staggering out of the darkness, her head twisted awkwardly to one side, her withered body jerkily moving beneath her nightgown . . .

. . . and her flesh began to sputter and run . . .

. . . and she began to scream . . .

. . . and suddenly Joseph was alone, in a dark place, moving resolutely forward. Up ahead, in the distance, there was a light. Abruptly, he stopped.

And waited. For the light. To come.

To him.

It came with a rumbling at his feet and in his ears. It came with a violent rush of wind, as if the light were a solid wall racing toward him. It came with such sudden, awesome speed that he almost backed away from it, his arms rising up to shield his face . . .

. . . *and then the thing was on him, tearing at him, raking its claws across his arms, his chest, his face. He struggled against it, his hands on its throat, holding back the teeth that now loomed before his eyes, long and sharp and glistening redly . . .*

. . . *as the light and the rumbling overwhelmed him . . .*

. . . and suddenly Joseph was sitting bolt upright in his chair, the gaping mouth of Bugs Bunny enormous before him on the TV screen, while sunlight streamed through the living room window.

"Balls," he moaned. It came out garbled. His throat was caked with dried phlegm; his body, weak from lack of rest and extreme dehydration, cried out for water and food. He rubbed one paw across his burning eyes and groaned again.

On the screen, Bugs was nose-to-nose with the Tasmanian Devil. They roared at each other. It hurt Joseph's ears. He winced, rubbed his eyes again, and dragged himself out of his chair. Behind him, something smashed loudly, and the cartoon monster howled in pain. Joseph jumped, startled, and whirled toward the set.

Jesus Christ! That's too loud! he thought, reaching for the volume control. *I'm gonna wake up. . . .*

And then he remembered.

Joseph stared at the television for a long cold moment, oblivious to the action on the screen. In his mind, he went back to the dream for a second: back to the head of the stairs, looking downward. Then he pulled himself out of it, backed away from the set, and just stood there with his arms across his belly.

"You can make all the noise you want," he informed Daffy Duck, who had suddenly appeared on the screen. "It doesn't matter any more."

Daffy and Bugs launched into an argument while the Tasmanian Devil watched them, dimly confused. They argued as to who would make the better, tastier victim. Joseph turned away from them, moving wearily toward the bathroom for a badly needed piss.

On his way, he paused at the doorway of his mother's old bedroom. The door was wide open; the room was dark. He hung there, hesitating for almost a minute, before he could bring himself to look inside.

At the empty bed, alone in the center of the dark room. At the deep groove that ran down its center, where the mattress had conformed to her shape over the course of endless months. At the clean, freshly laid sheets; at the night table, barren except for one lamp, no longer burning; at the blank walls, the pools of shadow, the shuttered window staring in at nothing like the eye of a corpse.

Then he proceeded once again to the bathroom.

Pausing, only once, to punch the wall.

* * *

The viewing was held in a small Brooklyn cathedral,
not far from Joseph's apartment. It was done largely for the
benefit of his mother's friends, who assembled in black to
weep and prop each other up in front of the open casket.

Joseph sat alone in the back of the cathedral, expressionless. The old women who had given their respects
passed by him silently, frightened by his stoniness, on their
way out the door.

He waited for all of them to leave.

All during the sermon, while the preacher waxed
sanctimonious on the heads of his sorrowful flock, Joseph
held it in. It wasn't easy. The impulse to scream, to rip the
pews right out of the floor and hurl them through the
stained glass windows, was almost more than he could
contain. But he did; it would have been pointless to do
otherwise.

So he sat there, thinking *this is so inspirational!* and
trying not to show how angry he was, while Father Drucker
spewed out platitudes from a leather-bound book. He
clenched his fists at the image of Jesus leading Mary Ellen
Hunter up the path to glory, surrounded by cherubims soft
as bunnies. He hissed through his teeth as the good Father
praised God for His mercy, His eternal love and comfort in
these, our times of greatest sadness, amen. He swallowed
bile at the thought of his mother's death being used like
this: as a plug for some dipshit in a black and white smock, a
chance to hype the Church.

And now, as the last mourners filed out of the chapel,
Joseph thought about what he'd do if *he* were God,
wandering into His house, confronted suddenly with this
mealy-mouthed Pillsbury Doughboy of a priest. He saw
himself glowering, eyes bright as all the flames of Hell, his
head nearly touching the ceiling. He saw Father Drucker,
cowering behind the altar, his raiments falling away from
the puffy flesh, ash before they hit the floor . . .

. . . then Joseph was back in the last row of the
cathedral. The mourners were gone. Drucker was alone in

the front, extinguishing candles. A replica of Christ hung on a cross of polished metal.

And his mother lay in a temporary box, awaiting the hot kiss of cremation.

Slowly, Joseph Hunter pulled himself to his feet. Slowly, he proceeded down the aisle. Drucker turned at the sound of his footsteps. Joseph scrupulously avoided the man's gaze, eyes focused on the pale white profile that jutted from the open coffin.

Then he was standing over her, his great hands resting on the coffin's rim, looking down at the hideous mannequin that the makeup artists had made her up to be. He trembled, a rush of emotion sweeping over him, sudden and unexpected as a sniper's first shot.

"I don't know what God's will is, Mama," he heard himself saying, "but it sure as hell ain't this." Part of his mind detached, saying *you're talking to a corpse, man. Cut it out.* But the words continued to come.

"It's insane," he said. "It's insane that you should die like this. It's not right. I mean . . .

"You were a good lady, mama. Not the best, but . . . Christ, who is? I didn't always like you. Sometimes I felt like I didn't even . . . even *love* you, Mama, but . . . you were my *mother*, you know? You were my *mother*, and . . ."

He paused, trying to get a handle on what he was trying to say. He could no longer ignore the tears that were streaming down his face, the chest convulsions that were making it difficult to speak, the round eyes of Father Drucker that peered at him from behind the altar. A high-pitched whine escaped his throat, absurd in a man so huge; after a moment, he abandoned himself to it like a martyr to his fate.

He didn't hear Father Drucker pad softly up beside him. He didn't see the pudgy hand reach out to rest gently on his shoulder. He didn't even feel the contact. Not until the priest's voice came sliding into his ears did he realize that the man had approached.

"Joseph," said the priest, all dutiful kindness, "is there anything I can do for you?"

Joseph took a moment to consider it; just long enough to control his breathing.

"Yeah," he said finally. "You could get the hell out of my face."

Drucker took a nervous step backwards. "Now, son . . ." he started to say.

"Now, son, my ass." Joseph had turned now to face the priest. His eyes were bloodshot and glassy and wild. His voice was level, the danger thinly concealed. "I just listened to you talk for half a goddamn hour or more, mister. I think my mother's name mighta come up two or three times, all told. Remember her? She's the one in the box."

Joseph indicated her with a jab of his thumb. Drucker hit the edge of the dais and teetered for a moment in awkward panic, eyes bulging. A grin flashed across Joseph's features like a switchblade's sharp flickering to life.

"She used to come out here a lot, didn't she? Sunday mass, church socials, fund raisers. . . ." Drucker went off the dais now, slowly, as Joseph advanced. "She used to spend a lot of time here, on her knees, listening to the same kind of holy horseshit that you fed us all today. Only today she couldn't hear it, could she?"

He reached out to poke Drucker in the chest. Drucker backed off, sweat beading up on his smooth forehead.

"Because somebody *killed* her, didn't they?"

Poking again, harder. The priest, staggering backwards and blubbering slightly.

"But we didn't *hear* about that today, did we?"

One last prod, forcing Father Drucker onto his ample behind in the first row of pews.

"No," Joseph said, towering over the priest, with a voice like ice and steel. "Today we heard about how great God is. We heard about the merciful heavens above. We heard that God is great because He has such a great place set up for us; and all we have to do is pray to Him, and believe in Him, and thank Him for everything He does.

"Then, when cheap punks rub us out on the way to the grocery store, we can thank Him for the broken bones, the internal bleeding, the stroke that lays us up for years and years. We can thank God that the punks are still running around, so that more of us can get up to Heaven even *sooner*. We can thank God that there are guys like *you* around, to tell us what a swell guy He is for letting us get down on our knees to praise Him! Right?

"Now listen." He hunkered down in front of the priest, face to face, with only inches between them. "There is something moving around in the subways right now. It's killing people. You might've read about it in the papers." Drucker nodded hesitantly, his eyes wide and full of terror, his sweaty forehead gleaming like a freshly varnished floor. Joseph nodded in response.

"Yesterday, I saw some things," he continued. "I saw some things that let me know we're not talking about any ordinary human. *Comprendo? Not an ordinary human.*"

He hesitated then, fishing for the words. A wily grin crossed his face, disappeared, then flashed again. Drucker was convinced that Joseph Hunter had gone mad, but he didn't dare say a word.

"It's a vampire, Father. Do you believe in them? It's a vampire, and it sucks the blood right out of your neck. It's a dead thing that walks around at night, killing people and turning *them* into vampires. I don't know if you were ever a kid or not, but I must've seen a billion of those things in the movies, and I never believed in 'em for a second.

"Until now."

The same violence in his voice, but something else as well, as he posed the question.

"But you're supposed to be a man of God. You're supposed to know all about this shit. So let me ask you: do you believe in vampires, Father? Do you believe in evil, the same way you're supposed to believe in good? Do you *believe*," hoisting Drucker up by the collar of his robe, "that Satan can bring dead bodies back to life; and if you do, can your God do anything to stop them?"

Drucker's jaws worked, but no sound came forth.

"Can He?"

Drucker's face began to darken, turn purple. Joseph was holding his collar too tightly.

"*Can He?*"

Joseph hurled him, gasping, back onto the pew. His eyes shone with triumphant contempt.

"I didn't think so," Joseph said, stepping back toward his mother. "This guy wouldn't know Jesus from a blank fucking check."

Behind him, Father Drucker was sucking air like a beached whale. Joseph ignored the great whooping sound. His attention was on his mother's face, drinking in the details for what he knew was the last time.

"Goodbye, Mama," he whispered.

His eyes closed then, involuntarily. He found himself seeing her the way she once was: when there was still vitality in her body, life and lustre in her eyes. He remembered them after Pappa's death: Mama & Joey at Coney Island, her smiling and stretching their meager budget to allow one more ride on the Cyclone; Joey stuffing his fat little pre-adolescent face with hot dogs and knishes and cotton candy. Mama & Joey, alone against the world, her working full-time days at Freiberg's and three nights a week as a *maid*, fer chrissakes, just to keep a too-small apartment and meat loaf on the table; Joey, the man of the house, leaving school to work so she could finally stop. "Joey" always protecting her, afraid to leave her, loving her too much to leave her, and hating her for it . . .

. . . and then, in his mind, he saw her as she was now: the features sunken, the complexion pasty and withered, the eyes forever closed . . .

. . . *and suddenly her eyes snapped open, blank and redly gleaming as her face turned, slowly, cold lips parting to reveal—*

"*No,*" he hissed, jerking back to reality by reflex, eyes riveted on the face in the coffin.

The cold, unmoving face.

She's just dead, he thought. *Just dead, thank God.*

*Whatever that means . . . Heaven, Hell, or nothing at
all . . . she won't be getting back up again.*

Thank God.

If there is one.

Then he turned, terror and rage coursing through him
like a slow infusion of embalming fluid, and left Father
Drucker to his empty house of worship: a place unsullied
by any living presence, any power, any flame.

CHAPTER 18

Business was slow at MOMENTS, FROZEN. It was
not atypical; it did, however, leave Danny Young with far
too much time to think as he wandered through the racks of
memorabilia.

All day, Danny had been thinking about Claire.
Nothing wrong with that, per se; he'd spent much of the
previous day doing exactly the same thing. It's just that,
while yesterday's thoughts consisted largely of nice romantic fantasies (and blue movies of the mind), today's were
dominated by fear.

It began when he awoke, a cold sweat rolling off of his
forehead to burn in his eyes. He couldn't remember the
dream, exactly . . . it slipped away at the borders of
consciousness, was gone before he had a chance to get any
sort of handle on it . . . but one image lingered, phan-
tomlike, in the rear projection screen of his mind.

It was Claire, a dark shadow looming over her, while
her eyes shone with something between horror and hunger.

That was remembrance enough. It nagged at him all
morning, while he got ready to go to work. It twisted in his
guts as he walked to the shop, squeezed at his temples as he
opened for business, wormed its way up his ass during the

first few customers of the day. It absolutely refused to leave him alone.

It was refusing still.

Danny wandered back to the cash register, checked the alarm clock behind it for the umpteen-millionth time. Almost three in the afternoon. *Oh, Hell,* he thought, nervously picking at his teeth with a long-nailed index finger.

Again, for the umpteen-millionth time, he glanced at the phone book. He'd sworn up and down that he wasn't going to look up that number . . . that he'd wait for her to come around, to demonstrate what a nonthreatening, go-with-the-flow kind of enlightened male lover he planned to be.

But that was before the dream.

He stared at the phone book. He moved, slowly, toward it. He ran his fingers across the cover like an infant discovering tactility. He waged war internally, logic versus intuition, fear of rejection versus fear of bodily harm or worse.

Or worse . . .

The image came, full-blown, of Claire cruising the streets of the Village by night. Charming the pants off any number of young, testosterone-bearing men. Taking them home, with a wink and a smile and a swivel of hip. Bedding them down, her flesh white and cool as a marble tombstone. Inviting them to take her. And then, when they had dropped their guards and succumbed to the lure, a sudden baring of fangs. . . .

"Forget it," he mouthed, barely aware that he had done so. His attention was on the pages that flipped past him as he searched for her name.

And, of course, her number wasn't listed.

"Son of a bitch," he moaned, slamming the phone book closed. He whirled, glaring at the blank wall behind him. "Probably isn't really her name," he informed it pointlessly. "Probably Dustin Hoffman in drag again. Probably . . ."

The door behind him opened.

He whirled again, face flushed, half-angered by the intrusion.

It took him a moment to recognize her.

"Claire?" he asked weakly, his fears confirmed with a moment's glance.

Claire Cunningham/a.k.a. De Loon stood framed in the open doorway, sunlight diffusing through the wild disarray of her dark hair. No elaborate makeup, no exotic garb: just an organic darkness around the eyes, jeans and T-shirt on a body that trembled, frightened and vulnerable, before him.

Without a word . . . without even closing the door behind her . . . she rushed across the length of the shop and into his arms.

She told him about Dorian. He thought *my God*, picturing the scene easily enough. His arms tightened around her instinctively, protectively; she snuggled against him and shuddered. The vibrations ran through him like waves.

She told him about her room, the book on the floor. He thought *my God* and urged her without a moment's hesitation to stay the hell away from her apartment. "Sleep at a friend's house. Get a hotel room. Go to the YWCA. You could even"—hesitating for the first time—"stay at my place if you wanted . . ."

She stopped him, abruptly, with a kiss. He thought *my God*, but he wasn't about to argue. They spent the next three minutes in wordless and total agreement.

Then, after their breathing had returned to normal, she told him about the guy at St. Marks Bar & Grill. He pressed her for a description. She gave it to him. He thought *my God* and froze up, a picture imposing itself upon him with chilling clarity.

The picture was of Stephen Parrish's friend. The creepy graffiti artist. Whatsisname.

The guy who disappeared. . . .

CHAPTER 19

Nigel was fine again.

Josalyn couldn't understand it. She had spent the night in the living room, on the couch, listening to Nigel slam himself against the bedroom door and wail like a banshee for hours. Finally, he had quieted down, and she had been able to catch a few hours of troubled sleep.

In the afternoon, she had awakened to the sound of his gentle mewling. He no longer sounded insane . . . at least not any more than usual. He sounded like archetypal Hungry Nigel, coolly allowing his wishes to be known.

She let it go on for a long time: tending to her wounds, where the red streaks of infection had begun to sprout along her abdomen; fixing a light meal that she barely touched; trying to write, with the stereo blaring in an attempt to cover his ever-more-piteous sounds. But the clock had spun around to six o'clock, and she'd found that her sympathy had begun to outweigh her fear of seeing him again.

Finally, she'd opened the bedroom door. Nigel had strutted out, every bit his old self. She found that, barring the scratch marks on the door, he had been a good boy.

Now he was eating, in his customary place on the kitchen floor. It was 9 Lives Super Supper tonight; she studied the empty can, laughing nervously, knowing what a great lecture she could give on the importance of eating his Super Supper and growing up to be big and strong.

If only she weren't so scared.

Nigel is fine, she told herself. *Look at him. I bet I could swat his ass silly right now and he wouldn't so much as growl.*

143

It's as if he doesn't even remember.

But she remembered. She had the scars to remind her.

And as darkness fell over the city, and the urge to lie down and sleep began to press more and more insistently upon her, she found herself dreading what the night might hold in store.

And she knew that, no matter how sweet he might appear at the moment, she couldn't allow Nigel to sleep with her tonight. She couldn't bring herself to trust him.

Not now. Not yet.

Not until something changed drastically.

One way or the other.

CHAPTER 20

*T*wenty rats, in a tight semi-circle around the mouth of the niche. Tiny eyes, glittering in the dim light from the tunnel walls. Twitching like a single wounded organism, moved by some impulse more basic than thought, as they watched.

The two great rats, facing off in the niche: the first one gray, bloated, monstrously scarred; the second smaller, leaner, entirely black. Sharp yellow teeth bared. Eyes glaring red. Fur standing up straight along their spines as they circled each other, making tiny-throated bloodhunger sounds.

The gray one moved first, lunging forward suddenly to lash out with powerful jaws. The second one ducked, crouching lower, driving up with its snout. Tasting of the flesh beneath the chin.

Then rolling, the both of them, a ball of thrashing raw meat motion and animal scream. Tearing holes in each other, sharp teeth and talons struggling for a hold, tearing

*away jaggedly and attacking again, imbedding deeper into
muscle that strained with the effort of its own offensive.*

*The others, growing in number, pressing closer, strain-
ing for a glimpse of some edge in the murderous blur, some
hint as to which one was closer to death.*

*And then it came: a sudden reversal, a grinding halt, a
final flurry of motion. The black rat on top, its jaws
clamped tight on the throat of the other, jerking it back and
forth like a dog with a bloody rag. The other, fruitlessly
kicking, eyes glazing over as its windpipe severed, sputtered, and sprayed . . .*

. . . and Rudy Pasko was kneeling in the dirt of the
niche, with a large dead rat in his mouth.

The other rats backed away now, as a body. Their
screeches of confusion and terror split the silence. Rudy
watched them retreat, mind swimming, not entirely clear
himself as to what had just happened.

Then it all came rushing back; and with a snarl, he
ripped the dead thing from between his jaws and winged it
into the tunnel. It struck the third rail with a wet splut,
flopped madly at the center of a shower of sparks and light,
then lay still in the dirt, smoking and sizzling like a burger
on a grill.

"LITTLE BASTARD!" he howled, wiping the warm
blood from his face with a contemptuous sweep of his hand.
His flesh stung in a dozen places, where the rat's teeth had
taken cold chunks from him that grew exponentially as he
regained human form.

But he did not bleed.

Rudy plopped backwards on his ass in the dirt, leaning
against the side of the niche. He was still breathing heavily
from the fight, his heart still pounding emptily in his chest.
"God, that was weird," he mumbled, letting his mind drift
back . . .

. . . *to a time outside of time, a flowing stream of
moments without perimeters that stretched on and on and
on. Time spent scrambling about on scrawny legs, belly
inches from the earth. Time spent trapped in the body of a
rodent, scurrying for cover in a world grown suddenly too*

huge, too huge for comprehension, while the threat of killing sunlight hung imminently like the fat knot of a hangman's noose over his head.

Then . . . who knows how much later . . . finding a subway entrance and making a mad dash for it. Failing to compensate for the change in size. Tumbling ass-over-elbow down the concrete steps in a series of uncontrollable flips, screeching with pain and terror.

Amazing himself by landing at the foot of the stairs, regaining his own footing, and racing past the platform into the safety and darkness of the tunnel beyond.

Lapsing, then, into the sleep of the dead: a sleep that was crawling with dreams. . . .

In his dream, time had rolled backward to that fateful night, a mere five days before. Defacing the posters. The dark train's approach. Leaping onto it, ignoring his soul's last scream for survival. Facing the small, dark shape that leered at him with its glimmering fangs. Hearing that soft, quietly mocking voice, as the dark shape approached.

And then he was dying, the thing fastened onto him, the blood rushing up to his throat and then out through the twin puncture wounds. It was meticulous, not at all like Rudy; it didn't miss a drop.

But while it drained him, it spoke to him. Not with its mouth . . . its mouth was busy . . . but with its mind somehow, using the same cool inflection to resonate, not in his ears, but at the core of his shriveling, dying soul.

Rudy, it said, knowing him intimately, more intimately than a lover, as it sucked the life from his veins. *You're not going to die. Not now. This is something far greater than death that you're experiencing. And far more interesting.*

You are fascinated by the darkness, yes? Rudy had tried to answer, then. He couldn't. There was no longer any air in his lungs. *So I thought. When I first saw you. Amazing what time can do for your perceptivity, if you apply yourself.*

A dry chuckle. *And you will have time, Rudy. Plenty of time. All the time*—and it chuckled again—*in the world.*

You will come to know darkness, in all of its subtle texture and gradation. It will be your essence and your environment: no longer just an obsession, but the state in which you dwell. You will know it as you know yourself.

If you are attentive. And if you are careful, Rudy. Careful. It paused then, emphatic. *For, just as surely as you will hunt down humans . . . as I have done, with you, tonight . . . they will be hunting you as well. They will cling to their tiny sparks of life, for as long as they last. They will recognize you as an enemy, and they will kill you if they can.*

The train was slowing. Rudy sensed it in a way quite unlike anything he had ever experienced before. Blind, limp, and nerveless . . . for all intents and purposes, a dead man . . . he was still intensely aware of the train's movement, the grinding of the brakes, the whole-body shuddering of the train as it lurched to a halt.

Then he was being borne, as if floating, across a dark expanse that reeked of metal and dust. How he could sense these things, he had no idea; but they were there, impressions more vivid than life. Of the tunnels. Of the arms that bore him. Of the vast, filthy concrete expanse where he was laid to rest.

And before it all faded out into perfect consuming blackness, he heard the voice coming to him from somewhere beyond, saying *you have power now, Rudy: enormous, untapped potential, just waiting for you to discover and develop. Things you would not have believed possible are now well within your grasp, if you will but learn to master them.*

But that requires discipline, which is a trait you sorely lack. You frittered away your potential in the last life, sneering at the very idea of it, mocking the techniques that would have allowed you to come into your own. You assumed that to be what you were was enough, as though the sheer raw force of your anger could bring empires to their knees.

That kind of arrogance has no place, Rudy. Not in Heaven. Not in Hell. Not in this world, so firmly between.

There is order in chaos, a dark hierarchy of power you can not yet conceive of. It will not smile upon your pretensions. It will not be impressed by your tacky bravura, your insolent airs.

See, now. I have taken you as I might a little girl: effortlessly. I could take you again, any time I so desired. I am your master. I shall always be your master. Forever and ever, you will bow before me. Remember that. Always.

But to them, Rudy, you can be like a god. As I am to you. If you will utilize the gifts that I have bestowed upon you . . . unlimited power, and unlimited time in which to gain control over it . . . they will have no choice but to bow before you. As you must bow for me.

The voice was fading, the darkness all-encompassing. Still, the last words crept into his consciousness somehow, reverberating with an eerie finality.

I must go now. You are on your own. I wish you better luck with this life, your last. If you are successful . . . if you do justice to what I have given you . . . I will be back to show you what lies beyond. If not . . .

Whatever came after was lost, as the blackness achieved completion. One last cold rush, moving through him like a skewer, and then . . .

. . . Rudy was back in the niche, sight refocusing on the moisture that beaded up on the dank concrete walls. His own forehead was damp and clammy with sweat. He found himself gnawing at his fingernails, and pulled them away abruptly, panic in his eyes.

He'd forgotten. He'd forgotten entirely. For days, everything from the point where he was bitten to the point where he woke up on the abandoned 18th Street platform had been a total blank. He assumed that he'd just been left there, and that was that. He thought he was a free agent.

Now, with the words still ringing in his ears, the picture had been turned around completely. Suddenly, with all the subtlety of a rapist's hands on his victim's skirt, Rudy's illusions had been stripped away. *I am your master,* the voice said, and a shiver rattled painfully through him.

He glanced over at the dead rat, still smoldering by the side of the third rail. An overwhelming hatred welled up in him, a hatred directed at all that lived: all the puny little scuttling things, racing pointlessly toward nothingness, dim lights flickering behind their eyes. It didn't occur to him that the hatred was really aimed straight back at himself, at his dream-induced feelings of insignificance.

He only knew that he wished the rat were still alive. So he could kill it again. And again. And again.

Rudy Pasko pulled himself to his feet, staggering slightly with the effort. The hunger. It made him weak, lightheaded. It filled him with rage as he moved out of the niche and into the tunnel itself, pausing at the edge of the tracks to look around and get his bearings.

He had gotten to know the tunnels quite well over the last several days. They had become his kingdom, his turf, his home. He knew them by heart, every lonely stretch and confluence, every subtle detail that set one length of track apart from the others. He knew where to sleep, when the hour was upon him. He knew where to hide, when the workmen drew near. He knew where to hunt, where the pickings were easiest.

But the time had come to change all that.

Rudy moved toward the Prince Street station on the Broadway line, hugging close to the wall. In jollier times, he'd have walked down the rails like a ten-year-old country bumpkin with a piece of straw in his mouth. But there was something burning inside of him that had sucked out all the joy.

Like a little girl, huh? The words, the words ate away at him now. They stuck in his craw like hot rivets, dredging up shame that translated as righteous indignation. *So I pissed away my whole life, did I? Just an arrogant little nobody who never got his act together . . . certainly no challenge for you, is that it? You bastard.*

A plan was forming, of its own accord, in his mind. A piece from here. A piece from there. A glimmer of inspiration, sudden and striking as poetry, shedding new light on the path that lay before him.

There was much to be done in the next several days. A lot of groundwork to be covered, before the real action began. And though Grampa Death made a big deal about there being all the time in the world, Rudy wasn't sure that he felt like taking all that much time.

Especially if he wanted to be ready when Grampa came back.

And I do, baby. I do, he thought, smiling now as he entered the gray foyer to the workman's stairs. Outside, the night had fallen conclusively. He could feel it.

Before anything else went down, there was somebody that he wanted to see. And he would see that person.

Tonight.

CHAPTER 21

A covert roll of the six-sided dice. A crafty, giggling glance from his lightly glazed eyes. A luxuriant toke. A malevolent grin. A lush cannabis cloud that he hissed through his teeth.

"Seven armed skeletons have just entered the chamber," he said.

"*Hooo-EEEE!*" Ian yelled, leaning into the table. His eyes were wild. "Alright! Poot's got his broadsword out. He rushes forward and swings into the first one's teeth."

Dice, tumbling like dislocated molars. Allan, nodding as he spied the result. "The skeleton's head is flying apart. The top of its skull just hit the second one in the face."

"Great . . ." Ian began.

"But it's still coming at you. It takes a swing with its double-edged battle-ax."

"*But . . .*" It was the sound of a bubble bursting.

Allan rolled again. "Poot parries the blow. Does he take another swing?"

Ian nodded fiercely. "Just under the ribcage, cutting right through the spine."

"Okay." Allan rolled again and passed the pipe to Ian. "Clean shot. The top half just fell off and shattered on the floor. The legs are still hopping around."

Ian took a deep toke and let out a maleficent leer. "Poot trips 'em," he croaked, still holding his hit. Again, the tumbling dice.

"They're down." Ian exhaled, grinning. "The second and third ones are coming up on Poot now. What's everybody else doing?"

"Well, Mighty Matilda's still a little bummed out about her broken sword arm. She's just hangin' back. Weaselface is hiding behind her." Ian turned to his silent partner and poked the stem of the pipe at him. "How 'bout your people?"

"They're freaking out," Joseph mumbled. He was staring at a ripple in the stuccoed ceiling.

"Even Wambo, the Warrior King?" Ian demanded incredulously. Joseph shrugged. A long pause. Ian stared at Joseph, exchanged woebegotten glances with Allan, and stared at Joseph some more. "Are you sure you don't want some of this?" he queried, motioning with the bowl again.

Joseph shook his head. Ian shrugged, eyes rolling like dice, and passed the pipe back to Allan. Another pause, equally long.

"Poot slices 'em off at their imaginary spleens," Ian said finally. His grin was tainted. He flashed it nonetheless.

"Right." Allan rolled again, a ponderous motion. His smile, too, was a teensy bit strained. "You got 'em. Bones are piling up all over the place."

"Hey!" Ian thumped the table exuberantly, shook his fist at the trembling air. "It's a hot time in the ol' dungeon tonight, boys! Yow!" This time, the grin was effortless and genuine. *It's fun to kill monsters,* he flashed, and thought about pointing that out to Joseph. Then he thought better of it; they were already walking on extremely thin ice.

"It's not over yet, boss," Allan informed him. "Poot's up

to his kneecaps in animate arms and legs, you know." A roll of the bones. "One of 'em just sunk its talons into his leg."

"Whoa . . . !" Ian jumped back a foot in his chair.

"And the other four skeletons are converging."

"Jesus!" Ian flashed a look of shock and betrayal at the dungeon master, who shrugged with godlike indifference. "What are you trying to *do* to me, man?"

"That's beside the point," Allan said. "*They're* trying to kill you. That's just what kind of guys they are." He put a torch to his Captain Black, sent a plume of smoke to hover loftily over Ian's head. "So what you gonna do, Poot?"

"Well, since the reinforcements don't seem to be coming . . ." This with a mock-disparaging glance at Joseph, who was staring into his beer. ". . . there's nothing left to do but back off, I guess."

Allan rolled. "He trips over somebody's ribcage and falls on his ass. The sword flies out of his hand." He rolled again. "One of the skulls just bit into his forearm, and a skeleton's coming at him with a spear."

"For Christ's sake!" Ian yelled at Joseph. "Do something, man! I'm gonna get killed!" Joseph stared at him blankly. "Have Saint Pompous give me a fucking protection spell or something!"

"Protection spell," Joseph muttered. Ian looked exasperated. Allan rolled the dice.

"Didn't work." A grave pronouncement.

"You didn't even *try!*" Ian howled.

"You've got three seconds before the spear comes down," Allan intoned. "You'd better get moving."

"Jesus!" Ian looked genuinely distressed. "Poot does a quick roll to the left and starts to scuttle away. . . ."

The tumbling die.

"I hate to tell you this," Allan said slowly, "but Poot just got a spear through his back."

Ian mouthed the word *no*, but no sound would come. Allan sighed heavily and nodded his head. Ian cleared his throat and squeaked, "All the way through?" Allan continued to nod. "Oh, God," Ian breathed, cupping his face in his hands. "Am I . . . am I dead yet?"

"Well, let me put it to you this way," Allan said, taking his friend gently by the shoulder. "If a mosquito bites you, it's all over."

"AAAAAUGHHHHH!" Ian screamed, falling back in his chair. His arms and legs flapped like the flags of conquered nations. "AAAUGHHH! AAAUGHHH!" He slid off the chair entirely, disappeared under the card table. "Saint Pompous! You gotta help me! I'M DYIN'!"

"Well?" Allan said, turning to face Joseph. "Is Saint Pompous going to do anything? A healing spell? Warding off of evil?"

"A magic booger with which to smite mine enemies?" Ian called from under the table. He was still thrashing feebly.

Joseph was still staring at his beer, the white-knuckled hand that clutched it. There was no trace of humor on his face. "Saint Pompous can't do shit," he said finally.

Beneath the table, all movement ceased. Silence, thick and ponderous as stone, descended over the room. Joseph continued to stare at his hand. Allan rubbed at his eyes, then folded his hands on the table and followed suit.

"Alright," came the muffled, weary voice from below. The sound of scuffling was, in context, extraordinarily loud. Then Ian was crawling back into his seat with exaggerated stiffness, like an old man abandoned to lethargy's weight. "Alright. We'll just wait around for rigor mortis to set in." He scowled, grinned, scowled again, pointed a loaded finger at Joseph's forehead, and said, "Dude, you don't seem to understand that we're trying to show you a good time."

Joseph sighed massively. His eyes continued to point straight down. "And *you* don't seem to understand," he said, "that it ain't gonna work."

"Terrific." Ian threw up his arms. "That gives me the courage to go on."

"Hey, I'm sorry," Joseph answered quickly. "I appreciate what you're trying to do, but I've got a lot of things on my mind, and I'm just not in a partying mood. You know? I mean, I had to say goodbye to my mother today.

She's a little pile of ashes by now. That gives *me* the courage to go on, right? I had to sit in that stupid goddamn church, listening to that stupid goddamn priest rattle on and on . . . man, I coulda *killed* that guy, he was such a friggin' idiot!" He paused to take an angry swig.

"And you know what the weird thing is? I kept waiting for her eyes to open. Not like she was still alive, but . . ." Turning to Ian. ". . . like that thing we saw yesterday. You told him about it, didn't you?"

Ian nodded. He and Allan were both staring at the table now, shamefaced and silent.

"Yeah, well. So then you know. There's this *thing* running around in the subway, killing people and making them get back up to kill somebody else! Regular punks and murderers aren't bad enough, I guess! Now we gotta have *vampires* to scare the shit out of us when we walk the streets at night! It drives me crazy!

"And while all this weirdness is going on, what the hell are we doing? We're sitting around in Ian's apartment, gettin' blitzed and playing Dungeons and Dragons, fercrissake! There's a *real monster* out there, killing *real people*, and I'm supposed to get all bent out of shape because Poot gets a spear stuck through him? Shit! It's like we don't have a goddamn brain in our heads!"

Joseph stared defiantly at his friends. They were unable to meet his gaze. He took another swig off his beer, caught himself in the act, and slammed it back down on the table violently. His eyes snapped shut, features tightening like a fist. Through clenched teeth, he hissed, "I can't stand it."

"Well," Allan asked him, "what do you want to do about it?"

"I wanna kill it. That's all."

"Whoa, Joseph. . . ."

"Whoa *nothing*, man! Don't you understand? *Somebody has to kill that thing!*"

Allan looked wildly over at Ian for assistance. He didn't get it. Ian had his elbows on the table, his face resting heavily in his hands. Very gently, he massaged his temples, a thin sheen of sweat on the forehead between. His eyes, when they opened, had that faraway look.

"Okay," Allan said, turning back to Joseph. "Somebody has to kill it, assuming that it's real . . . an assumption I'm not quite ready to make. But who says that it has to be you?"

"You got somebody better in mind?"

"There's always the police. . . ."

"Shit." Joseph dragged the word out contemptuously. "They wouldn't know what they were dealing with."

"And you do?" Allan leaned forward now, taking the offensive. "You've hunted vampires before? Or do you think that watching Dr. Van Helsing on the late late show taught you everything that you need to know? Come on, Joseph! Be real!"

"There's nothing real about this," Ian interjected suddenly, "except that it's happening. And it is, Allan. No two ways about it. The only question is: do we sit around on our asses, or do we act? And to tell you the truth, I've got to agree with Joseph. . . ."

"*Come ON!*" Allan screamed. "I thought you were gonna help me talk sense to this guy!" The look in his eyes went on to say *I can understand that Joseph's got a vendetta going, but I don't understand what the hell's gotten into you.* Ian saw the look, got the message; he nodded, held up one finger, and answered.

"It's like this, man. I think Joseph will agree with me." He glanced over to make sure that his big buddy was paying attention. The smile that he saw warmed Ian's heart. "Did you ever find yourself caught up in a situation beyond your control: something that really has very little to do with you . . . certainly not the kind of thing you'd pick as your favorite pastime . . . but that you suddenly find yourself stuck in the middle of, and know that you have a part to play in it? Of course you have. We're in one now." He winked at Allan, but the playfulness of the gesture was buried by something weightier.

"When that happens," Ian continued, "there's this very strange sense of inevitability about it. You can try to ignore it. You can try to escape it. You can hope that it'll just go away, or that somebody else will deal with it. But you know that sooner or later, whether you like it or not, it's gonna come back on you. Reminders will come up and tug at your sleeve; and in the end, you'll have to answer for what you did or didn't do.

"Well, it's like that now. The same way we feel about Joseph"—this to Allan exclusively—"trying to help him through this miserable time. Nobody paid us to lay out this evening's entertainment, such as it is. There are government agencies to help you cope with a death in the family. There are social workers. There are psychiatrists. But we know where *that's* at.

"The fact is: you see something that needs to be done, and a little voice goes off in your head that says *you know what to do, man. Do it. Don't wait for somebody else, because they either won't or can't do it, and by then it might be too late.*"

Ian paused to gauge his audience. Joseph was nodding emphatically; Allan's face was a portrait of grim resignation. Apparently, he too had sensed the inevitability of it. Ian smiled and went on.

"Joseph has got that kind of feeling about . . . the thing in the subway." *It's hard to say "vampire" out loud without feeling silly,* he mused privately, not breaking stride for more than a second. "It's pulling at him. It's eating away at him, every time he stops long enough to think. I know exactly what he means, because . . . to be perfectly honest . . . it's doing the exact same thing to me.

"I didn't tell you what happened to me last night, did I?"

Allan shook his head wearily. Something went off behind Joseph's eyes, though: a flash of memory, the spark of something undivulged that raced now toward the surface. *Ah ha!* Ian thought, eyebrows raised. *I should have guessed.*

The storytelling began.

And the net inexorably closed in.

* * *

It wasn't a dungeon, though the similarities were cheap and plentiful. It lay buried in the bowels of an imposing pile of brick and stone. It, too, was perpetually shielded from the light of day. Death was its stock in trade; corpses were its currency. Its unfortunate visitors were unceremoniously picked apart and trundled off by cynical technicians who whistled while they worked.

But instead of the acrid sputter of tallow-dipped torches, there was the cold blue-white hum and flicker of fluorescent lighting. Dank mold and matted straw gave way to springtime-fresh, industrial strength Pinesol; moist, pitted stone was replaced by miles of smooth linoleum tile. And while the dungeon marked the beginning of suffering and torment, the morgue at St. Vincent's heralded the end.

At 10:15, Rick Halpern was halfway through his customary egg salad-and-Bacos sandwich. His round, porcine features were blissful, serene. His thoughts were on the swinging late-night *soirée* with Sylvia Marx that he had planned for later. There was a dollop of yellowed mayonnaise at the corner of his lips and an unsightly tumescence in the crotch of his whites.

The double doors slammed open just as Halpern went for a big wet bite. He jerked slightly, and a sopping scrap of scrambled egg perched lazily on the tip of his nose. "Damn!" he yelled, setting down the sandwich and mopping at his face with his sleeve.

A big white body under a big white sheet wheeled into the room. A white tag dangled from the big right toe. "Guess who's coming to dinner!" Broome announced, following the stretcher into the room. He had a wide, toothy grin that Halpern occasionally wanted to pummel.

"You got my coffee?" Halpern wanted to know.

"You bet. Now you'll have something to dip your Twinkie in." Broome parked the body in front of his partner, reached under the sheet, and pulled out a styrofoam cup with a plastic cap. "Don't worry. He didn't drink any. He's just here for an autopsy and a steam facial."

"Broome, you are a sicko," Halpern muttered distastefully. His erection had dwindled in the last few seconds, and the coffee had become less appealing somehow.

"And you are a walking pork chop," Broome replied. He could talk; he had a weight lifter's body at the age of fifty-five. Nautilus. "In fact, you remind me a lot of this guy." He paused to pull the sheet away from the corpse's face. "Strong family resemblance. You might have fed at the same trough together."

"Gee, thanks." Now that he mentioned it, there was a marked similarity to their features. Halpern winced, and his first bite of egg salad came briefly back to haunt him. He was callused, by and large, but bodies that resembled him always touched a special nerve. "What got him?" he asked quickly, changing the subject.

"Heart attack," Broome said, pulling his own coffee out from under and then covering the face again. He took a little sip and contentedly *ahhhh*ed. "You know, it's kinda nice to have some people in here who died of natural causes. Every once in a while, an inexplicable murder can brighten your day. But enough is enough, you know what I mean?"

"Yeah." There'd been an awful lot of excessive nastiness going down in the last few days, and quite a bit of it had wound up at St. Vincent's. "If I have to see another one like our topless cutie, I'm gonna hang this up and get a nice job in Proctology."

"Birds of a feather . . ."

"Oh, you're cute, Broome. Cute." This was one of those times. The older man's teeth made a target almost too good to pass on.

"But you're right. That was depressing. I don't even wanna *know* what happened to her." Broome's gaze slid down the rows of roll-out drawers where the bodies were kept. "Marlowe, right? Man, she was a beauty. Things like that are such a damnable shame. . . ."

It was true. They'd wheeled Dorian Marlowe in the previous night, and absolutely nobody was joking about it. The cause of death had been clear enough, so they'd foregone the autopsy. What little blood remained had been drained out through her right foot, and then they'd cauterized her stumps. After that, it was the body bag, with the head tucked neatly under one arm. Her funeral would be a closed-casket affair. No matter how much they'd loved her, her friends and family would not want to see.

Broome meandered over to the drawers and started picking over the labels. Halpern brought the sandwich to his mouth again and let it waver there, poised. He was afraid that Broome was going to do something crazy, and he wanted his mouth free, just in case he needed to scream.

But Broome just paused in front of the designation MARLOWE, shook his head, and rapped three times, lovingly, on the metal door. "Hey, kid," he said softly. "Don't sweat it, okay? You're gonna make a beautiful angel."

And on the other side of the door, inside the pale gray body bag, the face of Dorian Marlowe contorted horribly at the sound. Her lips peeled back in a soundless snarl, and her eyes popped open, flickering once with the red-light spark of vestigial evil that would never come to fruition. Then it was gone.

But the expression remained. It was anything but angelic.

CHAPTER 22

The crumpled-up napkin sat on the bedside table. Stephen's eyes kept coming back to it, no matter how hard he tried to distract himself. A dozen half-finished chores surrounded him . . . dishwater in the sink, dirty clothes in a pile on the floor, a stack of notes and manuscript in the first phase of organization . . . all rendered abortive by a stupid piece of paper, designed to wipe the ketchup from a sloppy eater's face.

One stupid piece of paper. With one stupid phone number scrawled across it.

And one all-pervasive aura of terror.

"I can't handle this," he whined, fairly leaping from his seat at the kitchen table. "I can't handle this at all." He moved quickly across the apartment, grabbed the napkin up in one trembling hand, and stared at it, as if daring it to threaten him further.

The napkin, of course, was innocuous; the terror lay in what it brought to mind. Stephen felt like an idiot, standing there, even as the fear and anger coursed through him like twin jolts of Freon and fire.

And the thoughts came rushing back in a flood of images: Rudy on the train, those red eyes glaring out from the ghastly pallor of his face; the bloody handkerchief; the madness, not human, that flashed across Rudy's features at that moment. And behind that . . .

Dark eyes, glowering in the wide, primeval face. Massive fists, trembling with barely contained anger. A presence so formidable that you could punch it through a brick wall, staring at him across a distance the length of a barroom table.

Joseph Hunter read the name on the napkin before him. Stephen shook his head, overwhelmed by the metaphor. He could almost see Joseph, primitive spear in hand, running out of some cave to attack a saber-toothed tiger, and coming away wearing the animal's skin.

He's going to find Rudy, Stephen thought, *and then God knows what he'll do.* He could see Rudy snapping in two with very little effort on Joseph's part. And yet . . .

And yet . . .

Something had changed in Rudy. Stephen didn't know exactly what . . . he certainly didn't think that Rudy'd become one of the walking dead, as Joseph seemed to . . . but something had definitely happened. Something dark, and strange, and frightening.

I've gone all the way in, Stephen, the voice hissed once again in his mind. *I've gone all the way into the darkness, Stephen, and you know what I found there?*

"What did you find, Rudy?" he found himself whispering. "What did you find . . ."

The phone rang, loud and sudden as a fire alarm. Stephen jumped, his head whipping toward the sound, his hands jerking abruptly. There was a soft, tearing noise, and he felt something give. "Oh, no," he mouthed, but the words were a silent lump in his throat.

The napkin had been torn neatly in half, right down the middle of the number.

The phone rang again. Stephen stood there, mute and motionless as a ventriloquist's dummy, half a napkin dangling stupidly from either hand. A thousand voices screamed at him from the dark grooves of his brain, most of them his own.

The phone rang again. Somehow, the spell was broken. He let the flimsy pieces of paper waft to the ground and turned to the phone. On the fourth ring, he answered it.

"Hello?" he said, the shrill vibrato of his voice echoing back at him through the receiver.

"*Ah, Stephen.*" The voice was a thin, metallic whisper over the phone lines, but it thudded like a brass drum in his ears. "*You're home. I'm so glad. That's just wonderful.*"

The voice was the tip of a long cold stiletto, inserting itself into Stephen's belly with infinite, almost lackadaisical, slowness. The voice was a forkload of maggoty flesh, pressed insistently against his lips. The voice was a Checker cab, wheeling suddenly around some corner and straight toward him, with its bright eyes glaring over the ravenous, grinning grill.

The voice was a train. A long, cold train. Upon him now.

And he was powerless before it.

"*Listen, Stephen?*" The voice struggled for control, trebling upward at the end in a burst of lunatic cheer. "*We'll be getting together in the next few days. I'm not sure when. But I'll definitely let you know.*"

The line went dead. His breath sucked in sharply, and the receiver dropped like a stone from his nerveless fingers. A great, uncontrollable spasm of terror shuddered through him, and he dropped to his knees beside the dangling phone wire.

"Oh, my God," he whispered, eyes focused on nothing, a tidal wave roaring between his ears. He shook his head violently, and his vision came back, and he found himself staring at the napkin on the floor.

In two equal pieces.

With Joseph Hunter's number torn neatly, lengthwise, right down the middle.

"Oh, my God," he whispered.

CHAPTER 23

Rudy hung up the phone and leaned back against the door of his apartment, grinning beatifically. He had a definite buzz on, a consummate high; the weakness and the hunger and the anger were gone. His whole body tingled with strength and vitality. He felt absolutely tremendous.

"Tremendous," he whispered, his head lolling slightly. His eyes were closed; and in the absence of light, he concentrated on the feelings that rushed through him. The two old friends, now coursing through his veins.

And against the backdrop of darkness, in the private screening room of his mind, he watched the events of earlier this evening unfold in living color. . . .

His name was Dod Stebbits, but everybody called him "The Bod" because he had such an unusual one. He looked like a chicken on a spit, to be honest: little spindly limbs and a scrawny chest, attached to this enormous bulging belly and protruding ass. His neck was long and skinny; his head sat on top of it precariously, like a chunk of beef fondue on a toothpick. With his beak nose, bulging eyes, crooked grin, and puffy razor cut, he looked more like a Muppet than a man.

But Dod Stebbits consistently had good drugs. There was no question about that. Whatever else you could say about him, the kid was a walking pharmacy. There wasn't a buzz on the market that he couldn't get his hands on in the space of three hours, if he didn't have it on him already. He was a procurer *par excellence*.

Rudy always scored his speed from Dod the Bod. Anything from diddly-shit like black beauties and robin's eggs to first-class crystal Methedrine. All Rudy had to do was find him, and that was never too hard. The Bod was in business; he was always around.

Tonight, Rudy had gone to Dod's Bleecker Street studio apartment. Fortuitously, he'd gotten there just as Dod was splitting for the night. Rudy had dragged the dealer back inside and killed him instantly, scrawny arms and legs waggling impotently while all the life flowed out of him like a milk shake up a straw.

Then, sated, Rudy had gone through Dod the Bod's pockets, throwing the contents on the bed. He was staggered by what he found: a Baggie of Quaaludes, maybe twenty hits of blotter acid, and well over an ounce of coke, all cut down into grams. Not to mention miscellaneous doodads, $140 in small bills, and a .32 caliber Sterling Automatic. (Rudy checked Dod's wallet. No permit. "Tsk tsk," he mumbled.)

But that didn't begin to compare with what the kid had stashed in his apartment. Rudy'd found himself looking down at the white, lifeless thing on the floor and thinking *my God, man! You were worth this much?* It was like a year in Disneyland without ever having to leave your house. It was incredible. *You could've had your whole body rebuilt to look like Arnold Schwarzenegger, with that kind of money.*

Then the thought came: *what could I do with that kind of money?*

Followed by: *what could I do with a steady flow of that kind of money?*

Followed by what he felt to be a marvelous idea.

Within a half hour, he had Dod Stebbits' body securely
tied up on the four-poster bed, right in front of the picture
window with the lovely eastern exposure. He used rope
and strips of bedsheet, leaving Dod's bod awkwardly
spread-eagled, oversized head slumped to one side, moonlight twinkling on the two wet holes in the throat. Rudy
shoved a pair of Dod's dirty underwear into the dead mouth
and then taped it shut, just in case the guy came back
screaming.

During the course of this, Rudy also popped a pair of
robin's eggs and snorted a huge line of coke. He had not
slept well as a rat, and even the blood hadn't brought him
back to a full state of alertness. Besides, that was really
what he'd come to Dod for in the first place.

He wanted speed to stay awake. The amount of sleep
he'd been getting recently seemed like a total waste of
time. *And if I'm someplace where the sun refuses to shine,*
he reasoned, *there's no reason why I shouldn't be able to
work straight through the day.*

There was so much to do, after all. And he wanted it to
come down quickly.

Which was why he left Dod trussed up like a turkey in
front of the window. Which was why, just as he had loaded
up his pockets and readied to go, he leaned over next to
Dod's ear and whispered, "I'll be back tomorrow to pick up
some more goodies. Then I'll decide whether to feed you or
leave you like this. Depending on whether or not you're
worth having as a slave, you understand me? If you make it
worth my while, I'll let you live forever."

And then, keys in hand, he'd sealed Dod the Bod up in
the apartment that had become Dod's tomb.

Rudy let himself slide down the wall, giving in to the
euphoria. There would be plenty of time to work tonight
. . . and into the new day, if he so desired . . . but right
now, he just felt too good.

When his ass hit the floor, he grinned and splayed his
legs out, slouching back against the wall. He stretched,
sighed, and put his hands behind his head. His mind began
to soar across the brainscape, plucking up images and

toying with them briefly, then moving on, restless and fickle as a nursery-school kid in an overstocked playroom.

He saw himself riding on a black Harley-Davidson, leading the great dark parade of the damned down Fifth Avenue to Washington Square Park. There was a bonfire in the center of the plaza; he could see its radiance, flickering through the arch at the end of the road like the light at the end of a tunnel. A lot of things were burning in there. So many more to come.

He saw himself at the head of a banquet table at the Plaza Hotel, where the walls were festooned with his sanguine graffiti. His horde was feasting tonight on the staff of *People Magazine*, having already dispensed with *Time*, *Newsweek*, and *The Wall Street Journal*. For dessert, they would have the Channel 11 News Team and the entire cast of *All My Children*. To his right was Ed Koch, the first undead mayor in the history of New York City. To his left was Caspar Weinberger, who had the misfortune of coming into town for a U.N. address. Tomorrow, he would go back to Washington for a special meeting with the President.

He saw himself at the top of the World Trade Center, staring out over his kingdom. Below him, the dark trains were moving through tunnels and over bridges, spreading the word into Brooklyn and Queens, thundering out to Long Island and Newark, creeping into Jersey City and Hoboken like a death kiss blown on the breeze. And establishing Rudy Pasko as the master of all that he surveyed.

Then he saw himself in the imperial bedroom, done up in lavish red and black silks and satins. There was a girl writhing on the bed before him, bound to the four posts by delicate scarves, her nightgown open to reveal the soft white flesh beneath. Her hair had fallen across her face, burying it even deeper in shadow.

Rudy moved toward the girl. Sat down on the bed beside her. Reached down slowly, with mock tenderness, to brush aside the hair. . . .

"Josalyn." He whispered the word, and his eyes suddenly opened, and the fantasy world ripped away like a gossamer veil. Rudy was staring at a dumpy room on 8th

Street and Avenue B: dingy white walls that were fading gray, warped wood floor, two lousy windows that offered a stunning view of the alley.

And in the center of the room, a small gray rat, staring up at him with quizzical eyes.

"Come here." The words surprised him on their way out of his mouth. He sounded, to his own ears, like an American Sportsman talking to one of his prize retrievers. There was no anger in the voice, no hint of the loathing. Just a firm, almost friendly command. "Come here, okay?"

Slowly, hesitantly, the rat began to move forward. A strange light came into its eyes. It slunk up to his outstretched feet, then around them, stopping about five inches beyond his reach. Its whiskers twitched, and its head cocked to one side, as though struggling to comprehend its own actions.

"Come here, bay-bee," he said, motioning with his fingers. He giggled and adopted a whiny falsetto. "Oh, coochie-coochie-coochie, little baby, come to Daddy. . . ."

The rat cringed, then, snuffling at the air, as though a bad scent had just wafted into the room. Rudy saw this, and all the humor went out of his voice. "Come here!" he barked. "Come here right NOW. . . ."

And the rat stiffened suddenly, trembling on its haunches. The eyes flashed bright red for a second, then off; but what remained was glazed and blank. A thin stream of urine spritzed onto the floor. It formed a shimmering trail as the rat painfully began to drag itself forward.

And into Rudy's hand.

"Good, good," he cooed, cradling the animal to his bosom, stroking it absently as he settled back again and closed his eyes. "Little Poopsie's all done peeing on the floor now, right? *Nice* Poopsie! *Nice* . . ."

And his mind drifted back to that fantasy bedroom. He focused on it with all of his might, his hand still idly stroking the rat, his lips falling silent.

And then, very softly, he whispered her name.

In her dream, she awakened on a huge brass bed in the center of a dark room. She saw something glide through the shadows and vanish. She heard something, faintly. A whisper. Her name.

She tried to get up. Something tugged at her wrists. Fear exploded in her chest like an incendiary bomb, but all that escaped was a tiny choking cry. She was bound securely to the four posts of the bed, and all the struggling in the world wouldn't free her.

The figure in the shadow reappeared at her bedside. She whipped her head around to face it, and her breath sucked in sharply.

It was a silhouette, like a life-sized cutout in the shape of a man, rendered in a fabric so soul-suckingly black that it stood out in sharp relief against the darkness. The deeper she stared into it, the more she felt herself starting to drift, as though she were being sucked into an abyss, sent endlessly spiraling down. . . .

Then the thing reached for her. And her eyes snapped shut. And she started to scream.

He had connected with her. He could feel it. Part of him, detached from the process, was picking up on her terror from halfway across town. It accounted for the smile that lightly creased the corners of his mouth.

As he continued to stroke the rat in his hands. And his mind stabbed deeper into her dreams.

There were hands upon her now. Cold hands, raising goose-bump patches as they slid across her flesh. She writhed beneath them, not out of pleasure. The bonds would only give her an inch of leeway on either side. She whined and struggled harder.

Cold fingers, sliding up her inner thighs. Her legs, completely parted, shuddering with violent, helpless rage. Her hips, recoiling as far as they could go.

More hands. Coming up beneath her buttocks. And lifting.

More hands, then. More hands. Encircling her waist. Kneading her breasts. Raking their nails along her belly, describing circles around her painfully taut nipples. An icy finger, worming its way into her rectum, sending a horrible wave of nausea through her.

Something else . . . something terrible . . . poised at the mouth of her vulva.

And then the last set of hands, coming up on either side of her head and stroking her hair. Sliding down to the base of her skull. Moving ever so gently across the straining expanse of her throat.

Lingering there, for just a moment.

And then . . .

"Now," he said, fingers tightening and twisting. There was a tiny squeal, followed by a muffled wet snapping sound.

In the back of his mind, he heard a scream ring out sharply. It seemed to be coming from far away. Then it cut off suddenly, and silence reigned.

Rudy opened his eyes. The glare of the lights was painful. He squinted against it, and his right hand automatically came up.

The dead rat's head poked out from between his thumb and forefinger, thick red gore trickling from its ears, nose, and mouth. He had twisted its head completely around, without even knowing he'd done it.

"Blechhh," he said, grimacing. He tossed the body to the other side of the room, then wiped his hands disgustedly on his pants and got to his feet.

On his way to the bathroom to wash his hands the full impact of what he had done came rushing back to him. *I actually touched her!* he marveled. *I was there! I felt it! And she . . .* He smiled wickedly, dreamily. *She felt it, too.*

He thought about the quality of the image he'd sent, and a cruel chuckle escaped his throat. It transformed to outright laughter by the time he entered the bathroom and flipped on the light.

Then he remembered the rat's neck breaking; and in his mind, he heard the echo of a distant scream.

Rudy paused for a moment, questions flickering across

his mind. He wondered at the extent of his power. He wondered if Josalyn was . . . if he'd just . . .

He started to laugh again.

"Oh, well," he muttered, shrugging, as he turned on the faucets. "I suppose I'll just have to wait and see, won't I?"

As he washed the blood from his hands.

CHAPTER 24

Sunday morning. The air was muggy and oppressive, bloated with the potential for rain. It was the kind of day that invited inactivity and foreboding thoughts.

The calm before the storm.

Joseph Hunter was riding the D train over Manhattan Bridge, staring out over the harbor at the Statue of Liberty, wondering if and when he was going to get his chance. Allan was still crashed out on Ian's guest mattress, blissfully unaware that Ian was already up and making plans . . . plans that would drag them both into the mouth of the dragon.

Danny Young was lying in bed, one arm still draped around the naked shoulders of Claire "De Loon" Cunningham, who dreamed of moving through a Gothic castle that looked like something straight out of a Hammer horror film. She shifted uneasily in her sleep. Danny's expression shifted from joy to concern, then back again. He had made love to her . . . he *loved* her now, undeniably and irrevocably . . . and the emotion was a Ping-Pong ball being knocked back and forth between the light and dark sides of his mind.

T.C. Williams and Tommy Wizotski were at their respective homes, privately dreading the day's return into darkness. Armond Hacdorian was talking to his priest, his satchel loaded with an unusual amount of holy water.

Stephen Parrish was barely tasting the breakfast he had prepared for himself. He didn't know it, but he was just waiting for his phone to ring.

And at Josalyn Horne's apartment, the bedroom door was open just a crack. It helped, in a small way, to ventilate the room.

To air out the ripe, overwhelming stench of death.

CHAPTER 25

The phone rang.

It was now early afternoon. The same chores were still waiting to be tended, but Stephen was farther away from completion than ever. More dishes. More dirty clothes. A paragraph of something new . . . uncharacteristically, a horror piece . . . leaving even more unfinished prose on his desk.

And now the phone was ringing. Again.

Hesitantly, fearfully, Stephen pulled himself off the bed and moved toward the phone. On the stereo, David Bowie's *Scary Monsters* was blaring away at high volume. Stephen sidetracked to turn the volume down, lingered there for a moment, while his mind intoned *it's nothing. It isn't Rudy. There's nothing to be afraid of.* . . .

Then the phone rang again. His hand tightened on the volume knob, then jerked away abruptly. "You idiot," he whispered, ashamed of his cowardice. Still, two more rings went by before he could bring himself to answer.

"Hello?" he said, trying to mask the quiver in his voice.

"Hello, Stephen?" The voice didn't immediately register. It set Stephen off-balance for a moment. *But at least it isn't Rudy,* he noted, sighing inwardly with relief.

"Yes," he said, adding, "Who is this?"

"This is Danny, from down at MOMENTS, FROZEN."

"Ah!" The inward sigh made its way to the surface. He giggled on top of it, a bit crazily, and added, "Uh . . . what can I do for you?"

"Well, I . . . uh . . ." Danny's throat, clearing from the other end of the line. "I wanted to ask you about something. Something really . . . weird."

"Oh?" Something in the way Danny emphasized the word *weird* made Stephen tighten up suddenly. "What is it?"

"Well, it's about your friend. The one who disappeared." In the subsequent pause, Stephen practically swallowed the mouthpiece of the receiver. "You know who I'm talking about, right? I can never remember his name. . . ."

"No." Stephen heard the word come out of his mouth, but he didn't believe it.

"Oh, come on. The graffiti artist. Black Bart with eyeliner. What's his name?"

Stephen didn't answer. The phone trembled in his hand. He felt an overpowering urge to hang it up and then leave it off the hook, maybe rip it out of the wall entirely. He suppressed the impulse, but not its power over him. Not entirely.

"Stephen?" There was a slight edge of desperation in Danny's voice. "Are you there, man? Are you alright?"

No, Stephen thought, teeth gritted, eyes squeezed shut, his grip on the receiver tight as his chest's suffocating pressure on his heart and lungs. *No, I'm not alright. I'm losing my mind*, cried a tiny voice in his head. His own voice was silent.

"Stephen! Jesus Christ!" Danny yelled. "Can't you hear me, or what . . . ?"

"Yes," he managed finally. "I can hear you, Danny. I'm . . . I'm sorry. . . ."

"What's the matter?" Danny's voice quieted, dropped

an octave. There was concern there: mixed, to Stephen's ears, with a wee drap of suspicion. Stephen wrestled with the words that wanted to come out, two conflicting messages that grappled for position: *I'm fine. Rudy who? Go away* on the one hand; *I'm going crazy. What do you know about Rudy? Please help me* on the other.

It was a draw. "I . . . I . . ." Stephen stammered, his voice cracking. "I can't talk to you right now. I'm gonna have to call you back. I'm sorry."

"But wait! Just let me ask you something. . . ."

"I'll call you back. Really. In a couple minutes." *I have to hang up*, his mind warned him, emphatic. *I have to hang up now*.

"Just *wait* a minute, Ste . . ."

Stephen hung up the phone.

"Christ," he moaned, his hand still on the receiver. The phone rang again.

Stephen cried out, jerking backwards suddenly. Automatically, the receiver came up in his hand. He stared at it in shock and horror, as if it had just transformed itself into a lit stick of dynamite. Then slowly, very slowly, he brought it up to his ear.

"Hello?" he said, a trembling squeak.

"Stephen?" The voice was scarcely more than a whisper. He didn't recognize it, per se; but there was something in it he connected with immediately. A terror very much like his own. Only worse.

"Who is this?" he croaked, his own voice hushed.

"Oh, *Stephen* . . ." the voice cried out, and then broke apart in a series of heartrending sobs.

Stephen didn't know what to do. The caller was still unknown; he doubted that he'd ever heard a voice like that in his life. It sounded like a grade school girl who'd just watched her parents get skinned alive, aging ten thousand years in one horrifying instant.

He listened, helplessly. She cried . . . he knew, if nothing else, that the caller was female . . . for a solid three minutes before a word could come from either side. When it came, it was from the other end of the line: a plaintive moan, so utterly desolate that Stephen had to fight back his own tears at the sound of it.

". . . please help me. . . ."

And in that moment, Stephen knew precisely who he was talking to. The knowledge came like the serrated edge of a long bread knife, cold steel raking along his spinal column with inarguable yes-you-are-dead-now assurance. It came with an audible click in his mind, like the final closing of the morgue slab door. It came as a whisper that rang in his ears, saying *oh, God, he's going for both of us.*

"Josalyn?" he said, a weak hiss into the receiver. The crying from the other end intensified suddenly; he could almost see her sitting in her apartment, unable to speak, nodding helplessly at her blind telephone. The next question came automatically, before he had a chance to consider it.

"What has he done to you?"

The sobbing from the other end subsided as quickly as it rose, dying down to a trickle. He could feel her gathering up the power to speak as she cleared her throat and hesitated, then cleared her throat again.

He waited.

"He's . . . going to kill me, Stephen." The words seemed to have forced their way out of her throat by necessity. The struggle behind them was gruelingly clear. "I know he is. He killed . . ."

"Who did he kill?" He almost shouted it.

"M-my *cat*!" Josalyn screamed back. A fresh wave of sobs escaped her. She fought her way through them. "He k-k-killed Nigel, and . . ."

"Your *cat*?" He started laughing then: a horrible, cruel sound that seemed to be . . . no, *had* to be . . . coming from somewhere else. It scared the bejesus out of him, even as it gushed from him like blood from a spurting artery. "You call me because your stupid *cat* . . . ?" He was laughing too hard to continue.

Stunned silence from the other end. A sharp intake of breath that seemed to hold and hold forever, but only lasted a second.

And then she screamed.

"HE BROKE HIS FUCKING NECK!" Now she was like a mother, wailing over the corpse of her son. Stephen's laughter cut off abruptly, a cold sweat patina oozing suddenly from his pores. "BROKE HIS NECK AND THREW HIM ACROSS THE GODDAMN APARTMENT! I WOKE UP, AND . . ."

"Wait a minute." Stephen found himself waving away the mental cobwebs with his hand. "Wait just a minute. You mean that Rudy came into your apartment and . . ."

Josalyn paused for a moment; just long enough for her voice to drop down a couple of decibels. "It was a dream, Stephen. In my dream, it was happening to *me*. But . . ."

"Now, what kind of bull . . ." he began, the first ugly bubble rising to the surface and bursting.

". . . but when I woke up, Nigel was . . . he was flying across the room, and . . . and there was all this *blood*, and . . ." Her voice decayed into sobbing again, through which she barely managed to say, ". . . I still can't . . . I can't b-bring myself to . . . to *touch* . . ."

Stephen was silent as a stuffed moose head on a wall. The only sound in the room was Josalyn's anguish, pouring through the receiver, as he struggled to put his reeling thoughts in order.

The anger had gone back to wherever the hell it came from in the first place, another weird phenomenon to try and piece together with the other events of a life gone suddenly and completely haywire. Subway slaughter. Corpses staggering out of the tunnels, or rumors thereof. A friend who mysteriously disappeared, only to come back as a red-eyed, dead-looking sucker of bloody handkerchiefs who made cryptic, frightening phone calls in the middle of the night.

And who, it now appeared, could send out dreams that make you die.

It was a puzzle that should not be able to come together, like a model of the M.C. Escher waterfall that flows down and down until it reaches the top of itself again.

It should not come together. It should not make any kind of sense at all.

But it did. Somehow, suddenly, it did. And the room in which Stephen Parrish was sitting grew somehow, suddenly, extremely cold.

"Listen, Josalyn," he said finally. "I don't know what's going on, but I do know that something is definitely wrong. . . ."

"*No sh-SHIT!*" Her laughter, hysterical and shrill, cut through his words and her tears like an ice pick through terry cloth.

"No, no," he blurted defensively. Embarrassment flickered through him, then anger, both giving way to the memory of his cruel laughter from mere moments before. He swallowed it all and continued. "You're not the first one to come to me about Rudy in the last forty-eight hours. And I . . . had an experience with him myself. . . ."

"You . . . what?" That seemed to stop her for a moment. Stephen let an oddly triumphant smile flash across his face before continuing.

"Friday night. I . . . I ran into him on the subway. He was . . ." Searching for the right words. Compromising, in the end. "There was something seriously wrong with him. I don't know what. But he was . . . oh, shit. Listen.

"I think you should meet a couple of people tonight." There was an assurance in his voice, as alien as the laughter from before. Telling of the plan that had just arrived, full-blown and utterly unexpected, in his mind. "The people who have been calling me. Like I said, I don't know what's going on. But if it's all of a sudden as important as this, then maybe we'd better find out."

Silence, from the other end.

"Josalyn?" No sound. It made him very nervous. "Josalyn? Are you there?"

A long moment's pause. Then, in a frightened little girl voice, "You wouldn't . . . this isn't a . . . *trap*, is it? I mean . . ."

"No. Honest to God, no." He hadn't even considered it. But as he spoke, the image came to him:

leading Josalyn down to the West 4th Street station, down
the first flight of stairs to that ominous level between. And
there, in the darkness, his red eyes gleaming over that
ghastly self-satisfied grin, was Rudy: his pale hands outstretched, his voice whispering *well done, Stephen. You
have served me well.* . . .

"No," Stephen repeated, to himself this time. To
himself, and to the voice that giggled malevolently in the
back of his mind.

After he had gotten off the phone with Josalyn,
Stephen sat on the edge of his bed and thought. The
imaginary betrayal was still fresh in his mind, and it
bothered the hell out of him. Like the mocking laughter.
Like the fact that he had held out on Joseph Hunter,
automatically and wholeheartedly *against* what he now felt
to be his better judgment. Like a thousand other things he
had done in the past week, and . . . yes, now that he
thought about it . . . for as long as he could remember.

But that was far too much to think about.

Stephen found himself staring at the wastepaper
basket next to his desk, with the crumpled sheets of
manuscript and empty Tropicana orange juice containers
jutting above the rim. He knew that, not too deeply buried
in the debris, both halves of Joseph's number were waiting
him out. Waiting for him to rediscover his backbone, get
himself together, and dig them out.

He'd made a point of hiding the napkin from view, in
the hope that the old adage would hold true: *out of sight,
out of mind.* Well, it hadn't. Not a bit. He might as well
have glued the thing to his forehead.

And now it's come down to this, he thought. *I can't
even pretend to ignore this any more. The next mistake
might be the killing one.* He shuddered at the thought.

Then, slowly, he pulled himself to his feet and moved
to the basket. Knelt in front of it. Meticulously began to
remove the refuse, piece by piece, until he found what he
was looking for.

Stephen put the two pieces of napkin on the floor and

fit them together as best he could. Dampened to begin with, the thin, fibrous paper had pulled apart in the worst possible way: the numerals were blurred and stretched and jaggedly mangled. Joseph's handwriting didn't help matters, either: the least damaged number could have been either a one or a seven.

Frustration rippled through him in sickly little waves. "How am I supposed to do this?" he whined quietly, fidgeting with the pieces, knocking them out of alignment. "Oh, God*damn* it!" he yelled, throwing his arms up in a gesture of defeat.

That was when the tiny voice in his mind, very matter-of-factly, said *just dial the phone, stupid. Dial it until you get it right.*

He slapped himself across the forehead. "Why didn't *you* think of that, you dope?" he moaned; then he got to his feet with the napkin in hand, went over to the phone, and started running all the possible combinations.

On the first try, he got Antonio's Pizza. "Sorry," he said, hanging up. Next, he got a recording to the tune of *we're sorry, the number you have reached is not a working* . . . That made him nervous. He hesitated for a moment before trying again.

The third call put him in touch with a Mr. Weinstein, who claimed to be locked in a hotel room in Queens. "Where's Eddie?" Mr. Weinstein demanded. Stephen hung up without another word and tried again.

A sexy feminine voice informed him that he had reached Suzy's Erotic Fantasies. He tried again.

A little boy answered and started screaming in Vietnamese. He tried again.

"Hello? Is this Eddie? This is Mr. Wein . . ." Stephen shrieked and slammed the phone down on the hook. He stared heavenward, as if for guidance, all the while thinking *this is ridiculous, this is pointless, I'm never gonna get him, I might as well just forget about it.* . . .

But when he shut his eyes, dark things were in motion against a bright red backdrop. The light streaming through his eyelids from the bedside lamp was the color of blood.

He opened his eyes with a start, picked up the phone, and tried again.

And tried again.
And tried again.
Until he got it right.

CHAPTER 26

On the screen, somebody was getting disemboweled with an electric carving knife. Lots of blood. Lots of intestinal splatter. The audience hooted and screamed and chuckled while the poor victim yowled and thrashed, hokey synthesizers blaring and whooping it up in so-called musical accompaniment.

The name of the film was *Gore Feast*. True to its name, *Gore Feast* had been moving along at a ferocious clip, serving up fresh bodies to mutilate at regular five-minute intervals. Heads staved in with hammers. Eyes turned to pudding with eggbeaters. Torsos dangling from meathooks. Brains in blenders. Kidney pie.

It made Rudy very hungry indeed.

He was sitting in the balcony of the Cinema Village, where a special sleaze festival had been running all week. Eternal classics like *I Disemember Mama* and *I Spit On Your Grave*, *The Bloody Mutilators* and *Ilse: She-Wolf of the S.S.*, all gathered together under one roof for seven days of cinematic putrefaction. It was a big departure from the theatre's standard fare . . . Woody Allen, Monty Python, Stanley Kubrick, and Federico Fellini . . . but it had its audience of twistos and fans who would pay good money to see it.

Two such creatures were sitting right in front of Rudy: two zit-faced butterballs with greasy hair and horn-rimmed glasses, the lenses on them thicker than bulletproof glass. Their mouths had been in motion continuously, shoveling down popcorn and making little whiny criticisms with their mouths still full. They were the kind of people that you just want to hit.

But Rudy had a better idea.

The carving knife victim had been reduced to cutlets by now; the audience had settled down; the camera had wandered off to look at something else. Ostensibly spooky music droned softly in the background as the camera finally settled on a closet door that slowly, silently, opened.

From the widening crack, a chain saw poked its many-toothed head out daintily.

"Oh, *Gawd!*" griped the fat, greasy fan on the right. "Can't they do anything original? I mean, really!" Rudy felt his gorge become buoyant.

"Well, I have to admit that I never saw anyone get their eyes taken out with an eggbeater before," the one on the left quipped with snooty derision.

"But a chain saw? I mean, really! Gawd!" As he packed another handful of popcorn into his face.

Shut up, you fat fuck. I can't stand it. I mean it. Rudy's stomach felt hollow and coated with slime. He clutched it with cold, trembling fingers, rocking back and forth, just trying to get through the next few seconds without losing control.

But the chain saw extended itself out to its full length without making a sound. The drone built slowly in volume: far too slowly. Little clusters of impatient grumbling pockmarked the smoky air. Rudy gritted his teeth and sighed heavily, trembling. The moment dragged on and on.

"This is what passes for suspense in a Grade Z . . ." the second fan cleverly murmured.

And then the chain saw erupted into thundering action. The carving knife killer whirled just in time to watch the blade slice off the top of his head. Blood gushed out like paint from an overturned gallon can. He screamed. The crowd screamed with him.

The overall volume was more than adequate. Rudy

leaned forward just as the first fan recoiled with involuntary disgust. He took a handful of greasy hair and pulled the fat head over the back of the seat, stretching the throat out, laying it bare.

Without hesitation, he found the carotid artery and proceeded to tap it.

The dying kid's friend didn't notice. He was quite absorbed, despite himself, with the spectacle of a man getting his head chain-sawed in half with one neat vertical sweep that wound up at the collarbone. The two halves of head flopped to either side and dangled like wet rubber chickens from what was left of the neck. It was quite an impressive display.

He was about to comment upon it when a cold hand took him by the base of the neck and squeezed. What came out of his air hole was just that: air, a great whooshing burst of it, muffled as a fart under a thick pile of blankets. His thick lips flapped impotently in the breeze. The grip on his neck tightened.

And slowly began to twist his head around.

"*Mrgmph*," he managed, cow eyes bulging and bright with tears. They caught a glimpse of his dead friend's face: the flesh bone-white and puffy, the jaw moist and slack, the eyes glimmering dully in the thin beam of light from the projectionist's booth. He had just enough time to register the sight before a second hand came around from over his right shoulder to take him by the left side of the face.

"*Hey, squishy face,*" said a voice from behind him, a sibilant hiss that blew into his ear. "*How about this? Does this scare you alright?*"

A thin gurgle rose in the constricted throat.

"*I noticed that the movie wasn't doing it for you.*" The hand on his face began to push, twisting his head around to the right, while the other hand held his neck stationary. Something went *ping* at the base of his skull, and white-hot pain shot through him like a lightning bolt.

He twisted his body onto its side in the seat, momentarily easing the pressure. His knees came up and banged against the dead meat at his side, which sagged and drooped like an overstuffed garbage bag. He pushed at it weakly, trying to keep it from falling on him. A whimper twitched, still-born, on his shuddering diaphragm.

Then he was jerked around entirely, facing toward the back of the theatre. He gulped down one last breath before the hands closed around his throat, sealing in the air like a Ziplock bag.

Rudy grinned at him, their noses only inches apart. His fangs were long and capped with darkness, like the tips of fountain pens. His eyes were dancing pools of flame.

"Perhaps you'd like to offer some more criticisms," Rudy whispered, and his hands squeezed with all their might.

"Mrgmph," the fan tried for, but he hadn't the wind. His eyes rolled back under the purpling lids. His cheeks bulged like balloons. His zits darkened and swelled. He looked like an enormous pimple on the verge of bursting open.

Rudy glanced away for a moment, attracted by a sudden movement on the screen. Mr. Chain Saw was still at it, hacking poor old Mr. Carving Knife into teensy-weensy pieces. All four limbs had been severed. They lay flapping on the floor in a grotesque parody of what was actually happening in the seat before him. A line from a book popped into Rudy's mind . . . something about life imitating art . . . and he suppressed a chuckle as he turned back to the matter in his hands.

Dark, bubbling froth had appeared in the corners of the fat kid's mouth. His thick, blackening tongue lolled out stupidly. A wet *blatt* trumpeted from his cushioned ass-end as his bowels let go in his corduroy slacks. There was one last spasm that made the body jiggle like Jell-O on a spring.

And then it was over.

Rudy let go gradually, careful to keep the kid from sluicing all over him when the throat opened up enough to drain. Sure enough, a thick gout of something hit the floor next to him. His legs jerked away just in time. Then Rudy eased the corpse back into its seat and let go.

Abruptly, the theatre went all but silent. A quick

glance up revealed that the film had cut to a new scene, from the perspective of a table on wheels being rolled down a long dark corridor. Rudy watched, slumping back in his own seat and sighing contentedly. He felt ever so much better. The first guy alone was a meal and a half.

At the end of the corridor, there was a door with a small oval window at its center. Pale bluish light filtered through it. In the moment before the rolling table connected with the door, Rudy checked his face and hands to make sure that there wasn't any blood on them. There wasn't. His fastidiousness pleased him.

You're getting good, he told himself. *Getting better all the time.*

Then the door slammed open, and the camera moved into a great banquet hall. There, a vast array of kooky cannibals were munching out on the organs of their choice. Evidently, this was the much-heralded gore feast itself. Rudy smiled at the shrieks and shrill hilarity that ensued.

The chain saw killer appeared at center screen, leaning over the table that he'd just wheeled in. He removed the half-moon lid from a large circular tray, and there was Mr. Carving Knife's head . . . apparently glued back together . . . with a rosy red apple in his mouth.

Rudy took that as a cue. He'd have loved to stay and see the rest, but the smell of fresh feces was beginning to spread. He rose to his feet and moved toward the stairs, noting that he wasn't the only one walking out at this point in the proceedings.

Never realized that the movies could be this much fun, he thought, laughing to himself, and then headed down the stairs.

Behind him, the riotous roar of the crowd was like music, sweet music, to his ears.

CHAPTER 27

"So you say that this guy knows something about it." Allan was dubious and, what was more, discomfited. He looked like the man who picked Door Number Three and wound up with two tons of manure.

"Yep," Joseph said, not breaking his stride. "Like I said, he knows Rudy."

"And who are those other people we're going to meet?"

"One girl who says Rudy is sending her nightmares. One girl who thinks Rudy might have murdered her roommate. And some other guy, I don't know what his story is."

"He played basketball with Rudy back at Transylvania High," Ian said, prodding Allan in the ribs. "Cheer up, Squiggums. This ain't nobody's funeral."

Allan groaned and ground his teeth against the stem of his pipe.

They moved rapidly down Bleecker Street toward their rendezvous with destiny. The site of this encounter was slated as The Other End, a laid-back little bar and nightclub with two separate rooms. They had chosen the smaller room because the music was acoustic, not electric, and because there was no cover charge. "Besides," Stephen had stressed, "it's not a very busy place, and there's a big table in the back where we could probably sit all night."

"I'm less than thrilled by this whole idea," Allan grumbled. They moved past a NO PARKING sign, and he tapped out his pipe against it cheerlessly.

"We know, we know," Ian droned, mocking him.

"Some people just don't know how to have a good time. Right, Joseph?" He elbowed both of his friends in unison.

"Cut that out," Allan grumbled anew. Joseph just grunted and kept walking.

"So much fun, I've never had," Ian added, grinning wickedly. Then his eyes perked up, and he said, "There it is." He pointed at a dark green awning on the other side of the street.

They moved single file between a pair of parked cars and stopped in a line at the edge of traffic. The light, for the moment, was against them. Allan took the opportunity to make one last appeal to their senses.

"I'd really rather not go in there, if you don't mind," he said, "and I . . ."

"I do mind." Joseph had turned to face him, constrained by one strand of patience that was wearing very thin. "I want you to meet these people, because I want you to see just how serious this is. I want you to see that we're not just making this up. Okay? I want you to see for yourself."

"I . . ."

"*Allan*." The tone of his voice was unforgiving. "If you don't go in there with us, I don't even wanna talk to you."

"He's not kidding," Ian piped in, not as funny as he'd have liked. "It could mean the end of a beautiful relationship."

"This sucks," Allan said, staring down at his feet.

But when the light changed, and Joseph stormed across with Ian capering and grimacing monsterlike behind, Allan knew that he had no choice.

Very reluctantly, he followed.

"Are you sure this is the right room?" Ian asked once they got inside.

"In the back," Joseph answered, still forging ahead. They moved past the jukebox, the bar on their left. The room widened at that point, about thirty yards from the back wall and the little stage in the corner. As they stepped into the expanded space, Joseph glanced to his right and saw a very large table, catercorner to the stage. Four people were seated around it: two guys, two gals. Because the guys were facing away, it took Joseph a minute to peg the one on the right.

"Stephen," he said, stepping forward.

At the table, all four of them looked up at once, the men half-turning in their seats. Stephen's eyes lit up at once; it was hard to tell if the emotion behind it was fear, or relief, or both.

"Joseph," he said, standing up gingerly and gesturing toward the seats. It crossed his mind to offer his hand for shaking. It crossed back out again.

The two young women were seated on a long bench that ran along the wall. They both slid down, and Joseph seated himself beside them. The man on the left, a tall, gangly guy with glasses and a dark ponytail at the far end of his receding hairline, moved one seat over to remain abreast of the girl he had been facing: a sultry brunette with a lot of makeup on her pale, agreeable features.

Allan sat down between the two guys and across from the other woman. Because her eyes were downcast, he took a moment to study her: the short, dark hair, unwashed and disheveled; the sunken, slightly discolored flesh around her eyes; the deep worry lines on either side of her thin, trembling lips, corresponding to the furrows in her brow.

She looked like someone who'd just spent the last several days as a guest of the Spanish Inquisition. Despite all that, it was obvious that she was a very good looker, under ordinary circumstances. It tugged at Allan's heart, and he was forced to look away.

Ian, too, had been staring at her. Ever since they first looked up, his eyes had not left her face. He'd caught her gaze, in that moment, and a spark had gone off in the back of his head.

Oh, my God, he'd thought, something tightening up inside him like a wet washcloth being wrung out by hand. *What has he done to you?*

He caught himself now, still standing at the head of the table, awkwardly staring at a total stranger. He shook his head vigorously and grinned like an idiot at the wall, then turned to appropriate an empty chair from the neighboring table and seat himself, still at the head.

"Well," he said, grinning sheepishly around the table. "Where do we start?"

There was a brief, nervous silence, full of unrealized and semi-furtive glances. Stephen shifted uncomfortably in his chair. Even Joseph seemed temporarily at a loss.

"Okay. How about this? My name's Ian. And you are . . . Stephen?" Stephen nodded, smiling faintly. Ian nodded back and smiled, then looked to the other guy.

"Danny," said the other guy, grinning affably. Allan interjected with his name at that point, and Claire . . . the brunette . . . quickly followed suit with a breathy voice that bordered on the suggestive.

"And this is Joseph," Ian said, as Joseph didn't seem inclined to introduce himself: he nodded, expressionless, at the mention of his name, then leaned back on the bench and crossed his arms.

One person remained to be introduced. Her eyes were closed, her head tilted downward. She didn't speak, she didn't move. The new silence that sprang into being was as heavy as the knot on a hangman's noose. Not even Ian knew how to go on.

Finally, Stephen leaned forward and said, "This is Josalyn. She's had a very . . . rough experience. . . ."

That was when she began to cry.

"Oh, Jesus," Ian said, starting to reach forward with one hand. Allan echoed the gesture. They both stopped short.

It started as a sharp, sudden intake of breath that jerked her body once and then stopped. She sat there, straight-backed and rigid and motionless as a statue. The first tear rolled down her cheek as if by magic, from out of nowhere, like the stories of the bleeding Christ re-enacted.

From there, it took about fifteen seconds for the walls to cave in, and for her to collapse across the table, the air lightly shaken by her gentle sobbing sounds.

"Okay," Joseph said abruptly, putting one large fist on

the table as he leaned resolutely forward. "We got that out of the way. Now where's the goddamn waitress? I need a drink, and we need to start talkin'."

Nobody else knew how to react, but Ian and Allan both flashed him a look that had *you heartless cocksucker* written all over it. Joseph shrugged, not exactly apologetic. Josalyn, for her part, seemed not to have heard. Her head remained on the table. Her sobbing softly continued.

As if just slightly behind cue, the waitress appeared and asked them what they wanted to drink. "A pitcher of Bud," Joseph answered immediately.

"Make that two," Ian followed.

"No. Three," Allan added.

Danny smiled despite himself and turned to Claire. "You want to split one?" he asked. She nodded, smiling back. "Okay. We're up to four."

Stephen, apparently remembering his last drinking session with Joseph, said, "Just a mug, please," with an uneasy grin.

It was Allan who leaned forward and said, "Josalyn? Can we get you something?"

She paused for a moment, seemed to consider it, then lifted her head just enough to be heard and said, in a tone only slightly above a whisper, "Wine."

"Wine?" the waitress repeated, uncertain.

"Yes. White wine." She lifted her head and pulled herself upright, made a go of smiling around the table. It was close. Damn close. And her eyes, though bloodshot and cloudy with tears, were far more alive than they'd been a minute before.

"I'm sorry," she said, and looked down again.

"It's all right, kiddo," Ian assured her. "Not to worry. So long as you're okay, it's okay."

She looked at him, then. The second their eyes met, something moved between and through them like a quick jolt of electricity. It happened in a fraction of a second. That was all it took.

It didn't get past Danny. He knew a connection when he saw one. His hand reached across the table as if by reflex to close lightly around Claire's. She blew him a kiss and looked back at the others. She'd picked up on it, too.

In fact, none of them failed to notice the spark, though each had a different reaction: numb amazement from Stephen, mild jealousy from Allan, vast impatience from Joseph. The waitress, turning away to fulfill their orders, assumed that they were old lovers who'd fallen on hard times, and wondered why they were sitting so far apart.

"Can we get on with it?" Joseph growled, punching a hole in the moment.

Ian turned: startled at first, then smiling with a bit of his own cold annoyance. "Would you just relax for a second?"

"Hey," Joseph retaliated. "I just didn't know that this was the social hour. Somebody's getting their throat ripped out right now, but what the hey? Maybe we should all just go to the movies."

Ian rolled his eyes. His lips and shoulders tightened. He glanced at Josalyn, whose gaze dropped to the floor again, and then back at Joseph angrily.

"Okay. All right," he said, sweeping his gaze around the table now. "I guess we all know why we're here. Everybody's been having some weird experiences lately. Am I right?"

Allan was the only one who didn't nod assent. He was watching the proceedings with slit-eyed perplexity.

"Well, does anyone want to tell us what they think is going on?"

A long, shuffling, agitated silence.

"Right." Ian smiled nervously and cleared his throat. "Well . . ."

"There's a monster running around in the subways," Joseph interrupted. "Does everybody know that already?"

Josalyn looked stunned. Stephen looked miserable. Danny and Claire lit up like Christmas trees, like kids on a rollercoaster, with matching expressions of awe and excitement. They looked at each other and beamed.

"What, you think that's funny?" Joseph demanded, his fists squaring off.

"No, no," Danny said, still grinning despite the force of Joseph's anger. "It's just that we *knew* that's what it was! A vampire, right?".

Now it was Joseph's turn to look stunned. That was the last thing in the world he'd expected to hear from anyone else. He nodded thickly, mouth gaping, eyes momentarily dazed.

"What makes you think that?" Ian asked, leaning into it, his eyes sharp and leveled on Danny's. There was a little half-smile on his face that he wasn't even aware of.

"Well . . ." Danny began, and then the waitress returned with their drinks.

Josalyn could feel herself going insane. It was like the floor had opened up under her feet, plunging her downward toward the snake-filled pit of utter madness. Fear slid through her, cold and reptilian. Her flesh crawled, clammy to her own touch as she hugged herself in sudden desperation.

A hush fell over the group as the waitress distributed the pitchers and glasses. It was the kind of silence that falls over a room when a bunch of kids are plotting a prank and somebody's mom walks in: immediate, sly, and guilty as hell. It struck Josalyn with alarming force that she was caught up in some twisted children's game, a terrible make-believe that had ripped through the barriers.

A nightmare made flesh.

What are they talking about? she heard her inner voice screaming. Her eyes cast wildly about at them all. *Vampires? Vampires? What the hell are they TALKING about?* She shuddered painfully, and her fingernails dug into her bare arms.

The one named Danny poured himself a beer and started to speak again. She turned to face him. His eyes, behind the wire-rimmed glasses, looked distorted and far too large for his head. She suppressed a sob that nobody seemed to notice.

As the pit yawned, wider, beneath her feet.

* * *

"It started when we went to see *Nosferatu*," Danny said eagerly. "It's this great German vampire movie, directed by Werner Herzog and . . ." He saw very quickly that they didn't want to hear about the film. With a little nervous laugh, he continued.

"Anyway, we were both sitting there," indicating Claire, who nodded, "and all of a sudden, we both got hit with the same wild thought. We didn't even know each other at the time . . . we were just sitting next to each other in the theatre . . . when we both got hit with it at the same time."

"What if there were a vampire in the subways?" Claire said, re-enacting the moment. Danny laughed . . . the only one to do so . . . and continued.

"Yeah. Because there's this one scene where Nosferatu lands in England, and his ship is full of rats. That made us think about the big mass murder . . . I guess it was Monday night, or Tuesday morning . . . that happened on the subway. Remember?"

Everybody nodded but Josalyn this time. Danny noticed for the first time that she didn't look well at all; like she might shudder to pieces at any second. He looked away quickly and went on, a bit shakier himself.

"The whole back of the train was full of rats. That's what the papers said, anyway. And one guy had his throat torn out, like an animal did it. Vampires are supposed to be able to change into all kinds of shit. Like wolves, for instance."

"But did they find any people with the blood sucked out of them?" Allan asked, turning to face him directly.

"Well, no, but . . ."

"Well, then, why did it have to be a vampire? I mean, it seems to me like twin puncture wounds in the jugular vein would be the thing you'd want to look for, right?" When Danny didn't say anything, Allan's nod was grimly triumphant. "That's a pretty off-the-wall theory, if you ask me."

"The whole thing's off-the-wall," Ian said, his eyes thoughtful. "That doesn't mean that it's not happening."

"Yeah, but . . ."

"It might have been just because we were stoned, and we made some kind of subconscious association," Danny broke in now. "But like I said, it hit both of us at once; and it was a very strong, gut-level kind of feeling. We *knew* it was true. We just knew it. And then . . ."

"*What are you talking about?*" Josalyn stood up suddenly. Her eyes were wide and crazy; her face was flushed; she was shaking so hard that the whole table vibrated as she leaned her hands upon it. "*What is all this vampire garbage? I don't understand! What does this have to do with anything?*"

Nobody knew how to react. Ian mouthed the word *whoa* and sank back into his wooden chair. Danny gaped in silence. Stephen swallowed a lump of something nasty and cringed. Something nastier was on the way. He could feel it coming.

It was Claire who reached out to take Josalyn's arm and broke the silence.

"I'll tell you what this has to do with," Claire said, her voice level and almost chillingly controlled. "My roommate was murdered on Friday night. Her blood was drained, and her head was torn off." Josalyn twitched violently, but Claire retained her grip. "I saw who she was with earlier that night. Not too well, really . . . we were in a bar, and it was packed in there . . . but I definitely caught a glimpse of him."

"And when she described him to me," Danny added, "it sounded just like this guy I'd seen hanging around with Stephen."

"Omigod," Josalyn whispered, sagging back into her seat, her face bleaching out from the inside. "Omigod, omigod. . . ."

"And then I remembered," Danny concluded, "that Stephen was looking for him on the day after those murders in the subway."

"That was the day you called me up," Josalyn said, the words slow and ponderous, turning to stare at Stephen with numb, disbelieving eyes. "You said he disappeared, and . . . and that you thought he was *dead*. . . ."

"WHAT?" Joseph roared, slamming his fists against the table. Stephen practically flew out of his chair. "You little bastard! You didn't tell me!" He reached for Stephen's collar and missed by an inch.

Stephen slid his chair back a foot from the table before he even knew he'd moved. Ian grabbed onto Joseph's arm and tried to drag it back, nearly upsetting both of their pitchers. "*Hey!*" Joseph yelled, yanking violently free. They stared at each other, red-eyed and panting, for a long, dangerous second.

Then Stephen bolted from his seat and started to walk across the room.

"Hey!" Joseph repeated. He started to pull himself up from the bench; and for a second time, Ian grabbed him by the arm.

"Let me try to get him," Ian said. The anger had drained from his face. "He isn't scared half to death of me. Yet." Then he flashed a crafty, knowing grin, waited for Joseph to acknowledge it, and took off after Stephen.

"Jesus H. Christ," Allan murmured. The rest of them were speechless. Joseph reached for his pitcher and sullenly refilled his glass, draining it at a gulp. Then he filled it up again and set it down, staring defiantly around the table.

Suddenly, Josalyn started to giggle. Her hands curled up into little limp fists. She brought them up daintily and held them to her lips, as if they could hold the laughter in. Her eyes were glassy and remote and unreal, like two polished buttons on the face of a doll. When she spoke, her voice was squeaky as a rubber squeeze toy.

"So Rudy is . . . a *vampire,* huh?" A high-pitched titter escaped her, and a tear rolled down one cheek. "Oh, that's great. That's just fantastic. I . . . I can't believe all the *fun* we're having!"

The laughter got louder, more hysterical. Joseph looked at his hands, wondering if he should slap her. He decided against it, and emptied his glass instead.

* * *

"So where were you plannin' on goin', man?" Ian had caught up with Stephen in the doorway and taken him gently by the shoulder from behind.

"Leave me alone," Stephen practically whimpered, feebly trying to pull away. *I see what Joseph meant about this kid being a wimp,* Ian thought, but he kept it to himself.

"Look. You're the one who got us all together, right?" Stephen nodded hesitantly. "Well, you don't wanna run out on your own party, do ya?" Stephen shot him a sidelong glance that was crawling with terror.

"Yeah, Joseph's a scary guy, all right." Ian put as much empathy in his voice as he could muster. "But he's been through a lot lately . . . you wouldn't believe how much . . . and he doesn't really want to hurt you. He just wants to get at this Rudy character, you know?"

Stephen started to say something, then clammed up again. He looked like somebody'd dipped his nuts in a hot bowl of soup.

"Aw, come on," Ian urged. "Say it. I don't want to beat you up or anything. I just want to hear what you have to say. That's all anybody wants. It seems like you know more about Rudy than anybody else; and I, for one, would be much obliged if you'd share some of the knowledge with us."

Stephen finally looked away from his feet and brought his gaze up to meet Ian's. The tears were just biding their time behind the eyelids, ready to roll at any moment. But behind the fear and the sadness . . . it was obvious to Ian that both were a factor here . . . there was also a dawning element of trust. Stephen had seen who grabbed Joseph's arm in the nick of time; and he knew who Joseph would listen to, if anyone.

"You won't let him punch me out?" Stephen asked. It was almost a plea.

"Not a chance," Ian said, and hoped to God that it was true.

Slowly, Stephen let Ian lead him back to the table. Neither one of them noticed the figure that watched, with keen interest, from the street.

* * *

Allan was not happy. He was not happy when he came in, he'd become slightly *less* happy when Josalyn had first broken down in tears, and he had been getting less and less happy ever since.

In fact, the only thing that could have cheered Allan up would have been a telegram from God, informing him that the last several days had been a bad dream, and that he'd be waking up shortly. That, or the sudden admission by everyone present that the whole thing had been an elaborate gag, a practical joke with a punch line so boffo that it took a week of misery to build up to.

As it stood, he saw neither option looming up on the horizon. Instead, he found himself surrounded by people who had either blown a fuse or tiptoed into the *Twilight Zone*. Either way, it sucked the imperial whanger.

And the worst of it was, Joseph and Ian were right square in the middle of it. No *way* were they going to back off now. Not when they'd stumbled onto so much affirmation. *Christ,* he thought, decidedly unhappy, *I couldn't restrain them now with twenty feet of chain and a ten-ton weight.*

A damp and clammy silence had fallen over the table, sporadically broken by tiny sounds from Josalyn. She seemed to be alternating between sighs, sobs, and giggles at this point. Her head was in her hands, and she was shaking it a lot.

Joseph sullenly nursed his beer. He kept glancing in the direction that Stephen and Ian disappeared from, then back down at his hands. When he felt Allan's gaze upon him, he looked over for a moment; and Allan thought that he saw a trace of apology there, mixed in with the customary impatience and rage. Then Joseph looked away again.

As for the other two: Danny and Claire were staring off into space, no particular expressions on their faces at all. They were obviously uncomfortable. *And who wouldn't be,* Allan observed, *sitting at a table where someone is losing her mind?*

He took a pinch of Captain Black from its pouch, tamped it into his pipe with fingers that felt numb and weighted with lead. Everything about the place . . . the dim light, the dark wood, the ghostly strains of Blue Oyster Cult's "Don't Fear The Reaper" wafting over from the jukebox . . . seemed calculated to feed the atmosphere of gloom that enveloped them.

Suddenly, Joseph leaned forward slightly, and his eyes brightened. Allan turned to look; a moment later, Stephen was sitting down beside him. Ian followed, beaming; he flashed a look at Joseph that said *be cool, man. Don't start*. Joseph nodded almost imperceptibly, and Ian slid back into his seat.

"Okay," Ian said. "So where were we?"

"We were talking," Josalyn offered in a remarkably steady voice, "about Rudy being a vampire, right? We were suggesting that he's the one who's been killing all these people." She paused to take a first tentative sip of her wine. The glass shook in her hand. The effort behind her control was evident.

"Well, I think it's true," she continued. "Now that you've brought it up, I think that it's got to be true. Rudy's either a vampire or something like it. He's some kind of monster. He's got to be. Otherwise, he couldn't have done . . . what he did . . .

"To me." The words were almost an afterthought. She had been trailing off there at the end, sinking toward inaudibility. Now her voice came back, more powerful than before. "Do you know what that fucker has done to me?" she asked. "Do you know why I'm sitting here, freaking out like this?"

A shaking of heads, grimly urging her on. She sipped again at her wine, then obliged.

"I've been having dreams, for the last few nights. Terrible dreams: the worst I've ever had. I don't remember the first one too well, except that something came out of the grave for me . . ."

A discernible shiver ran through the group.

". . . but the last two nights, I remember. I remember them very well." Her face tightened into a vengeful, furious grin. Her eyes pointed down at the white knuckles of her delicate, fisted hands. The others were keyed in tightly, gauging her every word and gesture.

"For the last two nights, I've been raped and murdered in my sleep," she said. Claire, in particular, jerked in reaction. "I've been put through Hell, in dreams so vivid that I woke up screaming. And my cat . . . my cat . . ." She would not let herself cry. She would not allow it. She stiffened, shaking her head in a rapid, staccato pattern, and quickly changed the subject.

"Anyway . . . last night, I finally saw his face. Just for a second, just before I woke up, but the picture was very clear in my mind.

"It was . . ."

"*Well, well, well!*" a new voice interjected, and a cold hand pressed its weight on Stephen's shoulder. "What do we have here? A party?"

They looked up, startled. Josalyn froze; her pupils contracted to the size of pinpricks in a face gone suddenly paler than the bloodshot whites of her eyes. Her features slackened. Her eyes rolled up and out of commission. She teetered for a moment in her seat, then slumped against the wall in a dead faint. Nobody noticed.

They were all staring up, in varying degrees of terror and awe, at Rudy Pasko.

To Ian and Allan, the sight of Rudy set off a pair of diametrically opposed reactions. Whereas Allan found all of his skepticism dashed in a single second . . . logic be damned, he *knew* now that it was true . . . Ian took one look at that pallid, grinning countenance and said to himself, *Is that all there is to him?*

To Joseph, Rudy's presence made his hackles rise. It's the kind of fright you get when somebody steps out of the shadows behind you: a fleeting terror, but a total one in the moment that it strikes. Even more than Stephen, he could smell the death in the air.

To Danny, it was the kind of awe he'd have expected to

feel if he were suddenly sucked into one of his movie posters: the sense of stepping concretely into the realm of the impossible, both feet on the ground and head suspended at a dizzying height.

To Claire, Rudy looked even more gorgeous than he had at the bar.

Stephen seemed to be shrinking under the weight of that cold hand, those luminous eyes. His face was pale, as pale as Rudy's. The vampire grinned down at him in a mocking kind of palsy-walsy manner, and Stephen almost swallowed his tongue.

"What's the matter, Stephen?" Rudy asked him, feigning genuine concern. "I thought you'd be glad to see me! Umm . . . aren't you going to introduce me to all your nice new friends?" Stephen just stared at him, the color of Wonder Bread.

Joseph began to rise from his seat. Ian felt it coming the instant before it happened. Instinctively, the smaller man pushed his chair around so that he was facing Rudy. One leg kicked out to the right, tripping Joseph before the big man could get an inch from his seat. Joseph sat back down hard, whoofing slightly. Ian put his hand on Joseph's arm, pinning it lightly to the table, his eyes never leaving Rudy's face.

"So you're Rudy, huh?" he said. "I've been hearing a lot about you."

Rudy glanced over at Ian, then to Stephen, then back again. His face, which had contorted in anger for a moment, twisted itself into a calculating smile. "So you've been talking about me, have you, Stephen? I thought you might. How rude of you." His eyes engaged Ian's for a long crackling moment. Ian didn't even flinch. "And your name was . . ."

"It still is. Ian." An extended hand. A smile as phony as Rudy's own. "Pleased ta meetcha."

Rudy stared at the hand for a moment, perplexed. *Who the hell does this guy think he is?* Rudy wondered, unaware that Ian was thinking exactly the same thing. He

regarded the hand for a moment longer, considered taking
it, then dismissed the gesture entirely. "And what has our
friend told you about me?"

"He hasn't told us jack shit," Joseph cut in angrily. He
didn't like the idea of being restrained, not even by his best
friend, for all the right reasons. "We had to find out for
ourselves."

"Oh?" Rudy turned his attention to Joseph now,
regarding him coolly. "And just what did you find?"

"Oh, nothing," Ian interjected. "Nothing you don't
already know about, I'm sure. Just little mundane things,
really." He smiled sweetly, condescendingly. He was feeling
the fight build up inside him, like steam in a pressure
cooker, and loving every minute of it. "Nothing very
interesting at all."

Rudy didn't like that. Like a slap in the face, it knocked
him off-balance for a moment and made him come back
pissed. He glowered at Ian, no trace of a smile on his face as
he hissed, "You're a smart little shit, aren't you?"

Ian leaned forward in his seat, grinning wickedly.
"That's me," he said, nodding. "Got that right on the nose.
Coming from a squirmy little worm-faced fuck, that's
awfully darned astute."

"*What?*" Rudy's face reddened slightly. A burst of
helpless laughter swept the table, and Rudy once again
said, "*What?*"

"Hey! I thought you had X-ray hearing!" Ian griped.
His smile was almost big enough to park Joseph's van in.
"What about all those amazing powers we thought you were
supposed to have? Don't tell me it isn't true! I couldn't bear
to hear it!" He put his hands over his ears and winced
comically, eyes bulging.

Rudy was stunned. He couldn't believe what he was
hearing. The audacity of this human exceeded all bounds.
He felt like taking this Ian's face and grinding it into the
ceiling. "You're going to be sorry . . ." he began.

"Oh, I already *am!*" Ian's own ferocity had reached its
head and boiled over. "Believe me. When I heard about the
big bad monster that rapes and kills women, I got this

mental picture of somebody who was *really impressive*, ya know? And here I find that I got all worked up over nothin'! It's a big disappointment, let me tell ya."

At that moment, Josalyn started to come around. Her mouth opened, a low moan escaping. All eyes turned toward her. For the first time, they noticed her unconsciousness. Terror blossomed in Ian's heart like a mushroom cloud. Rudy smiled like the man who found Achilles' heel.

"You like her." A mocking pronouncement. "The high-buttoned bitch attracts you, I gather. Well, let me warn you: she likes men without backbones. She likes toadies that she can domineer. . . ."

"She likes *your* type, I take it." Ian had whipped around to face Rudy, no trace of a smile to mask the fury now. "She likes craven little scumbunnies who send bad dreams to do their dirty work for them. She likes peroxide pretty boys with yellow teeth and eye-liner who think they're the baddest thing since Attila the Hun. Yeah, I can just see her quivering with desire." All this at a steady low volume that cut all the more because of it. "Why don't you just *piss off*, Mr. Shithead from Beyond the Grave? Why don't you go take a sunbath and rot, like your last girlfriend did? Why . . . ?"

"That's ENOUGH!" Rudy's voice boomed like a gun-shot in an empty basement. It carried across the room, drowning out shouting matches at the far end of the bar the way a jet plane's landing would swallow a mosquito's drone. There was no earthly way that Rudy's diaphragm could generate such volume. Ian knew that, even as the sound pushed him backwards half a yard.

And the air around the table dropped thirty degrees in the space of a second.

"You're going to die," Rudy said. . . .

The darkness flared up like a sudden implosion of light. Their nostrils were flooded with the stench of death, a green haze of putrescence that hung in the icy air around them. Ian glanced sharply over at his companions, and with a sledgehammer jolt of horror he saw that they were

*all dead, their bodies twisted at impossible angles, flesh
discolored, meat exposed. His hands jerked up to his face
involuntarily, then away. A scream welled up in his throat
and died there, throttling.*

*He was staring at his hands: at the slim white cylinders
of exposed bone that showed through the mangled, pitted
flesh of his palms. For a second, the skin seemed to crawl of
its own volition; and then he saw that they were maggots,
grayish-white and puffy, burrowing in and out of him in a
timeless dance of birth and consumption and death.*

*His second scream raced upwards, trampling the
corpse of the first on its way out of his mouth. The vile,
gagging flavor was heavy on his tongue, as if he'd just taken
a big bite of something rotten. That was when he realized
that the mouth itself was decomposing, caving in on itself,
crawling with pale, bloated, carrion-eating life. . . .*

*And as his scream burst out into the open air, he felt
something shift behind his eyes, pushing against the backs
of them.*

Forcing its way through.

*And his vision went blank. And his screams stretched
out like a moldering tendril. And the moist horror oozed
down his cheeks . . .*

. . . and suddenly he was back in the room, and the
others were alive, and Rudy was standing over him with a
stupefied expression on his face. Sensation came rushing
back in a torrent of freezing sweat that seemed to burst
from every pore in his body. He rubbed his eyes quickly
and gaped at Rudy, at his companions, at the solid living
flesh of his hands.

"Omigod," he breathed, staring back up at Rudy again.
It struck him instantly that Rudy didn't know what happened, either; the look of confusion on that pale, ghastly
face was hysterically out-of-place.

Behind him, Joseph's voice croaked, "What the hell
did you just *do*?" The voice was phlegm-caked, numb with
shock. A dull murmur came from the rest of the group, and
Ian knew that they'd all just seen . . . something.

Ian's gaze leveled on Rudy. He started to laugh. He tried to control it. He might as well have tried to control federal spending. "He's like Bullwinkle!" he exclaimed, the words wiggling out of his throat like party streamers. "Hey, Rocky! Watch me p-pull a rabbit outta my h-h-*hat!*" He was laughing so hard he could barely go on. "N-n-nothin' up muh sleeve . . . ha ha ha . . . PRESTO!" He collapsed against the table, tears streaming from his eyes, convulsed with laughter.

Rudy took a few uncertain steps backward, frowning vaguely. Danny started to giggle. The others were too stunned to do anything but stare.

"Doncha *see?*" Ian looked up, met each of their gazes with his own red and watery one. His face was stretched in a grin so extreme that it looked unreal, like a nightmare clown in a fever dream. "Oops! Don't know muh own *strength!*" he shouted, Bullwinkle-style, and laughed again. Then he turned to Rudy and said, "Man, you'd be scary as *hell* if you weren't such a putz! You don't even know what you just *did,* do ya?"

Rudy stared at him blankly.

"You don't know your ass from a *hole* in the wall!" Ian shouted, leaping to his feet. He pushed Rudy's chest, sending the vampire stumbling backwards. "You're a *joke,* man! You're a million laughs! We oughta get you a rubber nose and call you . . . Count Bozo, Vampire!"

Rudy backed away from him, almost blindly. The red eyes swam in the white face like a pair of mud-puppies at the bottom of a river. A snarl formed on the pale lips but there was no force behind it. Rudy was on the defensive entirely: his body off-balance, his mind madly squirming.

Ian had gotten him halfway to the door, still pushing and prodding and leering obscenely. "Go on, man!" he shouted. "Get outta here before I laugh myself into a hernia!" He gave Rudy a final shove that sent the vampire skittering.

Everybody in the place was watching them now. Jeers and catcalls rose up from the ranks, reminding Rudy all too vividly of the crowd at the Cinema Village. He was poor old

Mr. Carving Knife, getting ripped to pieces in front of a howling mob, without a chance in hell of pulling himself back together again.

Rage, pain, and confusion churned like witch's brew in his eyes. He wavered there for a moment, then turned and pushed his way through the crowd, pausing at the door to lock vengeful, humiliated eyes on Ian. Then he was gone.

Ian watched him leave, still laughing hysterically, but all the humor had leaked out of him like air from a ruptured inflatable doll. It was almost a convulsive thing, like hiccups gone haywire, that wracked his chest as Rudy disappeared into the night before him.

For a moment, he forgot where he was.

And when he snapped out of it, Ian Macklay felt strangely drained and disoriented; as though he, too, had stumbled upon a hidden potential and then found it beyond his control.

When Ian came back to the table, he was greeted by the open gape of a dozen moon-shaped eyes. He grinned at them weakly and flopped down in his seat, brushing at the blond hair plastered to his forehead. His fingers trembled. He wrapped them around his glass and then paused, staring a hole in the table.

"That was amazing," Danny said. Ian looked up and saw that the guy was smiling and nodding with frank admiration.

"No fooling," Allan added. He, too, was obviously impressed. "Ian, man, I didn't know you had it in you."

"Aw, shucks," Ian replied, but his head was spinning. He looked at the others, trying to gauge their reactions. Josalyn stared at him the way a child might, watching Daddy perform some miracle far beyond a tiny mortal's ken. The same combination of fear, awe, and gratitude was at play on Stephen's face.

Joseph, on the other hand, looked darkly troubled. Ian puzzled over it for a moment, saw the way that Joseph averted his eyes, and understood.

He can't understand why he just sat there. Ian smiled,

nodding ruefully. *He's mad at himself for not doing something . . . and maybe just a little bit jealous of me.*

The only expression that he couldn't quite get a handle on was Claire's. She, too, refused to engage his eyes; and he didn't know her well enough to guess what that meant.

"Do you believe that?" he said at last. "Do you believe the way he went out of here with his tail between his legs? That was *weird.*" He shook his head, took a long-awaited swig of beer. "I'm amazed he didn't kill me."

"Rudy can't stand to be humiliated," Josalyn said. A bit more color, a bit more strength, had found its way back into her face. "If there's one thing he can't stand, it's for someone to point out his weaknesses. It drives him crazy. He thinks he's so perfect." She paused, looked down at her hands. "That's why he hates me so much."

"Why?" This from Allan, who pointed the stem of his pipe at her as he leaned forward. It had gone out during the altercation. He relit it as she spoke.

"Because . . . the night he disappeared, I had a big fight with him. At my apartment. We'd been . . . going out for a little while." She studiously avoided Ian's eyes. "He started jumping all over me. He did that a lot. And after a certain point, I just stopped taking it.

"So I started yelling back at him. I told him what I thought of him. I told him that he was an emotional eight-year-old: a selfish, egotistical prick who didn't give a good God damn *who* he hurt so long as he got his own way." She paused to pull a cigarette from her purse. Allan lit it for her.

"He got crazy. I got even crazier. I mean, I was just *screaming* at him after a while. And I realized that, after a little while, he just didn't know what to do any more. He couldn't react."

"He can dish it out, but he can't take it." Joseph chewed on the thought for a moment, his eyebrows uplifted. Ian watched him do it, smiling, seeing Joseph turn it to an advantage in his mind.

"So then what happened?" Allan asked, egging Josalyn on.

"I told him to get out," she said. "And he went."

"Wow." Ian boggled at the sheer simplicity of it. He looked at Allan and shrugged; Allan echoed the gesture. "So what do we do now? Insult him to death?"

"Embarrass him right out of Dodge?" Allan said. They laughed nervously.

"We gotta kill that son of a bitch," Joseph rumbled. "That's all there is to it. We gotta lay that boy out on a slab, and I mean *quick*. That's the whole reason I came out here tonight: to see if anybody wanted to help me." He glanced around the table. "I mean, really, we should be out there after him right now."

"C'mon, Joseph," Ian said. "We don't have any tools with us. I doubt if any of us even carries a cross." He looked around; nobody volunteered one. "Yeah. Maybe *you* could take him apart with your bare hands, but nobody else around here could."

"This is crazy," Stephen moaned suddenly. "This is absolutely insane."

"You noticed," Ian replied smartly.

"Why don't we just call the police or something?" Stephen's face was pinched and drawn. His eyes bugged out. He looked like Peter Lorre in a hall of mirrors, reflected in the long concave glass that makes beanpoles out of potato-shaped men.

"What? And cheat ourselves out of a vampire hunt?" Danny gasped, as if stunned. His eyes sparkled merrily behind his thick glasses. "You wouldn't want to miss this, would you, Claire?" She shook her head decisively, but her eyes were far away.

"Listen, wimpo," Joseph addressed Stephen. "I don't wanna hear that kind of guff from you. Especially after tonight. Man, if you had to wait for police protection, he'd be fittin' you for a coffin right now."

"Besides that," Ian added, "they're already looking for him. For the Subway Psycho, anyway. And if we told 'em who and what he is, do you think they'd believe us?" He laughed ruefully. "They'd go to any one of our apartments and find dope laying around; next thing you know, they're patting you on the head and getting out the handcuffs. 'Uh, sure, kid. Vampires. Tell us where you buy this stuff, we'll let you off easy.'"

"No way around it," Joseph emphasized. "We're gonna hafta get him ourselves. Lay a few traps out for him and nail that bugger good."

"So who's with us?" Ian asked. "Allan?"

"I'm thinking," Allan replied. He plucked at his beard with one hand and brought the pipe to his lips with the other, staring off into space.

"I'm with you," Josalyn interjected suddenly. The old resolve . . . a confidence that none of them had seen before . . . breathed fire into her words. "I want him dead. I don't want to . . . have to worry about him any more."

Ian met her gaze; and once again, the spark flew between them. This time, there was no omigod-is-this-happening jolt attached. This was a connection, pure and unwavering, completely free of static. They held it for a timeless stretch of seconds without perimeters, a wordless linkage of minds.

Yes. The word came suddenly, unbidden. *Yes.* It took a moment, stuck in time once again, to realize that it came from neither of them.

"Yes," Allan was saying. "I'm here, boss. I'm in the game."

That left Stephen. Stephen, who trembled in the spot between the rock and the hard place, with Rudy Pasko on one side and Joseph Hunter on the other. *Along with everybody else*, he thought, feeling the bond that was arising between them. Feeling very much apart from it. Feeling very much alone.

And wondering, suddenly, why that should have to be.

"All right," he said finally. It sounded, to his ears, like a stranger's voice: a part of himself that was only now coming to light. "All right. You can count me in, too."

As the net. Closed securely.

Over them all.

CHAPTER 28

Outside . . .

No moon. No stars. A thick, muggy haze, congealing in the heavens. Black clouds, draped like a shroud across the top of the Manhattan skyline.

On the streets . . .

A million souls, wandering down a million separate paths. Each one, distinct. Each one with a purpose.

That few of them had found.

At the uptown entrance to the Astor Place station . . .

He stood. Bent. An old man, shivering despite the heat. A tiny bottle of clear liquid, gripped tightly in his hand.

Muttering to himself. Eyes closed. Head bowed. Bringing the mouth of the bottle to his lips. Kissing the cold glass.

And dropping, ever so slowly, to his knees.

In his hands . . .

The tiny bottle. Its tiny cork, removed. One liver-spotted finger over the lip, keeping the clear liquid within. One liver-spotted finger, pulling away.

A last benediction.

Then: the bottle, tipping slightly. A trickle of dancing transparency, pouring out of the bottle and onto the grimy pavement below. Defining a straight line that stretched out in front of him for six inches, then stopped.

The process, repeated. Another line, bisecting the first. Bringing them together.

In the form of a cross.

On the old man's face . . .

Lines. Many lines. Lines etched in vitriol, carved by

time's scalpel, crosscutting his face like the folds of the brain. Each one distinct. Each one a memory.

This one, speaking of a day many years in the past, when the walls of the death camp had first loomed into view from the cattle car window. This one, and this one, for the man who'd been beaten to death with a shovel: first, when the right arm came away at the shoulder; second, when the forehead flattened and crumbled inward, body still teetering on nerveless legs.

This one, born at the moment that his wife had been led into the gas chambers. And this one, permanently fixed by the sight of his son, dangling from the rafters by a length of tawny rope.

All old lines. Very old.

And then *this* line, this *new* line, formed just three days ago. Formed in the subway, by a sight to blast Man's soul.

Screaming for that woman. That poor, poor woman. On the train.

Other lines, too. Deep grooves of exertion. Lines that formed around the mouth as he smiled with satisfaction. Character lines, achieved through a life both sweet and starkly painful. Lines that bloomed like flowers. Like graves.

As he dragged himself, slowly, to his feet.

Joseph was watching from the other side of the street.

He saw the old man perform his strange ritual at the top of the stairs. He watched the old man rise, with what seemed to be extraordinary effort, to his feet. He faded back into the shadows and observed as the old man turned toward him and began to cross that stretch of road where Fourth Avenue segued into Lafayette Street like two hit singles on a master deejay's console.

The old man shuffled across the flat concrete expanse at his own aged pace. He kept glancing furtively to his left. A pair of teenage hotdoggers in their respective souped-up Fords were idling noisily at the intersection, New Jersey plates glimmering in the glow of the street lamps, impatiently revving their engines. Joseph didn't trust them to wait out the traffic signal, and he could see that the old man harbored similar doubts.

The opposing lights turned yellow just as the old man crossed the center line into the second lane. Joseph noted with alarm that both cars had jerked into gear and were edging their way into the intersection. *They're gonna drag race*, his mind informed him wearily. *Jersey geeks. They can see the geezer in the middle of the road. They just don't give a damn.*

Automatically, he took a few short steps out of the shadows.

The light turned green.

Simultaneously, the cars peeled out. The engines roared, the tires screeched, like beasts in agonized flight. Great flatulent plumes of gray-black exhaust blasted out of their asses as they leaped forward, pedals to the floor.

The old man froze, nailed like a rabbit by the headlights. He was only about seven feet from the curb; if he hurried, he could make it with no problem. But it didn't appear that he *could* hurry, and valuable seconds had been lost in paralysis.

The cars continued to accelerate.

"HEY!" Joseph yelled, breaking into a run. The old man's eyes snapped over to him; the spell of the headlights was broken. He began to move again, far too slowly. The cars closed in like dogs on the kill.

They were thirty feet away. They were twenty feet away. Joseph reached the old man roughly a yard away from the curb, and they were ten feet away.

Nine feet. Eight. Joseph took the old man in a bear hug that straddled the line between caution and haste. He was afraid of squeezing too hard; he was even more afraid of moving too gingerly. It struck him in a flash of utter clarity that they could be reduced to several hundred pounds of hamburger in three seconds flat.

Joseph whirled and raced back toward the curb with his cumbersome burden. There was a white-knuckled moment of doubt as the headlights and the howl of the engines overwhelmed him. . . .

And then they were on the curb, the cars barreling past them and off into the night.

"Those stupid bastards," Joseph growled quietly, eyes locked on the motorheads as they disappeared around the bend. Then he remembered that he was still clutching the old man to his chest like an enormous sack of potatoes. "Oh, my God," he said, easing the old man to his feet. "Are you okay?"

The old man stood there, pale and shaking. His eyes were closed, and there was a peculiar look of concentration on his face. He looked like he was trying to hold it together, like someone who's had too much to drink and is keeping from vomiting through sheer force of will. There was a long, terrifying moment in which Joseph was certain that the man was going to have a heart attack and die on the spot.

But he didn't. Instead, he shook his head, smiled, looked up at Joseph with pale gray eyes that glittered like polished stones, and said, "I am fine. And I thank you."

"Those goddamn kids," Joseph blustered, masking his relief and sidestepping the old man's gratitude. "I don't know what the hell's wrong with 'em. They're crazy."

"They will learn." The old man's voice was calm, almost reverent. "Someday they will kill someone, or one of them will die. They will discover how frail we are, how easily shattered. They will see how delicately life is balanced. And then, perhaps, they will begin to think."

Joseph watched him, studied him as he spoke. An obvious intelligence sparkled in his eyes. His clothes, though slightly baggy, were nicely tailored; and aside from the patches of dirt on his knees, they were also clean. It was clear that this man hadn't been sleeping in gutters and pissing himself; it was clear that the man was sharp and sane.

So what was he doing, Joseph wondered in private, *on his knees, sprinkling water on the sidewalk and talking to himself?* The question took him off into his mind for a moment; when the old man addressed him a moment later, he popped back in with his thoughts akimbo.

"Uh . . . beg pardon?" he fumbled with his tongue.

"I asked you," and the old man smiled, "if you are often saving people's lives."

Joseph didn't answer. He couldn't. He looked into those eyes, and he knew that the old man was *seeing* him . . . *really* seeing him . . . with a preternatural clarity that cleaved to the heart of the man and knew what it found there. Joseph was not accustomed to being seen so clearly, so quickly. Joseph was practically floored.

"Did you see what I was doing?" the old man asked.

Joseph shook his head, slowly. "I saw you doing *something* . . ." he volunteered.

"Ah." The old man looked away then, enigmatically, grinning at the pavement. He sighed, cleared his throat, said nothing more. After thirty seconds, Joseph got the hint.

"Uh . . . what *were* you doing over there?" he asked.

Even as the question was posed, he knew the answer. He saw it in the old man's eyes as they came back up to lock with his own. He saw it in his memory, in the old man's stance and manner as he'd knelt and gestured in front of the subway stairs.

The subway stairs . . .

And he knew, suddenly, why he'd been watching so closely.

"Oh, my God," Joseph murmered, his lips curling upward.

"Exactly," said Armond Hacdorian.

CHAPTER 29

While Armond and Joseph discussed the consecration of entrances to the underground . . . while Stephen and Allan dragged themselves back to their respective homes, alone . . . while Danny and Claire got ready for the first bad vibes of their brief and bizarre relationship . . . while Rudy contemplated the intricacies of vampire suicide, temporarily sublimating his impulse toward revenge . . . while a creature that reeked of rotgut fed on human blood for the very first time, and a similar monster was born in its bedroom with secure bonds restraining its arms and legs . . . while, on the other side of the Atlantic Ocean, an ancient evil tooled down the streets of Paris in a limousine driven by a rotting thing . . . while all of this was going on, Ian and Josalyn were catching a cab back to her apartment on 25th Street and Park Avenue South. It had been decided that she should not travel alone tonight.

And between them there was much to be discussed.

They grabbed a Checker cab just beyond the arch at Washington Square Park, which they had meandered through as if there were nothing in the world to be afraid of. The thought had struck both of them, at different times, that death could be lurking behind any tree; but they had dismissed it, and nothing terrible had happened at all.

They got stuck at the light on 12th Street and 6th. All the way down the block, and to their right, several police cars and an ambulance were pulled up in front of the Cinema Village. Two stretchers on wheels were being loaded into the ambulance. None of them failed to notice that the sheets were pulled up over the heads of the bodies on the stretchers.

211

A chill fell over the cab.

Ian and Josalyn split the tab when they got to her place, tipping generously, and hopped out of the back seat. Then they turned toward the doorway to her apartment.

To the right of the doorway, at street level, stood a storefront deli with a garish green paint job. Josalyn had shopped there, for convenience, ever since she'd first moved to the city.

To the best of her recollection, its name had never made her shiver before.

"Very cute," Ian quipped; but the blackness of the joke sent a shiver through him, too.

The name of the deli, emblazoned across the storefront in bold pink letters bordered in crimson, was SWEET TEETH.

All the way up the stairs, Josalyn's mind performed twisty calisthenics. She was bringing a strange man home with her . . . a *good* man, from all the evidence, but a stranger nonetheless . . . on the heels of what might well have been the worst twenty-four hours of her life. She couldn't stop the pictures that her thoughts projected in the relative darkness of the stairwell: flashes of nightmare crosscut with the image of Nigel's body flying across the room, Rudy and Ian at The Other End, that moment when she'd looked around the table and seen that all of them were dead. She found herself questioning both her motives and her sanity; she found the answers, in both cases, to be nebulous at best.

Then Ian, behind her, said, "If I'd known you lived this high up, I woulda brung my rope and pitons." Josalyn laughed, amazed by how easy it was to laugh with him, and the tension broke. For the moment.

Typically, the light on the third floor landing was out. Ian moved to her side as she grappled with her purse for the keys, his eyes casting into the shadows for the slightest hint of movement. None. She found her keys, moved tentatively toward the door, located the lock through intuition.

She opened the door.

The phone rang.

"Oh, shit," she cried, quickly flipping on the light switch and rushing into the kitchen. Ian hesitated in the doorway, watching. "Come on in. Make yourself at home," he heard her call from around the corner. "I just have to deal with . . . oh, hell." The sound of her foot connecting with something plastic, sending it skittering and sloshing across the floor.

Ian stepped into the apartment, let the door close behind him. He moved to the kitchen doorway and saw the water bowl strike the baseboard, splashing up onto the cabinets. He saw Josalyn's spine tense, and her shoulders sag, and her hands come up to her face as she wavered in front of the still-ringing telephone.

He didn't know about Nigel yet. He didn't know about the half a dozen cans of 9 Lives that would never be eaten, the kitty litter in the bathroom that would never be shat in again. Nor did he know about the phone call from Stephen, only five days ago in tick-tock time, but still ringing wraith-like in her ears across a stretch of what seemed like eternity.

But he knew a crying woman when he saw one.

And as the phone fell silent, ringing its last, Ian moved slowly into the kitchen and took her gently in his arms.

She told him everything.

About Nigel. About Rudy. About Glen Burne, her long-lost, dangling boyfriend. About her studies, and the philosophical intaglio that led her to Rudy, then beyond him. About other things, obliquely connected, that she hadn't even known were bothering her until it all started to pour out in the presence of her new confidant.

And he listened, understanding the role that this night had prescribed for him. They snuggled together on the living room couch, and his own feelings had been walking the tightrope between platonics and passion. There were moments where their eyes locked, and their lips parted, and the ripe potential of their two mouths mating sent a tangible current through the air; but every time, something stopped them, like a Greek chorus rising up from the background with the chant *not yet. Not yet. If it's right, there'll be time. Not yet. Not yet. If it's right* . . .

Right now, she needed an ear. She needed a shoulder to lean on. Ian had two of each. He lent them to her gladly.

And the hours drifted by in a stream of conversation. And the soft weight of sleep began to press down on her eyelids. She settled into the crook of his arm as she would into a mound of pillows, yawning and squeezing him like a child. He held her, gently kneading her shoulders and neck, conscientiously avoiding her erogenous zones and grinning at the image of his libido on a leash, like a sad-eyed dog that longed to run.

Just before she slipped away, her sleepy voice wafted up to him, saying, "I hope the dreams don't come tonight."

"Don't worry," he assured her. "You're in good hands with All State."

She giggled and rubbed her cheek against his chest. He kissed the top of her head. They settled back into warmth and silence.

Sleep came to her, then.

And with it, the dream.

Josalyn.

Something in Ian's mind jerked to attention at the sound. Floating in the shadowy middle ground between darkness and dream, he heard: like a wooden stake, punching a hole in the mist. It was not a voice from his own mind, he knew. It was a cold voice. It filled him with dread.

Josalyn. A warm figure shifted beside him, and his consciousness slowly rose toward the surface, the waking world. The voice came from there, yet not from there. He trembled in the borderland, in the chill and billowing fog.

You little bitch. You'll get what's coming to you now.

The weight writhed against him then. Ian heard a low moan from light-years away; a dense aura of terror settled over him, crackling like the air before an electrical storm.

Suddenly, he knew where he was. He knew that, in

the waking world, he and Josalyn were asleep on the couch. The weight was hers. The terror was hers.

But the voice was not.

In the distance, he saw something move.

Man in a dream, he rushed forward, parting the mists with his arms. He moved deeper into the alien landscape. Desperate. Blind. Pushing through the clouds that whispered and danced like gossamer curtains in a harem girl's chamber. One after another another another and . . .

Nothing but darkness. Abrupt and total. He paused, peering deeply.

He saw the teeth.

Long teeth, sharp teeth, surging out from the vanishing point and racing toward him as if fired from a cannon. Sharp teeth, enormous teeth, already the size of the image on a drive-in movie screen. And still growing, still growing, as they got closer and closer . . .

. . . and thundered past him, above and below him, churning up the darkness like a hurricane . . .

. . . and he was staring into a room, a room far larger than life, the way a man in the front row of a theatre stares at the pictures on the screen. Josalyn was there, her eyes wide and screaming, her jaws mutely working as she stumbled backwards into the room.

And Rudy was there, the red glow of his eyes partially obscuring his features: too bright, too bright to look at. Rudy smiled, and his teeth were clearly visible. Long teeth. Sharp teeth. They glistened in the crimson light.

Now, Rudy said, in that same chilling voice. *Now. As his hand reached toward her.*

"NO!" Ian heard himself screaming aloud. Both Rudy and Josalyn turned, as if startled, and stared in his direction without seeming to see him.

"LEAVE HER ALONE, YOU SICK SON OF A BITCH!" Ian howled. Rudy took a step back, looking very much the way he had at the bar. "GET OUT OF HER BRAIN! GO CURL UP AND DIE!"

He felt himself growing; or perhaps it was Rudy who was shrinking. Josalyn was out of the picture entirely. All *he could see was Rudy's face, receding back toward that vanishing point and contorting with animal fury. A scream echoed out from the yawning darkness, dwindling down to nothing as the face disappeared . . .*

. . . and Ian Macklay was awake. Wide awake. Adrenaline coursed through him like a gallon of iced espresso, forcing the sweat out through his skin.

In his arms, Josalyn had settled back into peaceful slumber. He listened to the gentle susurration of her breath, her heart's even pulse, and he smiled. The dream had been averted. Tomorrow morning, with any luck, she wouldn't even remember that it happened.

But he would.

And like Rudy, who screamed and threw a tantrum and trashed the bulk of the previous night's work, Ian would not be able to sleep until the moonlight was devoured by the sun.

CHAPTER 30

"**I**'m out of practice," Danny offered by way of feeble explanation. "I'm sorry." Claire nodded and looked away, pressing the side of her face into the pillow. There was no point in trying to hide her frustration. He was all too aware of it as he rolled out from between her legs and flopped down limply beside her.

It wasn't like this last night, she mournfully observed. *Last night, he was fine. Last night was fantastic.* But the memory had faded to a ghostlike transparency in light of tonight's blown performance: a minute of vigorous slamming together . . . just enough to set off her own urgent climb toward climax . . . only a minute, before he started to hoot and shiver and shoot his load, then grow weak and flaccid within her.

Danny, for his part, felt absolutely terrible. Wimpy excuses aside, the fact of the matter was that he'd been barely even there: he ejaculated, but he definitely did not get off. Most women aren't aware that there's a difference; they assume that if a guy shot his wad, he got his jollies. Most men don't seem to grasp the difference, either. But Danny knew. He might have gotten to drain his scrotum, but *neither* of them were satisfied. It was almost as if his pecker had raced toward a premature ejaculation, just to get it over with.

Because something's wrong. He felt it, but he didn't have a handle on it. All he knew was that Claire had been no fun at all on the way back to his apartment; but once they'd arrived, she'd been all over him, dragging him to bed before the front door had a chance to swing shut.

And the sex itself had been weird: too wild, too fast. It had reeked of desperation in an unpleasant manner, as if she'd been trying to prove something and it had to happen *now. This instant.* He'd felt helpless before it, had wound up riding her like a body surfer on an enormous breaker, bounced and buffeted toward the shore. There'd been no joy in it from the start, he realized. Because something was wrong . . . something needed to be proved . . . and he wondered what it was.

That she loves me? he thought. *That's a strange way to prove it. That she can have me any time she wants? That's STILL a strange way to prove it. That she can make me cum in thirty seconds? Or that I can hold on for two hours under pressure?*

No, that's stupid. He shook his head, staring straight up at the ceiling, horribly aware of the fact that she could feel his movement through the pillows. It bothered him so much that he stopped, closing his eyes and tilting his head to one side, seeing nothing.

Saying nothing.

While Claire pondered the nature of fatal attractions, and toyed with the notion of a late-night rendezvous.

Knowing full well how crazy it was, how deep-down suicidal and outright stupid. She knew what she'd sound like if she tried to verbalize it. She knew how Danny would feel if she verbalized it to him.

But when she closed her eyes, she saw that face. Those eyes. That smile. She felt the power. It frightened and beguiled her. She felt it. She wanted it. And it seemed to want her, too.

So what am I supposed to do? she wondered. *Stay with Danny? Go back to an old boyfriend? Find somebody else who's nice and safe and . . . ?* She let it peter out.

If it weren't true, then how could I possibly feel this way?

She settled on that question, rolling it in her mind as she lay there, face pointing away from Danny and toward the bedroom window. Out there, the night was like black lipstick on one great ripe kiss, for her alone. One glorious kiss that went on forever, just waiting for her with . . .

Teeth.

Something fluttered by outside the window. She shuddered and closed her eyes.

Saying nothing. Like Danny.

Afraid to.

CHAPTER 31

Morning came on wings of sweltering humidity, bringing with it a painfully slow day for Your Kind Of Messengers, Inc. Allan bore it with the kind of grim stoicism that only comes with endless repetition, saying, "Nothing on the desk, boss" over and over to thirty messengers who didn't want to hear it. "I'm sweatin' my ass off for *nothin'*!" they screamed; and although he sympathized, he really didn't want to hear it, either. It heightened and expanded the headache that he'd awakened with at seven this morning. It did nothing to brighten his outlook on life.

So when Ian wandered into the office, sweat-drenched and bleary-eyed but grinning like a bandit, Allan was happy to see him.

Until he started to talk.

"Man, you wouldn't *believe* the morning I'm having!" he began, wiping his forehead for emphasis.

"Yeah, buddy. It's the pits," Tony said, shaking his head ruefully.

"Well, I've been running around like a goddamn lunatic," Ian said, laughing. "Hey, Allan. You're really busy right now, huh? Come here. I gotta talk to ya."

All at once, Allan remembered why he woke up with a headache in the first place. It made him groan as he rose, meeting Ian's wild gaze with his own beleaguered one. *It was this crapola, precisely. Sitting up all night, drinking and thinking about it. And now he wants to do it again.* He dry-swallowed another Tylenol, and hoped it would help.

"This has to do with your last run, right?" he inquired, hopeful.

"Yeah, right. That was two hours ago. I just wanted to know if I got there yet. Has anybody seen me?" Ian threw up his arms like the little lost princess. Allan paused to massage his temples. Nobody else responded at all. Ian, buoyed by his success, turned to Tony and said, "Ummm . . . think you can handle the phones without your side-kick for a minute?"

"Don't think so, buddy. The way these phones are ringing, it's driving me beserk." Everybody laughed at the dead silence of the switchboards. Allan shrugged, doomed, and followed Ian out onto the street.

It was ninety-two degrees in the shade of the doorway. The air was motionless, bloated with moisture. It hit Allan's head like a wet sandbag, making pain scream through his synapses like a school of electric eels. He winced and grabbed his head.

"Got a headache, huh?"

Allan nodded. "Severe."

"Why don't you use what doctors recommend most?"

"Oh, God . . ."

"Electroshock therapy! It really works!"

"Stop yelling, man. This really is bad." Ian was mollified. Allan winced again and continued. "So what did you want to talk about?"

"The horse races, shithead. What did'ja think?"

"Okay, okay, all right. I gotcha. Do you want to know what I think?"

"That might be nice."

"Don't count on it. No . . . *ouch*!" Waiting for the latest jolt of pain to recede. "No, I'll tell you, boss. I did some serious thinking last night, and . . ."

"You talked yourself out of it?"

"No, no. I came up with a good idea. A strategy for doing this crazy thing." Allan smiled through the pain. "I think you might like it, so I might as well tell you now."

"Yeah?" Ian sidled up against his friend and cocked one ear conspiratorially. "Shoot."

"Well," Allan said, warming up to the subject, "it occurred to me that we could coordinate the hunt a lot better from the dispatch room than from any other place in the city."

"You mean *here*?" Ian asked, incredulously indicating the door with his thumb.

"Yeah. We've got maps. We've got all the beeper numbers. We've got a whole switchboard to choose from. We could pretty well keep track of the whole troupe that way; and whatsisname, the vampire, too."

"That's *great*!" Ian yelled, beside himself with excitement. "That would take care of *every* . . . !"

"Please." Allan looked like he was about to cry.

Ian caught himself, went back to a normal volume. "That would take care of all our problems," he continued. "That was the missing link, right there. Do you think you could get away with it? Like, how would you do it?"

"Well, I'd have to make up some story about a client doing late runs. I mean, *very* late runs. That way, I could volunteer to handle it, and have the run of the office for the whole night. When the big boss comes in the next morning, we just tell him that the call never came. No muss, no fuss."

"That's great," Ian repeated, slapping his knee with the flat of his hand. "When do you think we could set this up for?"

"Not tonight. Tony's got a meeting with Mr. Big. They'll probably be in there all night, knowing them. Tomorrow would probably be the one."

"It's gotta be soon," Ian stressed, adding, "Did you see the *Post* this morning?"

"Yeah." Allan knew what he was driving at. The story about the two kids at the Cinema Village made the front page headlines.

"He probably killed 'em while we were sitting around, introducing ourselves and ordering beer." A frown creased his features. "That really sucks. It shows how pressing this has gotten."

"Yeah, I hear you." They nodded at each other solemnly.

Suddenly, a wave of dizziness swept over Allan. His head felt like a MixMaster set on puree. He teetered, leaned back heavily on the door, and moaned eloquently. Ian took him by the shoulders and tried to steady him. It worked, after a fashion.

"I think I'd better get back inside and sit down," Allan said.

Ian opened the door and helped him through. The cooler air from the air-conditioned office helped to clear his mind a little, but he still felt groggy as Ian led him back to his chair and sat him down easily.

A pair of phones rang. Chester and Tony answered them. Ian took this opportunity to lean close to Allan's ear and say, "You feeling better?"

"Yeah." Allan nodded weakly. It still hurt to move his head. "I didn't get much sleep last night."

"Tell me about it. I was up 'til like six o'clock over at Josalyn's."

"Bet that was fun." Allan managed a half-hearted leer.

"It was . . . very strange." Ian stared off into space

for a moment, came back. "I'll tell you about it later." He smiled. "You know what I've been doing today?"

"What?"

"Well, Joseph and I went shopping for all the things we're gonna need. You wouldn't believe some of the weird places we hit: occult bookstores, creepy little shops I never even knew existed. This one place was like a warlock Army surplus store: man, it was crazy! I think it's the only place I've ever seen where you could pick up a pair of wolverine testicles on sale." They laughed riotously, Allan clutching his head but helpless to stop. "No, seriously! They had all those little balls in jars. . . ."

"Shhh. Please. Stop." Something went *clang* in Allan's head and let off a thousand volts of sheer discomfort. His eyes locked on Ian's, pleading for mercy. It was granted.

"The only things we picked up so far," Ian said quietly, "were a bunch of these hefty crosses. Stainless steel. About five, ten pounds apiece. Vampire or not, you could definitely give that boy a concussion with one of these babies." He grinned wickedly. "And they're beautiful, too. I might hang one up in my room when this is all over."

"Didn't you get any wolfbane?" Allan asked innocently.

"Wrong monster, man."

"How about tanna leaves?"

"Jesus!" Ian slapped himself across the face. "For someone who's gonna be playing Dungeon Master with all our lives, you sure are a goddamn noodlehead."

That comment knocked Allan back in his seat. The headache gave way to a moving, pulsing wall of dread that wrapped him in its moldering folds. "Whoa," he muttered, blinking back the vision. "Whoa, I don't know if . . ."

"Sure you do," Ian said, insistent. "You're perfect for the part. It's just like Dungeons and Dragons, man. You move us through the twisty labyrinth so we can fight the dreaded bugaboo. Only this time, every corridor is a street down in the Village. Or a subway station. Or a tunnel."

"But I didn't *make* this dungeon . . ." Allan complained.

"Yeah, but you know how it's laid out," Ian countered.

"You're a dispatcher. You know this city better than almost anyone else in it. And you know how to keep track of thirty guys at a time. A dozen of us shouldn't be any trouble."

"Yeah, but I don't know where the monster will be."

"Yeah, but we're gonna kill the monster anyway, so it doesn't matter."

"Unless it kills *you*, boss." Allan's features pulled taut, earnest. "That's the consideration that nobody seems to be taking very seriously. This isn't a game of D & D, where you can get butchered by an ogre and resurrect ten minutes later with a roll of the dice. This is real stuff, Ian, and it scares the piss out of me. Honest to God, it does. . . ."

"What in the world are you two *talking* about?" Jerome interrupted suddenly. Ian and Allan turned, startled, to see that he'd caught them with their proverbial pants down. For all they knew, he could have been listening the whole time.

"None of your fuckin' business, Mary," Tony interjected, firing up a Parliament while another smoldered, half-smoked, in the ashtray.

"No, really!" Jerome wheedled. "I just want to . . ."

The phone rang. "Answer the phone, bitch. I heard enough of your fuckin' mouth to last me a lifetime, I kid you not."

"Don't call me a bitch."

"Answer the phone, whore."

The phone rang again.

"Don't call me a whore, either. Or a faggot, or a homo, or a queer. . . ."

The phone continued to ring.

"I'm a man," Jerome concluded emphatically.

"Answer the phone, Queen-fucking Matilda, I'll break your queen-sized fucking ass. Jesus Christ, you can't get that cunt to do *nothin'* around here without a fucking argument, I kid you not."

Jerome answered the phone. Ian stared at Allan in disbelief. Allan shrugged. "Are they always this charming?" Ian wanted to know.

"Fuck, fuck, fuck, fuck. Fuckin' sonofabitchin' *cunt*," Tony chanted, conspicuously pleased with himself.

"I gotta get out of here," Ian moaned. "These people are crazy."

"You get used to it," Allan offered. "I guess."

"Fuck you both, you scumbags. Who needs you?" Tony casually remarked.

Ian blew him a kiss and tiptoed toward the door. Allan waved prettily and called out, "Bye-bye, darling."

"Whores, faggots, and junkies," Tony mumbled to himself. "That's all I got to work with. Whores, faggots, and junkies."

"I'll talk to you later, man," Ian said to Allan as he opened the door.

"Yeah, later," Allan replied, smiling. Ian smiled back. The door closed behind him.

Allan Vasey watched Ian disappear into the street. He looked at the spot where his friend's smiling face had been, saw only the refracted light glaring at him through the window. It sent a white-hot sliver of pain through his forehead.

And the headache. And the dizziness. And the terror. Came back.

With a vengeance.

CHAPTER 32

Night fell, and the shadows took over, deepening as they swallowed the last of the sunlight. Street lights took over. And headlights. And neon. They twinkled like the jewel-encrusted scales of a dragon, poked tiny holes in the fabric. No more.

The shadows took over. They owned the night.

In Madison Square Park, an ominous figure moved between the rows of benches that lined its central promenade. The usual crowd of junkies, faggots, whores, and dealers were assembled on the benches and under the trees, making their moves with ritual abandon; but they faded back into the bushes silently . . . no pitches, no lines, no come-ons, no jive . . . when this one approached. They could sense the danger, like dogs scenting death, from twenty-five yards away. They were afraid to even breathe until he was safely out of range.

The dark man, the deadly man, moved to the farthest easterly extreme of the promenade. There was an unfenced section, between the benches, that allowed one to enter the tree-lined clearing that made up the center of the park. He stepped through the gap, squatted at the base of an enormous tree, looked up through the leaves at the ghostly haze of the moon, and smiled.

In one hand, he held a short, stout piece of wood. In the other, he held a very sharp carving knife.

"Tonight," he whispered. "Oh, yes."

Softly whistling a cheerful tune, he whittled away at the piece of wood until one end tapered down to an imposing point.

Meanwhile, further downtown, on a side street just south of Astor Place, a derelict was passed out on the cold gray of the sidewalk. He snored, the sound of a rusty ratchet being spun by a tireless child. A thin mist of fragrant spittle hovered around his mouth; his pants, as usual, reeked of urine. He could not see, or hear, or feel.

When it came, he didn't even know it.

Not until the cold hands took him by the shoulders and roughly shook him. Not until he felt himself rising from the pavement, the empty bottle of muscatel slipping from between his fingers and shattering at his feet. Not until the touch and the motion and the sound coalesced, forcing open his eyes, did the bum see what had found him.

"*Louie.*" A whisper like a charnel house breeze. "*Hey, Louie, I got a bottle. Hey . . . hey, Louie, I got myself SOMETHING TO DRINK!*"

One word . . . a name . . . strangled and died in Louie's throat. His rheumy eyes bugged out obscenely; his jaws locked open in a silent rictus of terror. He flailed at the air in a ludicrous backstroke, tried vainly to pull himself free.

"SOMETHING TO DRINK, LOUIE! COME ON! I'LL SHOW YA!" The left side of his face was a mass of scabs and protruding bone. There was a moist twinkle in the back of the gaping socket, a trick of light that made the nightmare visage seem to be winking playfully. The other side of the face was pale and withered, one eye glowing red above a hideous half-smile.

The throat had been gnawed open, forming a second crooked mouth that grinned with lips of black, scabrous meat. Louie took one look at it and pissed himself for the very last time.

"Nooooooooooo . . ." he whined, his famous last words.

And then Fred dragged his old buddy down the workman's entrance to forever night, where the serious drinking got done.

CHAPTER 33

Ian Macklay drained his third pint of Guinness stout and set the empty down beside his kitchen sink. He had a slightly-more-than-respectable buzz on, which suited him just fine as he whirled and headed for one last check in the bathroom mirror.

He saw himself: long blond hair and thick mustache, wide patriotic eyes (red, white, and blue), shirt three buttons open to reveal a stretch of unevenly tanned flesh that extended up to his scalp line.

He made faces in the mirror. He gawked. He leered. He preened like a model. He stuck a finger in either corner of his mouth and stretched the skin away, wagging a coated tongue at his reflection. His reflection gestured insolently back. He stopped clowning and checked himself out again, seriously.

I look drunk, he admitted. *My eyes look like meatballs. Other than that, I'm dashing as hell, but . . . maybe I should wear a pair of sunglasses.*

He giggled at the thought, but the reason for it remained. *I look drunker than I really am,* he confirmed unhappily. *Or maybe I just don't realize how drunk I really am. I dunno. Whatever the case, I look drunker than I want to when I'm going to see a lady.*

Or maybe it's just that I'm so tired.

That's the answer, he decided. *You get two and a half hours of sleep, you run around in the hot sun like an idiot for about eight hours, and then you expect to look like Prince Charming when 9:30 rolls around. Christ, Macklay, you're one clever son of a gun. No wonder all the girls are beating down your door.*

He had one more rueful laugh at his own face's expense and flicked off the light, turning back through the kitchen on his way out the door. He paused by the living room light switch, taking in the entire apartment in one sweeping glance. *It's a nice place,* he flashed. *A little on the shabby side . . . a little trashed-out . . . but, basically, really a nice place to live.*

Ian caught himself, wondered why he'd become so maudlin all of a sudden. "You're a rathole," he informed the room, lest his thoughts betrayed him. "You're a sleazy little fleabag apartment near the buttocks of modern-day Sodom." He thought of a thousand complaints he'd had with the apartment since he first moved in; but none of them could successfully contest the warm feeling he got as he looked around at his little niche in the world . . . the place that he called home.

"Weird," he said, feeling suddenly and decidedly detached, like somebody else watching a man named Ian Macklay stare around the apartment with eyes like a displaced baboon's. He shook it off, became one again, went through the door, and locked it behind him.

* * *

Just short of 14th Street on Seventh Avenue South, Ian picked up a 16-ounce Bud for the road. He popped it open luxuriously and poured it into his mouth, the cold, gold carbonation dancing over his tongue and down his gullet in a joyful flood. A thin tributary wandered down his chin and onto the front of his shirt. He cursed between his teeth, wiped it off, momentarily considered the wisdom of having yet another beer, and then brought the Bud back up to his lips again.

So sue me, he thought. *Tomorrow, we're gonna be chasing a vampire through the streets of New York City. I will definitely want to be sober for that. Joseph would mash my skull in if I wasn't.*

He drank to that, staggering slightly on his way to 25th Street and the East Side. He wove a semi-diagonal path toward the Flatiron Building, where 23rd Street happened by to catch the big intersection between Fifth Avenue and Broadway. Then he crossed the street, moving to the perimeter of Madison Square Park and wavering at the nearest entrance. The stern-faced statue of William H. Seward stared down at him from its pedestal; he stared at it for a moment, then doffed an imaginary hat in its direction and proceeded down the pathway to the center of the park.

Not more than thirty steps in, it suddenly occurred to him: *where is everybody? I've been in here for over a minute, and nobody's tried to sell me any drugs.* It was bewildering. He paused for a moment in the middle of the path to light a cigarette, taking in the smoke and the stillness together.

Nothing. No motion. Not even a breeze to rustle through the branches, stir the litter at his feet. Up ahead, he saw the new array of brightly colored benches. They were empty.

There was nobody in the park.

"Well," he told himself aloud. "At least I'm not gonna get mugged." He laughed a little, but the sense of strangeness pervaded his thoughts, telling him that *this isn't right. This doesn't make sense. I mean, it's a miserable*

*hot sticky night out, but . . . come on. I've seen people
out here through rain and snow and . . . come on!*

He took a troubled swig off his beer and stared into the
darkness, unmoving. His eyes adjusted to the intensified
shadow of the trees, and he looked deeper, saw blackness
within blackness, each level farther away from the light and
a greater triumph over it.

But no movement.

At all.

"Christ, this is weird." The flatness of the words didn't
fail to impress him. They sounded empty. There was
nobody around to hear them. *Nobody*. Spoken internally,
that word had weight. It thudded in his temples like a big
bass drum.

It occurred to Ian that he might want to get his bad self
out of the park. He might want to do it soon, before
whatever wasn't out there got him and turned him into
nothing, too. In his drunken state, he envisioned a big old
void sitting in the middle of the park, just waiting to suck
up anything that moved. The idea cracked him up; he stood
there, laughing in the middle of the path, until it wasn't
funny anymore.

Then he fell silent, and started thinking again.

"Well, Mr. Macklay," he informed himself in his
soberest tones. "Either you will retreat like a coward or
keep going like an asshole. Or you will stand here all night
like an idiot, which isn't much of a choice, either. So . . .
vich vun vill it be, eh?" he concluded in his best sinister
Nazi voice.

He wavered through a moment's indecision.

"So it's an asshole, is it?" he finally announced. "Well,
have at you!" And he moved deeper into the park, toward
the heart of the mystery.

He reached the area with the colorful benches and
paused again. There were little slogans written on them, a
different one for every bench. He took a moment to check
them out with growing curiosity.

WHAT IS THE BRIDGE BETWEEN YOU AND
YOUR GOVERNMENT? the first one read. Instead of
using the word *bridge*, they had a little stencil design of a

suspension bridge that seemed to be the recurring device in every little slogan. WHAT IS THE BRIDGE BE-TWEEN YOU AND YOUR FAMILY? WHAT IS THE BRIDGE BETWEEN YOU AND YOUR COMMUNITY?

On the bench that asked the question WHAT IS THE BRIDGE BETWEEN YOU AND YOUR HEALTH? some wiseguy had inked out the word *health* and substituted the word *death*.

WHAT IS THE BRIDGE BETWEEN YOU AND YOUR DEATH? the bench now read.

"Oh, that's cute," Ian observed. "That's just adorable." He moved closer, dragged his finger across the addition. It smeared; it was fresh. "Who wrote this shit?" he wanted to know.

The park answered him with silence.

And then he saw, way off to the right-hand side in the center of the park, that they'd actually *built* a bridge of sorts. It looked like something for kids to play on: a big wooden hulk, maybe thirty feet long, very cubic in design but still suggestive of a bridge's general contours.

Actually, it looks stupid, he noted. *Whose brilliant idea was this? Some civic organization, turning our city's parks into monumental think pieces that we can savor for generations to come.*

Except that the only people who ever come here any more are junkies, whores, bums, and dealers.

None of whom, he remembered abruptly, *are current-ly present.*

Ian glanced around the park again. He was at a much better vantage point now; the center of the park was essentially a clearing, and the central promenade extended away to either side of him. Still nothing. Still nobody.

"Well, obviously," he told himself, "this is a setup. They built this bridge because they knew I was coming. They did this just to confound me. You bet.

"Well, I'll show *you!*" he announced to the emptiness. "This isn't any garden-variety twisto you're dealing with here! This is *primo loco!*" He drained his beer, tossed the empty behind his back toward a handy waste receptacle, and actually made the shot. "*Ta da!*" He bowed for his nonexistent audience, did a sweeping gardyloo. Nobody applauded, and the joke wore thin. It occurred to him that Josalyn was probably worried by now; he was roughly forty-five minutes late, by his guesstimate. And here he was, posturing like a clown for nobody at all to enjoy.

In the middle. Of the deathly silence. Of the park.

A thought struck him, suddenly and reassuringly. It had the down-home tone of reason to it, firmly ameliorating the state of mind produced by his wilder flights of fancy.

There was probably just a big bust here, he reasoned. *A knife fight, or a big dope deal that brought the cops in en masse. And all that bridge shit really is the work of some stupid civic group, spending thousands of tax dollars on some idiotic renovation that they think is really clever because, gosh, they'll make us think about how lucky we all are to be rich Manhattanites with this kind of money to throw around in ludicrous fucking displays. Yeah, that's probably it to a tee.*

All the same, I think I'll check out yonder bridge there. See if they put a sliding board on it, or anything decent. Maybe Josalyn and I can come back here and have a little fun.

If da boogyman don't git us.

He hummed the theme to the *Twilight Zone* as he vaulted over the bench marked WHAT IS THE BRIDGE BETWEEN YOU AND YOUR DEATH? and into the center of the park.

All the way over to the bridge, he felt fine. There was an oddness to knowing that he was alone, and that civilization was getting farther away to either side with every step; but it wasn't anything grimly foreboding. No alarms were going off in his head. No cold chills were racing up or down his spine. He felt great.

He had shifted over to the *Perry Mason* theme by the time he reached the bridge, scrutinizing it from every side. No slides. No stairs. No fun stuff at all. He sighed in disappointment, realizing that namby-pamby community spokespeople actually *were* responsible for the whole silly affair after all: only well-meaning people could possibly build toys that were no fun to play with.

Oh, well, he thought. *At least it brought me to this side of the park. I'll write a letter to my congressman in the morning.*

He started to saunter away, toward Josalyn's apartment.

Suddenly, for some reason, a scene from Stephen King's *The Shining* leapt to mind. It was the one where Danny, the little kid, was playing in the snow outside the Overlook Hotel, and he found one of those big concrete tubes that kids like to climb through, and he got in, and suddenly he became aware of *something else* that was in the tube there with him: a kid who had climbed in there and couldn't get out, who had died there, who clamored toward Danny with a pathos that bordered on revulsion and then surpassed it, clearly wanting Danny to die there, too, to stay with him, forever. . . .

Ian found himself simultaneously wondering why Kubrick didn't put that in the film and thinking, *Momma, get me outta here, this place is starting to give me the creeps.* He was not surprised to find himself walking at a highly accelerated pace.

"This," he told himself aloud, "is ridiculous. Fucking Stephen King. This is all his fault." But he couldn't joke away the terror that was building inside of him, like a tornado gathering fury, as he moved step by step toward the promenade.

He reached the first of the inner ring of trees, a massive oak that could easily hide a man. He peered behind it cautiously, stepping away gingerly, though he knew that there was nobody behind it. There wasn't. He patted the tree like an old pal and moved beyond it.

And something stepped into his path.

"I knew you'd come," it said, with a voice both mellifluous and menacing. "I've been waiting here for you."

Behind the next tree, Ian's mind blurted irrationally. *It's always behind the next tree.* But he didn't show any of this to his assailant, opting instead for what he hoped was dispassionate cool.

"I don't suppose you baked me a cake," he said, freezing in his tracks and grinning like Dr. Sardonicus.

Rudy grinned back. His teeth gleamed in the diffused moonlight.

"No, I didn't," Rudy said, taking a long step forward. It made Ian recoil despite himself, made him edge backwards entirely against his will. "But I brought you something else that you might find reassuring."

He extended his hand toward Ian. His fingers were wrapped around a sharp wooden stake.

"That's what we're traditionally killed with, the way I understand it," Rudy said. "Since you think you're such a hotshot, I thought you might like to give it a try."

"I don't suppose you brought a hammer with you, either," Ian replied, shaking in his shoes and trying hard not to betray it. "What am I supposed to do: chase you around with that thing and wait for you to let me stab you? Come on. That's ridiculous."

"It certainly is," Rudy quipped. "That's why I wouldn't put it past you." *Touché*, said a sick part of Ian's mind: the craziest part, the one that's suicidal.

Ian wrestled severely with that part of his mind as he dragged out the best response he could come up with, under the circumstances. "You're a really funny guy," he said. "Why waste your time with this Bela Lugosi shtick? You should check out Robin Williams. He's got a lot more to say to the eighties."

"Keep laughing," Rudy said. "Keeping hamming it up. The fact of the matter is that I'm going to kill you."

"Unless you kill me first."

"Zat so?" Ian did his best to suppress the laughter, purely hysterical, that wanted to climb up through his throat. Some inner well of strength . . . the same one that had bailed him out the night before . . . whispered softly in his ear before exploding outward. *Be cool*, it said. *Buy time. Wait for your moment and get out of here alive.*

"Zat a fact?" he repeated, taking an unexpected step forward. Rudy jerked back a step by reflex, and Ian smiled. "Maybe we oughta just go back and forth for a while. I mean, hey! We could trip the light fantastic out here! Just you and me, baby: dancing the night away." He took another step forward and did a simulated cha-cha-cha.

Rudy didn't back off; Ian found himself suddenly closer than he liked. Fear rippled visibly through him; he stopped dancing and stood there awkwardly.

It was Rudy's turn to smile.

"You still don't understand what you're up against, do you?" He shook his head and went *tsk-tsk*. "You don't realize what I'm capable of."

"Do *you*?" Ian grinned fiercely, put on his best Cecil Turtle imitation. "Help, Mr. Wizard!" he yelled; then, in his regular voice: "Have you seen those cartoons, or am I wasting my time?"

"You're wasting your time," Rudy growled, taking several quick steps forward. Ian was backing off before he even knew it. "You won't make a fool of me tonight, my friend. Tonight, you're mine. Tonight, and forever after."

"You don't say." Ian's voice sounded remarkably calm and glib, but it was a façade. The cold hand of fear had wrapped itself around his nuts and was squeezing him slowly, flooding his guts with weakness and sickly discomfort. His heel struck an exposed tree root, and he stumbled, nearly losing his composure entirely. His mind told him to *be cool, buy time*, but there was a rising note of panic in the voice.

"You're not so tough after all, are you?" Rudy asked, stepping closer, keeping Ian off-balance and in retreat. "I'm a lot scarier when you're not with a bunch of your little friends, aren't I? Oh, yes. Much scarier indeed." His eyes flashed bright red, almost blinding, for a moment. "You little shit. This is too easy."

"Oh, YEAH?" Something snapped in Ian at that moment; he lurched forward, knocking Rudy back a couple of feet, and stood his ground in shivering anger. "Well, let me tell *you* something, pinhead! You're not *nearly* as scary as you are obnoxious! I oughta snap your ass in half!"

Rudy smiled boyishly, biding his time. "Then take the stake, hotshot," he said. "You'll need it."

"Piss off!"

"C'mon. Take the stake." Rudy slowly proffered it, point first. It looked extremely sharp. Ian eyed it nervously; every muscle in his body tightened.

And then he remembered his knife.

"For *you*, man?" Ian roared. "Don't make me laugh! You say that you're a terrifying vampire? Ha! I wanna see some fireworks!

"Let's see you turn into a bat, okay?" Rudy looked uncertain; Ian pressed on. "Surely you can pull *that* one off! It's the easiest trick in the book! Or how about a wolf, or a weasel, or a wombat? Boy, I'd *love* to see a wombat right now, if you could swing it."

"Shut up." Rudy's voice was a menacing hiss.

"Hey! How 'bout a rat?" Ian yelled, undaunted. "You've got all the requisite character traits. . . ."

WHAP! Ian didn't even have time to see the left hand come up and smack him across the face; it was that fast. He staggered backwards, his mind gone white-hot and blank for a minute. Then his vision cleared, and the pain set in. *God, that mother is strong!* he flashed, and then Rudy was advancing again.

"That's it," Rudy snarled. "No more games." He took another two steps forward. "It's time for you to die."

Ian backed up and into something large and solid. He jumped; his hands jerked back to see what he'd hit. *The tree*, he noted. *The first one. Oh, boy.* Automatically, his right hand slipped into his back pocket and wrapped around the hilt of the stiletto. He hoped that Rudy wouldn't notice.

Slash him and run, he thought, even as his voice said, "Get out of my face."

"Time to join your girlfriend," Rudy drawled malignantly. "Won't that be fun?"

"*WHAT?*" Ian yelled, all the air rushing out of him.

"She's mine now," Rudy hissed, watching the way that Ian seemed to deflate and loving every second of it. "I got her. . . ."

"*You LIAR!*" Ian shrieked, whipping out the stiletto. He made a roundhouse swing, the blade flicking out about midway to the side of Rudy's head and gleaming in the darkness as . . .

. . . something much too quick for the eye to catch whooshed between them, striking Ian's hand with sledge-hammer force. The knife went spiraling crazily off into the dirt. Ian stared in shock and pain at the stake in Rudy's hand, its point now hovering between their faces. Rudy had disarmed him with it, and brought it back around, before Ian even knew what happened.

Rudy lowered the stake and took a step forward, grinning.

I'm fucked, Ian's mind informed him in a voice that was strangely calm. His body started to twist away in a last desperate attempt at flight.

And something punched in through his belly.

Ian let out a strangled yelp of agony; his body doubled up slightly, then sagged and slumped back against the tree. His bulging eyes stared down in disbelief at the foot and a half of wooden stake that protruded from his belly, the oil-black gouts of blood that drenched the stake, Rudy's hand, the ground at their feet. His own hands came up weakly to clutch the wooden shaft. Rudy twisted it ever so slowly, pushed it in another inch.

Ian tried to scream; he gagged instead, and thick freshets of blood streamed out from his mouth and nose. He choked again, the pain receding now into merciful shock, his eyes glazing over. He looked up into Rudy's face. The image grew hazy, distorted, then blank . . .

. . . *and he was watching a stranger named Ian Macklay: an old man on a porch swing, with a corncob pipe in his hand and a gaggle of wide-eyed grandkids at his feet, spinning a yarn that held them in joyful captivity. He watched the man grow magically younger, slip backwards through a life that was marked by love and laughter, dance madly past the marriages of children, the births of children, the man's own marriage and then further back, further back, to a barroom where the young man sat with his good friends Allan and Joseph, to a bedroom where he coupled with a lovely young lady named Josalyn Horne on a hot, muggy night that seemed so far away. . . .*

He saw all the things that would never come to pass.

"Now," the voice hissed, right next to his ear. Ian jerked back instantly, the clouds rushing away. Much too clearly, he saw that Rudy's face was only inches from his own. He saw the eyes, bearing down on his like crimson headlights. He saw the teeth; they were the ones from the dream.

So long. So sharp.

"No," he burbled through a mouthful of blood. It sprayed in Rudy's face, sent tiny rivulets trickling down the cheeks and forehead. He brought his left hand up to Rudy's face and tried to hold it back. Rudy pushed forward, forcing the hand back slowly, until Ian could feel the cold breath on his throat.

And with his last dying effort, Ian brought his right hand up to grab Rudy by the balls and squeeze them with all his might.

Rudy bellowed and squealed and twitched like a bird on a high-voltage fence. Ian had just enough time for one tight-lipped grin of victory. Then Rudy's arm slammed forward.

And the point of the stake ripped through Ian Macklay's back, sinking four inches into the great oak behind him.

Josalyn sat at her desk, trying vainly to concentrate on her work. The typewriter was silent before her, a blank piece of paper jutting impotently from it. A Number 2 pencil, extremely sharp, trembled in her hand above some scratchily rendered notes.

All day, Josalyn had been unable to think straight. Ever since Ian awakened her this morning, and her eyes opened to see his tired-but-smiling face, the image had imposed itself at every opportunity. It simultaneously frightened and delighted her; her little heart was all a-twitter.

She'd spent the day making the apartment look nice,

cleaning and rearranging things with almost maniacal fervor. At a certain point . . . just as she'd caught herself rearranging the throw pillows on the couch for the fourth or fifth time . . . it had occurred to her that she was acting very strangely, not at all like her usual self. That was when she'd realized how much he'd come to mean to her, in just a very short time.

Then, after an hour of prettying herself up, she'd decided to do some writing while she waited. There was an hour to kill before he was due, and she couldn't just spend it twiddling her thumbs . . . although, as it turned out, that was exactly what she'd done.

It was now 10:40, and Ian was just slightly more than an hour late. Despite herself, she had begun to worry. There was probably a reasonable explanation, she knew; as crazy as he was, it wouldn't surprise her if he turned out to be one of the world's least punctual guys. But all the fears that she'd spent the day repressing bubbled up to the surface, unstoppably; her worst fantasies came to visit her, one by one.

I just wish he'd call, she thought, *and let me know what's going on. Even if he said that he wouldn't be able to make it, at least I wouldn't have to worry. This is crazy. Why doesn't he call?*

When the phone rang, she almost flew out of her chair. The pencil slipped out from between her fingers and went cartwheeling through the air. *It's him!* she thought, the first traces of a smile taking shape in either corner of her mouth . . .

. . . as she watched the pencil embed itself point first in the hard wooden floor, sticking straight up like the needle of a compass facing north. Trembling for a moment. And then standing completely still. . . .

The phone rang again.
Omigod, her mind whispered.
The phone rang again.
And again.
"I will not answer the phone," she said, under her breath. "I will not answer the phone. I will not. Leave me

alone." She backed away, shaking her head violently. The phone rang again. And again. And again.

You were expecting company? whispered a voice from her past: a horrible, sneering, mocking voice that laughed and laughed and laughed. . . .

The phone was still ringing when she hit the floor, unconscious. She didn't need to take the call.

She'd already gotten the message.

CHAPTER 34

Stephen was dreaming about a cold stone passageway in the bowels of an old dark castle. Thick chain clinked against the manacles that bound his wrists, echoing in counterpoint to the sound of their shuffling footsteps.

The men who dragged him forward, digging into his biceps from either side, had been dead for a long, long time. The flesh had rotted and fallen away in chunks, leaving a clotted slime coating on the bones, made of moldering muscle and sinew. Only the eyes had resisted decay; they flashed and gleamed like brake lights in their skeletal sockets. Stephen was too terrified to do anything but obey them as they pressed on down the corridor, escorting him with hatred in their death's-head grins.

Deep in the darkness ahead, he spotted the door. Light shined through the tiny window in its center and streamed onto the floor in a twisted rectangle, crosshatched with shadow cast by the window's metal bars. He heard the creaking of ancient machinery, the moaning of souls in pain. It was coming from there.

Stephen Parrish began to shriek and squirm. His heels dug at the stone floor with no success. The dead men's hands tightened around his arms as he struggled, punctur-

ing the skin and digging into the meat. He yowled and went
slack, blood running in jetties down his arms, his feet
dragging behind.

As they moved toward the door.

On the other side of the Atlantic, in a small Parisian
sidewalk cafe, a creature of extreme longevity and evil
sipped quietly at a snifter of expensive brandy and contentedly beamed at the world. Life had been wonderfully good
to it, for well over 800 years. Life had succored it in style.
Life had sated it, again and again, with beauty and bounty
to spare.

It thought back to a day, some five hundred twenty-
one years before, when it stood before a great roaring fire,
the light dancing merrily in its eyes. The fire burned
outside the Transylvanian city of Sibiu, and nestled deep
within that howling inferno were three hundred-eighty
chaste maidens of Sibiu, hair crisping and fat bubbling in
those charring flames. The Mad Prince himself had ordered
this blaze, and three others just like it, spaced a quarter
mile apart across the valley, having deemed it unseemly
that virgins be exposed to undue humiliation. Those whom
his soldiers had so rudely deflowered upon entering Sibiu
were no longer chaste, and thus were free to join the
remainder of their townfolk, who writhed on stakes,
arranged in festive displays for the amusement of Prince
Vlad the Impaler.

The ancient creature smiled. All in all, it had been a
merry day. Vlad and an army of twenty thousand had
crossed the border of Romania and attacked Sibiu for no
apparent reason. The slaughter was impressive: ten thousand dead or dying. And the carnage was just now winding
down, chiefly for lack of victims. The wind shifted slightly,
bringing a cloud of stinging, acrid smoke into the creature's
face. Its attendants coughed and sputtered and moved
away, but it remained transfixed, eyes absorbing every
pitiful movement from within the flames.

The ancient creature stepped away from the pyre. It
strolled through the neat rows of stakes upon which the

citizenry now twisted in their death throes. It marveled at the audacity of Vlad Dracula, at the increasingly ambitious displays he undertook in an attempt to curry its favor. Such a zealous pupil. So eager. It chuckled, low in its throat.

Vlad is a fool, it mused. Earlier that day the prince had personally decapitated the mayor and the city regents, their heads coming away like ripe melons plucked from the vine, and placed the heads on spikes outside the front gate. And when the creature had refused to acknowledge this bid for approval, Vlad had very nearly soiled his tunic. He later executed the men who witnessed his terrible secret.

Now, sitting at a sidewalk cafe in the oh-so-civilized twentieth century, it laughed and sipped its brandy and thought of how the great and dreaded Vlad Dracula, the Blood Count of Transylvania, was absolutely terrified of vampires.

A lovely French girl appeared at its table, her waitress's outfit flattering her form. The creature shrugged and grinned like a child, indicating that it was fine, its glass was full, it was happy. The girl nodded, a trancelike expression muting her features.

Later, after closing, it would have her for dessert.

But for now, she was allowed to wander back through her other tables, tending to mortal patrons with an uncharacteristic sluggishness. The ancient monster was in no hurry. It knew, without question, how little time means.

It sipped at its brandy. It stretched and sighed. It looked back over centuries of blood and growth, over wars and revolutions and breakthroughs in brutality that transcended its wildest, darkest expectations. And it realized that it had never been happier.

Oh, things are just dandy, it mused with glee. There aren't any heads on spikes any more . . . sometimes, I really miss those heads on the spikes . . . but all in all, things are going just marvelously. The new dark days are here, and I love them so much, it thought, sipping again at its brandy and smiling.

For some reason, its mind traveled back to New York City, its so-recent vacation. It wondered about the little seedling it had planted there . . . Rudy, his name was. It wondered how Rudy was doing.

He was a strange one, it recalled. *Not built to last, but quite intense, all the same. He may well have caused some interesting trouble by now. It might be entertaining to check on him.*

I think I shall.

It settled back in its chair then, eyes closed, relaxing completely, easing into that state where all physical laws are suspended and all barriers removed. There is a gateway to that realm, that reality: an imposing gateway, shaped entirely of fear. The monster passed through it effortlessly.

The monster began to fly.

Curled up on the floor in a trance, Rudy Pasko was in his glory. Though he still cupped his testicles gingerly in his hands, there was no pain. Gone, also, was his fury at having let Ian slip away into death so easily. All earthly cares were forgotten in the dreaming.

In the sending of dreams.

He watched from behind the Iron Maiden as Stephen was dragged into the chamber by the two rotting guards. It all looked suitably abhorrent: the guards, the victims, the layout of the torture chamber itself. Stephen, too, looked suitably terrified.

Which is just as it should be, Stephen. Rudy chortled in silence. *Since I'm doing this just for you.*

Rudy straightened his robe, brought himself up to his full height, and prepared to make his grand entrance. In his dreams, he was king. No one could cheat him of victory. No one could get off a cheap shot to the balls. No one could sully his vision or rain on his parade. And no one could resist him. He was master. He controlled.

He was not aware of the eyes that watched him with wicked and boundless amusement.

Ian was skewered to the wall, his feet dangling a few inches above the floor. It was the first thing Stephen saw as he entered the room; the steady pok-pok-pok of Ian's blood against the pavement drew his attention like a charm.

He looked away quickly. For a moment, it seemed that Ian had twitched; he didn't want to know if it was true or not. But the next thing he locked eyes on only worsened his terror. And the next one was worse. And the next one was worse.

Here, the death by boiling oil. Here, the beating and flaying alive, hung by the thumbs over a slow-burning fire. Here, the thumbscrews. Here, the rack. Here, the ancient Chinese "Death Of One Hundred And Twenty Cuts."

To his right, in the corner, a man sat chained in an upright position. His body kicked and flapped in spasms. A cage full of starving rats had been placed over his head. The rats were no longer starving, and the man no longer screamed; but he continued to jerk at his chains and convulse in a hideous puppet's dance, while crimson seeped down his bare chest and back.

Stephen screamed. He screamed again. He continued to scream as the guards led him forward, past the man with the hot irons thrust into his eyes and the woman with her entrails laid open for the dogs. He was still screaming as they hoisted him up over a crossbeam three feet in height, thrust his head and hands onto the grooves of an old-fashioned pillory only two feet high, and secured him there with his ass in the air and his legs waving uselessly behind him.

He looked down. This time, the scream froze solid in his throat. At the foot of the pillory, right under his face, there sat a basket full of severed heads and hands. Something moved inside the basket, and Stephen closed his eyes to blot out the horror.

The slamming of a huge iron door snapped him out of it. A muffled scream rang out and died in an instant. Stephen looked up, over the basket and straight ahead, at the Iron Maiden, with her inscrutable expression and the blood rolling out through the drains at her feet. He knew where the spikes were located; he did not need to see.

Hi, Stephen, *said a voice from behind the Iron Maiden.* And welcome to my humble abode.

Rudy stepped into view, resplendent in a full-length robe of black and red velvet. A pair of dead children, very much like the guards in terms of appearance, bore aloft the great folds of streaming fabric behind him as he approached.

This is darkness, *Rudy said, gesturing expansively to indicate the whole of their surroundings.* Not your penny-ante, long-suffering darkness of the mind, mind you. Not your minor-league depressions and sorrows. This is the real thing: no bottom, no end.

I wanted you to see it.

Rudy moved closer, stooping for a better view of Stephen's face. Stephen struggled against the pillory, trying to slide his hips off either side of the crossbar; all to no avail. The guards grabbed hold of his legs and held them steady, stretching him taut as Rudy squatted directly in front of him and riveted him with luminous eyes.

I'm going to break you in now, Stephen. *Rudy cocked his head to one side and smiled, appraising the reaction.* I'm going to let you know, once and for all, who is the master and who is the slave. You see, there are only two ways to approach the darkness: either you serve it, or it devours you. Your companions, here, are all doing the latter.

But you, little Stephen, *he said, tweaking Stephen's cheek painfully,* are going to serve me well.

Rudy rose to his feet then, his robe falling open. Stephen saw that Rudy was naked beneath it; the pale scrotum and thin, white erection dangled freely, only inches above his forehead. He watched as Rudy fondled himself for a moment, then walked around behind him.

At that moment, his own pants were wrestled from around his waist and dragged down to his ankles. There was the sound of tearing cloth and clinking steel. The pants were replaced by ankle chains that spraddled his legs apart painfully. In horror, he realized that his own phallus had swollen to the bursting point; to find himself aroused, in the face of such abomination, was the most debasing moment of Stephen Parrish's life.

Then Rudy was behind him, between his legs. He felt the cold hands drag along his inner thighs, sliding up over the tensed buttocks and then going off on separate missions: one to take his cock in its grip, the other to part the mouth of his rectum. Air hissed between his teeth; the screams of the dead and dying caromed off the walls and into his mind, mingling with his own as he waited for the first icy thrust . . .

. . . as a monstrous voice boomed, from out of nowhere, WHO IS THE MASTER, AND WHO IS THE SLAVE?

And suddenly Rudy was splayed out beside him, the screaming face and knotting hands run through an identical pillory. Because his head movement was limited, he couldn't see anything that went on behind; but he knew that Rudy had somehow been ripped out from between his legs and deposited in the selfsame position.

By something far more terrible.

LIKE A LITTLE GIRL, RUDY. *The voice was like thunder.* AGAIN AND AGAIN, IF I WISH. AND FOREVER.

Rudy's shoulders slammed rhythmically against the back of the pillory as something pounded into him from behind. He whined and mewled like a wounded animal, struggling desperately against his bonds, gasping in time with the brutal strokes that cleaved him over and over and over.

Stephen watched, slack jawed and dumbfounded, his own predicament forgotten. He saw the tears of rage and humiliation that streamed down Rudy's cheeks as the rape mounted in intensity. He looked into the eyes of the defiled and saw madness there: the same blend of self-hatred, pain, terror, and violence that had blown through his mind when Rudy'd been about to mount him.

THERE IS ORDER IN CHAOS. A DARK HIERARCHY OF POWER. *The floor shuddered in sync with the words and the thrusts. It had all become mechanical, lifeless.* THERE ARE SO MANY THINGS YOU MUST LEARN, MY PETITE ONE. AND THE FIRST OF THEM IS THAT . . .

Rudy howled in agony at some secret torment, hidden behind the wooden shackles.

. . . I AM THE MASTER. AND I ALWAYS COME FIRST.

The room started to fade. Stephen felt the pressure slip away from his extremities, as if his restraints were vanishing by degrees. His sight went out completely, but his mind was still flooded with the sounds of the torture chamber: Rudy's keening wail, that horrible voice, the screams of the dead and the dying. The tone of the latter had drastically altered.

It sounded like cheering.

Then Stephen drifted off completely, leaving behind him the frenzied applause of the damned as Rudy let out a final shriek . . .

. . . and the three of them awoke, simultaneously, from the dream: Stephen, caked with sweat and nocturnal emission; Rudy, with a very sore rectum to go with his very sore balls; and the ancient creature, who decided to let the little French waitress go home unharmed.

It had already had dessert.

CHAPTER 35

Tuesday morning's edition of the *Post* featured two stories of note, but only one of them caught Jerome's attention as he rushed to be late for work.

The other one . . . the one he didn't notice . . . involved a young man named Dod Stebbits. The *Post* didn't know whether to dub Stebbits' death a suicide or a murder, so it used both words in its headline and put a question mark at the end. The police, too, appeared at a loss to explain what had happened.

It would have helped if they'd known that Dod Stebbits had been turned into a vampire; that he had awakened, one night later, and found himself too weak to free himself from his bonds; that when the sun came up on Monday morning, the pain was so intense that Dod had finally succeeded in loosening one arm out of sheer desperation; that he'd used the gun to blow his brains out and end the agony; that he had *survived* the gunshot, flopped around on the bed with half his face missing for almost an hour of inconceivable suffering before dying; that it was the sun, not the bullet, that had finally polished him off.

Without that kind of information, though, nobody had been able to make heads or tails of the case.

Jerome didn't notice. His attention was locked on another story: just as strange and inexplicable, but much closer to home. *Unless it kills YOU, boss,* Allan's voice chanted in his memory. *Unless it kills YOU.* As he slowed to a stop.

Being late to work no longer concerned him. In fact, he dreaded the idea of showing up at all. "Oh, this is terrible," he moaned out loud. "Oh, I don't want to be there when Allan finds out. . . ."

But Allan already knew.

"I took the call at eight o'clock, when I got in to open up. The phone was already ringing," Allan droned. He was numb. He couldn't feel the words coming out of his mouth, and that was good. *If I just keep talking,* he thought, *I'll be fine. I won't feel a thing.*

On the other end of the line, Joseph said nothing.

"Somebody's gonna have to go and . . . identify the body," Allan continued, cracking just a little. He did his level best to keep his voice steady. "I can do it . . . or you can, if you want to . . . it doesn't matter. Somebody has to, that's all. I . . ."

"I'll do it." Joseph's voice: impossible to read.

"Okay," Allan said. "That's fine. That's . . . okay."

"We're on for tonight, man." A statement of fact. "There's no problem with that, right?"

Allan was unable to answer. His breath had started to come out in little machine-gun bursts. *I should have kept talking,* he told himself inanely. *Now I can't talk at all.* . . .

"Allan? Am I right?" Joseph's voice was insistent.

Allan cracked.

"*Are you crazy?*" he screamed into the receiver. "*Ian's dead! Ian's DEAD, God Damn it! Don't you understand?*"

"Oh, yeah," Joseph muttered. "Oh, yeah. I understand. I understand that I'm gonna kill the motherfucker that did it; and you're gonna help me, or I'll snap both of your . . . damn. Allan. I'm sorry. . . ." His voice trailed off in shame.

No longer numb, Allan suddenly felt everything . . . the anger, the pain, the sorrow, the outrage and utter disbelief that something so wrong could be allowed to happen . . . he felt all of it burst forward in a torrent of tears that could no longer be repressed or denied. For a full two minutes, it was the only sound to pour through the phone line. Joseph's shallow breathing was too soft to be discerned.

Finally, Joseph broke the silence. "Allan?" he said. "I didn't think. I forgot who I was talking to. I . . . I . . ."

"It's alright," Allan managed to squeeze between the sobs. "It's alright, boss. I understand."

"Well . . . I'm gonna go . . . to see him now. You think about tonight, and let me know. If you don't think you're up to it . . ."

"Joseph."

Pause.

"What?"

"We're on, champ. You just . . . get hold of everybody, and I'll set things up here."

"You're sure?"

"I'm sure." Allan's breath took on a semblance of normalcy again. "I don't want to say that we owe it to him, but I guess that's what I mean. I mean . . . if there was ever a time when I thought I could let this slide, that time is over now. We have to deal with this. We have to stop that son of a bitch." He paused for a deep breath, trying to calm himself, to stop the shuddering. "Now it's my fight, too. You know?"

Joseph sighed heavily. "You *know* I know."

"Alright." Strength came trickling back to him now: strength and resolve, from a reserve so private that he hadn't even known he had it. "Call me up a little later and let me know how it's going. I want to be on top of this. We want to do it right."

"You got it," Joseph said with unreserved admiration. "You got it, boss."

An hour and a half later, Joseph was driving his van through the Village. He had seen Ian's body, rolled out on the slab. He had identified it positively. And he had left the morgue in a state neatly torn between anguish, awe, and killing rage.

He was smiling, Joseph silently repeated for the fortieth time, still staggered by the implications. *That amazing little mother was smiling when he died: laughing in the face of death*. The courage in that single act, that single vindication of life, made him respect Ian more than he ever had before. It also, more than ever before, made him wish that Ian were still at his side.

That was where the anguish and the killing rage came in. He'd been careful to check for bite marks on the corpse, hoping against hope that there'd be none to be found. The idea of having to hunt down his best friend was more than he could bear; but as it turned out, that would not be necessary. Therein lay the victory, and the reason behind Ian's forever grin.

But he died anyway, Joseph privately moaned, *and nothing's gonna bring him back*. The loss was a flavor that sat heavily on his tongue: the flavor of bile and dust and blood. All he wanted now was five minutes alone with that wormy little sonofabitching punk. All he wanted was for Rudy to come apart in his hands.

And he would have that satisfaction. Or die in the process of getting it.

Tonight.

Joseph wheeled past MacDougal and pulled to a stop at the curb of West 3rd Street, directly in front of the window with the words MOMENTS, FROZEN embossed in bold letters across its surface. The window was too dirty to see through, but the door was open. He left the van idling and leaped out, running up the seven steps and pausing just inside the doorway.

In the back of the shop, Danny and Claire were having an argument. Other than that, there was no one in the room. Joseph cleared his throat loudly when he realized they hadn't heard him enter. They looked up sharply, and then fell into two distinct postures: Danny shamefaced and grinning sheepishly, Claire pouty-faced and staring holes in the floor.

"Hi. Joseph?" Danny stepped gingerly around Claire and the counter, looking both embarrassed and relieved by the interruption. "What's up?"

"Did you read this morning's *Post*?"

Danny looked confused. "Uh, no . . ."

"Read it." He looked over Danny's shoulder at the Rolodex on the counter. "I need Stephen's address. Do you have it?"

"Uh, no," Danny repeated, half-cowering as he backed toward the counter. "But I . . . uh . . . could look it up in the phone book for you. . . ."

"Fine." Joseph followed Danny to the back of the shop, watched him flip nervously through the Manhattan White Pages, and suddenly remembered that he'd left his van running. "Omigod," he yelled, turning to run back to the door. "Hang on a second. I'll be right back."

Joseph's feet pounded against the wooden floor and thudded to a halt in the doorway. The van was still there, miraculously; he considered going out there and shutting it off, then turned to see Danny writing something on a piece of paper. He paced for a minute, and then Danny ran up with the paper in his hand.

"Here you are," Danny labored, out of breath. "Uh . . . do you think you could tip me off on what's happening? I'd really like to . . ."

"I don't really wanna talk about it," Joseph replied gruffly. Danny's face sagged a little, and Joseph heard a voice in his head say *stop being such a prick, all right? This guy's on your side*. It was the kind of thing that Ian would have said; it was what Ian would be saying if he were . . . if he hadn't been . . .

"I'm sorry," Joseph said, looking away. He sighed and frowned miserably. "I'm sorry, man, but I'm, uh, a little wired-out right now, because . . . because Ian is dead, and . . ."

"Oh, God." Joseph looked over and saw that Danny was genuinely stunned. He was about to go on, to say that Rudy did it, but it had gone without saying. He experienced a flicker of gratitude for the fact that Danny intuited it, understood it, grasped and cared about it. If he were capable of expressing warmth . . . if he were not so ungodly wired-out . . . he would have done it.

"We're on for tonight," he said. "We'll need you at my office by 6:30. Here's the address." He dug a messenger receipt pad out of his pocket; the address and phone number were printed in bold type at the bottom of the sheet that he tore off and handed to Danny. "If you have any problems with that, call Allan at that number. Otherwise, we'll see you then."

"Thank you," Danny said. "We'll be there." Glancing back at Claire, who had been tuning in the entire time. She turned away at his glance.

"All right," Joseph said. He met Danny's gaze, saw resolve and a hungering for acknowledgment there. Impulsively, he extended his hand, and Danny shook it eagerly, smiling.

Then he turned away and tromped down the stairs,

heading for his van, the address that Danny gave him clutched tightly in his hand. He glanced at it, and an unpleasant smile creased his features.

Now for that little dick-licker, Stephen, he thought, hopping into the van and slapping it instantly into drive. *Now's when the boy pays up*.

Stephen was dripping tears on the difficult first draft of his suicide note when the fists started slamming into his door. He leapt out of his seat, and a fresh bout of bawling erupted from within him. His time had come, as he'd known it would; it had just been a question of day or night, Joseph or Rudy.

"OPEN THE GODDAMN DOOR!" howled the muffled voice from the other side.

Stephen didn't know how long he stood there, his fists clenched over his ears, the tears streaming down his cheeks. He wanted to finish the note, but it suddenly seemed pointless. He didn't deserve to live. He didn't deserve to have his last words immortalized in the *Daily News*. And the world had done nothing to deserve them, either.

The pounding on the door got louder and louder. He knew that Joseph was going to smash it down at any moment. Hiding in the closet occurred to him, as well as jumping out the window or slashing his wrists. Instead, he just stood there in the middle of the room, sporting nothing but a T-shirt and his BVD's.

"I HEAR YOU IN THERE, GODDAMN IT, STEPHEN! OPEN THE DOOR!"

Slowly, very slowly, Stephen turned toward the door. He watched it rhythmically bulge out from its frame under the steady rain of blows. He imagined one of those fists connecting with his face, and suicide became out of the question. He didn't want to die. Not like that. Not at all.

And certainly not like Joseph's friend, Ian.

He has every right to be furious, Stephen told himself. He's seen the story on the morning news, curled up in a ball on impact. There was no doubt as to what had happened.

Nor was there any doubt as to his complicity. He had withheld information; if he hadn't, maybe Ian would be alive today.

A moot point. Ian was dead, and the door frame was giving out fast. A couple of seconds, either way: it didn't much seem to matter. Stephen moved very slowly, like a man at a funeral, to the door; and in a voice that sounded absurdly calm, he said, "Joseph? I'm letting you in now."

He opened the door.

Joseph entered the apartment with his right fist first, laying into Stephen's left eye with such force that the art student spun full circle before hitting the opposite wall. Stephen collapsed with a groan, and Joseph was inside, slamming the door behind him as he stalked across the room.

"Get up," Joseph growled. Stephen rolled and moaned and clutched his head. "I said GET UP!" Joseph yelled, hoisting Stephen up by the collar and dangling him there by one hand while the other hand came up to slap him across the face.

Stephen yelped. Getting punched in the head by Joseph was worse than he could have possibly imagined. The world . . . what he could see of it . . . was blearily spinning. The flesh around his left eye already felt raw and puffy; it stung like crazy when he brought his hand up to touch it.

"Why I don't kill you now, I'll never know," Joseph rumbled in Stephen's face. "Ian was worth a thousand of you, you little putz. I *ought* to just kill you now."

Stephen whimpered and lolled his head.

"Oh, fuck it," Joseph grumbled, realizing that Stephen was too freaked out to waste his threats on. He tossed the limp form onto the bed, picked a pair of crumpled jeans off the floor and tossed them at Stephen, saying, "Put these on. And some shoes and socks. We're gettin' out of here."

"Wuh, wuh," Stephen gibbered, uncomprehending.

"We're *going*," Joseph hissed, leaning straight down into Stephen's face, "to your best friend Rudy's house.

You're going to show me where it is, because I want to
know, because I'm gonna kill him. And if you're lucky, I
won't leave you there as bait. Understand?"

Stephen nodded emphatically.

"Good," Joseph said, and started to turn away . . .
just as Stephen's nodding upward stroke went all the way
back to make his head strike the mattress in a stone cold
faint.

Fifteen minutes later, they were out the door, Joseph
dragging Stephen behind him as they clumped down the
stairs and out into the waiting van. Joseph shoved his
companion in through the driver's side, then violently
motioned for him to move over; a moment later, they were
rolling down the street. Only then did Joseph close the
door behind him.

They drove in silence, Stephen already having given
up the address. He inspected himself glumly in the
rearview mirror, probing tentatively at the full-blown
shiner that now graced his left eye socket. Deep reds and
purples adorned it in bold, splashy strokes; and the
moisture from his icepack gave it the appearance of a high-
gloss finish. He briefly considered turning it in as his next
art project, then stifled the thought. He was afraid to laugh
in Joseph's presence.

I'm afraid, period, he admitted to himself as they
rolled east on 8th Street toward Avenue B. *I'm afraid of
what we'll find in Rudy's apartment. What if he's there?
What if there's a big coffin in the middle of the bedroom?
And what if he's got somebody there to guard him . . . ?*

That last question seemed so pertinent that he almost
mentioned it to Joseph; but one look at the man behind the
wheel made him promptly reconsider. Joseph looked like a
solid mass of vengeance, staring straight ahead with flinty
eyes and a dangerous scowl plastered onto his features. He
smoked a cigarette mechanically, deriving no pleasure from
it whatsoever, just doing it to fill the seconds between this
place and Rudy's front door.

They reached Avenue B and screeched into the only

available parking space, moments before a middle-aged Oriental woman could negotiate her old Buick into reverse and parallel park there. She screamed at them in broken English and waved her scrawny fist. Joseph ignored her, shutting off the engine and motioning Stephen toward him. "This way," he said. "Lock the door. This won't take long."

Stephen obediently climbed out the driver's side, shrugging apologetically at the still-screaming woman. Joseph slammed the door and locked it with his key, then turned and crossed the street without a word. Stephen followed behind, looking nervously from side to side, drinking in the pomp and circumstance of Junkie Heaven.

Because Avenue B was the kind of place people were talking about when they mentioned a "bad section of town." Young men, not much more than Stephen's age, were passed out in the filth on the sidewalk. Little kids were running around, calling each other motherfuckers and shouting that they were going to "cut'choo up." Everybody either looked armed or too wasted to care any more. To someone like Stephen, who was already frightened and miserable, Avenue B was a singularly depressing and harrowing locale.

"This is the place?" Joseph asked, pointing at a doorway as Stephen scurried to catch up with him.

"I think so. . . ."

"You *think* so." Joseph turned to lay a withering glance on him.

"No, no!" Stephen blathered quickly, fading back a step. "I mean, I'm pretty sure. It's just that I never came here often. It's not really my kind of neighborhood."

"Right," Joseph said, and began to climb the stairs. Stephen followed closely.

They opened the outer door of the building and stared into a grimy foyer. The smell of derelict piss was ripe and pungent, cutting into their nostrils like ammonia. Joseph winced and brought one hand to his nose, then stepped inward to check the mailbox.

"Jackpot," he growled nasally, his nose still pinched shut. "Pasko. 3B. Let's go."

The inner door to the building was supposed to be

locked, but it pushed open easily. They found themselves faced by a ratty-looking stairwell, thick with the smells of greasy cooking and unwashed bodies. The stairs themselves were rickety; they buckled and creaked as the two young men climbed to the third floor landing. A television set was blasting game shows on the second floor, somewhere. It was the only other sound they could hear.

"This is it," Stephen said finally, leaning on the banister to catch his breath.

They paused for a moment in front of Rudy's apartment, gauging the atmosphere surrounding the door. It was *bad*: they both sensed it at once. It was the kind of aura that spoke directly to the nervous system, setting off chills and danger signals, prying the lid off the subconscious mind so that all the deepest mortal dreads could freely run amok.

Joseph stepped hesitantly over to the door, suddenly conscious in the extreme of how loud his footsteps were. He wrapped his right hand around the doorknob, retracted it abruptly with a startled hiss.

The doorknob was freezing. In ninety-plus weather, the rounded piece of plastic was colder than an icebox: so cold that it almost burned.

"Jesus Christ," Joseph whispered, rubbing his hands together briskly. Stephen's expression was frightened and quizzical. Joseph shrugged and took ten good paces away from the door before stopping, turning, and bracing himself.

"What are you going to do?" Stephen asked him.

Joseph rolled his eyes and shook his head wearily. "Take a wild guess," he said.

Then he thundered toward the door at full speed, bringing his left shoulder around in front at the moment before impact. Stephen's warning cry froze in his throat as the sound of splintering wood exploded in his ears. His eyes snapped shut reflexively, and he half-turned away.

Suddenly, a door behind him flew open. Stephen whirled to see a round Puerto Rican face pop out into the hallway and yell, *"Who's makin' alla this a-noise, eh?"*

"MIND YOUR OWN BUSINESS!" Joseph yelled, behind him.

"*I call they POLICE!*" the Puerto Rican squeaked shrilly.

"SHUT UP, OR YOU'LL NEED 'EM!" Joseph bellowed, banging his fist against the wall. The round head popped back through the doorway abruptly, the door following closely behind. There was the sound of multiple locks snapping shut, muted grumbling in Spanish that trailed off like vapor.

Then Joseph said, "Come here, Stevie," and Stephen turned to see that the door was dangling by one hinge from the frame. Joseph had his back to Stephen, peering into the darkness of the apartment. He was perhaps two feet inside.

"Come here," Joseph repeated. "You've got to see this."

Stephen dragged himself forward unhappily. About ten feet away from the doorway, his nerves started jangling alarm again. This time, it was accompanied by a genuine forty-degree drop in temperature and a strong, fetid, unfamiliar smell. It all served to make him shiver and flinch as he forced himself into the room.

"Check it out," Joseph murmured with cruel satisfaction. "This is the guy you were trying to protect."

Joseph turned on the light.

"Omigod," Stephen whispered, making almost no sound.

The room showed itself to Stephen in totality first: a single dead organism, reeking of evil, crawling with unnatural life. It flooded his senses with a chittering swarm of nightmare images, hammered down into one solid gestalt impression and left to burn in his mind forever. It gripped him for a long frozen moment of horror, bombarded him from every direction at once, oozed in through his nose and his mouth and his pores, raked his eyeballs with fire, filled his head with its infinite shrieking chorus.

Then slowly, piece by piece, it unfolded itself before him.

It showed him the writing. The blood. The walls. It showed him how the three had merged into a whole more hideous than the sum of its parts. It showed him the furniture, stripped-down and mangled. It showed him the boards, nailed up over the window, totally shielding the room from the sun.

Then it showed him the rats.

There were dozens of them. All shapes. All sizes. The sudden light and intrusion had stunned and confused them. They skittered across the floor in blind waves, screeching. They disappeared down secret holes, through doorways into darkness.

It showed him the shapeless pile of rags in the corner; the rats that surrounded it, reluctant to leave. The hatred in their eyes was a palpable thing as they slid away slowly, their tiny mouths working.

Then it showed him what they had in their mouths.

"Rudy Pasko," Joseph muttered, "this is your life."

Stephen puked all over the floor.

Joseph laughed. He couldn't help it. The insanity of the situation overwhelmed him. He danced to one side quickly, trying to avoid the splatter off the floorboards, and a machine-gun burst of clipped, humorless chuckles escaped him.

The shapeless pile in the corner was composed of more than rags. There wasn't much left, and most of it was so thoroughly trashed that it defied recognition; but Joseph could still distinguish the remnants of the two tiny pairs of pants, a sneaker, and a T-shirt with the word MENUDO tackily heat-transferred across its front.

And, of course, there were the bones.

Small bones.

Children's bones.

"You bastard," he muttered between clenched teeth. "You son of a bitch. God, I wish you were here."

Behind him, Stephen continued to retch. Suddenly, it wasn't funny: it was infuriating. A rush of mindless fury overwhelmed him. He moved around the pool of vomit and grabbed Stephen by the back of the neck, forcing the head upright.

"Two little kids," Joseph hissed in Stephen's ear. "Your buddy killed two little kids, used their blood to write all over the walls with, and fed 'em to the rats. What do you think about *that*, Stevie? Huh? How do you feel about ol' Rudy now?"

Stephen was unable to speak. He was remembering the two little children in his dream. He was seeing their dead eyes and moldering faces as they held up the folds of Rudy's robe.

He puked again, dry heaving this time.

"Hey! Maybe if I understood his philosophy, I would understand what he's all about!" Joseph was shouting the words into Stephen's ear now. "I could relate to his trip, maybe! Hey!

"What I should do," he continued, dragging Stephen forward with him, "is read his great words of wisdom here! It might change my whole life! Wutta ya say?"

Stephen coughed and sputtered and moaned. Joseph practically ground Stephen's face against the wall as they reached it, then dragged him backwards just a step. The writing on the wall refused to focus. There were too many tears in his eyes.

"Oh, yeah. This is great," Joseph said. His voice was quiet and deadly. "This is the work of a true fucking genius. I feel a lot better already. Are you reading this?"

Stephen tried to shake his head, but Joseph held the back of his neck too tightly.

"Read it."

A whimper, slowly burgeoning into a scream.

"I said READ IT!"

Slowly burgeoning into a scream, the sound welling up from his diaphragm and expanding into his lungs. Slowly burgeoning into a scream that cut off abruptly, as Joseph grabbed him by the throat and squeezed with both hands.

Stephen's bugged out, his tongue swollen and flopping, as Joseph violently jerked him around like a joystick. His face flooded with color, deepening to rival the purple welt around his eye. The scream sucked back into his lungs. His hands came up weakly, in futile resistance. The world began to gray out.

A strange sound came into his ears, then: by turns the roar of an ape, the rumble of a train, the howl of a baby at night. It was a mad chaotic sound that came from far away . . .

. . . and suddenly he was falling, the pressure around his neck released. His forehead cracked against the wall, and he crumbled to the floor, gasping for breath and clawing blindly at the air.

It took a full minute for him to begin to get his bearings. It was then that he figured out the source of the sound.

Joseph Hunter was crying.

Stephen looked up at him meekly, disbelieving. He rubbed his right eye and blinked the tears out of the other as best he could, trying to ascertain that what he was seeing was real. It was. Joseph had slumped to his knees, the massive body folding up like a switchblade while fierce spasms of sorrow racked him over and over. He was utterly oblivious to Stephen's presence now. He was utterly oblivious to everything.

Stephen crawled away from the wall quietly, staring up at the bloody smears upon it. His eyes could focus upon them now. His eyesight was clearing remarkably.

I AM KING
I AM GOD
I OWN THE KEYS
TO THE CITY

read the first stanza.

NONE SHALL ENTER
THE KINGDOM
EXCEPT THROUGH
ME

The column ended. There was more, written next to it. Stephen's eyes scanned over to the next section, while Joseph continued to cry.

I KILLED THE PIG
THAT TRIED
TO MAKE ME
CRAWL

There was more. There was more. Stephen choked down the fear that rose up sickly from his bowels, threatening to make him heave again. He steadied himself with his hands against the floor and read the last block of gore-smeared, artfully rendered print.

I WILL KILL THE CUNT, AND
I WILL KILL THE TOADIE
AND THE OLD ONE WILL FALL
BENEATH MY HEELS
AND THE SHEEP
WILL BECOME WOLVES
THAT WALK BEHIND ME

I AM KING

I am king. The words rolled around in his mind like living things. *And the sheep will become wolves that walk behind me.* Stephen closed his eyes, and the children were there: as they'd been in his dream; as they remained, in a pile on the floor beside him. Nothing on earth could spare him from those visions. They would haunt him for as long as he lived.

"Tonight, motherfucker," he heard Joseph Hunter sob. "Tonight is the *end.*"

And he heard his own voice, in the back of his mind, whisper *yes.*

BOOK 3

The Light At The End

CHAPTER 36

The clock on the wall said 6:05.

In the dispatch room of Your Kind Of Messengers, Inc., the last of the hordes were trickling out for the evening. Tuesday marked the end of the pay week, which made checkout time drag out to twice its normal length. Allan had forgotten about that; he cursed the luck that put Ian's death, the hunt, and weekly checkout all together in the same festive package.

There had been questions . . . too many questions . . . as the news of Ian's death worked its way through the messenger ranks. Ian was well-liked, by and large; and everybody knew how tight Ian and Allan had been. It was inevitable that the topic would come up, over and over, as each new handful of messengers wandered into dispatch.

And there were very few people that Allan really cared to discuss it with.

A handful of them were waiting outside, by the curb. Allan had asked them to wait around until checkout was done; he was pleased to see that they'd obliged him. He watched through the window as they passed an end-of-the-working-day joint around in an indiscreet circle and swigged on the beers of their choice.

Doug Hasken, the roller-skating messenger, was the last one to finish checking out. He and Allan were the only ones left in the office, now . . . Chester and Jerome having departed with the last big wave of messengers to leave . . . and Allan found himself looking at Doug more closely than he ever had before.

He's a good man, Allan noted. *Been with us less than a*

week, and already you can tell that he's gonna be an ace. Plus, he seems like someone you can trust.

I wonder if I should ask him?

Allan was still debating it when Doug called him over to look at a particularly weird run: thirty-five minutes of waiting time to pick up a fifteen-pound bag of self-help books and take them to three incorrect addresses. It was the kind of snafu that would make an ordinary messenger break into an animated war dance; Doug had taken it so gracefully that Allan wondered if the kid had been nominated for sainthood.

"Well, I guess I did alright, then," Doug said, staring at his totals for the week. "$150 in four days."

"If we were doing any business, you'd be clearing $250, easy," Allan assured him. In his mind, the debate had worked its way into a draw. *Speak now, or forever hold your peace*, it informed him unanimously. He decided to go for it.

"Uh . . ." he began, ". . . uh, I wanted to ask you what you're doing tonight."

"What I'm doing tonight?" Doug's eyebrows came up, a bit defensively.

"Yeah. Like if you had anything in particular going on, or . . . if you were going to be in the area."

Doug considered it for a minute before answering. There was an obvious conflict in his mind that he left unstated. *That makes two of us,* Allan noted bitterly, and then Doug began to speak.

"Yeah, I'll be hanging out in the Village for a while. Why? What's up?"

Now it was Allan's turn to be put on the spot. He wrestled with the words, with the idea of pursuing it at all . . . Doug's response so far had been less than heartening . . . then said *fuggit* to himself, motioned for Doug to wait a second, and moved across the room to rap on the window and beckon the others inside.

"I've got to ask you a favor," he said finally. "I'll tell you about it in a minute, when the other guys get in here."

Moments later, the door opened, and five crazy guys

came spilling into the room: Navajo, a lean black dude whose wardrobe tended toward leather, feathers, and beads; Dean, a lunatic biker with a perpetual wild-ass grin; Art Dodger, with his long blond hair and battered tophat, looking like he just stepped out of a Freak Brothers comic; Jimi, the sax player, blowing Ornette Coleman noise through a plastic kazoo; and Zeke, the eternally serious elf, letting an uncharacteristic guffaw rack his diminutive frame.

When these are your most trustworthy men, Allan mused with a private grin, *you're in serious trouble.* Even Doug looked crazy: with his knee and elbow pads, bike-racing helmet, and Road Warrior jumpsuit, he could have played a character in *Plan 9 From Outer Space.*

But they're the best. Aces, every one of 'em. I don't care how *weird-looking they are: not one of these guys has ever let me down.*

"So what's happening?" Dean wanted to know. "We blowin' up the office tonight, or what?" Before Allan had a chance to respond, three possible approaches to the demolition had been cheerfully advanced.

"No, no." Allan laughed, in spite of himself. "I'd rather not think about anything blowing up around here tonight, thank you."

"You're no fun," Jimi informed him flatly.

"I'm gonna *be* here all night!" Allan fired back. "And that's kinda . . . why I asked you all to hang around. I need for you to do me a favor."

"I knew it," Dean groused. "Overtime runs."

"Hey! You get paid double for that action!" Navajo yelled in his ear. "You doin' somethin' better with your time?"

"Well, it's not exactly overtime runs," Allan continued. "It's a favor for me. And there is a little bit of money in it for you."

The mention of money sent a tangible shiver through the room. It had been a bad week, and people were hungry.

"How much?" Dean queried, beady-eyed. Jimi elbowed him in the side and shushed him quickly.

"Well, it's like this," Allan said, pulling a small stack of Xeroxes out from under the counter and setting it down on top. "I need to find this guy tonight. I don't really want to tell you why, but it's very important."

He passed the Xeroxes around. They were grainy, black-and-white copies of a photograph culled from Stephen's collection. The shot was of Rudy. The pale face sneered up at them, seven times over.

"He ripped you off," Navajo ventured to guess.

"This has something to do with Ian, doesn't it?" Zeke suddenly inquired.

And a graveyard silence enveloped the room.

"We're pretty goddamn stupid, aren't we?" Dean mumbled shamefacedly. He spoke for all of them.

"I didn't really want to bring it up." Allan stared at his shoes as he said it, painfully aware of all the eyes upon him. "I hoped I wouldn't have to . . ."

"Hey," Art Dodger interrupted. "Don't sweat it, Allan. Really. We all loved Ian. He was a great guy. We understand."

Why Allan didn't start crying again, he would never know.

"You think this is the guy that killed him?" Jimi asked.

"Yeah," Allan admitted. "We're pretty sure."

The question flew around the room, unspoken: *you and who else?* Allan had the face of a man who'd already said far too much. Nobody was about to push him further.

"So what would you like us to do?" Doug inquired, speaking for the first time. Allan and the others looked over at him, pleased by how neatly the conversation had been turned around and put back on the track.

"Okay," Allan said, leaning his elbows against the counter. "We expect this guy to show up in the Village somewhere between nine and eleven tonight. What I'd like you to do is just cruise around and look for him. If you spot him, for God's sake don't get near him. Don't let him know you're watching. Just get to the nearest pay phone and call me here. That's all I want you to do."

"How about if we just grab him and knock his head in?" Navajo suggested.

"I'd love to grease that fucker's skids," Dean agreed.

"NO!" The violence of Allan's response startled them. "You've got to promise me to stay out of his way. Otherwise, forget it."

"Why?" Navajo spoke for all of them.

"Because . . ." He wanted to say *because you don't know what you're up against,* but decided against it. They'd go out of their way to prove how tough they were; he'd be forced either to deflate their collective machismo or explain that Rudy wasn't exactly human . . . and then they'd *really* want to be in on the action.

Which would be terrific, except that . . . I've already got enough people to fear for. I don't want to be responsible for any more.

"Because," he repeated, "we already know how we want to handle this. When you tell us where he is, we'll get him. That's just the way I want it done. Now, will you do that for me?"

The six messengers glanced back and forth at each other, considering it, weighing each one's reaction against their own, struggling toward consensus.

"I'll give you each ten dollars to kill the time with," Allan added, shrugging a bit foolishly at the piddliness of the sum.

"You already cut us out of the action," Dean pointed out abruptly. "Don't insult us by offering money."

"This is the guy who wanted to know how much," Jimi chided him.

"Actually," Art Dodger said slowly, embarrassed, "I don't even have enough money for a beer. . . ."

"I'll *lend* you the money, you heartless little twerp!" Dean yelled, but his grin gave him away. He turned to Allan, then, looking him straight in the eye and saying, "I don't know about anybody else, but I'll do it. You need a scout? You got one."

Jimi, Art Dodger, and Navajo were already nodding agreement. Zeke thoughtfully played with his beard, the eyes unfocused like a dreamer's. Doug watched him, also not decided yet, his own heavy considerations dangling before him.

Like *good* and *evil*, just for starters. Then on to *right* and *wrong*.

They were not considerations to be taken lightly. Not to Doug Hasken, at any rate. His continuing peace with God depended entirely on his obedience; and sometimes, it got awfully tricky to figure out what God's will actually was.

So when Zeke finally came out of his trance to answer in the affirmative, leaving Doug as the last one to commit himself by word or deed, he gave the only response that he honestly, safely could.

"I have something very important of my own to do tonight. It'll last until ten, I figure. As soon as I'm done, I'll give you a call." He shrugged. "That's the best I can do. I'm sorry."

Once again, as with Allan, the impulse was to ask him what was so godawful-damned important. Once again, the question was allowed to go unasked.

"Well, if that's it, then," Allan said, loudly sighing, "I won't hang you up any longer. I'll just need to start hearing from you around nine o'clock, okay?"

"You got it," Dean said, "speakin' for me and my cronies here." He made an unsubtle point of excluding Doug from their number.

Dean and his cronies departed then, noisily, leaving Allan and Doug alone in the office once more. Each of them had an unearthly secret that he dared not divulge to the other. But both of them wanted to. And both of them knew it.

"I really will call you," Doug said. His eyes were earnest.

"Okay," Allan answered. "That's all I can ask."

When they smiled at each other, it was in perfect understanding.

After Doug left, Allan slumped back in Tony's chair at the chief dispatcher's position. He thought about Tony and the rest of the guys in the office: the way they'd reacted after he gave them the bogus story about the late runs and asked them to back him up on it. "I don't know nothin' about it, buddy," Tony had said. "You took the call. That's all I know." Chester and Jerome had also agreed to silent complicity. But in all of their eyes, it was the same story again: the same curiosity, fear, and concern.

He thought about what was going to happen tonight: if they would find Rudy at all; and if so, what the final results might be. He wondered if anyone would die tonight; at the same time, he wondered how many. And who.

Then he thought about Ian again.

The clock on the wall said 6:20 now. That piece of information pleased him.

It gave him ten full minutes to cry and think and clear his mind before Joseph arrived, and the hunt began.

CHAPTER 37

Joseph's van pulled up in front of the office at 6:45. By that time, Danny and Claire had already arrived. They watched with Allan through the storefront window as Stephen and Josalyn piled out of the sliding side door, while Joseph came around to the passenger side and helped an unfamiliar old man onto the sidewalk.

"Who's that?" Claire wondered aloud, her eyebrows arching.

"A man that Joseph met the other night," Allan answered, barely aware that he'd done so. He, too, was staring in obvious surprise.

"It's Dr. Van Helsing," Danny quipped.

Claire laughed and smiled over at him. It had been very tense, all day, between them . . . at this point, she

wished that they'd never gone to bed . . . but Danny's
knack for keeping things silly was a trait that she really
admired in him. As much as it annoyed her, it charmed her
as well.

They watched as Joseph led the old man up to the
door, the other two following closely behind. For the first
time, they noticed the bright purple ring around Stephen's
eye; it was the second big surprise in as many minutes.
Allan laughed ruefully, knowing where it came from. It took
Danny a moment longer to figure it out. He wasn't quite so
amused.

"Joseph's not real crazy about Stephen, is he?" he
asked.

"You might say that." Allan chuckled, shaking his head.

"You mean . . . ?" Claire began, aghast. Allan and
Danny nodded in unison. She bit her lower lip and looked
at the floor. "I'm not so sure I like that," she mumbled. "It
scares me."

"It scares you," Danny echoed wistfully. He was
tempted to point out that her adorable vampire dreamboy
did a lot more than hand out black eyes. But the look she
flashed him let him know that she'd already gotten the
message. And hadn't appreciated it in the least.

Then the door opened, and the entourage began to file
in. Danny and Claire took one look at those eyes, and their
own problems shriveled into tawdry insignificance.

Such torment . . . such unspeakable gravity and
mangled emotion . . . they had never seen before.

The old man was the best. He smiled easily at them,
seeming very much in control. There was a sense of power
about him, an aura of wisdom and hard-won equilibrium
that struck them as he entered the room. But he was so old,
and the price of his victory so clearly etched upon him, that
his calm came off as chilling. He seemed to wear his own
death like a comfortable old suit, deriving satisfaction from
how perfectly it fit.

Stephen was next. He smiled weakly, unable to meet
anyone's gaze. He wore his bruise like the bare sleeve of a
court-martialed officer, after the stripes have been stripped
away. He was clearly a man who'd hit the bottommost trap-

door of his self-esteem: if he didn't bounce back up again now, there wouldn't be another chance. He'd just go down and down into that bottomless oblivion. And never come back.

But for sheer devastation, Josalyn was far and away the worst. Any life and strength and courage that she might have regained in the previous day had been wrenched away from her, as if a great talon had punched through her chest and ripped her heart out. When they met her gaze, it was like staring into the bottom of an empty glass.

And Joseph, who had held the door for the others and now closed it behind him, seemed to have aged twenty years in the space of a day. New folds and creases had popped up on his face, like tattoos rendered with an electric needle. His eyes were shiny and hard and cold: a pair of polished stones, glaring out of a rawhide mask. And his anger was a living presence in the air.

"Did those other guys show up?" Joseph asked Allan immediately.

"No, but they called again, about an hour ago. They should be here any minute."

"Good." Joseph turned back toward the door. "I gotta get some things out of the van," he said, over his shoulder. "I'll be right back."

As Joseph left the room, the old man approached Allan first, one liver-spotted hand extending in greeting. "My name is Armond Hacdorian," he said, an engaging musicality in his pronounced Slavic accent. "And you are . . . ?"

"Allan. Allan Vasey. Pleased to meet you." They shook hands.

"As I am pleased to meet *you*, my friend. Joseph speaks very highly of you; and for good reason, as I now see."

There was something vaguely disturbing about that statement, the smile and the handshake of the man behind it. It wasn't that Allan detected any hidden malevolence . . . far from it . . . but rather, it was the sense of being seen in a way that he couldn't even see himself. Being *seen through*, with wisdom and detachment. And being found, not to have a big booger hanging out of his nose, but to be of some mysterious value. It flattered and disconcerted him at the same time.

Armond left Allan to ramify in peace, turning his attention to Danny and Claire. *They are a pair of odd ones,* he concluded instantly. *Voyeurs in this enterprise: virgins who think that reading a book on the subject is the same as experiencing the act.* Their eyes, as he approached them, were wide as a hoot owl's; their awe amused him, even as it convinced them that they were entirely out of their depth.

He exchanged introductions with Danny first, found the young man to be extremely sharp and likable, but a bit quirky and unstable. Armond attributed it to drugs and rebelliousness . . . a stubborn refusal to let go of adolescence . . . that had stunted him in the subsequent years.

Claire was very much the same kind of person, hanging on to irresponsibility as if it were a freedom flag; but there was something else about her . . . a darker taint to her curiosity . . . that showed up in her ill-concealed fear of him. She had a secret reason for being here, with this group. And she was not to be trusted.

Not to be trusted. The thought made him nervous. So much was at stake. He hoped that he was better at concealing his emotions than she as he ran through the normal social amenities.

Then the door opened again, and he turned to see the two large men come into the office with Joseph. They were both dressed in dark clothing, and their nervousness radiated out from them in strong, jagged waves. Armond smiled at each of them in turn, automatically pleased to see them. Their experience with the horror was firsthand and genuine; he would not have to worry about coddling them. And they were, once again, very large, falling just short of Joseph in height and rivaling him in mass.

Joseph, typically, didn't bother to introduce them. He set two large duffel bags on the checkout counter noisily and paused to wipe sweat from his forehead. Then, without a word, he proceeded to empty the contents of the bag.

A dozen hefty stainless steel crosses: the ones that Ian

had been so impressed with. A dozen or so sharp wooden stakes, each one almost two feet in length, very much like the one that sent the life pouring out from Ian's nose, mouth, and belly. A dozen wooden mallets, the size of sledgehammers, at a third of the weight, suitable for driving in the stakes with deadly ease.

"Well, this is what we've got to work with . . ." Joseph began, when a muffled groan from elsewhere in the room stopped him cold. He turned just in time to see Josalyn's eyes roll back in her pasty-white face, her knees buckling beneath her. Allan was up and over to her in a second, catching her as she slumped toward the floor.

"Jesus Christ . . ." Joseph began again, impatiently.

"*Joseph.*" Allan hissed it between clenched teeth, trembling under the weight of Josalyn's body and his own' sudden anger. "Shut up. You aren't the only one here, all right?" He wavered for a moment, trying to get a more secure grip on her, while Joseph stared at him in silent shock.

One of the new arrivals . . . the black man . . . moved toward Allan and said, "Can I give you a hand, my friend?" Allan smiled tersely and nodded. The man picked up Josalyn's feet, and together they carried her over to the assistant dispatcher's chair, depositing her gently. Once the move was completed, they turned to each other and shook hands.

"T.C. Williams," the black man said.

"Alright. Allan Vasey. I spoke with you on the phone." They tightened their grips, solidifying the meeting, then disengaged. "And that's . . ."

"Tommy Wizotski," T.C. said, indicating his friend. Then he turned back to Josalyn's unconscious frame and asked, "She goin' to be okay?"

"Yeah, I think so," Allan answered, but his expression was rife with doubt. "She's just been riding the shitwagon too heavy for the last couple of days."

"I hear that," T.C. muttered solemnly. "And, hey, I'm sorry about what happened to your brother, you know? Ian was a good man." He paused for a moment, looking away. "Righteous," he concluded.

Allan nodded, looking away as well, wishing that he could just be allowed to forget about Ian for a little while. Every time the name came up, he weakened a little inside. And he couldn't afford to be weak. Not now.

"We are all here now, yes?" said a voice from behind him, and he turned to see Armond Hacdorian smile expansively around the room. A series of mute nods answered him, including Allan's own. "Then perhaps we can get started now. Too soon, the night will be upon us. We must be ready."

The statement, though addressed to them all, was specifically directed at Joseph. The big man hadn't said a word since Allan chastised him; he stood there, clenching and unclenching his fists, caught between humiliation and self-righteous anger. Now he looked up at Armond and saw the smile, saw the understanding of his predicament in the old man's eyes. Slowly, the tension within him decreased; he matched Armond's smile with one of his own.

Then he turned to Allan and said, "I'm sorry," waited for Allan to nod acceptance, ushered Tommy into the dispatch area with him, and added, "Now let's get this show on the road."

The meeting itself was short and to the point. Allan did most of the talking, of course: it was his plan, by and large, based on Ian's original ideas. Joseph stood beside him, nodding emphatically at each major point and making sure that everyone was paying attention.

The plan, in essence, was this:

Each of the hunters was given a messenger bag: a large burlap-and-canvas item with a shoulder strap. Each bag contained a beeper, a clipboard, a messenger manifest with the company's phone number printed across its top, a photocopy of Rudy's face, a pen, a cross, a mallet, a pair of wooden stakes, three vials of holy water, and a five-dollar roll of dimes.

The hunters would then split up into two groups: one led by Joseph, the other by Armond. They would stake out Stephen's and Josalyn's apartments, respectively. Both locations had phony notes planted on their doors: for example, Josalyn's note read STEPHEN, I HAD TO RUN TO THE STORE. I'll BE BACK IN FIFTEEN MINUTES. WAIT FOR ME. JOSALYN. This was intended to keep Rudy in one place long enough for dispatch to contact the other group and send them in as reinforcements.

Allan then explained about the messenger/scouts, their function as roving eyes for the hunting parties. He stressed the importance of the beepers, and of calling in to dispatch on a regular basis. "It's the only way we have of keeping tabs on each other," he told them. "Otherwise, we're all alone and in the dark. Also, it's the only way to cover an area the size of lower Manhattan."

It had been decided that Josalyn would remain in dispatch with Allan, to help him handle the phones and keep track of the hunt. She was obviously in no condition to be chasing Rudy all over the Village. There was some concern for Armond, as well, but the old man pshawed it, saying, "I am old, and I am slow; but I think that I may be of some use to us yet." No one could argue with that face, that voice, those smiling eyes.

The groups were then chosen, with a minimum of debate. Danny, Claire, and T.C. all went with Armond; Joseph's companions were Stephen and Tommy. Secretly, both leaders were pleased with the arrangement: Joseph wanted to keep an eye on Stephen, in much the same way that Armond felt about Claire.

After that, very little remained to be said. Tommy and T.C. emphasized the importance of being cool in the tunnels, if anyone happened to find themselves down there. "That's why we told Allan to have you all wear black," Tommy said. "If anybody catches us runnin' around down there, me and T.C. will wind up with our asses in a sling."

The clock on the wall said 7:45. In less than an hour, the sun would be well into its downward slide.

And the shadows would take over, devouring all light.

"Time to go," Joseph said abruptly. He was not surprised to see how many of them jumped.

By eight o'clock, Allan and Josalyn were alone in the dispatch office. To Allan, it was quite a bit like being entirely alone. Josalyn had awakened just before the meeting began, and she hadn't said a dozen words since. Her eyes were still focused on some spot in the unfathomable distance. She responded to sound; she sat upright in her chair; when he lit his pipe, she pulled a cigarette from her purse and followed suit. But she wasn't really there.

That was why he was so surprised when she turned to him suddenly and said, "Are they really going to kill him tonight?"

He looked at her, stunned. The soft lines in her face were taut with concern. The dazed expression was still in her eyes, but something was trying to cut its way through; the longer he looked into them, the cleverer they seemed to become.

"Will they really be able to do it?" she asked.

"I . . . I don't know," he said, flustered, regretting it instantly. *She doesn't need to hear that, stupid,* his mind chided him. "Yeah, I don't see any problem," he amended.

"Don't patronize me," she said with sudden force; and for a moment, her eyes were sharp as daggers. "A lot of people are going to die tonight. You know that, don't you?"

So much for that theory, Allan mused privately. "Yeah," he answered her. "I think I do."

"Do you think he'll kill them all?"

"No."

"Do you think"—and her eyes flared up again, this time with fear—"he'll find out where we are?"

"No way," he answered confidently. "We'll have him too busy running."

"But do you think they'll really be able to kill him? To make sure that he doesn't come back?" Her voice was loaded with so much emotion that he winced at the sound of it.

What do I think? he asked himself. *Does this stand a chance of working out? Can we actually kill a thing that's already dead, using pointy sticks and crosses, fercrissake?*

"I don't know," he said finally. "I really don't know."

The answer seemed to satisfy her. She turned away

again, silently puffing on her cigarette, while the distance crept back into her eyes. Leaving Allan, once again, alone in the room.

It was ten minutes after eight.

CHAPTER 38

Rudy, too, was waiting for the stars to come out.

He crouched, unseen, under a darkened workman's staircase on the low end of the Lexington Avenue line. His eyes were drowsy, thoroughly mad, and more redly luminous than the lit tip of the cigarette that he lazily dragged to his lips.

He had been waiting all day for the sun to go down.

Ever since the early morning . . . so early that it still deigned to be called the night, for dawn was far away . . . ever since he awakened from that terrible trance, with his rectum still throbbing memories from his pilloried violation, Rudy had been trembling on the near side of sleep. Several hits of speed, taken at regular intervals, had allowed him to maintain that uneasy state.

But it was the sleep of the dead that he deprived himself of. And the sleep of the dead is more demanding than the sleep of the living.

He twitched suddenly, the effects of the amphetamine that coursed through his almost bloodless veins. He didn't know how or why the blood left his system . . . it didn't seem to be coming out through his pores, and he had neither urinated nor defecated in eight solid days . . . but somehow it did, leaving him starving for more. And today, with no sleep to buffer the region between satiation and ensuing hunger, had been the most difficult of all.

Because he had been trapped down here in the

tunnels, with the slowly mounting emptiness alive inside his body. Because he had been helpless to do anything about it, pinned down by the sun and the busyness of daytime Manhattan. Never had he felt so restricted in the tunnels, so much like a prisoner wandering nightmare catacombs that offered no protection and no release. It made him crave surrender to the deeper darkness of sleep.

But he was afraid to sleep.

He was afraid to dream.

And so the nightmares had come to him awake, twisted fragments of imagining that skittered past him on spider-thin legs. Shadows, lurching out at him from nowhere. The ghostly echoes of ancient machinery, the timeless cries of men in pain. Strange flashes of light that yanked him away from the arms of slumber, like angels summoning him up to a place where he could never dwell. And wisps of laughter, terrible and familiar, that made the white flesh crawl over his bones.

Death without rest is a horrible thing. Rudy knew that now. An intimate knowledge. The Age of the Three-Day Creative Marathon was past. The Age of the Endless Party, as well: that surreal succession of barely glimpsed days that flipped past him like cards in a shuffling deck. Both of them, gone, as he grappled with the knowledge that he was in a strange place, where all the rules had been changed, and the path to Hell was the only road before him.

Most self-respecting vampires wouldn't touch speed with a ten-foot pole. They knew how badly they needed to forget, if only for a few hours. To forget how much worse it could so easily become.

Rudy's eyelids fluttered shut, pale membranes over the red luminescence. Now, with the sun's final surrender to the skyline, with the coming of the darkness that gave him life, he surrendered himself to death's whirlpool embrace. He let it suck him under, lapping over his head in dark whispering waves, lulling him as he settled into succoring folds, its replenishing depths.

As the seconds. Turned to minutes.

Into hours.

CHAPTER 39

The clock on the wall said 10:45.

And everybody was going insane.

"What do you *mean*, you still haven't heard anything?" Joseph screamed into the phone. "We've been out here for almost three fucking hours!"

"I know that, boss. I know that," Allan wearily replied. "I've been answering the phone for almost three fucking hours, and the only real thing that's happened is a vehicle run from Bankert and Company. Which means that not only do I have to listen to you guys scream at me I also have to put up with Vince."

"God," Joseph said, chuckling ruefully, the steam going out of him slightly. "You poor guy."

"Vince has got to be the biggest asshole in the world," Allan continued, gratefully playing on the change of subject. "Tell you what. After we're done with Rudy, let's take care of Vince, all right?" They laughed. "Bet you ten to one he decomposes on the spot. . . ."

The phone rang on another line. "Hang on a second," Allan said, about to put Joseph on hold.

"I'll get it," Josalyn said. She had gradually snapped out of it over the past several hours, the catatonia giving way to a deep depression. Allan wasn't sure that it was an improvement, but at least she was functional now.

"Josalyn's got it," he said into the phone. "So we were saying. . . ."

"Somethin' better happen soon." The tiny trace of levity had vanished once again from Joseph's voice. "There's starting to be some mutiny in the ranks. I can handle Stevie Baby: he gives me any more guff about going home, I'm

281

gonna knock his block off. But what can I say to Tommy, man? He's gettin' really tired of hanging around. If something doesn't happen, he's gonna take off, and I'll be left alone with the dipshit."

"I have Zeke on the line," Josalyn interrupted. "He says he wants to go home."

"Oh, Jesus," Allan muttered. He told Joseph to hang on for a second, then turned to Josalyn and said, "Ask him if he can hang out for another fifteen minutes. Just another fifteen minutes is all I ask." Josalyn nodded glumly and turned back to her phone.

"Tell me about it," he said, returning his attention to Joseph. "Armond's having the same problem with his people. And now all the messengers want to go home, too."

"Great."

"They've been doing a real good job for us," Allan emphasized. "Dean, Jimi, and Navajo have this really great routine worked out with their bikes. They'll rendezvous at one corner, mess around for a couple minutes, then fan out over a thirty-block radius and meet again on another corner a little further uptown. They've been calling every ten minutes since nine o'clock." He paused to empty his pipe. "And Zeke and Art Dodger have been busting it out, too. So it's not like they're not trying. It's just that . . ."

"He's nowhere." Joseph finished the sentence. "The sonofabitch has vanished from the face of the earth."

"Sorta looks that way, doesn't it?"

Joseph grunted a response.

"Would almost be nice if it were true," Allan continued.

"Balls. It'd be nice if he'd never been *born*." They laughed unpleasantly. "But I don't want him to get away that easily. I won't be happy 'til I nail him to the wall." Joseph's voice dropped down conspiratorially, and he added, "You know, I really hope that nobody else gets him. I really do. I understand why we need so many people . . . it's too big an area for me to cover all alone, and all that . . . but if anybody else gets him before I have a chance,

I'm gonna feel like I got ripped off. You know? Like some-body else got the prize that should have gone to me."

"Whoa, Joseph," Allan breathed. "The important thing is to *get* him, not . . ."

"Yeah, yeah. I know." Joseph sighed heavily into the receiver. "It's stupid, but I can't help it. I want his hide. He's mine. He's been mine ever since I saw that poor girl come out of the subway; and now, after what happened last night . . ." He let it trail off.

"I got you, boss. I'll do my best. We'll just have to see what happens, that's all."

"Yeah. Well." Allan heard the sound of a match being lit on the other end of the line. "If something doesn't happen pretty soon, I'm goin' down into the tunnels to look for him. Fuck this sitting around."

"Give it another half hour before you do anything. Okay?"

"All right."

Joseph hung up. Allan sat there, staring at the receiver for a minute. *This is turning into a disaster,* he thought. *A first-rate bomb. We're gonna sit around all night, waiting for something to happen, and then pick up tomorrow's paper and find out that the Subway Psycho has moved to Queens.* It was a discouraging thought; but everything about tonight had been discouraging, so far. It wouldn't have surprised him to find out that Rudy had rented a U-Haul and moved to Boston, where the subways were cleaner.

But not nearly as funky, he thought, reaching for his pouch of Captain Black . . .

When the door behind him opened.

Allan whirled, an inarticulate shout on his lips, the pipe flying out of his hand and striking the wall. Josalyn, too, whipped around suddenly with terror in her eyes. Both of them were all too aware that the remaining weapons were halfway across the room. *How did he find us?* Allan's mind was shrieking. . . .

"Hello?" Jerome piped in meekly, poking his head in through the doorway.

"Jesus Christ!" Allan yelled. He and Josalyn both slumped back heavily in their chairs, exchanging wide-eyed glances of relief. "You just scared the *hell* out of us!"

"Perhaps I should have knocked first," Jerome suggested, grinning mischievously. "May I come in?"

"Who *is* he?" Josalyn wanted to know. The cigarette between her fingers did the jitterbug with wild abandon.

"Some guy who works here," Allan informed her, still shaking like crazy himself.

"Some *guy!*" Jerome harrumphed. He turned to address Josalyn, Allan having sunken beneath his contempt. "I'll have you know that I'm the single most important person in the company's history. . . ."

The phone rang. All of them stared at it for a moment, as if it were an alien thing. Then Allan said to Josalyn, "Could you get that, please?" She obliged him, and he turned back to Jerome.

"I was worried about you," Jerome said, anticipating the question. "I've been worried about you all day. Finally, I just couldn't take it any more. So when I walked by the office, and saw that you were still here. . . ." He shrugged his shoulders.

"Dean says the guys want to go home now," Josalyn cut in. "What should I tell him?"

"This is just like work!" Jerome exclaimed. "Everybody wants to go home!"

"Ask him if they can hang out for just ten more minutes," Allan said.

"This *is* just like work!" Jerome re-emphasized.

"Shut up, Mary," Allan said, doing his best Tony impersonation.

"Now don't start," Jerome warned.

"They'll call back in ten," Josalyn said, hanging up the phone.

"Good men," Allan declared. "Aces, every one of 'em."

"So . . ." Jerome let the word drag out. "Is there anything I can do?"

"Well . . ." Allan let the word drag out twice as long.

"You could bring me a couple six-packs of beer if you wanted. I'm dying of thirst. Josalyn?"

"I'll have some beer," she said. "My nerves are going crazy. And I'm almost out of cigarettes."

"What do I look like?" Jerome demanded. "An errand boy?"

"No, you look like the fairy princess of my dreams. Now, if you can make the beer materialize with a wave of your magic wand. . . ."

"You can wave my magic wand, if you want to," Jerome interrupted, coy.

"Oh, God," Josalyn moaned, grinning for the first time tonight. It pleased Allan to see it.

"Just go get the goddamn beer before I stuff you back in your lamp," Allan grumbled.

"*You* can stuff me any old time you . . ."

"JUST *GO!*" Allan roared, and Jerome promptly tiptoed out the door.

"And don't forget my cigarettes!" Josalyn hollered after him. He peeked back in. "Salem Light 100's!"

Jerome disappeared, the door closing behind him. Allan and Josalyn looked at each other for a moment, then broke up laughing. "See what I have to put up with around here?" he said.

"I like him," she mused aloud. "He's funny."

"Yeah, but he's slow. By the time he gets back here, hot as it is, we'll be able to fry eggs on the beer cans." They laughed some more, fully aware of how badly they'd needed to. Privately, both of them thanked Jerome for coming in and breaking the ice. It had been a long, slow, nerve-wracking night.

Very soon, they would wish that it had stayed that way.

The time was eleven o'clock.

CHAPTER 40

At ten minutes after eleven, Doug Hasken finally freed himself from the endless spew of dogma that had detained him for the past four hours. It had been a singularly unpleasant experience . . . more so than he had expected . . . and it left him feeling more confused than when he went in.

If that's possible, he mused bitterly. *I was pretty messed up to begin with.*

He tarried for a moment longer in front of the Community Church of Greenwich Village. Through the storefront window, he could still see them: their lips in constant motion, prattling on and on about what marvelous sheep they were. It made him queasy, looking at them. It made him queasy to think about being identified with them in any way, shape, or form.

But I will be, he was quite sure. *I always will be. As soon as people find out that I believe in Jesus Christ, they'll lump me with every dumb Bible thumper who ever walked the Earth. They always have, and they always will.*

Goddamn it.

As if to punish him for using the Lord's name in vain, a design gracing the sign above the door called itself to his attention. It was such a typically tacky little piece of Christian fluff that he'd never really looked at it before. But he saw it now. And it weirded him out.

It looked like this:

"Godspo Hasken," he read aloud, then laughed uncomfortably. "I suppose I'll have to change my first name to Godspo now. Right, Lord?" He looked up into the silent, brooding sky for an answer. He didn't get it. He was not surprised.

Doug Hasken turned away from the Community Church of Greenwich Village, and all the madness surrounding it, roller-skating east on Bleecker Street toward the center of the Village. On his left, he watched a butcher shop whip past him, the meat hooks in the window speaking bluntly about their part in the endless slaughter. Just beyond it, at 257 Bleecker, a large sign confidently asserted: YOUR TRUE CHARACTER IS REVEALED THROUGH ASTROLOGY.

"Jesus," he moaned. It was more an invocation than a profanity, though it contained elements of each.

Doug paused at the center of Bleecker and Sixth Avenue, watching a pair of stranded punks dance in the middle of Father Demo Square while cars whizzed by them from every side. *Who's crazier?* he found himself wondering. *Those nuts out there, or the ones I just left behind? One group denies everything but its own senses. The other group denies its own senses to believe in a book. So who's crazier?*

It occurred to him strongly, and not for the first time, that the entire spinning universe was mad. It was not a thought that he was comfortable with, no matter how often it struck him. He pushed away from the curb, then, leaving both the corner and the question behind him.

Doug crossed Sixth with the traffic and wheeled rapidly down Bleecker. There was a bit of gridlock at MacDougal Street. It allowed him to pass the line of honking metallic insects with pathetic ease. "Get a pair of skates!" he yelled at one particularly grumpy man in the tie-up. The man responded in kind, suggesting to Doug that getting hit by a truck would be far too gentle a fate for a "cocksuckah like you." Doug waved bye-bye and left him in a very small cloud of dust.

On the other side of MacDougal, Bleecker was absolutely free of traffic. Doug took advantage of it, whipping down the middle of the street at full speed. He could do twenty miles an hour on his skates with no problem. He pushed it a little and wondered precisely how fast he *was* going. All he knew was that Sullivan Street was coming up on him with a speed many people would find alarming.

And that nothing, in Heaven or Earth, made him feel as good as the simple act of pushing himself to do more, go faster, be better.

Nothing, he thought, and then Sullivan Street was upon him.

He brought himself to a rapid halt, angling his right foot against the street and drawing a tight-yet-casual 360-degree turn. The effect was jarring and exhilarating all at once. He grinned, sighed, and pounded his chest with his fists like Tarzan before dutifully looking both ways. *Of course, nobody's coming*, he thought. *The day I don't look is the day I get nailed*.

The cars were coming up behind him on Bleecker now. He moved over to the sidewalk as he crossed Sullivan on the right-hand side. Skating among pedestrians was the slowest way to go, because most of them seemed to be the descendants of slugs. Even in New York City, where the average strolling speed looks like cross-country racing to the rest of the country, he always felt like he was surrounded by extras from *Night of the Living Dead*.

Which was an interesting thought for him to be having. Because, just as a trio of extremely fat tourists forced him to stop completely for a moment, he happened to glance across the street at a small, sleazy dive called Mills Tavern. The front door had just opened, allowing a discordant jangle of poorly performed rock music to tumble out into the street.

Something else was coming into the street.

Rudy.

Doug fell back against the wall, no longer interested in passing the tubby tourists. He recognized the face from the photocopy. Even in the shadow of the open doorway, eyes hidden by a pair of wraparound shades, there could be no mistaking it.

You forgot about Allan completely. You moron. You promised him that you'd call. All of those thoughts and more ran through a secondary channel in his mind. He heard them the way you can't help but overhear snatches of conversation from an adjacent dining room table. They were overwhelmed by his gut reaction, the sheer force with which it made itself clear.

That's the most evil-looking man I've ever seen, his gut informed him. And he knew, without a doubt, that it was true.

Doug watched in terrified fascination as Rudy emerged fully onto the sidewalk. He had a girl with him, Doug saw . . . a trollop, to be precise . . . who seemed to be having a hard time maintaining her balance. Rudy dragged her along behind him, grinning nastily as they moved back toward Sullivan Street.

At the corner, they paused, and he whispered something in her ear. Her head bobbed up and down like a cheesy dog-shaped dashboard ornament, and her shrill, drunken laughter rang in Doug's ears. It shot pain through his head, like biting down on tinfoil, though he had felt wonderful just moments before.

Why can't she see it? his mind screamed at him. *Why can't she feel how bad he is? What the hell is WRONG with her?* Once again, he looked up toward the heavens for guidance.

And was answered by the distant sound of thunder.

By this time, Rudy and the girl were crossing onto his side of Bleecker, moving downtown on Sullivan. He ducked into a doorway, mortally afraid of being seen; and he remembered Allan's insistence that the messengers stay out of the man's way. Suddenly, the urgency that Allan had shown made all the sense in the world.

I've got to call him, he realized. *I've got to call him now. Something terrible is going to happen if somebody doesn't get here right away. That girl is going to* . . . He didn't even want to think about it.

Doug peeked his head out of the doorway and looked down to the corner. They were gone. He wheeled back onto the sidewalk and moved quickly to the corner, peeking once again toward Houston Street.

Midway down the block, he could see them. She was still laughing and staggering; the man was practically holding her up as they moved rapidly toward SoHo, on the south side of Houston. Doug quickly skated across Sullivan and up to an unoccupied pay phone, digging in his pocket for a dime. A quarter availed more quickly; he singled it out, brought it up to the coin slot, put the receiver to his ear, and . . .

The phone was dead.

"Damn," he growled to himself, slamming down the receiver. There was another phone, right next to him, but it was occupied by a bony, white-skinned woman with bloodshot eyes and great dark smears of runny mascara down either cheek. Judging from the beret on her jet-black rectangular hairdo, she was an artiste of some sort. Judging from the way she twitched and shuffled around on her feet, she was either having a nervous breakdown or eating cold turkey.

He noticed all these things, but he didn't stop to think about them. The dark man and the girl were at the corner of Houston now, getting ready to cross. "Excuse me," he said to the woman on the phone. He tapped her on the shoulder, and she whipped her head around to smite him with dagger eyes.

"I have an emergency . . ." he heard himself weakly saying.

"YOU DON'T THINK THIS IS AN EMERGENCY?" she shrieked in his ear, shrill as a buzz saw down the length of his spine. "YOU DON'T THINK THAT MY WHOLE LIFE IS FALLING APART?"

Again, he heard himself mumbling apologies with an eerie sense of detachment as he backed away from her. A very un-Christianlike part of his mind was saying *I don't really care about your stupid problems, lady. Somebody is going to die because of your stupid problems.* But those thoughts would remain unspoken. The woman would only understand that she was being attacked, and he didn't have time for an argument. Especially not when . . .

They had disappeared.

"Oh, no." He stared down the block at the empty intersection for a long cold moment. *Could they really have crossed that quickly?* he asked himself. He didn't believe it, but the fact remained: they had disappeared, somehow, into the night.

He abandoned all caution now, blasting down Sullivan in reckless pursuit. Around him, the streets and sidewalks were empty. There was nothing to detain him as he pulled out all the stops, whipping down the cracked and potholed pavement that led to Houston and beyond.

He slowed at the intersection, letting the last few cars zip through the yellow light, taking a minute to scan the length of Houston. Nothing. If they had turned in either direction, he would have been able to see them; he was positive of it. Across the four-lane expanse of Houston, Sullivan Street receded into darkness, yawning before him like the mouth of a tunnel.

"That's where you are," he whispered aloud. "That's where you're hiding. I know it."

Doug took a last moment to look for a phone on any of the four corners. No such luck. He stifled the impulse to use vulgarity and moved across Houston with the light. At that point, his caution returned to him, and he slid up onto the right-hand sidewalk, deliberately slowing himself down.

He passed in front of Saint Anthony's Rectory, glancing across the street at the illuminated storefront of an all-night Laundromat. There were a few women inside, their laundry bags proportionate to their own body sizes: a fat lady with an enormous load, a scrawny old gal with a satchel so thin it looked like an understuffed sausage. The dark man and the girl weren't among them, not surprisingly.

Every other doorway on the block was lost in shadow.

The businesses were closed; the homes were locked and shuttered for the night. Doug paused for a moment, gauging the neighborhood, trying to spot the hole through which they had to have slipped. Then he rolled forward, very slowly, up to the edge of the rectory grounds.

From somewhere behind him, a moan.

Doug whirled. His eyes flashed on a human form that loomed above him, arms outstretched. Reflex knocked him back a foot and dragged a startled gasp from his lips. The shape remained poised, as if biding its time. His paralysis snapped, just as his mind fully registered the nature of the thing before him.

A very small statue of the Virgin Mary faced him, arms outstretched, head bent in supplication to the Lord. Doug stared at this symbol of mystical innocence for a long time, chiding himself. *You sure got a bad case of the heebie-jeebies, all of a sudden, getting scared half to death by the mother of Jesus.*

He took two short rolling steps backwards, still looking at the statue, not paying attention as the blackened stairwell to the rectory basement opened up to the left of his feet. He was only just turning to glance at it when the hand whipped out from the darkness and wrapped around his ankles.

Everything happened in the space of five seconds. He saw the girl, leaning against the wall with her blouse undone, her breasts exposed, the hips thrust outward, her ear pressed to the wall as if listening in on a neighbor's squabble. He saw the black cascade of blood that slithered down from her neck, tracing the contours of her bare shoulders and chest with wet skeletal fingers that grew before his eyes. He saw her mouth open as another moan escaped her: a weak, piteous, dying sound.

He didn't see the hand that was locked around his ankle, but he heard the sound of snapping plastic, felt the viselike pressure increase, screamed as a single claw burrowed into the muscle of his calf and sliced through the skin.

He yanked away desperately, the fingers sliding on the

plastic shinguards, losing their grip. The imbedded thumb-nail sliced a bloody four-inch arc around the side of his leg before ripping free as well. Doug staggered backwards, out of control. His arms flailed as his skates carried him off the edge of the curb, sent him stumbling into the street.

The Checker cab was moving down Sullivan Street, doing a cool 35 mph. At a distance of roughly five feet, the driver had virtually no reaction time. When the dark shape suddenly appeared in the center of his headlights, all he could do was slam on his brakes and shut his eyes.

The cab clipped Doug with its left front fender, sent him spinning crazily into a parked VW van. He slammed against the side, bounced, hit it again, and grabbed onto the sideview mirror before his skates slipped out from under him. He hung there, his legs splayed out behind him, his right hip curiously numb but unbroken.

"ASSHOLE!" the cabbie screamed at him, punching the accelerator. The Checker lay a squealing patch of rubber in its wake as it thundered down the street and away.

Slowly, Doug began to upright himself, sliding his feet forward to line up with the sideview mirror that he still clutched desperately in his hands. He was dazed, the numbness spreading through his entire body now, dulling his senses and muddying his thoughts. He achieved an awkward balance, steadying himself with difficulty. Only then did he look back in the direction of the horror.

The dark man was coming.

Like a corpse rising out of its grave, Rudy climbed to the top of the stairs. Every step made him appear to grow larger, more terrible. The cloud-smothered light of the moon played across his white features, twinkling on the dark wet slick around his chin, the merciless black slash of his wraparound shades.

Doug was frozen in place. He couldn't move. He couldn't breathe. He watched in helpless terror as Rudy stepped onto the sidewalk, gaining his full height, and moved to the edge of the curb.

"I *see* you!" the dark man called in a terrible, sing-songy voice. "Allee-Allee-*out's*-in-free!"

Then Rudy smiled. And his hand came up. And he slowly removed his glasses.

Doug's knees gave out as the red eyes bored into his own. His mind went totally blank for a second. His skates slid out from under him.

He hit the ground hard, landing flat on his ass. Awareness flooded back into him: sharp pain, sudden terror. His eyes snapped back into focus as his mind clicked on; he saw that the dark man was laughing hysterically, and a voice in his head said *get out of here NOW!*

Doug scrambled to his knees and got his wheels under him before Rudy had a chance to think. He was up on his feet and moving before Rudy had a chance to leave the curb. He closed his eyes and pumped his legs with every bit of strength he could muster. His teeth tore into his lower lip; his ears rang with the sound of rapid footsteps behind him, the sudden roar of inhuman rage that grew fainter and fainter as he pushed himself to go faster, go faster. . . .

And he opened his eyes. And Prince Street was before him: twenty yards away and closing fast. He slowed himself down and did a neat 180-degree turn. Far behind him, less than halfway down the block, a dark figure hollered and waved its fists.

"You can't have *me*, you bastard!" Doug yelled, laughing, out of breath. His voice didn't carry; he was too happy to care. "Too quick for you, huh? Just a little too quick. . . ." Before he even knew it, the laughter had turned to tears. Tears of joy. Tears of relief. Tears that shouted triumphantly, *I'm alive! I'm alive!*

Then he remembered the girl in the stairwell, and his own proximity to death. He remembered the pressure of the hand around his ankle. The sudden glare of headlights. Those eyes: the devil's own. The full monstrousness of the encounter came back to him; and the tears turned bitter, scalding in his eyes.

Quickly, he turned away and rolled forward to Prince, took a left at the corner and started heading east. At the corner of Prince and Thompson, there was a pay phone; he could see it, rather faintly, through the tears. He moved toward it, digging once again in his pocket for a dime.

He reached the phone, brought the receiver to his ear. *It works*, he marveled, managing a grin as he dropped the coin into the slot.

The phone rang. It rang again. *"Come on,"* he hissed into the mouthpiece, looking over his shoulder to make sure that the dark man hadn't followed him here. The phone rang again.

On the fourth ring, Allan answered. "Still nothing, damn it," the dispatcher grumbled.

"I found him!" Doug shouted into the receiver, half crazy. "Oh, God, Allan! Oh, Jesus! You didn't tell me how *bad* . . . !"

"You did WHAT?" Allan's voice screamed back in his ear. Doug shook his head, heard Allan shout something unintelligible to somebody else, felt the adrenaline rush through his system again. Then Allan was back on the line, speaking to him in a level voice of manufactured calm. "Who is this?" Allan asked.

"This is Doug!" he yelled. "And I found that guy . . . that *thing* . . . God, I don't know. . . ."

"Where are you, boss?" Allan interrupted him, voice crackling with intensity. "Just relax, and tell me exactly where you are."

"P-P-Prince Street," he stammered. "I'm on Prince Street and T-Thompson." Trying to be calm was much harder than shouting. He listened as Allan rattled off the coordinates. Someone else's voice distantly echoed the words. Listening to them talk made him crazy, and he shouted, "What the hell *is* he, Allan? You've got to . . . "

"I think you'd better come into the office now, Doug." Allan's voice was a drone. "I'll explain it to you here."

The women in the Laundromat were afraid to venture near the window. They huddled in the back, with the heat from the dryers baking the sweat onto their bodies. They would not so much as glance toward the street.

They'd come running at the sound of the squealing

brakes, seen the cabbie drive off, and felt vaguely disappointed. Then the dark man appeared from out of nowhere, rekindling their interest.

When he took off his glasses, one of the women screamed, and they had all recoiled in horror.

And when the wild howling had erupted from the street, they had moved to the rear of the building, where they remained.

Later, when a half hour of silence has passed, they will slink furtively up to the window and look. Seeing nothing, they will venture out into the street. A more observant one will notice the strange new fresco on the rectory's white wall: a frenetically rendered mishmash of scribbled words and images.

Then all of them will notice the yards and yards of pale white entrails, glistening in the moonlight like fat strands of tinsel, draped over the outstretched arms of the Virgin Mary and then streaming back down to the stairwell and their source.

Then all of them will scream, and several of them will faint, and one of them will find it in her to call the police before blacking out herself.

Thereby alerting the city to Rudy's first victim of the night.

CHAPTER 41

At 11:43, when all the beepers started going off at once, Armond's hunting party was deep in the grip of a long and protracted silence. The joking, the theorizing, the brief personal biographies had gradually given way to complaints, brief flirtations with mutiny, and conflict. At just the point where everybody's control was threatening to snap, the silence had set in. It was the only thing that kept them from each other's throats. It was a blessing in a very uncomfortable disguise.

Even Armond's patience had been wearing thin, listening to the chatter. Danny's glibness, Claire's catlike detachment and T.C.'s blunt impatience had become an annoyance, like the buzzing of flies in his ears. What made it worse was the fact that they seemed to be missing the point; everything they said seemed so extraneous. They seemed to have no sense of how *real* the situation had become . . . how *real*, their proximity to genuine evil. Listening to them, they could have been kids waiting to be picked up for a show, pissed off because their ride was late. Despite Armond's best efforts, it was really starting to get under his skin.

That was why he was grateful for the silence: it gave him the chance to realign himself, to be ready when the moment came.

That was why, when Danny's beeper erupted into song, Armond was already moving out of the shadow and over to the phone before Danny had a chance to turn it off.

Suddenly, all of their beepers were beeping together. It sent a shock wave through the group, set off a flurry of motion. T.C. and Claire grappled with their messenger bags, trying to locate the little buttons that would shut off the sound. Armond let his beep for a minute, patiently punching dispatch's number into the pay phone. After several hours of repeated dialing, he had it down pat. Only after the phone had begun to ring did he calmly silence the beeper.

Josalyn answered on the second ring with a nervous, "Hello? Who is this?"

"This is Armond. You have heard something, yes?"

Allan clicked instantly onto the line, heard the tail end of the question. "Armond?" he said, and his voice was profoundly agitated. "Good. We've spotted him, not too far away from here."

"You are certain?" Armond, trying hard to restrain his own rising excitement.

"Oh, yeah." Allan's quick laugh had the taint of hysteria. "The kid who saw him is half-scared out of his mind. There's no question about it. It's Rudy, all right."

"Where?" Armond heard a rustling of paper behind him, turned to see that the others were gathered by the phone. Danny had his pen and clipboard ready.

"In SoHo, right around where Thompson hits Prince. That's where he was spotted. . . ."

"Wait a moment," Armond interrupted, repeating the location to Danny. He could see that the others were studying their maps closely. "Yes," he said finally. "Go on."

"Just look for him in that general vicinity. Joseph and the others will be down to help. Just look for him, and *stay in touch*. If we can pin him down now, it's all over."

"How long ago was he seen?"

"Less than five minutes. He couldn't have gotten far."

"Thank you," Armond said, and hung up.

"We're supposed to go look for him?" Danny asked. His eyes were huge as Armond nodded.

"We need a cab," T.C. muttered, sourly scanning the length of Mercer Street.

"Lots of cabs on Broadway," Claire pointed out. "It's only a block over this way."

"That's the wrong way to Thompson," Danny interjected whinily.

"We need a cab, man," T.C. reiterated, nodding at Claire. "Let's go for it."

They all looked at Armond. He nodded and said, to Claire and T.C., "If you would run quickly to hail a cab, Danny will accompany me. Yes?" They nodded and took off toward Bleecker, disappeared around the corner. "Come," he said to Danny. "We must go as quickly as I can."

Danny grinned and paced him as they moved slowly toward the corner.

Danny's smile did nothing to hide his terror. Armond had considered talking seriously with him about Claire, urging him toward caution and a watchful eye; but it was clear now that Danny would come apart like a rag doll. As it stood, he was hanging together by a thread.

So instead, Armond reached up to take the young man gently by the forearm and say, "You will be fine, Danny. Of that much, I am certain." Danny looked down at him questioningly. Armond smiled back at him. "I cannot see the future, my friend. But I can feel things coming. I can sense them in the air. And I feel very good about you now."

Danny didn't know what to make of this information, coming from the old Van Helsing surrogate. He didn't know whether the old man was being legit, or just making it up as he went along. Armond, too, was momentarily confused. He'd started by just trying to comfort Danny; but when he'd started to talk, a very clear picture had come into his mind.

A picture of Danny, laughing and pointing at something that signified victory, comforting another in their time of deepest despair. . . .

And then it was gone.

They rounded the corner in silence now, each one lost in his own private speculative Hell. They had not gone more than ten feet when Danny noticed the Checker cab backing toward them, T.C. hanging out the back window and waving at them. They exchanged tense smiles, and Armond squeezed Danny's arm once more for good measure, before the cab pulled up in front of them and they hopped inside.

The chase was on.

The time was 11:55.

For the next fifteen minutes, they conducted a fruitless search of SoHo, whipping up and down every side street within a ten-block radius of the sighting, alternately shouting conflicting directions as the poor, disgruntled cabbie did his weary best to oblige them. He was right on the verge of kicking them the hell out of his cab when Armond slipped him a ten-spot and assured him that it was very important. Grudgingly, the cabbie accepted it. The search continued.

Armond's beeper went off just as they hit Lafayette Street on Houston, one block away from dispatch. They briefly considered just stopping by the office; while they debated it, the cabbie pulled over to the curb and put it in park, impatiently drumming his knuckles on the dashboard.

That was when a sudden cry from Danny ripped through the cab like a poison-tipped spear. That was when they turned to stare in the direction of his trembling, pointing finger. That was when they noticed the dark figure that moved slowly up Lafayette, with the street light dancing briefly on the bleached blond pompadour that crowned his head.

"Omigod," Claire whispered.

"Let us out here, man," T.C. told the cabbie, nudging Claire toward the door.

"Wait a minute!" the cabbie yelled. "You owe me . . ." He looked at the meter; it added ten cents before he shut it off. ". . . seven-anna-half bucks, buddy!"

"Here," Armond said, slipping another ten dollars through the slot. "We thank you for your kindness."

"Let's go," T.C. said, nudging Claire again. She snapped out of her little trance and opened the door, stepped numbly onto the pavement. They piled out after her, slammed the door, caught a glimpse of the cab driver's head shaking exasperatedly as he peeled out and away from them.

Leaving them on the corner, across the street and a block away from the dark figure that disappeared now, slowly, into the uptown entrance of the Bleecker Street subway station.

"We got to move fast," T.C. muttered, "before he gets away again. We be chasin' him all over town."

"I'm embarrassed . . ." Armond began, looking up at T.C. with a sheepish grin that made the big man pause. "I am so slow, and so small, and . . . and I wanted to ask you . . ."

T.C.'s woolly features cracked into a smile. "You want a *lift*, my man? You got it!"

"I thank you so much," Armond responded as he was hoisted up and cradled to the big man's chest.

"I promise I won't break ya, all right?" T.C. said, laughing, as he stepped out into the street at a rapid clip. Armond was pleased to see that Danny and Claire were smiling as well; in that moment, he found that he both loved and feared for them very much.

It was the first, and the last, warm moment that they would ever share.

The uptown local was coming. They could feel and hear its thunderous approach, shaking the pavement beneath their feet as they rushed down the subway stairs.

"Damn," T.C. moaned, puffing and panting between the phrases. He still had Armond cradled in his arms. "Anybody got a token?"

"I've got slugs," Danny offered, panting just as much without the extra burden. Armond gave him a funny look. "Black market duplicates. Work just like the real thing. At five for a dollar, you can't beat 'em."

"Where you get those things?" T.C. wanted to know.

"You just have to know the right people," Danny answered, winking.

They hit the bottom of the stairs. T.C. set Armond down in front of the turnstiles, and Danny doled out the bogus tokens, just as the train stuck its nose into the station. They moved quickly onto the platform and turned toward the sound. Rudy was there, near the end of the platform, alone.

"Claire," Armond said quickly, turning to her. "I want you to stay here and call the office. . . ."

"WHAT?" she yelled over the roar of the train. A red flush crept into her features.

"Please," he said. "There's no time. You must call Allan and have Joseph pick you up. We will need you all at the next station. Please."

"IT'S NOT FAIR!" she yelled. The tears were starting to come now. She glanced down the platform at Rudy, saw that he was watching them with smug detachment. Without being fully aware of it, she gave him a desperate look. Rudy frowned and cocked his head.

"You better do what he said," T.C. growled. He didn't miss the exchange. It filled him with a sudden and deep distrust.

Before them, the train shuddered to a halt.

"Please," Armond said, but it was not a beseechment. "Believe me; it is for the best."

Claire looked at Danny for help, but he refused to meet her gaze. The tears had arrived; her hands were balled up into fists of helpless fury. T.C. watched her with impassive eyes. Armond nodded grimly, sympathetically, and conclusively.

The doors opened.

"I'll do it," she said finally, her voice cracking under the strain. "But I'll never let you forget it." Then, addressing this last part specifically to Danny, "You fuckers!"

Danny took it like a slap across the kisser. He started to protest weakly, but she would have none of it, turning away to watch as Rudy boarded the second car from the rear. Armond took Danny's arm gently and said, "Come." Then he led the young man backwards onto the train, T.C. beside them.

"I'm sorry . . ." Danny called after her.

As the doors slid smoothly shut.

Claire "De Loon" Cunningham stared at her shoes as the train rumbled slowly away from the station. Only once did she glance up, just in time to see a flash of Rudy's face staring out the window at her with something like confusion. Then he was gone, the last car whipping by her, gradually picking up speed as the dark mouth of the tunnel sucked it in.

Leaving her alone in the Bleecker Street station.

"Be careful," she whispered, very quietly. "Please be careful." She was not at all sure to whom the statement was addressed.

It was now 12:25, precisely.

Rudy Pasko was alone in the second-to-the-last car. The two young couples that had shared it with him, for all of forty-five seconds, had moved to the safety of the next car up. Like Doug, they had never felt such evil; unlike Doug, they had no interest in checking it out. Later, they would remark to friends that every hair on their bodies stood on end when he walked through the door, and that the car had seemed to turn cold as a meat locker. "If we hadn't gotten out of there," they'd say, "he would have killed us. We just *knew* it. . . ."

But in fact, Rudy had barely given them a second thought. He was thinking about the Bleecker Street girls: the one that now decorated St. Anthony's Rectory, and the one that remained at the station behind him. The former gave him no problems; that was a jolly bit of fun; he'd like to do it again some time, maybe take a dozen slaves up to St. Patrick's Cathedral and whip up something *really* creative.

But the second one bothered him. He wanted to know why she got on the platform if she wasn't going to get on the train. He wanted to know . . . not out of humanitarian reasons, of course, but because he sensed that it was somehow important . . . why she was crying.

And he wanted to know where exactly he'd seen her before. There was something hauntingly familiar about that face, something that stood poised in the back of his brain like a word on the tip of his tongue. He *knew* that he knew her, and it was driving him crazy, and there was absolutely nothing he could do about it.

Because Rudy's mind was not working properly. Rudy's mind was like a train derailment, irreparably twisted and battered, an Independence Day pig-out of fiery explosions. It had more kinks in it than Plato's Retreat. Killing the girl, and the couple hours of sleep, had helped a little. Now he just felt like someone on a bad acid trip, as opposed to a baby left abandoned on the doorstep of Hell.

He stared out the window at the dark walls of the tunnel, trying to get the night in order. *First Josalyn, then Stephen*, he thought; but beyond that, things started to get hazy. He didn't know where to hide the bodies, for one thing . . . how to keep them safe from the sun, and under his control. Should he lure them down into the tunnels, save himself the trouble of trying to find good stash places? Could he actually lure them anywhere, now that he'd spent so much time scaring them half to death? Could he, perhaps, control them in wakefulness the way he controlled them in sleep? Could he *make* them come to him?

He didn't know. He wasn't sure. Nothing was coming out the way he'd planned it. Everything was going ka-blooie, blowing up in his face like a loaded cigar. The last twenty-four hours had wreaked serious havoc on more than his balls, brain, and bunghole; they had also done a serious number on his confidence.

Like a little girl, I take you, the ancient voice regaled him; and then Ian, as Bullwinkle, saying *watch me pull a rabbit outta my hat!* And again, more recently, not in words but in pictures, the roller-skating one-that-got-away. The mocking sounds and visions ganged up on him, made him feel cheap and shitty as they kicked him around.

So Rudy was not in peak form when the door at the front of the car slid open. He whipped around suddenly, wired-out and startled; when the three men stepped in and closed the door behind him, fear massaged his chest like a cold set of hands. He took an automatic step away from them, watching their faces. They were staring at him.

They were seeing him clearly.

It was the one in the middle that scared the piss out of him. Not the one on the left: he looked like a gimp, a sixties throwback, threatening as a toothpick and almost as thin. Nor the one on the right: he was big, he looked strong, but size and strength weren't the problem. If they were, the little old man in the middle wouldn't have rated doodle-e-squat.

But he does. Rudy knew it. It was something about the eyes. They saw him, they knew him, he could feel them bore into him like hot steel pokers.

But they did not seem to fear him in the least.

Rudy trembled under their gaze. The thought of the ancient one who called himself "Master" leaped into his head, and he almost cried out. For a moment, he was sure that the monster had found him; the chill started at his rectum and worked its way up his spine. Then he realized that, no, it was just a man, just an old man. . . .

Just an old man with something very strange about him.

It's just an old man, Rudy chastened himself. *You could waste him in a second. Relax.* He forced himself to look tough and detached, insofar as he could; and his voice trilled slightly in the higher frequencies as he said, "Who do you think *you're* lookin' at? Huh?"

Of course, it would have to be the old man who answered.

"We're looking at you . . . Rudy," he said. And smiled.

T.C. reached into his messenger bag and pulled out the .357 Magnum, just as Armond was unzipping his satchel. Danny stood to the right of them, mute and motionless, his hands as limp as his eyes were wide.

Rudy grinned at the round mouth of the Magnum's barrel as it raised to a level with his face. He sneered, exposing his teeth; and T.C.'s aim teetered slightly as he recoiled in shock.

"You don't think you could hurt *me* with that thing, do you?" Rudy said, laughing. "Don't be silly. I could bend it over your head."

"They're silver bullets, Rudy," Armond kindly informed him. "And they're blessed."

"*So?*" He tried to act indifferent, but some doubt seeped into his face.

"So you wanna find out?" T.C. offered, flicking off the safety and steadying his aim.

Rudy looked extremely uncertain and not at all happy. Armond watched him wrestle with the fear, was amused by it. *He truly does not know himself,* the old man mused. *What makes him live. What makes him die. Joseph's friend was right: the monster is a motherless child in the wilderness.*

But so dangerous. He reminded himself not to forget that. *So dangerous.* As his hand reached into the satchel.

"Danny," he said quietly, nudging the gangly longhair with his elbow. "Danny. Now." Danny started, his eyes blank for a moment; then he opened his messenger bag and pulled out a mallet and stake. Rudy shrank back, all question removed from his face. Armond nodded his head somberly.

And held up the cross.

Nothing in either life or death had helped Rudy to prepare for the pain that followed. It burned in his flesh like the heat from a building in flames; it ripped through him like shrapnel, like great shards of exploding glass; it screamed through his nervous system like a 220-volt injection. But that was not the worst of it, by any means. The worst of it was to look.

It was like staring into the heart of the sun.

Rudy whirled and screamed, his hands clamped over his eyes. *I'm BLIND!* his mind shrieked. *I can't SEE! I can't SEE!* The train hit a bad bump and shuddered violently. He stumbled, reaching out, and his eyes jerked open just as the floor came up to meet his face.

Then everything, all his senses, became very clear. He could hear the footsteps, rapidly approaching. He could smell the adrenaline rush. The floor was crawling with bright dots of white light, big as beach balls; but he could *see* the floor, behind the dots, stretching all the way down to the back of the car.

All the way down to the door . . .

. . . the open door . . .

. . . and suddenly he was scrambling toward it, getting to his feet before the first startled roar erupted from behind him, on his feet and *running* now, *running*, as the train threw him from side to side and the chorus of shouting voices mounted in intensity and the first shot went off, a thunderclap followed by a whistling past his ear that turned into a *pwinging* and a *pwinging* and a shattering of glass as the bullet ricocheted off one wall, then another, and then smashed through a window, but none of that mattered because he was running, running faster, and the door was right in front of him, he could see the floor buckling on the platform between it and the door that lay beyond it, also open, also waiting for him as he went through the first door and leaped across the space between and landed in the last car of the train with both feet, still running, still running, toward the back . . . .

. . . toward the end. . . .

There was a window in the back door of the uptown local: a goodly sized, rounded, porthole type of affair. A stout iron bar, several inches in diameter, ran horizontally through the dead center of the circle. The back door, of course, was eternally locked; its window was designed to remain shut forever.

As T.C. and Danny raced into the last car, they didn't notice the half-dozen staring commuters who speckled the seats to either side. Nothing to either side of them held the tiniest bit of interest.

They were totally and exclusively engrossed in the spectacle of Rudy Pasko, bearing down on that big fat bull's-eye in the middle of the door. Even as they barreled toward him, dodging the poles in the middle of the aisle, their eyes helplessly locked upon him.

They knew what he was going to do.

"STOP, MAN!" T.C. yelled, dropping back and drawing a bead on the junction between Rudy's shoulder blades and spine.

Rudy kept on running.

"I SAID STOP!"

He kept running.

"MAN, THAT'S *IT*!"

Rudy hurled himself forward, like an arrow, toward the window.

T.C. fired.

. . . *and he felt himself flying, a remarkable sensation, as the twin thunderclaps went off in unison, one from behind him that shot the whistling out past his ear again, the other wrapping around his ears like a symphony as the*

*top of his head struck the stout iron bar and bent it,
stretched it, snapped it in half, while the glass sprayed and
tinkled all around him like confetti, like the brightly
colored crystals of a kaleidoscope that was being spun as
he was being spun, end over end, by the impact and the
wind and the force of his own momentum, carrying him
outward into the darkness of the tunnel, sending him
downward in a mad loop-de-loop, spiraling crazily toward
the tracks. . . .*

Danny's face was framed squarely in the shattered
window opening. He saw, with exquisite clarity, the way in
which Rudy hit the tracks, flipped over precisely five times,
landed on his feet, regained his footing, and continued to
run as if nothing had happened.

Running back the way he came.

Behind him, T.C. was yelling something about how
nobody better say a *word* about this, not a goddamn word
to *anyone*. But Danny didn't hear him.

There was only one thing on his mind.

Claire was still alone on the uptown platform. A dime
was poised uneasily on the lip of the coin slot as she leaned
against the pay phone, the receiver to her ear. She listened
to the dial tone for about thirty seconds, shook her head,
hung up the phone, sulked for a few more seconds, picked
up the phone, and listened to the dial tone. She had been
doing this for the last three minutes. It had worked itself
into sort of a routine.

I feel so stupid, she thought. *Standing around like
this.* But she couldn't help it. She was genuinely torn, her
mind at war. The fact that one side was completely insane
did nothing to mitigate its power and influence.

Especially when the other side had just finished
pissing her off.

Her arguments for outrage were many and varied,
beginning with the obvious (why did *I* have to be the one
that called? Why couldn't somebody *else* have done it?),
moving on to the politics of gender (women *always* get left

behind, those macho sexist assholes, they'll want me and Josalyn . . . The Amazing Collapsible Woman . . . to make them coffee when all the fun is over), wading knee-deep into jealousy (what does he *see* in her, anyway? Why do *men* get to have all the excitement?), and winding up in the Grand Corral of Spite (you left me holding the bag, I hope you screw it up and die).

But the bottom line, once all the petty dross was swept away, came down to this:

> 1) the monster is horrible, and it needs to be destroyed;
>
> 2) the monster is gorgeous . . . and if they kill it, I'll never know what might have happened. . . .

Come on, Cunningham, said a voice in her mind. *Shit or get off the pot, alright?* The voice startled her for a moment, largely because it was not her own, and also because it took a moment to recognize. It had only been four days, but it seemed like forever.

Maybe it was because she'd never really liked Dorian all that much. Dorian was much more of a slut than Claire would ever be, and Claire resented it in a strange way. It was, like, Dorian seemed to feel that she was playing the only game in town: if you were with her, you *had* to compete. And Claire would always lose.

In a way, she wanted to win the game that Dorian lost.

But if you lived with a person, whether you liked them or not, you got close to them. Little things became precious . . . in a very subconscious manner, of course: you adjusted to them, they became part of your world, you came to see the bits of diamond in the coal. It was like living in a harsh environment: a desert, a jungle, a city. Oppressive conditions at every turn, but how many people would ever think of leaving?

Claire never really did like Dorian that much, but she did like her a little. Enough to live with her since January, and consider renewing the lease.

She saw Dorian's head on the floor, in her mind, and knew that she'd liked Dorian better than *that*.

Shit or get off the pot, alright? Dorian used to say that all the time, when they were alone together. *You want him? Go get him. Shit or get off the pot, alright? Somebody's gonna jump his bones if you don't hurry up. And it might be me.*

She was saying it again, her head on the floor. Claire heard it, and saw it, very clearly.

Claire put the dime in the phone.

On the second ring, Allan answered. "Armond?" he said.

"No. Claire. Listen . . ."

"Why hasn't Armond been answering his goddamn beeper?"

"Because he hasn't had a chance. Now listen a minute."

Allan paused, apparently listening.

"I'm at the Bleecker Street station, where the 6 train comes. We followed Rudy down here. . . ."

"WHAT?" Allan shrieked. It was hard to tell what he felt.

"We followed Rudy down here," she repeated, refusing to be cut off, "and the boys went on the train with him up to Astor Place. I'm supposed to get Joseph to pick me up so we can all drive up there together. . . ."

"Jesus Christ! How long ago did this happen?"

"Oh, about . . ." She decided quickly not to lie. "Four minutes ago."

"Why didn't you call sooner . . . ?"

"My dime was stuck in the slot." Not *entirely* a lie. "You better call Joseph, and . . ."

"He's on another line," Allan said impatiently. "Hang on."

He put her on hold. She sighed, listened to the complete absence of sound coming from the receiver, and turned toward the front end of the station.

Just as Rudy appeared in the mouth of the tunnel.

* * *

"I've been driving around for *twenty minutes!*" Joseph screamed into the phone. "Why didn't they call you sooner?"

"I guess they just didn't know any sooner, boss." Allan was freaking out, but trying hard to contain it. He wished that Josalyn would get out of the bathroom . . . not that she'd been in there long, just that she had to pick *now* to do it, with everything going berserk.

There were two empty Buds next to his phone. He swigged heavily on the third.

"He's probably up there already!" Joseph's voice hollered tinnily in Allan's ear.

"Excuse me . . . ?" Pulling the can from his lips.

"Up at Astòr Place! I gotta get there!"

"But what about Claire . . . ?"

"Fuck Claire! She's safe, isn't she?"

. . . and he was climbing now, climbing . . .

Two more phones rang. Allan desperately eyed the bathroom door. Josalyn was not forthcoming.

Two phones? Allan marveled, flustered. *Who else could be calling?*

"Hang on," he said, and put Joseph on hold.

. . . climbing up onto the platform . . .

He was climbing up onto the platform now. Claire watched him, not really believing, the dead phone still pressed to her ear.

"Hello?" the voice said. "This is Vince. . . ."

"OH, JESUS CHRIST!" Allan screamed, slamming down the hold button. "JEROME! WOULD YOU DEAL WITH THIS IDIOT?" His voice remained at a uniform pitch throughout.

There were three lines on hold now, and one line still ringing. Allan reached for the ringing line and punched it in.

* * *

*. . . and she was down there, he could see her, in the
center of the platform . . .*

"Allan! Allan!" He could hear Armond's frantic voice,
but not well. It was obscured by the sound of a moving
train.

"You're at Astor Place?"

"Yes, yes!" Armond sounded terribly agitated. "You
have heard from Claire?"

"Yes, she . . ."

"Is she safe?"

"Yeah, but . . ." Allan's face screwed up in puzzlement. "What do you mean?"

Another train, much louder, rolled by, completely
drowning out Armond's response.

. . . and he was moving toward her . . .

He was moving toward her. She watched him, en-
tranced. It was like a dream. Like a dream. The way he
moved toward her. So slowly. So slow that it seemed like
the whole world had shifted into low gear. Like time had
slammed on the brakes. And the moments were stretching.

Claire's eyesight was not very good. She had worn
corrective lenses since she was eight. Her contacts helped a
lot; but she still had a problem with details in the distance.
As Rudy moved toward her, he looked to her eyes like a
punked-out Prince Charming. *He's coming back for me,* a
little voice in the back of her mind squealed delightedly.

Then he got a little closer, and he didn't look quite so
good.

She remembered the dead phone, still pressed numbly to her ear.

"Hello?" she said quietly into the mouthpiece.
"Hello?"

"*What?*" Allan yelled over the roar of the train, and
then Armond's voice came back in.

"Rudy has escaped through the back window of the train, Allan! Danny saw him running back . . ."

"Toward Claire." Allan finished the sentence. "Oh, my God . . ."

. . . and he was getting closer . . .

The bathroom door opened, and Josalyn stepped out, looking confused. "GET ON 09, QUICK!" Allan shouted at her, and she hurried over to the switchboard, grabbed the receiver up with one hand, pushed the wrong button with the other.

". . . but, Vince, you don't understand . . ." she heard Jerome saying.

"JESUS CHRIST . . ." Allan roared.

. . . and he was very close now, very close, so close that Claire could see with exquisite and soul-blasting clarity that Rudy was not Prince Charming any more, not even remotely, with his hair mussed up and his clothes in tatters and his sunglasses smashed so that the red of his eyes showed through, so bright that it was like looking down into two active volcanoes, two matching round portals to Hell . . .

. . . and the thing that she thought was a smile was a snarl . . .

. . . and the thing that she thought was desire was . . .

"Please help me," she whimpered into the dead receiver and then let it drop from her hand. He was too close now, too close. Finally, she began to back away from him; it was a case of too little, too late.

At the last moment, Claire "De Loon" Cunningham dipped into her messenger bag and pulled out her cross with a trembling hand. She held it up before her. She prayed for it to save her.

Rudy smacked it aside, as if it were nothing.

And then he was upon her.

* * *

Allan and Josalyn, at their separate controls, pressed the same button at the same time and clutched the receivers to their ears.

Just in time to hear the screaming.

"Claire?" Allan said. Josalyn's voice was frozen in her throat.

There was a clicking sound, and then the screaming came in again, wailing out and out over the tiny speakers. The phone clicked again. The scream. The click.

"Omigod," Allan said.

Then Josalyn screamed, too.

Click. Scream. Click. Scream. Click.

And a mechanized voice came over the line, saying, *"Please deposit five cents for the next three minutes . . ."*

". . . or your call will be interrupted."

Back and forth. Back and forth.

"Five cents, please."

The receiver was swinging on its cord.

"Five cents."

Back and forth.

There was blood on the receiver.

"Thank you."

The blood was everywhere.

Click. *"Claire? Claire?"* Tiny voices, from the other end of the line.

Claire didn't deposit five cents.

Click.

A dial tone.

Back and forth. Back and forth.

It was now 12:32. And seven seconds.

Precisely.

CHAPTER 42

Joseph didn't waste any time with common courtesy. He drove like a maniac, running red lights, cutting people off, chasing pedestrians out of the way, honking his horn and screaming like a lunatic. At one point, a bunch of kids in a Trans Am were stopped in the middle of the street, talking to friends. Joseph came up behind them and told them to get their butts out of the way. The driver slipped him the finger. Joseph slammed into the back of the Trans Am, jumped out before the kids had recovered, and ran toward the driver's window. The driver decided that, yes, maybe he'd move after all. The Trans Am took off. Joseph got back in his van. The encounter took less than a minute.

He pulled up to the entrance of the Bleecker Street station at 12:43 on the dot.

The ambulances were already there. And the police cars. Apparently, they hadn't wasted any time on the way over, either. He envied them their sirens, their automatic priority status. He wished he could just put out an APB of Rudy right now . . . on the condition that Rudy be handed over to Joseph personally.

That's the bitch, he mused bitterly, and left it at that.

"You know she's dead," Stephen moaned from the passenger seat. Tears glistened on his cheeks, strobing red from the police car lights. He spoke as if he were telling Joseph something informative.

"Yeah, and you know it, *too*, doncha?" Joseph countered, cutting the engine and pocketing the keys. "You and your darling buddy-boy." Then, before he felt compelled to go on, maybe wind up punching the little twit again, he got out and walked over to the uptown entrance.

315

The crowd had gathered there, as usual, to soak up the bloodshed. He could see that the police were holding them back and parting them down the middle; some guys in bloodstained paramedic suits were trying to get a stretcher up the stairs. The sheet was pulled all the way up; no questions there.

Something lumpy and shapeless and extremely dead was sticking to the underside of the sheet. Joseph was grateful for having been spared the sight of it. *At least she won't be coming back*, he noted, sourly nodding. *There's not enough left of her.*

That was all he really needed to know; her death was a foregone conclusion. He circled slowly around the outside of the crowd, scanning the faces . . . no Rudy, of course . . . and made his way to the phone.

Danny didn't take it well. Nobody expected him to. Nobody attempted to offer him the tiniest bit of consolation, because there was nothing to say. She was dead, and there wasn't anything even remotely alright about it.

They had gotten out of Astor Place as quickly as possible: T.C.'s warning notwithstanding, the word had gotten out, and transit cops were starting to appear as they headed up the steps. The first thing to pass them on the street was an empty cab; they snagged it and rode it almost aimlessly all over the East Village, waiting for the sound of a beeper.

It came.

And Danny wasn't taking it well. Armond and T.C. could do nothing but watch while he crumbled to pieces on the corner of Prince and Elizabeth, sagging against the street lamp and letting out terrible whooping sounds.

When he wheeled around suddenly, blindly, incoherently, and began to stagger off in the general direction of home, neither of them did anything to stop him. Both of them knew that there was nothing they could do for him . . . or he for them . . . until his grieving had run its course.

"Be well," Armond whispered after him. "Take care."
T.C. nodded in silent agreement.

They would never see him again.

The time was one o'clock.

CHAPTER 43

Rudy rounded the corner onto Mercer Street at 1:20, hugging the shadows. A van was pulling away from the curb. The words stenciled across the back door meant nothing to him. He had never heard of Your Kind Of Messengers, Inc.

The occupants of the van failed to notice him, too, as they rumbled away.

It had been that kind of a night.

Rudy moved quietly up Mercer Street, probing the air with tendril-like senses for any hint of movement, the glint of watchful eyes. Nobody, nothing. It both pleased and disappointed him.

If anybody sees me, I'll have to kill them, he knew. It was good to not have to kill anybody right now, because he was already splattered with blood, and he didn't need to be made more conspicuous. But it was too bad, because he'd have *liked* to kill somebody right now, feel them come apart in his hands and teeth.

He paused in the middle of the block, staring across the street at the windows of Stephen's apartment. The living room light was on. Rudy smiled, the dried blood cracking on either side of his lips. "This is it, Stephen," he whispered to the windows.

"I'm coming to get you now. . . ."

He crossed the empty street, made his way quickly to the front door of the building, stepped inside. He looked at the buzzer marked PARRISH, brought his finger to the button, and stopped. *A surprise visit would be nicer, don't you think?* he asked himself, and found that he couldn't agree more.

By some fortuitous breach of security, the inner door of the foyer had been left unlocked. Rudy was positively beaming as he stepped through it and moved up the stairs to the second floor landing. There he paused, staring down the hall at Stephen's door, confusion washing across his features.

There was a note on the door. He moved slowly toward it, and the words came into focus. He stopped, reading it. His smile came back, magnified a thousandfold.

The note read:

> *Dear Josalyn,*
> *I had to step out for a minute. Please wait for me. I'm sorry. I'll be back as quickly as I can.*
> *Stephen.*

BOTH of them! The thought made his heart go pitter-pat. *Together! Tonight! In living color!* He rubbed his hands together with glee, pondered the implications: no having to traipse around, tracking them down; no hiding the corpses in separate locations: no muss, no fuss, we deliver to your door, the whole thing wrapped up tight as a gnat's ass on a silver platter.

And handed over. To him.

He tried the doorknob. It opened to his touch, as if by magic. He took a step inward, then remembered that Josalyn might already be inside. It gave him a moment's cunning pause.

"YOO-HOO!" he called, a high-pitched singsong. "OH, JOS-A-LYN!"

No answer.

"ANYBODY TO HOME?" he tried once again, but the effort was halfhearted. He was talking to the walls. Slightly disappointed, he stepped inside and closed the door behind.

I can wait, he thought. *I can wait all night, if I have to*. *It'll be worth it*.

The trap had worked perfectly.

To no avail.

CHAPTER 44

While Rudy amused himself, digging through Stephen's papers and rinsing the blood from his body and clothes, the following things were going on:

Josalyn and Jerome were exchanging troubled glances as they watched Allan slowly descend into drunkenness, while Doug tossed and turned on the couch in a shock-induced slumber;

Stephen was being led by Joseph and Tommy, very much against his will, down a workman's staircase to the forever darkness of the underground;

Danny was wandering alone, broken and wailing, down streets without name or number, completely cut off from the others and the relentless ticking of the clock;

one Detective Brenner was contemplating the connection between three extremely dead girls, with particular attention to the strange collection of objects found amidst the ruins of the late Claire Cunningham, and the still-stranger murder suspect sought for the Sullivan Street killing;

and T.C. was listening with rapt attention to the horror stories of the old man in the cab beside him as they rolled resolutely from station to station to station. . . .

"You have heard of Treblinka?" Armond asked. T.C. shook his head slowly. "So few seem to know about it. Such a tragedy, for so many to have suffered and died unknown. How is it that . . . ?" He stopped himself, made a game attempt at a smile, struggling to control his voice. "Not your fault. Not your fault," he said. Whether he was addressing T.C. or himself was a question that not even he could answer.

"Treblinka . . ." T.C. gently prodded.

". . . was a death camp in Poland, where the Jews of Warsaw were taken to be exterminated during the Holocaust," Armond continued. His tone was level, almost as if he were reciting a childhood lesson from memory. "Others were taken there, too, caught up in the machineries. Others like myself, my wife, and my son. Political martyrs."

Armond shuddered. His companion was unable to speak. In the front seat, separated from them by a sheet of transparent plastic, the cabbie drummed his fingers on the steering wheel while salsa music clattered tinnily through the dashboard speakers. It played in obscenely cheerful counterpoint as Armond resumed.

"I was there for just two months short of a year. My son celebrated his eighteenth birthday there, two weeks before he . . . died." An undecipherable expression crossed his face for a moment: maybe fondness, maybe pain. T.C. wasn't sure. "My wife died almost instantly . . . within an hour of our arrival. The Nazis were that efficient: several thousand per hour, eight hours a day, seven days a week."

T.C. lit a cigarette. It was the only thing he could think of to do. His hands were shaking ever so subtly: it took three matches to do the job, with all of the windows closed.

"You see, as soon as we were unloaded from the trains . . . they brought us in on the trains, of course, like cattle to the slaughter . . . as soon as we were unloaded, the men and women were separated and herded off to different locations. There we were made to strip off our clothing, and all of our possessions were taken.

"They spent a bit of time on the men: long enough to determine who among us was strong enough to work, to survive. But they wasted no time with the women. They had no use for them. I was still being beaten and stripped and appraised when I saw the women . . . naked, their

hair shorn and their bodies bent, the Nazis raining blows
upon their backs and heads . . . when I saw them being
driven down what they called 'The Road to Heaven.' I saw
my wife among them. I almost didn't recognize her. She
was running. Her head was bowed. A club . . . one of
those men, those monsters, those Nazis . . . a club hit
her on the back of the neck, and she staggered; but she
continued to run. I saw it all."

He paused. T.C. could see the tears welling up in the
old man's eyes, the way his body jerked with emotion like
an ancient marionette on an abandoned stage, left dangling
by strings to be buffeted by the storm winds. T.C. wanted
to say something, but there was absolutely nothing to say.

Armond continued.

" 'The Road to Heaven' led to the gas chambers, of
course. My wife ran very bravely to her death. She did not
cry . . . she did not cry out . . . not even when she
stumbled and almost fell. I was watching her face. . . .

My God, WHY AM I TELLING YOU THIS?" he
wailed: so suddenly, so abruptly, that the cabbie involuntarily slammed on the brakes and yelled, "Everything all right
back there?"

And Armond laughed.

Like a bell. Like the purest tinkling crystal. Like a
glorious cascade of rainfall from heaven, in consummate
correspondence with the tears that trickled down his
cheeks.

"Oh, yes!" he cried out. "All's right! All's right with the
world!" He laughed again. "Drive on!" he encouraged the
cabbie, who shook his head and stepped back down on the
gas pedal. Then the old man turned to his companion and
smiled, face radiant with tears and inner light.

"I don't need to burden you with all the horrible
details," he said. "I am sorry to have said so much already.
The important part of the story . . . the part that lives on,
as part of our history . . . is this: Treblinka was over-
thrown by its own prisoners, and burned to the ground. I
was there. I took part in that victory. And I survived
. . . quite an accomplishment, I think . . . as less than
fifty of us are still alive."

"Jesus . . ."

"*Evil can be defeated.* Never doubt that for an instant: if you doubt, you will be lost. And we will lose as well.

"I had a dream, quite recently . . . the night of the murder, that woman on the train, the one whose head you found . . . yes. That night, I had a dream. I dreamed that the monsters had come back, and I was in Treblinka again; but Treblinka had been moved to New York City, and the Nazis all wore Rudy's face. Instead of leading us to the gas chambers, they led us to their dining rooms. One by one, we joined them.

"Just before I awoke, my wife and son appeared to me. They told me that I was to come with them. Their eyes were like coals, and they were drooling. . . ."

The cab pulled over to the curb and idled there. "Grand Street," the driver said wearily. His passengers jumped and stared blankly at their surroundings. "You wanted all the subway stations? This is Grand Street. You want it or not?"

"Thank you," Armond answered finally. "I will only be a moment." He got out and moved slowly to the subway stairs. T.C. watched him, running the images back through his mind. He knew what the moral of Armond's story was; the old man didn't need to say another word.

If we don't kill Rudy, that's all she wrote. The monsters will take over again; and everything he did . . . his revenge, his survival . . . won't mean a thing. That's why he won't rest 'til we nail that sucker: he can't rest 'til it's done.

An' I guess I can't, either. Not knowin' what I know.

"I don't wanna be nosy," the cabbie turned to him and said, "but what's he doin' out there, anyway?"

Savin' yo' ass, T.C. was tempted to say, but he restrained himself.

"Don't ask," he suggested instead. "You'll be glad you didn't."

From there, they moved on to the East Broadway station, doubled back along Canal Street to hit all sixteen of the entrances there, and gradually crisscrossed their way down to the tip of the island.

It would be three o'clock before they reached their final destination.

CHAPTER 45

In the tunnels . . .

They moved slowly down the outside of the tracks, holding close to the wall, in single file: Tommy, then Joseph, then Stephen. Tommy's flashlight filled the tunnel with capering shadow-dances as its thin beam played off the rough-hewn supports and arches, casting suggestions of furtive movement that heightened the apprehension.

Stephen's watch put the time at 2:45. *We've been down here for over an hour,* he thought. *We're not going to find anything, we haven't found anything yet, my God I want to get out of here now.* . . . But the words were skewered to the tip of his tongue, going nowhere. The last hour had been spent in virtual silence, moving first along the uptown side of the space between Bleecker and Spring, now doubling back on the downtown side; in all that time, the only words had been whispered commands from Joseph. Stephen was not about to press his enormous good fortune by opening his mouth; all he could do was hope that Joseph would give up on the tunnels and take them back up to the street.

Another train was coming. In many ways, that was the most terrifying thing of all: standing so close to those thundering wheels, that massive crushing power. Worse than his fear of finding Rudy . . . Stephen severely doubted that he was down here; worse than his fear of Joseph, most certainly. Joseph could flatten him, but not like that. He pressed his back to the wall and slid along it, though the train was still out of visual range and only faintly audible.

"*Listen,*" Joseph whispered, stopping. Tommy turned and looked at him confusedly.

"*What?*" Tommy asked. "*The train?*"

"*No,*" Joseph hissed, his eyes suddenly blazing. "*Listen!*"

For a moment, there was nothing but the distant rumbling of the train. Stephen skrinched up his face, as if by sheer muscular exertion he could push his hearing out further, extend its range. Then the sound reached him, below and apart from the drone of the wheels.

Quiet sounds. A low moan. A muted, rusty cackle like the snapping of twigs.

And feeding sounds.

"*Come on,*" Joseph whispered. "*Real quiet and slow. The train will cover us.*" He stepped around Tommy and began to lead.

Stephen met Tommy's gaze, terrified as his own; and for a moment, something flickered between them. An impulse, a beam of thought that translated as *he's crazy, let him go, let's get out of here.* The impulse flickered and died in an instant, leaving their eyes like two sets of dull mirrors, reflecting each other's resignation.

They followed.

Twin snakes of light slithered up the tracks toward them, reflecting from the headlights of the oncoming train. The roar of its approach mounted steadily, more than keeping pace with the rise in volume as they drew nearer to the dinning sounds. Stephen heard a loud smacking, sharp and distinct, that whipped a nervous spasm down his spine.

Less than thirty feet ahead, there was an opening in the wall. He became aware of a low, steady thrumming and decided that it must lead to a generator room. The sounds were unmistakably coming from there. A mad picture came into his mind, of MTA guys sitting down with their ham sandwiches and beer, jumping out of their shoes when Joseph walked in with a cross in one hand and a stake in the other.

Then he heard a sound like a drowning scream, a gurgle crossbred with a yowl of anguish, and the picture evaporated like piss on a skillet.

The snakes of light whipped past them, beyond. The train poked its nose through the hole at the end of the tunnel, nailing them with its nightmare gaze. Stephen could feel the breeze that it pushed before it, chill and lifeless and ripe with decay. It screamed in his nostrils and put goose bumps on his flesh; he stopped, shuddered, fell back against the wall and tried to keep the tears from falling.

Something tapped him on the shoulder. Tommy. He watched Tommy say *come on, man*, but the moving lips made no sound. He watched Tommy turn away, proceed with silent footsteps. He watched his own feet, soundless as well, dragging themselves forward. They looked and felt like somebody else's.

The train had gotten much closer, its presence overwhelming. There was no sound but the thunder, shuddering through the earth and air. He watched Joseph's brightly lit silhouette disappear into the doorway, promptly followed by Tommy's. Fear of being left alone, more than anything else, forced him to race forward and duck around the corner, moments before the train blasted by him.

Three feet into the doorway, he slammed into Joseph's shoulder and stopped, halfway expecting to be hit; but Joseph didn't even seem to have noticed. The big man's eyes were locked on something ahead of him; Stephen's eyes, partially blinded by the headlights, struggled toward focus.

Then he saw what Joseph was looking at.

And he felt himself starting to scream.

There were three of them, hanging on to the bag lady's still-thrashing body. They were derelicts all, and the stench was overwhelming: they were already rotting before they died, and un-death had done nothing for their personal hygiene. They reeked of sewage and sun-puckered meat, of booze and bile and blood. Just seeing them, and smelling them, was more than bad enough.

But to realize what they were doing . . . to force the mind to believe that what it was seeing was true. . . .

They're spiking her, Joseph thought, the words stamping themselves indelibly into his brain. Like suburban drunks at a backyard barbecue, dumping vodka into a watermelon and sucking it out through straws . . . except that she wasn't a watermelon, and they weren't using straws, and this definitely wasn't the suburbs.

One of them . . . the one with only half a face . . . was emptying a bottle of muscatel down the bag lady's throat. The other two were holding her down, teeth buried in the soft undersides of her arms. Thin rivulets of cheap wine and blood coursed down her arms, neck, and shoulders; still, she continued to writhe and kick feebly, her eyes glazing over, her mouth burbling pink.

Joseph felt rather than heard the train, six feet behind him; he felt rather than heard the tiny, high-pitched squeal of terror, rising up to the right of his shoulder. *Stephen*, he thought. *You little jerk.* He whirled, one hand coming up to wrap around Stephen's face . . .

. . . and the back of the train flew past the doorway, almost instantly cutting its volume in half . . .

. . . and Stephen's wretched whine cut off abruptly, his own hands coming up to throttle the sound . . .

. . . and Joseph whirled again, looking back at the vampires. They went on with their business, undisturbed. For a long cold moment, there was only the sound of their smacking and slurping, set against the ghostly farewell echoes of the train.

Then Tommy's beeper went off.

Fred looked up. Through his one hazy eye, he could see the three dark figures framed in the doorway, jerked suddenly into motion by the steady *beep beep beep*, shouting and flailing impotently like bank robbers who'd just tripped the alarm.

He glanced down at his two companions: Louie and the nameless one, the one who went "blgy blgy" all the time. They continued to feed, too involved to notice.

He glanced back down at the bag lady's bulging, swimming eyes, the pasty pallor of her flesh, the twitching nerves behind.

He looked back at the figures in the doorway.

Fred let the empty muscatel bottle slip through his fingers, pulled his legs out from under the bag lady's head. The bottle clinked against the floor and rolled to one side; the bag lady's head made a dull thud and lolled to the other; Fred scuffled against the pavement and dragged himself awkwardly to his feet.

"Oboy," he said.

And smiled at them, advancing.

Tommy let out an inarticulate cry and instantly vented his bladder.

Stephen backed away, eyes like billiard balls, fists crammed halfway into his mouth.

Joseph stepped forward, his right hand dipping into the messenger bag and coming up with the wooden mallet. The half-faced vampire closed in, smecking and leering, its arms outstretched like a long-lost lover's. The mallet whipped back, then around and forward in a single blurred motion.

The right side of the vampire's skull caved in slightly at the temple, making the already-empty socket seem to stretch all the way around the side of its head. It slumped to its knees, moaning, clutching itself. Joseph kicked it in the face and sent it sprawling on its back; then he straddled its belly, sitting down with all his weight.

And with his left hand, he pulled out the first wooden stake.

It was all automatic. No thought. No delay. Just the placement of the stake with one hand, the raising of the mallet with the other, a sudden sharp sucking of air as he hammered down on the blunt end of the stake, driving its point through the vampire's chest, not pausing to watch as the monster yowled and spurted and floundered like a capsized beetle, but rather raising the mallet again, high over his head, and bringing it down. . . .

* * *

Louie scuttled backwards across the floor in a lopsided, drunken crab-like walk. His blood-slick jaws were slack with terror. Near the door, Fred was already beginning to decompose. Louie whimpered and burbled and backed into the wall.

The killing black shadow was rising now, rising up off of Fred's body and looming over them all. It turned toward him, fixed him with its murderous eyes, thundered slowly forward.

The other one . . . the blgy-blgy man . . . was still crouched over the bag lady, still feeding. He didn't see the enormous killing shadow cast itself upon his back, didn't see the nightmare hands descending. Louie couldn't bear to watch it, either. He curled up like a fetus, clamping down the lids over his murky red eyes. When the shadow pounded the stake in, with a sound like a tomato mashing against a barn door, Louie gritted his teeth and crawled blindly toward the stairs.

He crawled. He crawled. A voice bellowed behind him. He ignored it. He crawled. His forehead struck the bottom step, stunning him. He staggered back on his haunches, his eyes twitching open . . .

. . . and then the hands were upon him, the hot killing hands, and he was flipped over on his back, slamming down hard against the concrete floor. staring up into the face of the giant dark death-angel, black killing shadow, coming down like an avalanche of knees, like boulders on his stomach, making him rise up gasping at the waist to meet the sharp tip of the stake that forced him back to a prone position as the mallet came up and came down . . .

. . . and this time the sound was inside of him: his own heart, bursting like a water balloon as the wooden shaft plowed through him and thudded against the pavement on the other side. . . .

And Joseph Hunter pulled himself back up to his feet, wobbling slightly, like a sleepwalker awakening at the edge of a cliff. Stephen watched him, detached, also like a dreamer; *this can't be real, this can't be real*, his mind told him over and over.

But Joseph had turned, moving toward him now; and behind him, Tommy's baritone sobs were echoing arrhythmically against the hard walls. Stephen distinctly remembered the march down the tunnel, the three of them together; and unless it had *all* been a dream, starting back on the night before Rudy's disappearance, or maybe before, then it was real, it was all real. . . .

And Joseph was moving toward him, eyes shimmering like black moonlit pools, the face curiously expressionless in its frame of sweat-matted hair. The face was blank, but Joseph's posture told a different story. The spine was stiff, the movements rigid. His hands were fists, the right one still tensed around the handle of the mallet.

Stephen watched, numbed by the horror; his mind registered every detail of Joseph's advance, but failed to make the connection. Not until the dark killing shadow was upon him did he begin to understand.

By then it was too late.

"Your turn," Joseph said, grabbing Stephen by the wrist and yanking him forward. Stephen yelped and stumbled, weak-kneed; but the big man dragged him relentlessly toward the center of the room.

Where the bodies were.

"No," Stephen whimpered. He tried to dig in with his heels, wound up skidding across the floor like a reluctant water-skier. Desperately, he turned back to Tommy and silently pleaded for help.

Tommy turned away from the wall then, saw what was happening. A newer, deeper alarm nailed itself to his features. "Wait a minute . . ." he croaked, the words barely formed and scarcely audible.

Joseph didn't appear to have heard. He plowed forward, Stephen still in tow.

"Wait!" Tommy yelled, pushing away from the wall.

He minced forward like a girl in an ultra-tight skirt, his urine-soaked pants clinging unpleasantly to his legs.

Joseph stopped and whirled, just long enough to paste Tommy with a menacing glare. "Stay out of this," he growled. "I mean it."

"But you can't . . . !" Tommy persisted, though he froze in his tracks.

"What do you think I'm gonna do? *Kill* him?" Joseph laughed, a dry thunder devoid of humor. Tommy and Stephen stared back at him with eyes like glazed ceramic eggs. "No, no, no. It's just that Stevie and I gotta finish the job."

Before Stephen could respond, he was sliding forward on his heels again. Finally, horribly, he understood what was about to happen. "NO!" he screamed, struggling violently. To no avail.

Joseph came to a stop in front of the bag lady, yanked Stephen up beside him. Slowly, he intensified the pressure on Stephen's wrist; slowly, he lowered himself to his knees, forcing the other to join him.

"You know what's gonna happen to her?" he said, indicating the bag lady with his free hand. "Tomorrow night, she's gonna wake up. She'll crawl around the floor for a while, and then she'll drag herself to her feet; and then, after a while, she'll go out and get something to eat.

"You know what she's gonna want to eat, doncha?" He shook Stephen's arm vigorously, prompting a response. "You know what she *is* now, right?"

Stephen looked at the bag lady. Her head remained as it landed, facing away, the tongue lolling out, eyes focused on nowhere. She was no longer breathing. Stephen shuddered uncontrollably.

"She's dead. . . ." he managed to say.

"Not dead enough," Joseph answered, acerbically grinning. "Not dead enough for me."

"Joseph . . ." Tommy began, still frozen in the doorway to the tunnel.

"Shut up!" Joseph snapped, loud and over his shoulder. Then, to Stephen: "This one's yours, Stevie."

Stephen moaned, the tears welling up, his face going slack and pasty white. He shrank back as Joseph squeezed his wrist with one hand and brought the mallet over with the other.

"Come on," Joseph wheedled, patronizing. "Put the widdle hammer in your widdle hand now." Stephen desperately clenched his fist. Joseph clenched his teeth, holding back with extreme effort, and methodically pried Stephen's fingers apart. Stephen whinnied. Joseph forced the mallet into the palm of Stephen's hand, forced the fingers to close around it, held them there.

Then, with his free hand, he pulled out another stake.

"Gimme your other poodie, now," Joseph continued in the same tone of voice. Stephen squealed and wildly shook his head, eyes the size of softballs. "GIMME YOUR HAND!" Joseph hollered, dispensing with any cuteness. "NOW!"

Stephen brought up his left hand, not bothering to clench the fingers together, knowing what would happen if he resisted. Knowing what was about to happen, no matter what.

Stake in the left hand. Mallet in the right. Joseph's hands, wrapped around his own, like a puppeteer's strings made flesh as the big man forced Stephen to bend over at the waist, left arm reaching out to place the stake, right arm coming up to land the blow, all in a grotesque parody of free will.

"Now you're gonna know," Joseph said, very quietly. There was no anger in the voice. Like the voice of a god. "Now you're gonna learn how to do what you have to do."

Stephen let out one last, tortured gasp.

"I'm sorry," Joseph whispered.

The mallet came down.

CHAPTER 46

"*NO!*" Rudy screamed, awakening from the nightmare into the harsh light of Stephen's apartment. For a second, it was all still there: the black smoke, the puckering holes, the rain like lava. Then the dream pictures were gone, and he was staring at the wall, and the clock put the time at exactly 3:07.

"Shit," he muttered, rubbing his eyes. Weird jagged-edged patterns flew across the darkness behind his eyelids. He opened his eyes. The pattern danced and hovered in the air.

I gotta get home. The thought came unbidden, fighting its way through the fog in his mind. It pinged there like a clapper striking the bull's-eye bell at a shooting gallery. *I gotta get home.* An echo of certainty. A tightness in his chest that left no room for doubt.

Something was wrong at his apartment. He could feel it, he could taste it, like a hot copper penny at the tip of his tongue.

Rudy jumped to his feet, rushed toward the door, and stopped. *There isn't time!* his mind screamed. Harsh statement of fact. In his mind's eye, he could see himself running down the street. He could see himself, arriving too late.

The thought filled him with billowing, shapeless terror. *What is it? What's happening? What am I gonna do?* His mind reeled, like a severed tire rolling crazily down a steep embankment. He turned away from the door, staggered toward the window, threw it open and stood before it, pulled by an instinct he didn't even begin to understand.

I gotta get home, he thought once again. . . .

* * *

. . . and suddenly he was flying, the air whipping past him as he rose up over the skyline on leathery wings. And though he had never seen the city from this angle, through these blind eyes, he knew where he was going. He knew how to get there. Some inner system of guidance, indigenous to the form he had taken, zeroed in on the target unerringly.

While his tiny lungs and sharp-fanged mouth pierced the night with a chittering song.

To the left of the front steps, smothered in shadow, T.C. Williams lit his twenty-third and final cigarette of the night. He was thinking about his children, his ex-wife, his family and friends. He was thinking about what it would be like to see them shambling, undead, through the streets of Harlem. He was thinking about how much he loved them . . . how he'd die before he ever allowed that to happen. All that, as his eyes combed the street.

He didn't think to look skyward.

He never even saw it coming.

When Rudy was finished with the wet, broken thing, he left it in the shadows and started racing up the steps to his apartment. Fresh blood coursing through him, his human shape restored, his body felt strong as an athlete's in training; but his mind was still chaotic, bubbling over with panic.

Above him, on the third floor landing, Armond Hacdorian was gingerly opening the broken front door to Rudy's apartment. It was a difficult task for a man his age. He was uncomfortably aware of the pounding in his chest. A short jolt of pain in his left shoulder startled him; his vision swam for a moment, and the door slipped from between his fingers.

They heard each other at almost exactly the same time: Rudy's pounding footsteps, coming up off the second floor landing just as the door hit the wall, slid, and crashed at Armond's feet.

Rudy let out a tiny shriek of terror and raced madly up the last flight of stairs. Armond backed slowly into the room and reached a trembling hand into his bag, coming up with several vials of holy water.

Both of them were praying that it wasn't too late.

Rudy rounded the last corner and stopped short, panting. The door was open, and a faint light was playing across the floor of the landing. He edged toward it nervously. His forehead began to ache.

"*Son of a bitch,*" he whispered. Two feet short of the door, he moved to the wall and edged along it like a spy in a hoky forties melodrama. Something was happening in there that terrified him, but he wasn't sure what it was.

Then a splash and a hiss, and the glow from the doorway increased in brilliance, and it seemed as if the walls themselves were beginning to moan now with an agonized life of their own. Something about it nagged at the back of his head, telling him that *this* was the horror he'd come to avert. Quickly, then . . . desperately . . . he leapt through the doorway.

And fell back, hissing.

Blind.

"Ah, Rudy. You've come." Armond seemed genuinely pleased. "I was afraid we'd lost you."

"You'll *wish* you had, you bastard!" Rudy howled, averting his eyes and sidestepping painfully forward. "What are you doing to my *room?*"

"Not your room anymore, Rudy." Armond smiled. "Never again."

The light was coming from the old man's hands: from the tiny glass vials in his trembling grip. Already, the back wall was spattered with radiance. Now Armond sent a thick sprinkling shower of it out in an arc before him, neatly bisecting the floor, cutting a thin line of protection between himself and the vampire.

To his eyes, the floorboards seemed to sputter and steam, as though the holy water had become a highly corrosive acid. But to Rudy, yowling now with rage and terror, it was the stuff of his dreams: thick green-black plumes of smoke, gushing from a thousand tiny puckering craters, miniature volcanoes too bright to look at, opening up at his feet like sores on a ripe, deceased body.

"YOU BASTARD!" Rudy screamed. "I'LL KILL YOU!"

Armond smiled. He didn't know what Rudy was seeing, but he knew that it was far more intense than what his own eyes revealed. He intensified it further, crisscrossing the first line with another. It opened up the right side of the room for him, let him get closer to the door, while Rudy screeched and jumped back toward the far left corner.

"I'm not afraid of you, Rudy," he said. "I've seen human beings commit crimes against God that you will never rival in a million years. By comparison, they make you seem quite puny." He let the empty vial shatter on the floor, quickly uncapped another. "Like a troublesome child," he continued.

A plan was forming in his mind. He hadn't thought of it before . . . hadn't really expected Rudy to show up at all . . . but now that he thought of it, it just might be the final solution to their problems.

If I can trap him in here, he thought, *we'll have won. Either Joseph can come and enjoy his moment of glory, or we can leave Rudy for the morning sun. Either way, it will be over.*

If only I can trap him.

It didn't seem to be too difficult: Rudy was still backed up in the corner, hissing, and Armond had a clear shot to the door. But the pain thudded again in his left shoulder, making the world gray out for a long cold second. And when he snapped back out of it, he felt himself gripped with a mortal terror that had nothing to do with Rudy.

"Please," he heard himself praying. "Please, no." The confidence began to seep out of him like water from a leaky glass. Another jolt hit him, and he staggered back slightly. When he looked up, he saw that Rudy had moved closer to the door.

There's still time, he thought desperately. *If I can only . . .*

Then it hit him like a wrecking ball, his chest seeming

to explode with fiery agony, his knees buckling, his bowels releasing. The room disappeared; in its place, there was *pain*, unimaginable pain, tearing through him like earthquake fissures in a tortured earth. He didn't feel his hands open convulsively, didn't hear the vials of holy water shattering around him. He didn't realize that he was falling, the floorboards racing up to meet him. He didn't even know when he hit.

But when Rudy's teeth punched in through the soft tissue at the jugular vein, he knew.

The pain was incredible. A second that stretched forever, racing over the white light barrier, feeling it burn up through the soles of his feet and go *zzzzzzzttttttt!* through his nervous system like a lightning bolt. Then it was over, and he was dropping to his knees over little fucking Grampa, rolling the wrinkled old bastard over, watching the savage spasms that made Armond Hacdorian dance like a bug on a pin.

"Now," Rudy said. "It's *your* turn to be scared." And he bared his fangs. And he sank them in . . .

. . . *and he was on the speed-of-thought roller coaster of Armond Hacdorian's dying mind, racing back through history and the experiences of a lifetime, getting spitfire glimpses of the years, ticking backwards, a film in reverse, with a camera eye that missed nothing, missed nothing. . . .*

. . . *and he saw himself as Armond had seen him, experiencing the revulsion as if it were his own, hating himself and wishing only to plunge a stake through the heart of a Rudy Pasko that was suddenly not himself, but a terrible and demonic other . . .*

. . . *and then the calendar pages flipped back over years like dross, mere filler between consequential events, a long, long stretch of mundane struggle for survival that dragged on and on and on, in reverse . . .*

. . . *and there was a mounting descent into madness, converse of the recuperative process undergone by an Armond Hacdorian who had aged far, far beyond his years, young by time's standards but never to be young again . . .*

. . . and then he was watching Treblinka, in flames. . . .

Rudy wanted to pull away from the convulsing body beneath him. *I'm not afraid of you, Rudy,* the old man had said. He didn't want to see things more horrible than his wildest dreams. He wanted to pull away.

But he couldn't.

. . . and the walls were burning, the towers were burning, there were bodies twisting and shouting on their feet to the syncopated groove of machine-gun fire, bodies crisping and smoldering at his feet, bodies cutting frantic swaths across the smoky landscape as they raced toward freedom in the form of death or the woods beyond . . .

. . . and there were bodies in the trenches, tens of thousands of them, meticulously stacked, the thin ones arranged at the bottom like kindling, the fat ones on top, so that the mass incineration might operate at peak efficiency in these, the final days of the camp, all evidence of the slaughter reduced to fine gray ash and hidden forever from the eyes of Man . . .

. . . and Rudy was a passenger in Armond's mind, a prisoner in his body, helplessly reliving an atrocity many years past, standing at the edge of a trench, systematically transferring the deadweight of murdered child after murdered child from the pile behind him to the pit before him, where even less fortunate men crawled over the bodies already laid down to receive the new ones and painstakingly arrange them while the Nazis looked on, unspeakably cold and calculating and brutal, shouting out orders and dealing out blows to the shrunken, emaciated, subhuman drones who scurried and moaned and averted their hollow eyes as they handled their dead like sacks of garbage, loading them in and spreading them out . . .

. . . and they were leading him down "The Road to Heaven," that pebble-strewn path from the processing section to the gas chambers to the trenches . . .

. . . *and they were coming for him in the green section, where the clothes of the new arrivals were sorted, beating him to his knees in front of the large bins where the sweaters were separated from the shirts and blouses . . .*

. . . *and he was in the slave barracks, his son crushed tight to his bosom, and his son had a great purple welt below one eye, and any mark on the face was instantly translated into a trip to the "hospital," and a bullet to the back of the neck . . . and so he gave his son a boost, the young man tying the other end of the rope around a broad wooden rafter, and then his son's legs did a shuffling tap dance of death, two feet above the floor . . .*

. . . *and his wife was running naked down "The Road to Heaven" . . .*

. . . *and in the last moment of Armond Hacdorian's life, he flipped forward once again to the end of Treblinka, and he had the machine gun in his hands, and the Nazis were jerking like disco dancers under a strobe light, and one particular pale Aryan face stared back at him in horror, and the face was unmistakably familiar. . . .*

Rudy came up screaming, his teeth tearing away from the lifeless throat beneath him with a sound like shredding paper. Blood spurted, steaming, from the open wound. There was still quite a bit of blood left in the body.

Armond Hacdorian would not be back.

Under any other circumstances, Rudy would have been furious. Three times, now, he had been cheated of victory, tripped up at the finish line: first by Ian, then by Stephen and the one who called himself Master, and now by this one. Under any other circumstances, he would have been smashing down the walls.

But his mind's eye was still focused on a single image, dangling before him like a freeze-frame at the end of a movie. The last thing he saw before Armond died and took his nightmare visions with him. The only thing that Rudy could see.

That was me, a voice informed him. *That was my face. . . .*

Then a sound like a busy signal pried its way into his

consciousness, slipping in gradually, chiseling away at the picture until he was back in his apartment, in his body, looking dumbly for the source of the noise. . . .

And finding it in the dead man's pocket.

Whafuck? he thought, fingering the cold metal and plastic of the beeper. His thumb slid over the button and silenced it, quite by accident. *Why would an old man be carrying a thing like this?* he wondered, rolling it over and over in his hands like a stymied puzzle-freak with a Rubik's Cube.

Rudy pondered it for a full minute before the sharp pains in his forehead reminded him of where he was, what had happened. Distantly, he heard the sound of approaching sirens. Absently, he pocketed the beeper and pulled himself to his feet. Their soles throbbed, the pain punctuating his every step.

Without a backward glance at his light-spoiled sanctuary, Rudy Pasko moved quickly down the stairs, out into the morning's final hours of darkness.

It was now 3:45.

By 4:15, Brenner had seen just about enough.

The body out front was pretty grim, just for starters: throat laid open, left arm wrenched loose and dangling, a series of vicious clawmarks on his shoulders and the back of his neck. The victim's name was Terrence C. Williams. He left a sizable corpse. Evidently, he'd been working for the Transit Authority, judging from the receipts and check-cashing card in his wallet.

But he'd been carrying a messenger bag when he died. It was identical, in style and contents, to the one they'd found with the remains of Claire Cunningham.

That was for starters. Then he had gone up the stairs and found the old man, Hacdorian. The body wasn't mangled, at least . . . though there was no getting around the puncture wounds in the neck . . . but his simple presence there was both illuminating and disturbing. Brenner remembered Hacdorian well: the man who remembered nothing. Apparently, he'd remembered enough to get himself killed.

Armond Hacdorian carried no messenger bag, but he did have a satchel with a large cross inside it, identical to the others. And it wasn't too hard to figure out what all those little glass vials had contained.

After that, he'd studied the writing on the wall, the pile of tiny bones in the corner. There was a terrible torn moment, where the exhilaration almost overwhelmed the revulsion. He fought it down. *Neither the time nor the place*, he thought, *for a celebration*.

Though there was cause for one. They had the identity of the Subway Psycho. The trail of bodies had led them to his door.

Now, as he headed down to the street, he had seen just about all that he cared to. It was time to dig through the files for any mention of a Rudy Pasko. Get a decent description from the neighbors. See if it matched up with the Sullivan Street killing (he was willing to bet that it did). And put out an APB. They would stake the place out, too, though there was doubt that he'd be back. It was all Brenner could do, at the moment.

He wanted to know more about the deceased, however. He wanted to know how they'd tracked down Mr. Pasko, *why* they'd done it, and why they'd chosen such arcane methods of self-defense. Claire Cunningham's bedroom flashed back at him, replete with every piece of half-wit paraphernalia on the subject. *I can see one flako as an accident of Fate*, he mused. *But three, and it's a movement*. Brenner could not, for the life of him, figure out what a big bad dude like Terrence C. Williams was doing with a wooden stake and mallet. Or how they had gotten together. Or why they'd kept all that information to themselves.

"Oh, but if you were alive," he mumbled, addressing all three of them, "I'd interrogate the living piss out of you. I'd . . ." He pushed open the front door and cut himself off. There were people out there. A lot of them.

Six squad cars and an ambulance were blocking Avenue B. The police barricades were up, and patrolmen lined the perimeter. Their hands were full. Almost twenty after four on a Wednesday morning, and there were close to a hundred lowlifes, scuttling out of the woodwork for a

better view of the carnage. "Jesus," he murmured, wishing
. . . as he often did . . . that the people he served didn't
make him quite so ill.

They had scooped up the hefty carcass of Mr. Williams,
God rest his heathen soul. Brenner watched them load it
into the back of the ambulance and scanned the crowd for
reporters. None. He let out a sigh of relief and paused to
fish a cigarette from his breast pocket. They'd be coming
any minute, he knew. He had to have his bullshit ready.

"Detective?" Brenner turned. A young cop . . .
rookie, name of Ellison . . . was walking toward him.
Ellison was a serious, studious kid. A good cop. Brenner
asked him what he wanted. Ellison gestured back to the
street with his flashlight.

"There was a guy here a minute ago," Ellison said.
"Huge guy. 6'5" maybe. Brown shoulder-length hair. Dark
beard. Dark eyes. Looked like a lumberjack or something."

"What about him?"

"He was at the last murder scene. The Cunningham
girl."

"You're sure about this?" Brenner lit his smoke,
squinting past the flame, his eyes locked on Ellison's face.

"No question about it. I'd know that guy anywhere.
He's pretty hard to miss."

"Where is he?"

"He took off in a dark-colored, late-model van. It was
halfway up the block, so I couldn't see it clearly, but there
was something written in big white letters on the side."

"Terrific," Brenner said, blowing out an unhappy cloud
of smoke. *He's one of them*, he mused. *I can feel it.*
"Couldn't see his license, I guess."

"I'm sorry, sir," Ellison said. He looked slightly
deflated. Brenner felt momentarily like a heel.

"Don't worry about it, kid," he said. "You did what you
could. You did fine. Listen." He thought for a moment.
"Get that description down on paper. We'll put out an
APB."

"You really think he has something to do with it?"

"What do *you* think?"

"Absolutely." With no hesitation.

"Alright." Brenner smiled, and the rookie beamed back. "Good job," he added, and Ellison swaggered slightly as he moved back to the barricades.

So there are more of you, huh? Brenner thought, dragging heavily. He cast his gaze skyward at the billowing storm clouds. It was going to rain like a son of a bitch soon, adding insult to injury. Tonight was like one big holiday in Heaven.

How many more? he wondered. *How many more of you am I going to find?*

He sighed into his smoldering Camel and tossed it. *And will any of you be alive to explain it to* me?

CHAPTER 47

Doug Hasken was wide awake. No trace of the shock or confusion remained. God had sent him a vision . . . a vision of himself . . . that shimmered in the air above him like a glowing grail.

Hours earlier, when he'd returned to the office, Allan had promptly set him down on the couch, shoved a beer into his hand, and embarked on a lengthy explanation. The beginning of it had been lost on Doug; he *had* been very nearly in shock then, his mind an old piece of Silly Putty that no longer retained images. But by the end of his second beer, just before he'd lapsed into welcome unconsciousness, it had started to come clear.

Then had come the dream, and the vision.

Now Doug was wide awake, sitting upright on the couch, his full attention on the three solemn figures at the switchboards. The time was 4:05.

"That was Joseph," Allan told Jerome, the mute receiver still dangling limply from his hand. His words were faintly slurred. "He just went over to Rudy's apartment. The police were there. He says that Armond and T.C. are dead."

"Oh, my God," Jerome muttered. Josalyn stared at the wall, dumbly shaking her head. All three of them looked like they'd just undergone electroshock therapy: pie-eyed, pasty-faced, slack and moist as unbaked dough.

Doug could sympathize. He'd felt exactly the same way himself. But his shock was over now. The vision had replaced it. Watching them, he knew all the things that they were unable to say: *three dead, only three hunters left, three dead and it's all been for nothing, we'll never find him, we blew it, it's over.* The air thrummed with the force of their despair.

But Doug knew better.

Quietly, he slipped on his skates. The others were unaware of him, locked in their own silent universes of grief. He laced up quickly, pausing only a moment to check out the series of cracks and holes where Rudy's fingers had snapped through the hard plastic of his shin guard. *God, he's strong,* Doug thought. *It won't be enough to save him, but God damn if he isn't strong.*

On the checkout counter, a small cache of tools and weapons was neatly displayed. He stood, shouldered his messenger bag, surreptitiously rolled over to the counter, and deftly palmed four vials of Armond's holy water.

Then he rolled over to the door, glancing over his shoulder as he did so. They were all looking at him now; whether they'd seen him lift the holy water or not, he didn't know. When they found out what he was doing, he felt sure that they wouldn't mind.

"See ya later," he said. Allan nodded vaguely, Josalyn and Jerome didn't even respond. He went out the door.

Five minutes later, he dropped a dime in the slot and punched their number. "I'm on the street," he said, "and you have my beeper number. By six o'clock, we'll have him. I promise."

* * *

"GODDAMITALL!" Rudy bellowed, staggering backward, bringing one hand up belatedly to cover his eyes. "BASTARD! YOU BASTARD!" The words ricocheted madly against the shuttered windows and row-house walls, echoed and boomed down the length of Delancey Street.

He was standing at the mouth of the subway stairs, shuddering with helpless rage and mounting apprehension, wishing that he had Armond here to kill, again and again and again.

White light beamed up at him from the pavement at his feet. Two five-foot strokes of blinding radiance, in the shape of a cross.

The last three subway stations had been the same.

"YOU BASTARD!" Rudy howled one last time before limping away. The enormity of the old man's farewell effort was dawning on him now. If all the subways were sealed off, and he couldn't go back to his apartment, then . . .

What am I gonna do? his mind whined at him like a spoiled brat in a toy store. *The sun's gonna come up in an hour or so, and I'll be stuck out here, and . . .*

He had traveled less than twenty yards when the lone figure came whipping around the corner behind him, moving so quickly that he didn't even have time to place the sound, he didn't even have time to react . .

. . . as the steady whir and pock-pock-pocking of hard little wheels against the pavement closed in on his left, and an unfamiliar voice shouted, "Rudy!" in his ear, and he turned toward the sound . . .

. . . just in time to see the thin stream of dancing fire dots writhing in midair like a dying snake as it whickered toward him. A scream began to form in his throat. His right hand came up, once again, to shield his eyes . .

. . . and then he *was* screaming, a raw full-throated trumpeting of unspeakable pain, as the holy water made contact with his flesh.

The first drop struck him on the left earlobe. It sizzled and smoked like bacon grease, eating away half the lobe, leaving the other half to dangle and flap in the breeze. The second drop burned a canker sore in the corner of his taut upper lip. The third drop bored a hole in the bridge of his nose, exposing bone. The fourth, fifth, and sixth put round, shimmering rings on the fingers of his right hand. The next eight tattooed an oozing daisy chain down the length of his forearm. The rest whistled harmlessly off into space.

Nothing . . . not even dying . . . had ever hurt so much. Rudy yodeled and pinwheeled sideways, slamming into a wall, not even feeling it. The agony didn't stop on impact; it seemed to eat its way inward, twisting and mangling the soft tissue beneath like a soldering iron. He waved his right hand wildly, as if it were on fire, and black putrescent drops sprinkled the pavement.

He was only dimly aware that the roller-skating messenger of death had turned around and doubled back toward him.

He was the Doug Hasken of the dream: an avenging angel, smiting the unrighteous with a chain of shimmering gold. The wind roared in his ears like the voice of God, urging him onward, cheering him in his moment of glory as he power-skated toward the tortured figure of the evil one. The first vial was spent: he dug into his bag for another and uncapped it easily.

Rudy looked up at him then, with those baleful red eyes, but this time Doug was unimpressed. This time, he knew what he was up against. This time, he knew what he was. And in the war between Darkness and Light, he knew which was the stronger.

Rudy stumbled forward in a feeble attempt to rush him. Doug almost laughed, seeing the desperation in the move. He emptied the second vial of holy water in a clean arc that sliced Rudy at gut level. The vampire doubled up, screeching like a stuck pig.

Doug wheeled around smoothly, dropping the second vial and pulling out a third. He didn't bother to uncap this one, wrapping his fist around it instead as he closed it once again.

"This one's for all the people you killed!" he yelled, letting loose with a vicious sidearm throw.

All through his spotted high school career, Doug Hasken had been Dallastown High's premier relief pitcher, with an unbroken string of thirty-two hitless innings culminating his senior year. Everybody expected great things from him, especially Coach Stambaugh, who always claimed that Doug's fastball could "scare piss out of the devil."

Coach Stambaugh would not have been disappointed. The vial shattered on the crown of Rudy's head, soaking his scalp. The greasy blond hair began to crackle and shrivel and glow like a pile of burning twigs. Rudy screamed and fell, frantically clawing at the top of his head. Then a fresh note of horror came into his voice, and he stared disbelieving at the bubbling, blistering palms of his hands.

Doug circled in for the fourth and final time, uncapping the last vial of holy water as he moved to within a foot of Rudy's prostrate form, hoping to hit him in the eyes this time, leaving a blind and helpless creature for the hunters to polish off.

"And this one's for . . ." he started to shout.

That was when Rudy leaped forward, one still-sizzling hand latching hold of the strap on Doug's messenger bag, sending the messenger on a crazy tailspin even as the strap broke and the bag collapsed to the pavement. Doug hit the curb and landed flat on his face, the loud snap of his nose breaking shadowed by the terrified chorus that screamed between his ears. There was a white-hot moment of blindness and pain; then he was staring at the sidewalk, at the growing pool of his own blood, and the sight jerked him back into motion.

Rudy was crawling toward him now, staggering with effort to his feet. Doug rolled over, got his legs under him, then maneuvered up onto his wheels. Rudy lunged forward, tickling the air around Doug's ankles as the latter pushed away, legs pumping madly, pushing like he had never pushed before.

Doug Hasken was up to 15 mph when the pair of hand-holding faggots rounded the corner onto Delancey. Doug instinctively swerved to avoid them, realized his mistake too late, sucked his last breath of air just as the stairway to the Delancey Street station yawned before him like a dragon's mouth and swallowed him darkly, wheels spinning on empty space, body firing headlong toward the cold concrete below.

He hit the far wall at something like 12 mph. His head pulped like a melon. His ribs turned to shrapnel that acted upon his vital organs like a shredder, ripping them to tatters. He stuck to the wall for a horrible split second, then smacked down on the floor like a cold sack of shit. Beyond the first second of pain, he didn't feel a thing.

His dream, his glimmering vision, hadn't shown him how it would end.

God's funny like that.

The faggots had taken off running, the way they came. A wise decision. If Doug's kamikaze plunge hadn't been enough, the sight of the red-eyed thing before them was enough to send them hightailing it back to SoHo.

Rudy, for his part, was cackling with a twisted, savaged sort of glee. The pain was still there . . . the pain showed no sign of diminishing, as yet . . . but his eyes were intact. And though he couldn't get close enough to the subway entrance, couldn't see through the barrier of hateful light, couldn't actually go down the steps and play havoc on the corpse of his tormentor, he had seen the nosedive. He'd heard the crash.

It made him happy.

He began to rummage through the contents of the messenger bag. He saw the clipboard, the blank manifests upon it. They didn't mean anything.

Then he saw the beeper, and something clicked unpleasantly in his head. He dug into his pocket and pulled out Armond's beeper, held the two of them up side by side. They were identical.

Then he found the pad of messenger receipts. With the words, Your Kind Of Messengers, Inc., spelled out in bold letters near the bottom. Below that, an address. And below that . . .

A phone number.

"Ah," he hissed. And again: "Ahhhh." His smile lit up his whole face, crazily, the color of the cold moon above.

Then he rose, taking the receipt pad with him, leaving

the rest on the sidewalk behind, and moved away from Delancey Street on Essex. He wanted to put a little distance between himself and the scene of the crime.

And then he wanted to check on something.

At seven minutes to five, one of the customer lines on the switchboard went off. It was the first time that a call had come in on that line since the hunt began, some nine hours before. Allan was in the process of nodding out and if Josalyn hadn't been in the grip of a powerful yawn, eyes squeezing down to slits, she probably wouldn't have reached for it.

But she was, and she did. Just as she pushed down on the button, the yawn ended. She saw what she was doing. The fleetest stirring of dread and confusion prickled at the base of her skull, and then she was saying "Hello?" into the receiver.

No answer. Silence, like a void at the other end of the line.

"Hello?" she repeated, and the cold fear welled up again, huge this time. "Is anybody there?" she blurted, instantly wishing she hadn't, a voice in her head saying *hang up the phone, why didn't you hang up the phone, hang it up*. . . .

"Josalyn?" Jerome said, coming up behind her. She barely heard him: no more than a ghostly echo of the voice coming over the phone.

"*Josalyn*," he whispered, drawing out the word, running his tongue along it playfully. "*Well, isn't this a wonderful surprise*."

Now it was the *other* end of the line that had gone silent, graveyard-still. Rudy beamed wistfully at the cold plastic receiver in his hand, as if she could see him through it. *Maybe she can*, he thought. He suspected that she could at least feel it. He dearly hoped so.

"*I'm smiling*," he informed her, just to be sure. "*I'm smiling because I'm so happy. I'm so happy because I know where you are now. And nothing can stop me from coming for you*."

"R-Rudy . . . ?" her voice came whining out at him, trembling in the upper register, threatening to unravel like a poorly knitted scarf.

"*Yes, my darling,*" he breathed, then giggled. "*Soon. Before you have a chance to run. Too soon, we'll be together.*"

She started to cry. A wonderful sound.

"*Forever,*" he cooed. "*Won't that be nice? Our last night together will never end. It'll just go on and on and on. . . .*"

Then he blew the receiver a kiss, chuckled softly into it, ripped it out of the phone, and dropped it to the pavement. He gave it a little kick, sent it skittering into the gutter.

In less than an hour, the sun would come out. Already he could feel its approach, prickling his cold flesh with the faintest intimation of heat, like the first hint of a mounting fever.

But the office was only eight blocks away. Maybe less.

Quickly, he staggered west on Stanton Street. Heading toward Spring Street, and the deepest darkness before the dawn.

CHAPTER 48

At 5:15, it began to pour. For days, it had been threatening, climbing in humidity, trickling occasionally, carefully building up pressure. Now it let loose in a torrential flow, shattering the still-dark sky with thunder and buzz-saw bolts of lightning.

Danny Young could barely make out the shape of the phone booth through the driving rain. He ran toward it, bowleggedly hopping over the pools and streams that constantly formed in the street. In the fifteen seconds it took for him to step inside the booth and shut the door behind him, he was thoroughly soaked.

"Son of a bitch," he mumbled absently, hugging himself. He dug into his breast pocket, pulled out three soggy packs of matches and his joint case, its metal and stone exterior dripping. "Damn it!" he yelled, flipping the case open. There was only one joint left. He noted with relief that it was only slightly damp.

Danny had been wandering the streets for just over four hours, shuffling and smoking and mumbling to himself. Sleep had been out of the question. Going home had been out of the question. All he could do was think about Claire, play it over and over in his head, until the stretch of hours and the dope-smoke haze combined to make the memory fade into something like a dream.

Now, with the rain pounding all four glass walls of his coffinlike enclosure, he found himself staring at the telephone. His own mind seemed suddenly clearer; much clearer, in fact, than it had felt since . . . since . . .

Since she died, he thought, and then all the other thoughts came piling back with renewed clarity, and then his eyes were staring deeply into the narrow darkness of the coin slot while questions began forming in the bright space behind his eyes.

What went down after I split? he wondered. *Did they get him? Are they still after him?*

Are any of them still alive?

The coin slot of the pay phone stared back at him like a single winking eye. There were, he knew, plenty of dimes left in his pocket. All he needed was one. One phone call. And then he'd know.

"I'm afraid," he whispered out loud. He laughed. "No *shit*, I'm afraid!" he chided himself. But his fingers were digging into his right pants pocket.

When the phone rang, Josalyn expected it to be Joseph or Doug. She'd been beeping their pants off for the last three minutes, punching their numbers in over and over with steadily increasing desperation, her gaze flipping back and forth between the door and the switchboard. "Come on, Goddamn it," had hissed through her teeth so many times that it had almost become a mantra. So when the phone rang, she let out a nervous, triumphant whoop and snatched up the receiver like a starving woman at an open buffet.

"Joseph? Doug?" she shouted.

"Danny," said the thin voice from the other end. "Is this Josalyn? I . . . I'm sorry, but . . ."

"Danny?" Josalyn actually had to stop for a second, remember who Danny *was*. Then it came back, and she practically gibbered into the phone, "Danny, where are you? Can you get in here right away? *Please.*"

"What?" Danny's voice was a tinny squeak. "What's going on?"

Josalyn bit down on her lower lip to keep it from trembling while she pulled herself together. "Rudy's coming," she said finally. "He's on his way here. I don't know how he found us, but he did, and he's coming, and we need everybody out here *now*. Can you get here? Can you do it?"

A moment of silence, from the other end.

"Can you do it?" she repeated, forcing calm, keeping her voice level with the last remaining threads of her composure. If Danny didn't answer, she was going to scream.

But it wasn't necessary. Danny's voice squeezed through the tiny speaker, sounding suddenly clearer, stronger. "I'm on my way," he said. "Don't worry. I'll kill that bastard myself, if I have to."

"Thank you," she breathed. All the teeth in the world couldn't stop her lips from trembling now. "Hurry. Please."

"You got it," Danny said, and hung up.

Josalyn just sat there, mutely, clutching the receiver. Which was a good thing, as Joseph called only a moment later, briefly complaining that every phone he hit for the last five minutes was out of order.

"Joseph and Stephen are on their way," she informed Jerome a minute later. "Tommy's gone. Something hap-

pened . . . I guess we'll find out later." She lit a cigarette
with trembling fingers. "And Danny's coming, too. I don't
know what his story is, either."

"And Rudy's coming." Jerome's dark eyes were moist
and frightened. They could have been her own; *would* have
been, if the responsibility hadn't been thrust upon her now.

Allan was down for the count. All the energy had
drained out of him over the last twenty minutes. He'd been
working on his fifth beer when it happened; it lay, half-
empty, on the desk beside his folded arms, the head resting
upon them. Everything . . . the beer, the tension, the
endlessly stretching hours . . . had finally worn him
down. And he was out: deeply, sonorously *out*.

They'd tried shouting at him, shaking him, sitting him
upright. The best they could get was a mumbled *whuz-
zizis?* a blank ten-second stare from his bloodshot eyes.
Then he was gone again.

"What are we going to do?" Jerome was asking. Josalyn
shrugged, sighed, wiped sweat from her brow; she glanced
over at Allan, back over to the door, and then up at Jerome
again. He was dancing lightly from foot to foot. She looked
at him quizzically, and he forced a grin, saying, "I have to
wee-wee."

"Well, for Christ's sakes, do it now!" she yelled,
managing a weak smile of her own. "And while you're at it,
fill up one of these empties with water. We can pour it on
his head, if we have to." Gesturing at Allan. "We have to be
ready when Rudy gets here."

We've got to be ready. Jerome nodded, grabbed up an
empty, and hopped over to the bathroom. The door closed
behind him. Josalyn watched, fighting down the icy chill
inside her, clammy fist clenched around the base of the
metal cross. *We've got to be ready when Rudy comes. We've
got to hold him until Joseph gets here. If anyone can kill
him, Joseph can.*

There was no choice in the matter, no question in her
mind. Fate, the night, and whatever gods there were had
chosen her as living bait for the final confrontation. She had
to be ready. No falling to pieces, no running away, no

passive acquiescence to the end. She would live, or she would die, but she would do them fighting.

Like Ian. . . .

She winced, blinking back the image of him that was starting to form in her mind. She looked at Allan . . . the washed-out features, the dark and puffy eyelids in repose, the slack and gently snoring mouth . . . and a sudden wave of compassion stole through her. She wished that she could just let him sleep, awaken in the morning to a neat and happy resolution, unblemished by the horror to come. She wished that there were some way to spare him . . . to spare them *all* . . . from any further unpleasantness.

She closed her eyes, and Ian was there: his voice, his presence, very much like he was in the dream, long ago, saying *it's alright, he can't hurt you, he can't touch you now*. She moaned, low in her throat, wishing that it were true and not just a dream brought on by the hour and the stress, wishing he were really there beside her. . . .

There was a sound at the door.

Josalyn's eyes opened. For a moment, she couldn't see anything through the mist that clouded the glass. Then she spotted the red eyes, peering in through the window. The eyes like beacons.

That summoned her forward.

A tiny voice in the back of her mind screamed, *NO! NO! DON'T LOOK AT HIM, FOR GOD'S SAKE, JOSA-LYN!* Then the voice cut off, and her body went rigid, and her mind went completely silent of thought.

Come here. His voice, from the emptiness within. *Come here, bay-bee.* A giggle of glee. *Oh, coochie-coochie-coochie, little baby, come to Daddy. . . .*

She rose.

Nice Poopsie.

A blank thing, sucked of will, Josalyn moved toward the door.

Pretty Poopsie.

The cross slipped, unnoticed, from her hand and clattered to the floor.

Nice . . .

Her empty hand closed around the doorknob, twisted it. She couldn't hear the sudden howl of wind and rain, the flush of the toilet behind her.

When he took her in his arms, she couldn't feel a thing.

Allan awoke in a cold, stinging sweat. His vision was bleary, and his head felt like it was packed full of mud; but an alarm had gone off, somewhere at the core of him, jolting him into sudden, sharp awareness. He stared at his folded arms, the switchboard, the wall. He remembered where he was. "Josalyn?" he muttered thickly . . .

. . . and the alarm went off again, strong this time, more shrill and incisive. He knew, before he turned, what he was going to see.

"NO!" he shrieked, riveted to his seat. Rudy grinned back at him, slick as a water rat, and then sank his teeth into Josalyn's neck.

Something snapped in Allan Vasey's brain. He jumped up, still shrieking, and broke into something between a stagger and a run. His hip slammed into the edge of the checkout counter as he rounded it. It didn't faze him. He kept on coming.

Josalyn's back was arched, her head thrown back. Rudy was making a thin sucking sound, her blood jetting into him, fainter than a whisper. Allan's left hand found a handful of Rudy's hair and yanked back sharply; his right hand grabbed Josalyn by the shoulder and ripped her away from the vampire's arms.

"COCKSUCKER!" he screamed, rearing back with his right, still clutching Rudy's hair with the other. He swung with all his strength, catching Rudy in the jaw. Rudy staggered backwards, looking stunned.

Then he smiled.

"Nice try," he said, and attacked.

The bathroom door opened just as Allan slammed flat against the countertop, Rudy astride him. Josalyn just stood there like a mannequin, staring dully, as Rudy grabbed Allan by the beard and pulled his head back viciously.

Jerome yelled and rushed forward, grabbing Rudy in a headlock and trying to knock him off the counter. Rudy whipped his head around suddenly, raking his teeth along the soft underside of Jerome's forearm. A black puckering chasm opened up in the dark flesh, and Jerome wailed like a dying baby.

It may have been the scream, or the fact that Rudy's attention was distracted. Josalyn had no way of knowing. But she found herself standing there, staring, while Rudy rode Allan like a rodeo star and Jerome collapsed to his knees.

My God, she mouthed, no wind behind it. *My God, my God*. There was a dull throbbing pain in the side of her neck. Her hand went up to massage it, came away with a thin smear of blood. "Omigod," she croaked, staggering back a step in horror.

Then her gaze fell upon the cross: on the floor, less than five feet away, where she'd dropped it. It shimmered faintly in the overhead light.

Slowly at first, then madly faster, she moved past the struggling figures and wrapped one fist around the cross. It seemed to pulsate in her hand like a living thing: warm and vibrant and deadly.

And then she was coming up behind Rudy, both hands on the cross, hefting it like a Louisville Slugger. She wanted to call his name, to make him turn, so that he would see her face when the moment came. But she didn't want to blow her chance; if she did, they were all dead, and she knew it.

Rudy was mechanically pounding Allan's head against the counter. The dispatcher's arms flapped limply down either side; his legs were no longer even kicking. It occurred to Josalyn, fleetingly, that it might already be too late to save him. She thought about his twinkling eyes, his constantly burning pipe, his smile. She flashed back over the hours spent at his side, manning the phones, weathering disaster after disaster, sinking deeper and deeper into helplessness and despair and persisting despite it. She saw him in the moment that the call had come in about Armond and T.C.; she saw him comforting Doug, compassion burning in his eyes; she saw him on Bleecker Street, just outside The Other End, tight-faced as he gave his final good-night hug to Ian. . . .

All this, in the second before she swung forward with the cross and struck Rudy squarely at the base of the skull.

The world went white with pain. If a billion gibbering demons were set afire inside his head, their cumulative scream would have been no louder than the one that went off when the cross hit, knocking him forward, not even aware that his hands had slackened and set Allan free, not even aware that he was falling. He did a clumsy flip off the counter, landed on his neck with a sickening crunch that would signify a broken neck in a mortal man. There was no sight. There was no sound. Just a pain so intense as to be an abstraction, something beyond a nervous system's ability to comprehend . . . something to stagger the mind of God.

Rudy scuttled backwards across the floor, howling insanely. He didn't see Josalyn come around the counter, didn't see the fixed expression of vengeance on her face, didn't see the incandescent golf swing as the cross came around again, slamming upward into his face, breaking his nose, burning its shape into his flesh, lifting him off the floor and crashing him backwards through the storefront window.

And then he was on the sidewalk, in the rain; and though the pain still screamed through him like smelting iron, he could see Spring Street stretching out in either direction. Mindless, he struggled to his feet. His knees gave, cracked hard against the pavement. He didn't feel it. Something else had taken over. He got back up and staggered east, his breath rasping like gravel down a chute, his dead heart pounding.

Staggering east, dangerously close to the first rays of dawn that threatened to cut through the dense cloud cover.

It was now 5:30, precisely.

Josalyn was tending to Jerome when the van pulled up, three minutes later. She had soaked a paper towel in holy water and was cleansing the wound, having already mopped up most of the blood. Her hunch had paid off: they were both amazed by how quickly the pain and swelling receded.

They weren't quite so confident about Allan's recovery. He wasn't dead, but he was unconscious, and his breath susurred weakly between the pale lips of his chalk-white face. Josalyn checked for any visible wounds, found none. In a way, that scared her more than anything. She had wiped his brow with holy water, and then she had called for an ambulance.

So when the van pulled up, she half-expected a stream of paramedics to file through the door. Instead, Joseph and Stephen raced in, blankly staring at the destruction, Joseph's mouth and fists working in a spastic display of frustration and rage.

"THAT WAY!" she hollered, pointing east. Her mind gave her a spitfire image of herself, decked out like a saloon maid in a cheesy Western, yelling *they went thataway, sheriff! Head 'em off at the pass!* But giggling was out of the question.

Joseph whipped around and headed back toward the van. Stephen hesitated, fidgeting like an eight-year-old who hadda go to the baffroom, a question molding itself across his face as he stared first at Allan, then Jerome, then Josalyn.

"NO, STEPHEN!" she bellowed, half-guessing the question, not really caring whether or not she was right. "JUST GET HIM!" She pointed a finger at the van like Jesus, directing the moneylenders to the door. Her gaze, when Stephen met it, was a bolt of crazy, imperative fire. He turned and ran, as much to get away from her as to try and find Rudy. She frightened him, in that moment, as much as anything he'd ever seen.

Josalyn watched Stephen disappear around the side of the van, saw it peel out and blast away a moment later. Then she looked down into Jerome's eyes, saw her own dull shock reflected there. Then she looked away.

"We've got to tend to that neck of yours," he said softly.

"I'm all right," she said, turning back to him.

"No, you aren't. Here. Let me." He took a dry paper towel from the stack in her hand, emptied a vial into it, and gently held it to her wounds. It burned like a bastard for a few seconds, then began to feel very, very, good. Jerome's touch was tender, like a woman's. She didn't try to stop him.

Presently, the sounds of the storm were cut by a siren's distant banshee wail. Another joined it, then another. *It's almost over,* she thought. A nameless emotion washed over her. She couldn't have named it if she tried.

The sirens came nearer.

CHAPTER 49

"Figures," Joseph growled, gunning the engine. "Every time, we just miss him. Did you notice that? Every time, we get there just in time to see 'em scrapin' up another body, man. I can't stand it." Staring straight ahead at the road, dimly visible through the rain that pounded against the windshield and the pavement, he didn't see Stephen's eyes upon him. "But this time, we'll get him," he continued. "Cocksucker is *not* getting away this time."

Stephen just looked at him, outwardly responding not at all. Part of him was still down in the generator room, hands drenched in the last black heart blood of the bag lady whose eyes had flown open at the second of impact and riveted on his, squirming with an evil life as yet unborn. Part of him was still down there in that undead abortion clinic, kneeling over the body, his hands still on the wood of the stake and the mallet, the full reality of the situation striking home at long long last.

She was already dead, his mind informed him for the umpteenth time. *I didn't kill her. I killed the thing that was going to take her over. I killed the monster.* He needed to keep telling himself that, even though it was true, even though he already knew it. *I killed the monster.* He had to keep telling himself that, or he was going to go insane.

"Gonna get him," Joseph repeated, paying no attention to Stephen, talking mostly to himself. He slammed on the brakes abruptly, skidding to a halt at the intersection of Spring and Bowery, blindly looking both ways through the fogged-up windows.

He didn't even see the figure that raced up to the van until it started slamming against Stephen's door.

"YAH!" Stephen yelped, flying sideways out of his seat and right into Joseph's side. Joseph pushed him roughly back and said, "Roll down your window, dumbshit." He could tell right away that it wasn't an attack; even dimly seen, the figure pounding on the door looked nothing like Rudy.

Just then, the door flew open. Stephen's screams stifled in his throat; Joseph leaped forward expectantly. Danny Young grinned in at them and started shouting hysterically, his long hair plastered to his skull, his glasses beaded up with steam and water.

"All right!" Danny shouted. "He's right over there!" Pointing south down the Bowery, behind him and to their right. "Running like crazy! Are we gonna get him now?"

"Hop in," Joseph said, already starting to roll. Danny jumped in and slammed the door behind him in one graceful motion, landing on Stephen's lap as the van wheeled the corner and plowed down the Bowery. Stephen whoofed out air and struggled uncomfortably underneath.

They spotted him about halfway down the block, scuttling over the narrow concrete median strip, cutting over to Broome Street on the other side. "*Son of a bitch!*" Joseph howled, whipping the wheel around suddenly to the right, parking the van haphazardly at the curb. "Lock it up!" he yelled, cutting the engine and pocketing the key in one swift motion, his door already opening, his bulk surging out into the street. Danny leaped out, Stephen scrambling after him.

Then they were running, the three of them, running

catercorner across the Bowery and up to Broome, then around the bend and east. Overhead, a bolt of lightning like a neon chain saw sliced through the clouds; and halfway down the block, they saw him.

The sun! Rudy thought as the lightning shed its flicker-flash of brilliance. He half-expected to be fried in an instant, run the flesh-to-bone-to-ashes gamut that poor old Christopher Lee ran so many times in the old Hammer horror films. Then it was dark again, and he was still running, so he knew that it wasn't over yet.

But he could already feel the sun, slowly baking its way into his skin. It felt like sunburn: a faint impression of heat that became a tingling and then graduated into burning pain. It was only starting to tingle now, but it would get much worse in a few minutes; and the wounds in his head, hands, and belly felt like somebody was poking them with red-hot tweezers. Even with the cool rain pounding down on him in freshets, the heat was getting worse.

Rudy whipped around the corner, off of Broome and onto Chrystie. Up ahead of him, at the end of the block, lay the subway entrance to the Grand Street station. He slowed for a moment, blinking back rain, searching for the arch above the entrance. His left heel landed on a formless wad of sopping cardboard. He slipped, almost lost his balance, waved his arms like a circus clown on a high wire, howling and cursing the pain.

That was when he saw the three figures racing down the street toward him.

"Jesus Christ," he whined, and abruptly his tongue felt like a lump of burning coal. He shrieked, an inferno inside his head, and bolted down Chrystie Street like Richard Pryor in freebasing flames.

Behind him, the three figures were closing in.

Joseph was in the lead, teeth clenched, breath hissing warmly through them. He was a huge man, not built for speed . . . not since high school, in fact, had he been

forced to do anything more than hustle across a street
. . . but he was moving at a speed that would have surprised him if he thought about it. If he'd had anything but
vengeance on his mind.

Behind him, Danny and Stephen were laboring to
keep up. He didn't hear them; he was scarcely aware of
their existence. His eyes were set like the cross hairs of a
bazooka's sights on Rudy, less than thirty yards ahead and
closing.

I got you now, shitheel, he thought, pushing even
harder, feeling the distance between them diminish with
every step forward, every thundering step. Twenty-five
yards. Twenty. Fifteen, as Rudy passed the fireplug that
marked the last third of the block. Ten, as Joseph passed it
seconds later.

Five yards, as Rudy rounded the corner and limped
frantically toward the stairs. Three, as Rudy stopped
suddenly and brought his hands up to shield his eyes. Two,
as Joseph lumbered forward, not aware that Rudy had been
blinded by Armond's ultimate closing gift: a cross of holy
water, compounded by the rain to form a phosphorescent
pool that spanned the width of the subway entrance. Then
one yard. Then none.

Joseph roared, twirling Rudy around by one shoulder,
and the vampire's fist came around so hard, so fast, that
Joseph didn't even know he was falling until he smacked
the sidewalk. The big man shook his head, trying to clear it;
his peripheral vision caught a glimpse of Rudy looming
overhead, lips snarling in the horrible face . . .

. . . and then Stephen rushed past him, not slowing,
not braking, running full-tilt and straight into the vampire,
who grunted with surprise and then staggered backwards,
tripped over the top step, and tumbled end-over-end down
the steps.

For a micro-second, it looked like Stephen would be
able to stop. Then he, too, was pulled downward by
momentum, plummeting after Rudy without so much as a
whimper, the two of them vanished from view.

* * *

. . . *and he was falling, he was falling, very much like a dream, the repetitiveness of the move smacking of unreality as he hit a step, bounced, hit a step, bounced, tumbling over and over all the while, a jagged gray continuum streaking by his face but never striking it as he rolled and bounced and tumbled and fell . . .*

. . . *and hit the floor on his left side, skidding several feet before breaking into a roll again that came to a stop when he hit the wall. He looked over, dazed, and saw that Rudy was next to him, propped up against the wall, looking like a man who'd just had the rug pulled out from under him.*

Their eyes met.

And he was not seeing Rudy, he was seeing a monstrous white-face caricature of Rudy, a portrait of Dorian Gray made flesh, every sin clearly etched across the features in holy water firebursts of blistering horror, in the cross-shaped brand across the face that warped contusively above the broken nose, in the blackened bald spot where the hair had burned away at the crown of the head, in the roaring red fire of those inhuman eyes.

He heard himself saying I'm going to kill you *and reached automatically into his messenger bag. He felt the heft of the cross in his hand. He felt it light up like one of those gag light bulbs that you get at novelty stores, the ones that run on batteries and glow at the push of a button. He felt the cross rise up out of the bag, so bright that even he winced reflexively against it.*

He saw Rudy's face peel back in terror, saw the vampire whirl suddenly and blunder to its feet.

He heard the footsteps hurrying down the steps.

He felt himself starting to rise.

Rudy took off in a stumbling run toward the turnstiles. The others were close behind him, but the rumble of an oncoming train overwhelmed them in his ears. It was coming from the staircase on the left-hand side. He veered that way, reaching the turnstiles and vaulting over them, landing awkwardly and teetering for a long dangerous second before moving on.

Stephen was next to hit the turnstiles. He barely heard the shouts of the guy in the token booth as he hurtled over the metal crossbar and raced after Rudy.

By the time Joseph leaped over the top, the guy from the token booth was on an intersect course with Danny. "HOLD IT RIGHT THERE!" the guy screamed, and Danny skittered to a halt.

"B-But . . ." he began.

"You gotta pay for all *those* guys, buddy!" the token vendor roared. His face was red, his nostrils flaring. Danny thought briefly of the subway slugs in his pockets, caught himself in the nick of time, and then flipped the man four one-dollar bills.

"Keep the change," he said, and vaulted the turnstiles.

Downstairs, the train was thundering to a stop. Stephen saw Rudy round the foot of the stairs and head toward the front of the train. Stephen jumped the last six steps and took off after him, still clutching the cross.

He wanted to scream something . . . a threat, Rudy's name, an oath to God . . . but it was all he could do to keep the breath pumping in and out of his lungs as he ran, limping drastically now, the tumble down the stairs finally catching up with him. He kept apace of Rudy, pushing as hard as he could but unable to gain any ground. The tears were starting to come; he cursed at them, tried to shame them away. They bided their time, waiting.

The doors opened. Nobody else was on the platform. Ahead of him, Rudy continued to run. Stephen pursued him.

All the way to the front of the train.

Joseph hit the foot of the steps and turned. Way down at the end of the platform, Rudy and Stephen were a pair of frantic bug-sized specks. He looked at them, knew that he wasn't going to catch them, and stopped.

There was an open door directly in front of him. Joseph looked at it, looked at the train it was attached to. The beauty, the perfection of it, struck him in a single clear bolt of brilliance.

He smiled.

And stepped onto the train.

"D train to Coney Island," the conductor's voice came over the loudspeakers, a robot with a Brooklyn accent. "Watch the closing doors."

They reached the front of the train, Rudy crossing the threshold of the furthermost door just as the conductor made his speech. A shudder went through the train as the doors slid mechanically shut.

Stephen was just a second too late.

"*NOOOOO!!!*" he wailed. His fist came up, pounded against the glass windows. He slammed his full weight against the doors. They refused to budge. "*NOOOOO!!!*" he wailed again, jamming his fingers into the space between the rubber lips that buffered the doors from one another. He pulled at them with all his strength. They refused to budge.

The train began to move.

"*NOOOOOO!!!*" he wailed, one final time. He fell against the door as it began to skid past him. On the other side of the window, Rudy was laughing and laughing and laughing. Stephen kept pace for almost thirty seconds as the train ground slowly forward. Then it picked up speed, and the metal door frame slammed into his shoulder, bouncing him back slightly and sliding away . . .

. . . and then the train was whipping past him, section after section coming by so quickly that the details began to blur and then vanish into the tunnel, while Stephen screamed impotently at the unfeeling metal and the unfeeling Fates that harbored evil and propelled it into the darkness like loving guardians. . . .

A hand came down on his shoulder. He whirled, every single nerve threatening to leap out through his skin.

It was Danny.

Danny was laughing.

"*Don't you see it? Don't you see it?*" Danny yelled, pointing at the train, practically doubling over with the force of his laughter.

"*See what?*" Stephen screamed back hysterically. "*What the hell are you laughing about?*"

"*It's a D train!*" Danny bellowed over the roar of the train. "*D as in Downtown! D as in Death! D as in Decomposition . . . oh, man, don't you see what's going on?*"

Stephen looked at him blankly, dumbly.

"*This is the last stop in Manhattan, stupid! Don't you know what that means? This train is going to Coney Island, man! This train is going over . . .*"

But Stephen had already figured it out. He started to laugh. They laughed together.

And as the last car lumbered past them, they saw Joseph framed in the window of the back door. He appeared to be laughing, too, just before the darkness swallowed him.

CHAPTER 50

"**O**h, you bastards," Rudy chortled, his cold breath steaming up the window glass. "Oh, you bastards. You thought you had me. You thought you had ol' Rudy nailed, didn't you? You cocksucking bastards . . . oh, ho . . . oh, ho . . ."

The laughter was harsh and dry as dust. It was a nervous reaction, superficial and false; not even he was fooled by it. Underscoring it was a thick dark line of terror: *the proverbial bottom line*, he thought, giggling despite himself, transparent as before.

"But I got away, didn't I?" Filling the air with noise, with his own mad babble. "Couldn't get me, couldn't *catch* me! Too fast, too fast for you, you bastards. . . ." And for the first time, he realized that he could relax now, it was over, his enemies were back there at Grand Street with their thumbs up their asses, Stephen and the others. . . .

Stephen. The memory slapped him across the face like a cold, sobering hand. Who would have thought that Stephen would turn like that, get crazy, try to kill him? Who would have believed it possible? *Not me,* Rudy thought. *Never in a million years.*

And Josalyn. That bitch. Josalyn almost *did* kill him with that fucking cross. He would never have believed that, either. *It's all going wrong,* he mused bitterly. *It's all screwed up, and I don't know why. . . .*

There was laughter, suddenly, behind his ears. Ancient laughter. Terrible, gleeful, mocking laughter that came to him from across an enormous distance, like a transatlantic phone call locking in with startling clarity. And a voice . . . ageless, timeless, infinitely evil . . . said *I tried to warn you. I told you that they'd come. You were careless and arrogant, and now it's all over. Too bad for you.*

"No," Rudy moaned out loud, his hands coming up over his ears to muffle the sound.

Yes, the voice said, behind his ears. *Look at what they've done to you, Rudy. Look at where you are. It's over. All over.*

"YOU DID THIS!" Rudy shrieked, his fingers digging in and yanking on what was left of his hair. "YOU DID THIS TO ME!"

The ancient vampire just laughed, not dignifying the accusation with an answer. The laughter faded, grew faint and ghostly with distance. *All over,* the voice whispered, and was gone.

Leaving Rudy alone to stare at the window, vainly searching for a reflection that wasn't there. It made him crazy. He put his fists through the glass, watching it disperse into a billion glittering shards that were caught up by the wind and sent tinkling against the wall of the tunnel.

All over, the voice echoed in his ears as he staggered back to the middle of the aisle and looked out the front window into the forever darkness of the tunnel. . . .

* * *

They loaded Allan gently onto the stretcher and carried him out to the ambulance. The educated guess was that he had a concussion and multiple contusions. Jerome went along, his arm nicely bandaged. The ambulance sat on the street, its lights strobing and pulsing off the rain-slick streets. Josalyn sat with Detective Brenner and two uniformed cops who took turns looking at the shattered window and the vampire-hunting paraphernalia on the counter. A paramedic busied himself with the wound at her neck.

"That was really stupid, you know," Brenner said, putting a match to his unfiltered Camel and then wearily shaking his head. "You should have called us when you first suspected."

"You wouldn't have believed us," Josalyn maintained, blowing out smoke on an intercept course with the cloud that Brenner was forming in the air. "Ouch!" She winced and cast an irritated, weary glance at the medico. She fished a vial of holy water from her pocket.

"Here, use this . . . it's great stuff." The paramedic looked at Brenner. He nodded.

"We would have checked out this Rudy Pasko a long time ago," he countered. "At the very least, we would have connected him with the disappearance of the two little girls and nailed him *yesterday*." He slammed his fist down on the table and she jumped, caught herself, glued herself back down in her seat with her eyes boring sullenly into the carpet. "We would have had him before all . . . *this* . . . went down." He gestured toward the broken window.

"What you don't understand," she said, her voice tight and controlled, her eyes still on the floor, "is that Rudy isn't an ordinary human."

"Don't give me that . . . ." he started to say.

"Rudy is a *vampire*," she cut in, clipping each syllable off between clenched teeth. "What were you going to do: arrest him? If you know all about this case, you know what a monster he is! You . . . ."

"Young lady, I have been scraping Rudy's victims off

the pavement for over a *week* now! And tonight was the worst, believe you me. Do you know how many dead people I had to look at tonight, Miss Horne? Do you know how many people would still be alive if you hadn't tried this dumb stunt?"

"Do you know how many policemen would be dead if we hadn't? And he'd *still* be out there!"

Brenner stopped cold on that one for a moment, sucked smoke, blew it out in a slow-motion cumulus cloud. His eyes tracked it as it wafted across the room toward the broken window.

"Do you have anyone else out there?" he said finally.

She glanced quickly at the switchboard, then away.

"Don't play games, Miss Horne. I saw that one coming." He leveled a paternal, almost kindly gaze at her and then continued. "Bring them in, please. Call them. Beep them. Whatever you do, do it. This has gone on long enough."

"But they might get him . . ." she said, and her eyes went vague, and she saw Joseph and Stephen in matching pools of gore, splayed out like Allan and Armond and Claire and all the others . . . like Ian. . . .

"Let's not hold our breath on that, shall we?" he said, seeing through her, knowing that he'd won.

Josalyn nodded almost imperceptibly at him, acquiescing. Then she sighed and turned wearily to the switchboard, where she proceeded to punch in first Stephen's number, then Joseph's. She was tired. Very tired.

Get him, Joseph, whispered a voice inside her mind. *Don't let them stop you. Nail him down.*

There was something wrong with the tunnel.

Rudy's face was pressed to the glass of the front window, panting shallowly. The fear was building up inside him, inexorably squeezing and fusing his innards like a vise in the hands of an infinitely patient executioner. It had seemed that the train was rolling a long time without stopping; and when he first saw the light up ahead, he had assumed that they were finally coming to a station.

But he was wrong.

He was wrong, and the ancient vampire was right, and he knew it now. He knew it with one last glimpse of the dim light ahead: a light so faint as to be merely suggested, already too bright for him to bear.

I've gone all the way in, Stephen, he heard himself saying in a long-ago, faraway voice. *I've gone all the way into the darkness, Stephen*. . . .

A scream, boiling up from the depths of his soul as he turned to run at last.

And you know what I found in there?

Running. Running madly. Toward the back of the train.

Know what I found in there? in there? in . . . the voice echoed madly.

Whimpering now, throwing open the door, running through it, running faster, toward the back of the train.

Found the other side.

Throwing open the door.

Found the other side, Stephen.

Running.

The other side, Stephen.

Throwing open the door.

Found the light.

And running.

Found the light at the end.

And running, and sobbing, and throwing open the door. Too slow.

The proverbial light at the end of the tunnel, old buddy, old chum.

Too slow.

My friend.

Too slow, hating himself for being too fucking slow as he ran, madly, toward the back of the train.

And away from the light.

At the end.

Traffic was light on the Manhattan Bridge at six o'clock on a Wednesday morning. A few trucks and delivery vans, a few lonely motorists beating the rush: a mere foreshadowing of the traffic to come. It was a beautiful morning to be making the drive; the clouds were dispersing; the rain had left the air smelling crisp, clean, crackling with life.

And the sunrise this morning was absolutely breathtaking.

The center of the bridge began to tremble, and a low raucous thundering sound came up from out of nowhere to bury the noise of the six o'clock traffic. Only a few of the morning's motorists were disoriented by the mounting rumble and shudder: all tourists and out-of-towners, at that. The rest of them naturally took it for granted.

Trains went over this bridge all the time.

The downtown D express to Coney Island poked its nose out of the tunnel and into the light just as Rudy boarded the third car from the rear of the train. By the time he reached the second-to-the-last car, one-third of the train was exposed to the sun. It was roundly bisected into light and dark halves before Rudy made it to the end of the car.

When the last door flew open, Joseph was waiting for him.

"NOOOO!" Rudy screamed. Joseph grinned wickedly at him, showing teeth. The messenger bag dangled from one massive hand. Joseph let it drop to the floor and kicked it.

"No weapons, bucko. With my bare hands. Right now." Joseph dropped back against the rear door, bracing himself with spraddled legs, coyly motioning Rudy forward. "Come and get it, Rudy! *I'm waiting for you!*"

Nobody could have foreseen the speed with which Rudy raced forward at that moment: not Joseph, not Rudy, not even the ancient vampire whose whimsical joyride set the whole grim tableau into motion. Maybe it was a sudden burst of last-ditch survival adrenaline; maybe it was the fact that the train lurched to a sudden, grinding halt. Whatever the case, Rudy Pasko flew the length of the car as if he'd been fired out of a cannon, slamming into Joseph Hunter so hard and so fast that the glass starred and sagged behind the hunter's back, threatening to give way altogether.

Joseph didn't even appear to feel it. His grin was undiminished. His hands clamped down on Rudy's shoulders, hoisting the vampire up to dangle at arm's length and two feet in the air.

"C'mon, you little supernatural sonofabitch," Joseph said. "Let's take a walk."

He took a step forward, Rudy still in tow. The train lurched suddenly, sickly, back into motion. Joseph staggered forward in a series of awkward little dance steps, slamming Rudy's back into a pole.

Rudy went apeshit.

And Joseph's beeper went off.

Beepbeepbeepbeep. Rudy clawed at Joseph's arms like a wildcat, raking out great bleeding divots of fabric and flesh. Joseph winced back pain and leaned forward, pressing Rudy's spine into the pole, trying to fuse them. *Beepbeepbeepbeep*. Rudy flailed out with his feet, catching Joseph in the thighs with a volley of vicious kicks that sent cramps screaming through the muscles of his legs. *Beepbeepbeepbeep*. Joseph folded up slightly. Rudy's hand snaked out, grabbed a handful of Joseph's hair, and pulled with brutal, incredible strength.

Beepbeepbeepbeepbeepbeepbeep as Joseph howled, the world fading out in a brilliant white flash, white flash turning red, red flood turning back into Rudy's snarling face, cold, spittle lips . . . red, rolling eyes. *Beepbeepbeepbeepbeepbeep* in his ears, driving him crazy, filling his mind with hate that boiled up and out of him like a geyser of cold, oily blackness. Hate the job. Hate the city. Hate the sound of the beeper. Hate the lousy motherfucker in my hands. Hate this pain. . . .

And Rudy kicked and thrashed and wailed and ripped out the handful of Joseph's hair, then dug his nails into the raw meat of the scalp. And the beeper went on and on and on. And the pain and the sound and the sheer effort of holding Rudy up weighed down on Joseph, making his knees start to buckle, making him choke down the terrible fear that he wouldn't be able to keep it up, he was going to lose it, he was going to die and it would all have been for nothing. . . .

"*NO!*" he screamed, throwing all of his strength into one last desperate surge forward. . . .

. . . and sunlight streamed in through the windows, a solid wall of light that rolled down the length of the car like a bulldozer's blade. It swept over them just as Joseph pinned Rudy back against the pole. It drowned them in its radiance.

Rudy began to decompose.

It began with the x-shaped brand at the base of his skull, the blistering bald spot at the crown: a mottled, red-black scum oozed up to the surface as if squeezed from a tube. It slopped over his shoulders and down the sides of his head as he jerked and stiffened like a man being pulled apart by horses. His head lolled back, face contorted with agony. Sunlight hit the crosshatched tattoo across the broken nose, the sore on the lip, the dangling earlobe. A pale slime, like blood and blobs of curdled milk, spilled down into his open mouth.

. . . *and he was plummeting face-first into a vast, oily blackness, his disembodied awareness shrieking in terror as the hot, fetid wind choked him and roared like a million roasting souls, drowning out all thought as he fought to lose consciousness, to abandon all awareness of the horror yawning before him.* . . .

Rudy screamed: burbled at first, then pushing through, a deafening air-raid siren of anguish that warbled and screeched and raked at Joseph's eardrums like needles, while a geyser of pale, rank fluid arced outward from the mouth and splattered all over their shoes. When Peggy Lewin died, it was like a single soul being doused with gasoline and lit; Rudy's was more like the scream of legions, of the hundreds of thousands who died at Treblinka all screaming in unison. It was a sound that no single dying human could make.

. . . *and the roar of the wind was laughter, hideous*

and all-consuming laughter that laid his soul bare, peeled away to reveal the sour core of his arrogance and his ignorance, and the void parted its thick, acrid clouds to reveal a huge demonic maw, opening wide to receive him as he fell, buffeting against the finely veined membrane, screaming as he plunged down and down and . . .

Rudy kicked and clawed like a wind-up puppy, blindly thrashing at the air in mechanical frenzy. His face swelled up, turned gray-green and murky, like a layer of scum on a stagnant pool. The red light faded from his eyes, leaving behind a pair of yellowish hard-boiled eggs that had no pupils, no irises, no veins.

Still he screamed, the sound spiraling up into ultra-sonic frequencies, cutting through the rumble of the train like a dentist's drill. The flesh around the mouth sputtered and frayed, stretching across his jawbones like molten rubber bands. Something started to bubble up behind the eyes.

. . . and he was blind, he was blind, the hot howling wind robbing him, deafening him, sealing him in with its molten kiss, deaf to his own choking screams, screams that pulsed with the madly staccato beepbeepbeepbeep *that seemed so very far away. . . .*

Rudy's wind-up motion was grinding down to the last few turns of the key. His scream broke up into a grotesque parody of the beeper's shrill, steady pulse, out of phase and painfully distorting. The meat of his shoulders went soft and spongy under Joseph's hands. Joseph gripped them harder, pushing Rudy against the pole. Something snapped, and Joseph's fingers tore through the fabric of Rudy's shirt, sinking to the hilt in writhing, rotting meat and muscle. Thick clouds of sickly green vapor spewed hissing from the punctured flesh. Rudy's eyes exploded suddenly like tiny pus-filled water balloons.

Joseph screamed, finally able to stand it no more, slipping helplessly over the edge into madness. He jerked his hands away frantically. Rudy stuck to them. A thin animal squeal ripped itself from Joseph's throat; Rudy flapped and flopped at the ends of his arms as Joseph tried desperately to shake the body loose.

. . . and all was fire, all was pain, raw fear and madness spiraling upward and echoing back as his soul crisped and rolled and fell, like a shooting star, across endless plains of molten fire where the countless writhing hordes of the damned paused in their suffering to applaud the spectacle blazing through the vaulted heavens above them; falling, falling, the tormentors jeering and pointing with long, crooked fingers as the dying soul of Rudy Pasko arced headfirst into oblivion. . . .

Rudy finally came loose with a sputtering sound, slapping back against the pole and then slithering down its length like a warm stick of butter. Death rattled in his throat, a stopwatch ticking off the final seconds with pitiless precision. His moldering hands clenched and unclenched in a farewell spasm as he folded up on the floor, settling into himself like freshly mixed batter.

Then the maggots began to squirm in Rudy's eye sockets, and Joseph fell back blindly against the rear door. His hands pushed through the weakened window glass, sent it flying outward in a meteor shower of crystalline fragments that twinkled and sang as they plummeted toward the tracks and the East River below. A blast of air pounded into his face, buffeting him backwards like an enormous hand. It may well have been the only thing that kept him from going the way of the window.

It was certainly the only thing that kept him from puking.

Got him, he thought, and then the merciful black glove of unconsciousness wrapped around him, lowering him gently to his knees, to his side, to a brief, restful moment of blessed oblivion. . . .

Less than a minute later, Joseph Hunter awoke to the sound of his beeper. His hand automatically snaked across the floor, groping for the goddamn alarm clock; it touched something wet and unpleasant, snapping him back into his surroundings just as his hand recoiled in revulsion.

"Jesus Christ," he moaned, struggling to his knees. The taste of bile was still heavy in his throat; the stench of decay was still heavy in the air. He kept his gaze clear of the thing on the floor; in a big way, it was the last thing in the world that he needed to see.

Instead, he pulled himself to his feet and looked out the window at the morning sky. In spite of everything . . . or because of it, perhaps . . . the sunrise had never seemed quite so beautiful, bright red and orange gracefully segueing into a washed-out blue that the next hour would ripen into brilliance. The color patchwork reflected warmly off the thousandfold windows of lower Manhattan, making the skyline shimmer and gleam like the jewel-studded spires of a fabled city in a fantasy tale.

It's over, his mind informed him with a silent sigh of relief. *It's finally over.* A curious calm, just this side of emptiness, stole through him like a midnight prowler. Part of it was exhaustion, of course: twenty-four hours on the razor's edge tend to do that. And part of it was, just as surely, the calm that follows the storm.

But more than anything, it was the simple fact that it was *over,* in so many ways. More than just Rudy had been put to rest, at long last and forever; something more than just evil had been overcome. Joseph's memory skimmed over the events of the past eight days, back to the day when his mother had first been stricken down. He ran a silent inventory of all the pain collected, the suffering sustained, the violence taken in and meted out, the guilt and fury.

It still hurt. Just not as badly. And he had a feeling that it was going to get a whole lot better. In time.

He smiled.

On the downhill side of the Manhattan Bridge, the D express to Coney Island lumbered steadily toward the tunnel mouth of Brooklyn. A barge drifted slowly through the water below, heading westward into the depths of upper New York Harbor. To Joseph's right, the sun cast spiderweb shadows through the suspension cables of the Brooklyn Bridge, was reflected by the waves. Beyond, the Statue of Liberty was a child's toy soldier in a wash of white footlights, no bigger than his thumb. Why it should strike him as so unspeakably beautiful, all of a sudden, was something that he wouldn't even try to explain.

But *damn*, it felt good to be alive, riding on the train, having waded through the wall of fire without a burn that couldn't be healed. The next station stop was DeKalb Avenue: only seven blocks away from the apartment that he shared with no one. Not even the ghosts. He would be there in less than fifteen minutes.

The stench of death was still upon him, but it would wash off easily enough. And then he would answer the beeper that he silenced now, finally, with a flick of his gore-smeared thumb.

And then, perhaps, he would go through his belongings: what to pack, what to sell, and what to throw away.

The nightmare was over.

And Joseph Hunter was free.

The Other Side

No charges were pressed. In the end, it was easier to construct a myth from whole cloth, using only the inescapable snippets of reality. There was no getting around the victims, of course, and no way around Rudy; but the survivors of the hunt were encouraged to disappear for a while, lick their wounds, recuperate behind a swaddling screen of welcome anonymity. They were happy to oblige.

Twenty-nine deaths had resulted directly from that first late-night joyride on the RR train. Of those, nineteen were credited to Rudy Pasko. Some, like Peggy Lewin and Dod "The Bod" Stebbits, were just as easily swept into the bottomless caseload of murders *not* committed by Rudy Pasko; others, like the derelict vampires, were never even brought up at all. At the same time, much was made of the butchered roommates, the rats and dead children in his apartment, the decapitated bag lady, the writing on the walls, the splatter-film slayings, the staking of Ian Macklay, and the "indiscriminate savagery" of his final killing spree.

The pièce de résistance, of course, remained the carnage on the "Terror Train." Detective Brenner and the others who were pressured to create more palatable fictions for the public were at least free to admit that "We have no idea how he did it. We'll probably never know. It's our guess that they'll still be wondering in 150 years."

Rudy Pasko was captured and killed, as the legend would have it, by a pair of veteran patrolmen named Sweeney and Anderson. For their imaginary heroics, they got a lot of publicity, a nice set of brownie points, and a free boot up the ladder. Brenner ate a lot of shit, spat it out in sanitized form, performed to everyone's satisfaction, and took his benefits under the table.

For almost three weeks, Rudy's name enjoyed the kind of notoriety that he'd always hungered for in life. His picture was in all the papers, along with sketchy and highly speculative recountings of his sordid life and times. He joined the lofty pantheon of celebrated psychos, became one with the likes of Charles Manson, Jim Jones, Ed Gein, Jack the Ripper, and the Boston Strangler.

TV docu-dramas were conceived and announced: one of them boasted its "sensitive, upbeat portrayal of the tough, courageous cops who risked everything to stop the 'Subway Psycho.'" Ed Koch brought him up in speeches. Johnny Carson made Rudy Pasko jokes in his opening monologues. Jimmy Swaggart and his Bible-thumping hordes branded him a "demon from Hell" and made up wild stories about him; oddly enough, they were much closer to the truth than anyone dreamed.

His moment in the sun, as it were, took endless forms. His name popped up at cocktail parties and American Legion posts, flicking off the tip of every waggling tongue in the civilized world. He even made his way into the common street parlance, where guys like Three Card Monty would come back at hecklers with lines like, "Who do you think you *are*, blood? Fuckin' Rudy *Pasko* or sumpin'?"

Then the weeks turned into months, and the public imagination was inevitably diverted. New robberies, rapes, and murders. Wars and rumors of wars. Rising interest rates. Dwindling attention spans. One disaster after another, all trotted out in front of the collective eye like ducks in a shooting gallery, given their fifteen seconds in the light, then banished to the oblivion on the other side.

The press conferences were over. The families had assembled, the funerals had been staged, the bodies were long in the ground. The blood had been scoured and sandblasted off. The phosphor dots flickered and faded away.

Rudy Pasko was all but forgotten.

* * *

On the hill . . .

Autumn, and the year's slow skidding on the downhill side. Trees, many trees, rapt with deathly metamorphosis, resplendent in their funeral attire. A light breeze, rippling through the raiments. A mellowed sun, softly sustaining their glow. And the colors: the bright orange and rich red and yellow, the gold and the brown and the lingering green.

In the clearing . . .

A rolling plateau of freshly manicured lawn. A narrow road, winding through it like a thin, gray ribbon, trailing down to the bottom of the hill. A few scattered wreaths. A few severed bouquets.

Rows and rows of sculpted stone, carved and autographed by death.

In front of the grave . . .

Joseph stood, for a moment, in silently thrumming indecision. He'd been fine on the drive out, without a crack in his outward composure; but standing there, with the moment finally at hand, he wavered slightly on his feet and in his will to see it through.

The breeze tugged gently at the collar of his denim jacket, ran tentative phantom fingers through his hair. *It's nice out here*, he thought, smiling faintly. *Man, you could've done worse than to have family in Monroe. Why you left this place for the city is something I'll never understand*. He got a sudden vivid flash of the cemeteries in Queens . . . Calvary, New Calvary, Mt. Zion, Evergreen . . . and he shuddered, picturing the endless acres of cramped and anonymous tombstones, in tight little rows that stretched for miles.

He remembered cruising with Ian once down the Brooklyn-Queens Expressway, and Ian had said, "Jesus, it must be *standing room only* in that place! I mean, look at the way those things are packed together!" He'd smacked himself across the forehead, flashed a typical wild-ass grin, and added, "If I ever wind up in there, make sure they put down S.R.O. instead of R.I.P., okay?" It had been funny at the time.

"Wiseass," Joseph muttered, and his voice brought him back to the present. Looking down at Ian's grave, it was almost funny again; and he laughed, less from genuine amusement than from simple need. "You crazy little bastard. Nothing sacred in *your* book. That was for sure."

Ian's headstone stared back at him, mute and gray. Joseph took a last drag off his cigarette and then hunkered down on his haunches, grinding the butt out on a patch of ungrown soil. He set down the paper bag that was in his other hand, and it faintly tinkled: the sound of glass on glass.

In the valley, in the distance, a lone car was approaching. The size of a horsefly, from where he crouched, but already he could hear the mellow drone of its engine. *Sound really carries in the country,* he mused. It was something that he planned on getting used to, very soon.

He opened the bag. There were two cool pints of Guinness inside. He took them out, set them down, crumpled up the empty bag and stuffed it into his back pocket. Then he reached into his jacket, palmed his Swiss Army knife, and used the bottle opener to uncap them. A thin white mist wafted out from their open mouths.

"I'm leaving today," he said, turning back to address the grave. "I am finally going. All my stuff's in the van." He smiled, a brief and bittersweet muscular reaction.

"Yeah, I can hear you now," he continued, and then pulled off a passable Ian Macklay imitation. "'So what the hell took you so long, might I ask? Sensitivity training through the Learning Exchange? Advanced Toe-Sucking seminars three times a month?'" Again he laughed, head ruefully shaking. "Fucking smartass."

God, this is weird, Joseph thought. *He can't hear you. You know it. You spend too much time talking to tombstones these days.* Below, the car was getting closer. He hoped that it wouldn't come up. Performing the ritual was hard enough; he did not want an audience.

Joseph pocketed the caps and the butt, then picked up

the pints and stood. He took several steps to the right before moving inward; there was something about the idea of walking over Ian's body that made slugs seem to crawl in his stomach. At the tombstone, he stopped and eased himself down, sitting cross-legged beside it.

"Yeah. Well. So here's how it is," he said finally. "I couldn't leave without saying goodbye to you, champ. I just wanted to tell you where I'm going. So you'd know." He snorted and smiled, gently mocking himself and the scene's slow unfolding. "I just really wanted to talk to you. That's what it boils down to. I just really wanted to talk.

"I . . . I brought you somethin'."

Joseph held the pints aloft, watched them glisten in the sun. He leaned one shoulder against the tombstone, rubbing briefly against it as he might have with his friend in a rare, tipsy moment of intimacy. Then he grinned and clinked the bottles together.

"To us, man. Forever. To The Defender and his faithful teenage sidekick, Butch S-S-Sampson. . . ."

He was starting to cry a little, and that was just fine. The last few months had seen his emotions move closer and closer to the surface. He no longer felt caged inside himself, and the weight on his shoulders was gone. It was easier to laugh, easier to cry, and both were somehow sweeter than they'd ever been before. Slowly but surely, he was making his peace with the world.

With a jittering right hand, he poured about three ounces of Guinness on Ian's grave, then set the bottle down at the foot of the tombstone and swigged deeply on the pint in his left. He fought to speak clearly, without tears.

"Allan's got a cousin who owns a print shop down in Lancaster, Pennsylvania." Joseph cleared his throat. "Says he can give me a job. Delivery, print-shop assistant, that kind of thing. Doesn't pay as much, but it's cheaper out there, and I've got a couple thousand from Mama's insurance to hold me over 'til I'm on my feet. Should be okay. . . ."

The wind blew, a faint chill rustling through the grass. Joseph paused, to light another smoke, cupping the flame in his hands. He looked at Ian's mute grave, smiled, and shook his head.

"You know, ol' Stevie might be a man yet." He laughed. "He split town right after the hunt, went back to stay with his parents. I thought that was the last I'd see of him; but the little fucker called me two weeks ago, said he was in New York to pick up the rest of his stuff, wanted to take me to dinner.

"It was all right. He looked a couple of thousand years older for the wear, but he's not such a geek anymore." He snorted, took a swig. "Just wanted to thank me. Turns out he's up in Stamford now, studying computer programming. Figures, huh? Christ . . ."

The sun was starting its majestic descent into the horizon, tinting the underside of the clouds with broad sweeps of purple and gold, beaming heavenly spotlights down into the valley. The sound of the car was very close now, though he'd forgotten completely about it; and he looked up to see a long-faced family drive slowly past on the narrow cemetery road. He waved to them, and they nodded in return; theirs was a passing communion, not an intrusion.

Wonder who they're mourning, he thought, and the echo of the words washed through him in waves of longing and loss and love. He paused, steeling himself. The car rolled off into the sunset.

"Josalyn and Allan are very tight these days." This was going to be the hardest part, he knew. "Allan's in a neck brace, but he's okay. Makes him look like a giant ring pacifier." He laughed, took a short swig, and paused. "Josalyn saved his life, you know. You would have been proud." He leaned forward, grinning fiercely. "She kicked Rudy's ass, Ian. She really cleaned that pinhead's clock."

He finished his Guinness, reached for Ian's, thought better of it. His smile faded.

"She and Allan are . . ." *Say it. Get it out.* "They're getting really close, buddy." He lowered his voice. "They still see too much of you in each other's eyes to be more than just close. But they will. That's my guess."

The sun's last rays were playing across the sky, a magnificent spectacle that went largely unnoticed by the solitary figure on the hill. The air bit ever so slightly as Joseph stood and flipped the collar of his jacket up. Tonight would be chilly, no doubt about it.

He choked a little, back in his throat.

"Time heals, my man," he said. "The pain fades, if you let it. They won't ever forget you . . . hell, it's half love for you that brought 'em together in the *first* place.. . ." He let it trail off.

From Ian's grave, silence.

"You understand, don't you?" Expecting no answer. Gauging his own feelings for a sense of right-or-wrongness.

He felt fine. He felt . . . clean.

"They'll never forget you, boss." A tear rolled down Joseph's cheek. He let it. "And neither will I. You're a fucking hero, and don't you forget it. I . . .

"I love you, Ian. Wherever you are, you'll always be right here." He thumped his denim-covered chest. "Rest in peace, man. And if you're still kickin' around somewhere . . . be happy."

Joseph Hunter took one last look at the trees, the hill, the silent grave. He would not need to come back. It was done. He smiled, acknowledging it at last.

Then he turned. Fished the keys from his pocket.

And walked away.

ALL FALL DOWN

by John Saul

A terrifying story that weaves medical fact with ingenious scientific speculation – a tale of fear . . .

Something is happening to the children of Eastbury, Massachusetts. Something nameless that causes healthy babies to turn cold in their cots. Something that touches every mother's secret fear that she may have passed on to her child some terrible, life-taking flaw.

A small town, a family in jeopardy, a sudden terror . . . Against this backdrop, John Saul has created a compelling, terrifying and chilling psychological thriller.

0 552 12298 X   £1.95

NATHANIEL

by John Saul

Prairie Bend. Brilliant summers amid golden fields. Killing winters of razorlike cold. A peaceful, neighbourly village, darkened by legends of death.

WHO IS NATHANIEL

For a hundred years, the people of Prairie Bend have whispered the name in wonder and fear. Some say he is simply a folk tale – a legend created to frighten children on cold winter nights. Some swear he is a terrifying spirit returned to avenge the past. And soon . . . very soon . . . some will come to believe that Nathaniel lives still – darkly, horrifyingly *real*.

NATHANIEL

For young Michael Hall, newly arrived in isolated Prairie Bend after having lost his father to a sudden tragic accident, Nathaniel is the voice that calls to him across the prairie night . . . the voice that draws him into the shadowy depth of the old, crumbling barn where he has been forbidden to go . . . the voice – chanting, compelling – he will follow faithfully beyond the edge of terror . . .

NATHANIEL

0 552 12568 7   £1.95

BRAINCHILD

by John Saul

Muttering softly, his eyes blazing with fury, he started towards Mrs. Lewis, and began killing her.

Alex remained still in the corner of the kitchen, his eyes glued to the scene that was being played out a few feet away. He could feel the pain in Mrs. Lewis's neck as the dark-skinned boy's fingers tightened around it.

And he could feel the terror in her soul as she began to realize that she was going to die.

But he could do nothing except stand where he was, helplessly watching, for as he endured the pain Mrs. Lewis was feeling, he was also enduring the pain of the thought that kept repeating itself in his brain.

It's me. The boy who is killing her is me . . .

BRAINCHILD

An excursion into absolute terror
by the bestselling master of fear
John Saul

0 553 17171 2   £2.50

GHOST HOUSE

by Clare McNally

You won't be able to stop reading until the nightmare is over . . .

A dream house that traps a family in horror.

The beautiful old mansion on Long Island's South Shore seemed the perfect home for the Van Burens and their three young children. What happened to them inside that house is an experience you'll pray couldn't happen to you.

At first the Van Burens believed there had to be some natural explanation. Before it was over, they were fighting for their children's lives against an obscene manifestation of evil that engulfed them all in a desperate nightmare.

Not even *Flowers in the Attic* prepares you for

GHOST HOUSE

0 552 11652 1 – £1.75

GHOST LIGHT

by Clare McNally

In the blood of the innocent burns the flame of evil . . .

Pretty little five-year-old Bonnie Jackson was the darling of all the stage world. Until the night she found herself wandering, terrified, through the darkness of the Winston Theater – a night that would end with evil consuming the innocent girl in a horrible, fiery death.

Now, sixty years later, Bonnie has returned. And she will command the spotlight once again. For pretty little Bonnie Jackson is about to perform her show-stopping act of revenge . . .

0 552 12400 1   £1.75

GHOST HOUSE REVENGE

by Clare McNally

The Ghost House horror lives on . . . for revenge.

Only nightmares and broken limbs remained to remind the Van Burens and their three children of past terror. And when the physical therapist and his shy daughter arrived, the family dared hope for a return to normal life . . .

But somewhere within the ancient Long Island mansion, something was laughing, mocking, plotting . . .

They prayed it wasn't the same as before. It was not – it was much, much worse. Soon they were fighting for their lives against a shape-shifting horror of insatiable evil. A malevolence that lusted with hideous pleasure, and killed with raging delight . . .

0 552 11825 7   £1.75

Other Horror Titles Available From Transworld Publishers